DISCERNING INSIGHT

Book Eight of The Extraordinaries

MELISSA MCSHANE

Night Harbor Publishing

www.nightharborpublishing.com

Cover design by Amalia Chitulescu https://www.amaliach.com

This book is dedicated, with thanks, to the many authors who wrote about psionic and psychic talents before me, and whose work provided the foundation for the magic of The Extraordinaries

CONTENTS

CHAPTER I

IN WHICH LYDIA'S DISCERNMENT MATTERS LESS THAN HER KEEN HEARING

At nearly midnight, Lord Ormerod's ballroom was a mad crush of dancers whirling through the complex steps of a quadrille, pressed in on all sides by others who drank punch and conversed loudly so they might be heard over their neighbors. The beautiful room was hot as a summer day and smelled of perfume and warm bodies and sweat and candle wax that occasionally dripped from the three chandeliers whose brilliance added to the warmth of the room. Lydia could not imagine a more perfect night.

Perfect, in fact, for espionage.

She tilted her head back to regard the famous ceiling, painted to look like a blue sky dotted with clouds gave the illusion of a cool spring morning, far from London. Gilded moldings rimmed the blue expanse, reflecting the chandeliers' light in tawny stripes. Lydia felt she was looking through a golden window at a sky that knew nothing of the rains and dreary chill of early March. Perhaps birds might soar into view, tracing patterns of white or gray across the blue.

The foolish notion brought her to herself with a start. She hoped that had not been too extended a reverie. It would not do to appear eccentric in this gathering, not when her goal was to seem nothing more than an ordinary young lady.

Neither of her companions commented on her distraction, though; their attention was fixed on a group of young men nearby. Lydia's Extraordinary Discernment sensed the ladies' emotions easily, their excitement at the possibility of being singled out by one of the men. She also perceived that the young men, for all they seemed indifferent, were keenly aware of the young ladies, their emotions just as excited and tinged with romantic anticipation.

Miss Rogers clasped Lydia's hand in hers. "I believe they are looking this way," she whispered. "They are all so handsome, I declare I do not know which I prefer!"

"Do not be foolish," Lady Amelia whispered back. "They show no interest in us." But she flicked a glance at the tallest of the men, Mr. Hopewell. Though he still appeared indifferent, he noticed the look, for Lydia sensed his interest sharpen.

Not for the first time, she wished she had a Coercer's talent to guide the emotions she Discerned. Surely it could not be evil to enhance someone's already existing feelings? In Lydia's experience, the men at these dances often failed to approach the ladies who were most interested in them, mostly out of uncertainty at their possible reception. As Lydia could also not inform the gentlemen which ladies' hearts beat faster at their proximity, what she perceived frustrated her more often than not.

"I believe you are mistaken," she said. "He pretends to ignorance, but I have seen him watching you." An idea occurred to her, and she put a hand on Lady Amelia's wrist. "You should walk near him. Alone."

Lady Amelia gasped. "Alone?"

"Of course! We three together are daunting, for how is he to single you out?" Lydia ignored the embarrassment rising in Lady Amelia. "Simply walk past him and stop a few feet away. I am certain he will ask you to dance."

Lady Amelia's cheeks were pinker than the warmth of the ballroom could account for. "I cannot—"

"No, it is the perfect solution!" Miss Rogers said. "In fact, I believe we should all separate." She immediately put her suggestion into action, turning and walking toward the group of gentlemen. Lady Amelia squeaked and hurried after her, not too close. Lydia watched them go, basking in the sense of pleasure and nervousness that filled both her acquaintances.

Mr. Hopewell watched Lady Amelia walk past, and a new emotion flowered within him, the pale green of attraction and mild desire. Moments after Lady Amelia came to a stop, he approached her. They were too far away for even Lydia's keen hearing to make out their conversation, but as Lady Amelia's desire matched Mr. Hopewell's, hearing was unnecessary. Lydia smiled as Lady Amelia took his arm and walked with him to where couples were forming up for the next dance. There was nothing so satisfying in the world as the sensation of love beginning to flower.

Swiftly, she walked away through the crush, buoyed up by her sense of the crowd's enjoyment. She herself had no intention of dancing. She had never been fond of the activity. Now that she had control of her talent, she was aware of how many men felt nothing but lust when they contemplated dancing with her. The ones who felt cloyingly romantic were only slightly preferable.

But that was not why she needed to remain free of a partner. She could not accomplish Mr. Rutledge's task if she was occupied with a dance.

Contemplating the responsibility he had handed her left her torn between excitement and fear: excitement that she had an important task to accomplish, fear that it was perhaps not so important as all that. She sometimes suspected Mr. Rutledge gave her tasks that did not truly require an Extraordinary Discerner, or worse, were insignificant in the grand scheme of the great spymaster's plans. But she could not do less than her best and risk the possibility that they were vitally important. And it had only been two months since Mr. Rutledge had enlisted her as his agent; that was not enough time to make any kind of judgment.

She was aware of her sister-in-law's approach, her emotions always so strong and coherent in a way unique to her, well before Clemency took her arm and said, "This is a sad crush; you are not indisposed, I hope?"

"No, it is exhilarating," Lydia replied. It was true, she found the collective emotion of a hundred or more people as satisfying as floating in a sea, tugged at by currents but unmoved. "They almost all feel plea-sure, even if it is tangled with other emotions, and those who do not are few."

Clemency walked on, drawing Lydia with her. "I cannot imagine anyone feeling anything but pleasure in this gathering. Perhaps discomfort at the heat and noise, I suppose."

"Not everyone enjoys such gatherings. There are some who are annoyed, and several who are indifferent, and one or two who sorrow." Lydia had steered clear of the latter. She knew enough of her own sorrows to recognize that it was an emotion that did have the power to overcome her. "And there are others—but I should not be indelicate."

"I can guess," Clemency said, amused. "The ones who are on the hunt for a husband or wife. They stand out?"

Lydia nodded. "Their emotions are like knives, bright green and sharp."

"Your world must be so vivid, if you see color when you Discern emotions." Clemency felt no criticism or mockery as she spoke, only the placid blue acceptance that Lydia perceived what she could not. It was one of the things Lydia loved most about her. She herself did not understand why emotions had color; she only knew that, for example, excitement was yellow and peace was blue and love was a deep emerald green. She did not question it; her instincts told her those colors meant sanity.

"Well, I will not press you to tell me who those people are, however curious I am," Clemency said with an arch smile. "I have not seen Sir Anthony."

"Nor have I." It was the most either of them would say publicly in allusion to Lydia's assignment. Clemency understood the need for secrecy as well as Lydia did.

Mr. Rutledge's Voice had assured her Sir Anthony Michelson would arrive early to Lord Ormerod's ball and stay only briefly. She and Clemency had been among the first to arrive for that reason. Now Lydia wondered if Sir Anthony and Lady Michelson had chosen to remain home instead. She tried not to permit that possibility to dishearten her. Even if she could not complete her assignment, she was enjoying herself. And the Voice had always been right before, so she should not give up hope so easily.

"You know his appearance, do you not?" Clemency scanned the room as if searching for Sir Anthony.

"I do. The Voice showed me his face."

Clemency frowned. "I dislike you being in Spoken contact with a stranger. He might be anyone, Lydia, and suppose he uses his talent to impose on you?"

Lydia shook her head. "Mr. Rutledge would not permit it. And the Voice only Speaks to me on matters of business. It is not as if we are carrying on a courtship."

In truth, she knew the identity of the Extraordinary Speaker Mr. Rutledge occasionally delivered his instructions through, though she had not let on to anyone, not even Mr. Rutledge, that she knew the secret. Keeping secrets delighted her. She loved ferreting out what others chose to conceal and loved even more never telling a soul what she had learned. Gossip was abhorrent to her; a beautiful secret deserved to be kept.

So, she never revealed that not only was the apparently vacuous Lord Ravenscroft secretly an Extraordinary Speaker, he was also not the frivolous man about town he appeared to be. It made perfect sense to Lydia that someone as fond of intrigue as Alexander Rutledge would cultivate such a person as his secret Speaker advantage, especially since he also took advantage of the fact that very few people in London knew Lydia was an Extraordinary Discerner. Therefore, she went on referring to Lord Ravenscroft simply as Mr. Rutledge's Voice, even in the privacy of her own head.

This time, the Voice had given her a clear Spoken image of Sir Anthony that now resided in her memory as if she had seen the baronet face to face. She also remembered clearly the instructions that had come three days ago with the invitation to this ball: *Sir Anthony is in collusion with someone over fraudulent notes of hand. Identify his partner in crime.* No signature, and no more detail than that.

"Very well, I realize you know your own business," Clemency said. She patted Lydia's arm and released her. "Come to me when you have accomplished your task, and do not pretend to less fatigue than you feel. There is no shame in acknowledging when one has worked oneself to weariness."

"I understand," Lydia said, casting her eyes down so demurely Clemency laughed.

"And now I am behaving like a mama whose daughter is barely out," she said. "I hope you will dance at least once!"

Lydia smiled, but said nothing. She had never told Clemency why she did not like to dance. Before her three years in the Magdalen Asylum, her untamed Extraordinary Discerner's talent had meant she was incapable of distinguishing between her own emotions and those of everyone surrounding her, throwing her into confusion and eventually overwhelming her into madness. Physical contact had worsened the effect, even the brief contact of hands clasping hands in the course of a dance. She could not even imagine waltzing with someone.

It occurred to her that she now defined almost everything in her life by its relation to her stay in that asylum. Before Magdalen. After Magdalen. During Magdalen—but she shied away from those memories. Sanity had been hard won, but she did not for one moment believe living surrounded by those whose emotions were fragmented or overpowering was the only way she might have achieved it.

She made herself focus on her memory of Mr. Rutledge's note. The first time Lydia had received one of these terse communications, she had been so nervous she had nearly failed to discover the information Mr. Rutledge desired. Now, she was accustomed to his preference for brevity and conciseness, though anxiety still reared its head whenever she saw his handwriting on a note addressed to her. He believed her competent enough not to need extensive direction, and his respect for her compelled her to prove him right.

The yellow sea sang within her, tinged here and there with blues and pinks and awash with the green of passion—and then, a note of drab brown, a sensation completely out of place. Lydia floated toward it, not paying much attention to her surroundings. Guilt or remorse were muddy brown, a swirl of complex emotions that were for Lydia the easiest to distinguish from her own. Not like the red of anger or the grey-black of pure despair, which could sweep her away entirely.

"Miss Wescott?"

Lydia, startled, let out a gasp and blinked. Her surroundings came into focus. She had nearly achieved the ballroom door, there were few people nearby, and someone had just addressed her. "I beg your pardon," she said automatically.

"I seem to have startled you," the man said. "May I ask the pleasure of the next two dances?"

Lydia examined the man. She did not recall him being introduced to her, but his innocent pleasure and faint green admiration did not bear the tinge of guilt at breaking social mores, so it was her own recollection that was faulty. Inwardly, she said words she had learned from her fellow Magdalen inmates that her brother Colin would be appalled by. She could not refuse without drawing attention to herself, and being noticed might lead to being revealed as an Extraordinary Discerner.

"Of course," she said with a smile. "How kind of you to ask."

"The pleasure is mine, I assure you," the man said. He was neither too old nor too young, not too handsome or too ugly, and had she not wished to be elsewhere, Lydia might have genuinely enjoyed dancing with him. It was so rare to encounter a man whose emotions did not bear some palpable attraction to her. She knew it was unkind of her to resent men for finding her attractive, and she did her best not to hold her knowledge of their emotions against them, but truly, there was no romance in knowing to the exact degree a man's feelings for her.

Swiftly, Lydia looked past him in the direction of the sensation of guilt. And there he was, Sir Anthony Michelson, his thin but florid face and narrow nose exactly matching her induced memory. Brown mist engulfed him, but she would have known he felt guilty over something anyway, so pronounced was his stoop and the flickering gaze that never lingered on anything for more than two seconds.

His wife, Lady Michelson, had a pleasant smile and felt only a placid blue calm. That might become a problem, if Lady Michelson saw the event as nothing more than a social obligation; her lack of enthusiasm might take both her and her husband away before Lydia identified his co-conspirator. But that was, unfortunately, a problem for later.

She accepted the man's arm and permitted him to lead her to

where the couples were forming up for the next dance. Fortunately, it was a country dance, and she and her partner would go down the line so often she need not converse much. The dance would give her the opportunity to pay attention to that spot of guilt that now moved around the ballroom in the direction of the card-rooms.

The gentleman spoke rarely, which satisfied Lydia as she was preoccupied with the pull of Sir Anthony's presence. More concerning was that the tenor of his comments indicated that he expected her to remember their introduction. Lydia told herself it did not matter. This young man was no one of consequence, and if he discovered Lydia had forgotten him, he would be disheartened, but his emotions were unimportant compared to her assignment.

She smiled at her partner, but did not speak, every time they came together at the head of the line. Sir Anthony did not move. Lady Michelson drifted through the ballroom, her calm blue presence as easily distinguishable as her husband's guilt. When the dance came to an end, Lydia curtsied and was about to walk away when her partner said, "It is nearly midnight; will you accompany me in to supper?"

The obscenity nearly escaped her lips that time. Lydia opened her mouth to reject the man. Then she stopped, arrested by her sense of his pleasure in her company. For the first time in years, remorse filled her, not someone else's but her own natural emotion. "I would enjoy that very much," she said.

The man's smile widened. "It is my pleasure, I assure you, Miss Wescott. I had begun to imagine you had forgotten my name."

At that moment, Lydia Discerned Sir Anthony's approach. "I," she began, and Sir Anthony swept past them both, jostling her partner in his haste. And a second guilty emotion blossomed not ten feet away. Lydia peered through the crowd to identify the man—but no, it was a woman, one who watched Sir Anthony in a tangle of guilt and desire.

"Excuse me, I was distracted," Lydia said. She accepted the gentleman's arm. "That man was in a terrible hurry, was he not?"

"I have never known Sir Anthony when he was not in a terrible hurry," her partner replied. "Shall we go in?"

Sir Anthony had passed the guilty woman without more than a brush of the shoulder, and the woman did not look after him, but her guilt and desire redoubled. Lydia's suspicions that in this instance Mr. Rutledge was wrong about his target grew. "I am unfamiliar with that lady," she said, nodding in the woman's direction. "The one with the lovely coiffure. Do you know her?"

Embarrassment tinged her partner's emotions. "She is Mrs. Dexter," he said.

"She seemed to know Sir Anthony well," Lydia said, though Sir Anthony's interaction with Mrs. Dexter had not been an intimate one.

The embarrassment spiked yellow and green twined together. "I do not know of their connection," the gentleman said. The discordant knot of his lie was so palpable in his emotions Lydia might have giggled if she were not so despondent. Sir Anthony's guilt was not over a conspiracy; it was nothing but an illicit love affair. If he was guilty of fraud, he did not intend to meet his partner here.

"Well, it is of no matter," she said. "Pray, let us go in."

She listened with half her concentration to her dining partner, barely registering that his conversation was droll and entertaining. Her enjoyment of the evening could not prevent her experiencing despondency at having failed—though it was the failure of Mr. Rutledge's intelligence and not her own abilities, so she should not feel so. It still seemed like a waste of her talent.

Her distraction did not prevent her responding to her partner's remarks, nor from idly assessing the men and women surrounding her. Her Extraordinary Discerner's talent operated at a distance of some fifty feet in every direction from herself and saw no obstacle in walls or ceilings. Everyone had come in for supper, their emotions damped to a mild pleasure at the excellence of Lord Ormerod's table. Lady Michelson herself remained the one cool blue spot in the entire room. She would not be so placid if she knew her husband's emotions—or perhaps she knew and did not care.

Lydia became aware that the ladies were rising from the table, following Lady Ormerod's lead, just as her partner said, "It has been a pleasure, Miss Wescott. I hope our time together has not been displeasing to you."

She suddenly and miraculously recalled his name. "Not at all, Mr.

Bannister." Lydia impulsively offered him her hand. "I am glad to have met you."

"That gratifies me." Mr. Bannister smiled. Too late, Lydia felt his pulse of emotion deepen into something beyond mere interest. Her heart sank. She discovered she liked Mr. Bannister, but it was nothing more than liking. She had no desire to encourage him to believe she returned his interest, and yet spurning him felt cruel.

"Please excuse me, I see I am being summoned," she said quickly, and retrieved her hand. She fled before Mr. Bannister could say anything else.

Safely outside the dining room, she trailed along behind the other women, listening to the sound of the men rising from table as well. The general excitement that had muted to pleasure during the meal was growing again, but Lydia's own emotions did not rise to meet it. She reminded herself that she was not here for pleasure and walked faster, hoping to politely avoid Mr. Bannister.

She settled herself in one corner of the card room and contemplated the possibilities. She could learn no more from Sir Anthony, but she did not like to make Clemency leave early. She might join one of the card-tables, but her ability to sense the emotions of her opponents meant most card games were dull and far too easily won. Sitting in this quiet corner would be a pleasant respite.

Then, somewhere in the distance, she Discerned the tingling flood of guilt tangled with excitement, the rush of someone doing or plotting something forbidden.

It was not Sir Anthony, she knew immediately; Sir Anthony's guilt outweighed his pleasure, and it was tinged with shame. Whoever this person was, his emotions verged on the brink of delight. Lydia followed his progress as he moved from the entrance hall through the ballroom—a very latecomer, and one who moved with purpose. As he moved, Lydia Discerned another whose emotions shifted from ordinary pleasure to the same forbidden, guilty feeling of the first. The two converged on each other, and Lydia rose from her seat and headed for the card-room door.

Her own emotions once more warred within her. She had, in a sense, achieved her purpose, even though she had only discovered Mr.

Rutledge's intelligence was wrong; these men or women, whoever they were, were not her responsibility to investigate. But she did not experience the warm rush of success that would have contented her to let this mystery go. It would be but the work of a moment to see whether those guilty, elated emotions meant anything Mr. Rutledge would care about. And if they did not, well, she would simply add another secret to her hoard.

She drifted past men and women who ignored her until she reached the ballroom. Lydia had realized years before that no one usually noticed her, slight and pale as she was, unless she deliberately drew attention to herself. Far from disheartening her, the fact gave her a warm contentment that at least in this, she had some control over her life.

Presently, she caught sight of her new quarry, or rather both of them. One was dressed sprucely, almost too sprucely, in an elegant frock coat and shoes with very high heels, and his hair was as elaborately arranged as his neckcloth. The other gentleman was not nearly so well turned out. He was not slovenly, but his neckcloth gave only the barest nod to fashion, and his calves were not padded and likely should have been. Lydia took note of their appearances, in case she was required to describe the men later, but most of her attention was caught up in the men's tangled emotions of guilt and elation.

Both stood to one side, their heads together, conversing in voices too low for Lydia to make them out over the general clamor. She drifted nearer, pretending her attention was fixed on a cluster of women who were the men's nearest neighbors. Neither man paid her any heed. Though both continued in heightened emotions, the unfashionable man with the scrawny legs was more agitated than his conversational partner, his gestures and intensity of speech revealing his state to anyone who chose to look. Lydia kept her attention on the women. She was almost near enough to overhear the men, or might have were the music and general clamor not great enough to prevent it.

Then, with a final skirl, the musicians brought the dance to a close, and for a moment, the clamor ebbed. The two men had clearly not expected the quiet, and to Lydia's ears came the faint but unmistakable words *will kill the king*.

CHAPTER 2

IN WHICH A SECRET INTERROGATION REVEALS MUCH

Lydia did not flinch. She continued to walk, pretending to ignore the men. The well-dressed man gripped the other's arm, tightly based on the fear and anger that shot through the unfashionable man. Out of the corner of her eye, she observed them, hoping they did not suspect her of being close enough to eavesdrop. But instead they had their attention fixed on a handful of men standing nearby, laughing and teasing one another. To Lydia, that group's interest in the women in attendance was clear, and she could tell they had heard nothing, but the two conspirators walked wide of them as they moved off into the crowd.

Lydia found a quiet corner and closed her eyes, willing her heart to slow. She followed the men's progress through the ballroom, circling the dancers. She did not know what to do—no, what she was obligated to do. A scrap of overheard speech was not enough to justify making accusations in public. She might be mistaken, and those words meant something innocuous, some comment on a historical matter or a play in which a king was killed. They need not mean a plot.

But the emotions she had Discerned were unmistakable.

She reminded herself that whatever those two men intended, they could not carry out a threat against the king here and now. Even were she physically capable of apprehending them, there would be no point in doing so, not so long as their actual purpose remained unknown. Lydia was not large or strong, and she had no talent that would permit her to capture them. Clemency, an Extraordinary Mover of considerable skill, might be able to prevent them fleeing; were Colin here, he, a Bounder, might carry them away to Mr. Rutledge's house or the Catterwell Prison. Lydia had only her own Discernment to rely on— but, she considered, it might be a more useful talent than either Moving or Bounding in these circumstances.

Maintaining an awareness of her two quarries and their distinctive emotions, Lydia went in search of her sister-in-law. She found Clemency speaking with two women Lydia did not know, their emotions revealing that they were engaged in gossip.

Clemency saw Lydia approaching and immediately left her friends to meet her. "Are you enjoying yourself?" she asked. This was an agreed-upon phrase that meant *Have you accomplished your task?*

"I am, but I wish for some quiet," Lydia said. This, too, was a phrase with meaning beyond the surface.

Clemency's eyebrows rose, and she said, "Let us find you a quiet place to sit, then, unless you have the head-ache and wish to leave?"

"No, I simply need rest." Lydia smiled at the other women, who were annoyed with her interruption but were too well-bred to show it. Another benefit to being small and thin and pale was that no one ever questioned her claims to illness or weariness. She was far stronger than she appeared, but playing on her fragile appearance was sometimes useful.

She and Clemency returned to the card room, where Clemency made a show of finding Lydia a seat. "If you have achieved your goal, we need not remain," she said under her breath.

"I...am not certain," Lydia said. She decided Clemency did not need to know what she had learned and what she now intended. Clemency rarely interfered in Lydia's assignments, but Lydia was certain this situation was one Clemency would not approve of Lydia's involvement in. "Do you know either of these men?" she added, describing the conspirators.

"I do not recognize the first, but the second is Mr. Norris,"

Clemency said. "His spindly legs are, perhaps unjustly, the subject of much mockery behind his back. I know him to be of no very great intellect, but harmless."

"Do you suppose you might introduce him to me?"

Clemency's pleasure dimmed to uncertainty. "I do not know. He and I are not close acquaintances, and he is not precisely the sort of man who should be introduced to young women."

Lydia tilted her head inquiringly. "*You* said he was harmless."

"In the sense of not having a vicious or violent temperament, yes. That does not make him an appropriate companion."

Lydia shrugged. "It is what I endure for the sake of my assignment, and it will not be so terrible."

Clemency bit her lip, and her uncertainty grew. "I feel this is a mistake."

"I am in no danger here in the middle of Lord Ormerod's mansion." Lydia hoped that was not a lie. "Please, Clemency. I am not fragile, you know."

Clemency sighed. "I know. Very well."

She drew Lydia's hand through her arm and led her back to the ballroom, skirting the dancers and avoiding those who showed signs of wishing to engage the Countess of Ashford in conversation. Lydia saw Mr. Norris and his companion almost immediately. The two men were again deeply engaged in conversation, though the noise of the music and the dancing and the many other conversations made it impossible for Lydia to make out their words.

Clemency drew near to the pair, who broke off their conversation in startled surprise that shot through them like orange spikes. The unknown man tried to walk away, but Mr. Norris put a restraining hand on his arm.

"Lady Ashford," he said, his polite smile concealing the agitation her approach had thrown him into. "What a pleasure."

"Mr. Norris, how are you this evening," Clemency said with the brilliant smile that had confounded so many men. "And...I beg your pardon, we have not been introduced."

"Lord Deverell," the other man said with a bow. "Your servant, my lady."

14

"I realized you and I, Mr. Norris, have not spoken in weeks—oh, I beg your pardon." Clemency gave an excellent impression of someone genuinely interested in both men. "Miss Wescott, these are Mr. Norris and Lord Deverell. Gentlemen, Lord Ashford's sister, Miss Wescott."

Lydia curtseyed politely. "It is a pleasure to make your acquaintances," she said, shyly casting down her eyes. Lord Deverell's guilty elation dimmed with mild annoyance, but Mr. Norris' emotions became green-tinged with desire. Lydia wished again that she had a Coercer's talent to influence the emotions she Discerned. She could not guarantee that Mr. Norris' slight interest in her would be enough to compel him to ask her to dance.

"Miss Wescott is new to London, and I enjoy her companionship when I attend such events as this," Clemency continued. "She is very fond of dancing."

"Indeed?" Mr. Norris said, his interest deepening, and Lydia blessed Clemency for her subtle suggestion. "Then perhaps I might solicit your hand for the next two dances, Miss Wescott?"

Lord Deverell's mouth opened, and Lydia, Discerning his growing annoyance at this interruption, said quickly, "Of course, Mr. Norris, I should like that very much."

They strolled in the direction of the dancers, and Lydia said, "I hope I did not interrupt any important conversation, sir. You and Lord Deverell seemed quite intent on your discourse."

The guilty elation surged again, this time with guilt predominant. "Oh, it was nothing," Mr. Norris said. "Merely discussing an upcoming house party with friends."

To her surprise, it was not a lie. "How exciting," she said as the music drew to a close and she and Mr. Norris took their places. "Though I imagine the weather is still too cold for many outdoor activities—or am I wrong, and it is not a house in the country?"

"Lord Deverell's house is in Surrey, yes," Mr. Norris said. The music swelled, and then the figures of the dance swept them apart, making further questioning by Lydia impossible. She calmed her nerves and told herself there would yet be time for more subtle interrogation.

When they once more joined hands, Mr. Norris said, "And your brother is the new Lord Ashford. I declare, that was a most peculiar business, was it not?"

"Lady Ashford's inheritance as an Extraordinary meant she elevated her husband to her rank," Lydia said, annoyed at this irrelevancy. "Unusual, but not peculiar. I do not see why a lady who inherits in her own right might not grant her title to her husband."

"I beg your pardon if I gave insult," Mr. Norris said, embarrassment spiking through him. "Of course I wish Lord Ashford the best."

"Certainly." Lydia cast about for any subject that might redirect the conversation. "Lord Deverell must be quite well to do if he has property in the country. Do you visit him often?"

Mr. Norris laughed, a somewhat nasal, braying sound. "Such questions! I ought to be quite downcast that you are more interested in my friend than in me."

Lydia blushed, and hoped he would interpret it as embarrassment rather than the irritation she actually felt. "I meant only that you seemed good friends, and I know so little of London society it is all very interesting to me."

"Very well, so long as I alone may hold your entire attention for the space of our dances." Mr. Norris brayed his laugh again. "Lord Deverell is popular, and fond of hosting parties for our many friends. Even the Prince Regent has been known to attend."

Lydia made mental note of "our" and tilted her head in a way she knew made her look more innocent than usual. "The Prince Regent is quite busy, I hear, so that seems a remarkable coup for your friend. I am not much out in society, so I am certain the names of those who will attend mean nothing to me."

"Oh?" Once more, they separated, and Lydia inwardly cursed losing that line of interrogation. But when they joined one another again, Mr. Norris said, "I am certain these men are prominent enough even you have heard of them." He reeled off a list of some ten or twelve names, only two of which Lydia knew. She gave Mr. Norris a wide-eyed, impressed gaze that gratified his pride and memorized the list.

"Your friends are indeed important," she said, sounding awed. "No wonder the Prince Regent finds their company congenial." Of the Prince Regent, she knew only what gossip, rumor, and innuendo said, but she was certain his preferred lifestyle of indolence and gluttony had nothing in common with the men Mr. Norris called friends.

"Will he attend this party, then?" she continued.

"Oh, naturally, though his time is quite occupied," Mr. Norris said with an airy casualness that covered a deep satisfaction at having such a connection to greatness. "He will grace us with his presence at least once."

Lydia nodded, and they separated again. She could think of nothing else to ask, nothing that would not seem strange coming from a wisp of a girl with no experience in society. She knew Lord Deverell and Mr. Norris were plotting something about the king; she knew their plotting was related to this house party; she knew the names of several who would be in attendance; and she knew Mr. Norris hoped for the Prince Regent to visit, though she guessed that hope might be a vain one. It was enough to hand over to Mr. Rutledge.

She spent the rest of their dances wishing to be home already so she might send word to Mr. Rutledge. Mr. Norris' conversation, when not directed by her, was dominated by his desire to impress her with his many social connections, most of which Lydia guessed were one-sided. She was certain Lord Ormerod, who was an intelligent and compassionate man deeply interested in art, did not count Mr. Norris among his closest friends as Mr. Norris claimed. Lydia pretended to wide-eyed awe and left Mr. Norris at the end of their dances with an innocent smile even he could not believe meant she was interested in him.

Lydia immediately went in search of Clemency and, with a weak smile and a theatrical hand to her temple, ruthlessly extricated her from the conversation she was having with the still-placid Lady Michelson. Clemency asked no questions, merely took Lydia's arm and guided her to where they could take their leave of their hosts.

"Tell me truthfully," Clemency said at the door. "Are you ill, or was that a ruse because you wish to return home?"

Lydia opened her mouth to deny illness, and then realized her head did hurt and her bones ached with weariness. "I am fatigued, yes."

"Lydia, you should have spoken sooner," Clemency said, concern flashing through her. "Mr. Rutledge cannot expect you to exhaust your-self in his employ."

"I am well enough, do not fear." Lydia wrapped herself in her cloak and followed Clemency to the carriage. "I do give heed to my own condition, you know."

"I know, but—oh, it is unimportant." Clemency accepted the foot-man's hand, though as an Extraordinary Mover with the ability to Fly, she frequently assisted herself into the carriage. "You know how concerned Colin and I are for you, but we should not coddle you like an infant."

Lydia settled herself across from Clemency and folded her cloak more closely around her shoulders. "You would not appreciate such behavior yourself."

Clemency laughed. "No, I would not. Forgive my concern."

Lydia nodded, but said nothing. In her heart, the words spoken by Lord Deverell or Mr. Norris, words that might indicate a conspiracy against the king, echoed and struggled to be free. Clemency was a good confidante and was almost as careful of secrets as Lydia. But Lydia guessed this was not something Mr. Rutledge would wish her to share, not even with her family. Although Clemency knew something of Lydia's role in Mr. Rutledge's organization, she was not privy to the details of the information Lydia Discerned, and this was potentially explosive information.

They rode in silence. Lydia's weariness threatened to overcome her, and Clemency was preoccupied with thoughts of Colin—or, rather, tender emotions that would embarrass her if Lydia drew attention to them. Lydia felt nothing but joy when she Discerned them. Her brother had spent so many years working himself to the bone for her sake, he deserved every happiness.

The jostling of the carriage kept Lydia from falling asleep, but her eyes frequently slid shut, and she felt the sort of dissociative numbness one experienced in the moments between sleeping and waking. When the carriage drew to a halt, she blinked herself awake and then realized Clemency was steadying her with her Moving. "I am well, and I am not asleep," she said, "but I am not certain my body knows it."

Clemency chuckled. "I know you dislike being carried, so prove to me that you are alert."

Lydia surreptitiously stretched her limbs, then climbed down and walked steadily the few short steps to the door of Emeraude House. "You see?"

"Very well." Clemency paused on the front step, regarding Lydia closely. "Sleep well, and do not feel obligated to wake early."

"I never do," Lydia said. It was true, she enjoyed a leisurely, late morning. But she had something to attend to before she slept.

In her bedchamber, she changed into her nightdress with the help of her maid, Ellery, but did not climb into bed. Instead, she took a candle to her small writing desk and penned a note for William the footman to deliver to Mr. Rutledge in the morning. She handed it to Ellery. "Good night," she said, "and I hope you dream of your young man."

Ellery blushed. "I never know what to say to you, miss," she said. "You know how I feel before I do."

This was not true, but Lydia had gone through four maids before Ellery, from elegant Frenchwomen to girls barely qualified to tend her wardrobe, and all of them had left her service out of discomfort and fear at having their emotions laid bare. Lydia did not like to draw attention to her talent by correcting Ellery's misapprehension. "There is nothing wrong with feeling an attachment," she said. "And I am certain he feels the same about you."

Ellery blushed harder, bobbed a swift curtsey, and let herself out.

Lydia climbed into bed and pulled the covers close to her chin. She wriggled her toes against the warming pan wrapped in flannel with deep satisfaction. In a month or so, the frigid chill of winter would lose its grip on the world, and the warming pan would be unnecessary. Lydia liked spring, the feeling of the world waking from sleep, but this sensation of being warm when the air beyond her bed was cold satisfied her as well.

She once more contemplated what she had learned, but her weary mind failed to hold the knowledge in order, and after only a few moments, she drifted off to sleep.

CHAPTER 3

IN WHICH MR. RUTLEDGE'S
SUPERIOR IS NOT WHAT
LYDIA EXPECTED

Mr. Rutledge's response to her note came at breakfast, delivered by the butler, Slater. The idle blue-gray hum that indicated this task was merely one of many for him that morning suffused his emotions. "Thank you, Slater," Lydia said, smiling, and a quick pulse of satisfaction ran through him. Lydia already knew he felt a paternal affection for Clemency that extended to the members of her household, but it still satisfied her to feel it directed at herself.

The note bore a single line in Mr. Rutledge's familiar handwriting said *I will send a carriage at noon.* Only a few simple words, and yet they thrilled through her. Lydia reminded herself that she owed Mr. Rutledge no servility, but her desire to prove herself ran strong enough within her that it took an effort of will not to devour her meal in a rush.

The carriage arrived one minute after noon by the clock in the entrance hall. Lydia had been ready for ten minutes before that. She told herself it was courteous to be prompt. Mr. Rutledge would not know if she had been eager, and could not Discern her emotions in any case. Her eagerness still embarrassed her somewhat.

She sat in a corner of the carriage and closed her eyes. The rapid pace of the carriage meant the emotions of those they passed flowed over her with remarkable speed, dizzying her as if the carriage spun like a top instead. Many people, intent on their destinations or their conversations, felt nothing stronger than a bland beige hum, a combination of placidity and mild interest in whatever it was their attention currently focused on. Brighter colors, here and there, shot through the hum: delight, or anger, or sorrow.

Lydia shied away from the last. Sorrow was almost the most intense of human emotions, cousin to despair and powerful enough to draw her in. Lydia had known enough sorrow in her life that others' sorrow resonated within her and threatened to overwhelm her. She did her best to ignore the emotion, but she was not entirely comfortable until the sorrowing person, whoever it was, had passed beyond the range of her Discernment.

Mr. Rutledge's house was on a quiet street lined with other houses, all of them large and elegant. Lydia contemplated the portico, which was of a Grecian design, pillared and supporting a frieze of women dressed in Greek robes. Up and down the street, she Discerned men and women within the houses, going about their business. Two within the house across the street burned deep passionate green, which amused Lydia. Likely Colin would be shocked at her knowledge of human desire and how it was expressed, but she felt no shame at vicariously enjoying pleasure. Emotions were the most natural aspect of the human experience, and how foolish to label some of them as inappropriate or shameful.

Mr. Rutledge's butler, Darrow, opened the door for her and showed her inside. "If you will follow me, miss," he said after accepting her cloak and bonnet and handing them off to a footman. "You are expected."

Darrow's emotions, Lydia reflected, always hummed with annoyance at her visits, though he showed no outward sign of disquiet. She had Discerned his annoyance at other guests, and had deduced he disliked having his time wasted in greeting callers. Lydia had once considered sharing this information with Mr. Rutledge and had instantly been appalled at herself. She was not in the business of giving away others' secrets, and Darrow's behavior was always perfectly proper, so what did it matter how he truly felt?

Darrow led Lydia to the room she privately called the Lair, though Mr. Rutledge called it his study, and bowed her inside. The Lair was larger than the Eastern drawing room, which was the other room she often met with Mr. Rutledge in, and furnished in heavy, dark woods, oak and mahogany and ebony. It had no windows, and two walls were entirely taken up by bookcases that reached the ceiling and required the use of a little footstool to reach their upper shelves. The bookcases were full of leatherbound books, not ones shiny with newness and disuse, but worn, with chipped gilded letters embossed on some of the spines. Lydia had never seen Mr. Rutledge read, but she had no doubt he knew the contents of every book in the Lair.

Though the corner was taken up by Mr. Rutledge's enormous claw-footed desk, there were no uncomfortable chairs facing it the way Lydia would have expected the spymaster to require, seats for under-lings to occupy if given permission to sit while they reported. Instead, two very comfortable sofas upholstered in drab green and brown brocade faced one another across from the desk. A low table placed between them gleamed with furniture polish, the least intimidating object in the room.

At the moment, the right-hand sofa was unoccupied, and only one person sat on the left-hand couch. Mrs. Rutledge, an attractive woman with ruddy hair and a fair complexion, smiled at Lydia. "Miss Wescott, good morning," she said.

Lydia's attention immediately fixed on Mr. Rutledge, who stood near the bookcases with his gaze roving the shelves. His tall, imposing physique gave him the appearance of an elemental force of nature, though Lydia had never seen him behave with anything but perfect propriety. He had been speaking to the stranger standing next to him, whose head was tilted attentively toward Mr. Rutledge. Both men turned to face Lydia. She shut the door nearly in Darrow's face, making his irritation spike into anger for the briefest moment, and curtseyed.

Mr. Rutledge and the stranger felt an irritation similar to that of Darrow, though Lydia had Discerned it as she ascended the stairs and knew it was not directed at her. "Miss Wescott," Mr. Rutledge said. "I appreciate your circumspection in not committing details of your discovery to paper, but you have wound my curiosity to the breaking point. So. You have learned something of grave urgency?"

Lydia's gaze flicked briefly to the stranger, who appeared to be in his mid-thirties, his brown hair curly, his nose aquiline. He looked short next to Mr. Rutledge, who was well over six feet tall and broad in the shoulders and chest, but he would still tower over her. Brown eyes regarded her intently, but unlike Mr. Rutledge, whose irritation was laced with an unexpected anger, curiosity threaded through the stranger's emotions. Lydia could not tell whether he was curious about her, or about the news she brought.

Her hesitation went on a moment too long. Mr. Rutledge gestured impatiently at the sofa. "Have a seat, Miss Wescott, and leave off silently criticizing me. Do you believe I would have you reveal sensitive information before someone not entitled to hear it?"

Lydia blushed, first with embarrassment at his accurate assessment of her thoughts, then with a consciousness that her blush was quite vivid on her pale skin. The stranger smiled, a thin twist of the lips that matched his inner amusement at her distress—though it was not mockery, she Discerned, but bore traces of nostalgia, as if he were recalling times when he, too, had been caught out in such a way. Curious, Lydia took a seat opposite Mrs. Rutledge, facing the two men.

"Miss Wescott, this is Lord Craythorne," Mr. Rutledge said, taking pity on her. "Lord Craythorne is a member of the oversight committee to which I report. Lord Craythorne, Miss Lydia Wescott, Extraordinary Discerner."

"My lord," Lydia said, inclining her head politely. "I apologize if I implied you were not trustworthy."

"It was a reasonable reaction," Lord Craythorne said, "and one Rutledge ought to admire, suspicious as he is. But Rutledge is correct; he reports to me, and therefore anything you tell him will eventually reach my ears." He turned away from Mr. Rutledge and paced around the end of Mrs. Rutledge's sofa, but did not sit. "We both judged your information important enough that I should hear it directly."

Under that intent gaze, Lydia's uncertainty grew. "I hope that is true," she said, "that is, I hope I am not mistaken. I never mean to waste anyone's time."

"I was given to understand your Discernment is unusually accurate," Lord Craythorne said, his irritation rising. "Most Discerners are erratic in their behavior and not always at home to reality."

It felt like a criticism, and before Lydia could remind herself that he was a peer of the realm and meant no such thing, she snapped, "You may dislike not being in control of a situation, my lord, but as you are no Discerner yourself, your fear of losing control should not permit you to disregard another's talent."

Lord Craythorne's eyes widened. Mrs. Rutledge covered her mouth to hide a smile. Mr. Rutledge grunted, and his satisfaction surged in a blue-green wave that rushed all through Lydia. "Are you satisfied, Craythorne? Take a seat, and let us hear what Miss Wescott has to say."

Another blush flooded Lydia's cheeks, and she tried vainly to suppress it. She considered apologizing—and yet she had been honest, so why should she apologize for honesty? But Lord Craythorne was astonished rather than angry or insulted, and traces of chagrin ran through him, which told her an apology would be a mistake.

He took a seat beside her, his attention fully on her, and to distract herself from her embarrassment, she turned her gaze to his hands, which were well-shaped and masculine, not quite slender and not quite sturdy. Light glinted off the signet ring of heavy gold he wore on the smallest finger of his right hand as he rested that hand on his knee.

To her surprise, his astonishment at her words was fading, diminishing as if he had a Coercer's control over them. Only two kinds of people were capable of such a thing: those with true self-mastery, and those whose pleasant demeanors concealed the kind of madness she had seen too often in Magdalen. Lydia told herself Lord Craythorne must be one of the former, for surely Mr. Rutledge would not give such respect to a madman.

Mr. Rutledge sat beside his wife. "Tell me what you learned, if it is not the identity of Sir Anthony's partner in forgery."

Lydia drew in a calming breath. Lord Craythorne's attention on her, however muted his emotions, made her uncomfortable. "I discovered evidence—perhaps 'evidence' is too strong a word—at any rate, I believe two of Lord Ormerod's guests are plotting the assassination of the king."

Sharp orange surprise spiked through all three of her listeners. Mr. Rutledge said, "Astonishing. How did you come across this evidence?"

Lydia clasped her hands loosely in her lap. "It was by happenstance. Mr. Norris and Lord Deverell were guests of Lord Ormerod, but I believe they intended to meet there to have their discussion. But that is why I am uncertain. Why would two men plotting something so dangerous meet in a public gathering in someone else's home rather than in a private setting?"

Lord Craythorne shifted to face Lydia more directly. "Such meetings often occur when the two conspirators have no reason to meet intentionally, and can justify a supposedly accidental meeting in a gathering when both have been invited separately. But I believe Norris and Deverell are known to be friends, and therefore should not need such subterfuge."

"Let us first establish whether they said anything I should take notice of," Mr. Rutledge said, "and worry about the peculiarities of their meeting later. Tell me their exact words, Miss Wescott?"

"I heard only four words, 'will kill the king,' and I was not close enough to hear which of them spoke," Lydia said. "But my interrogation of Mr. Norris revealed more."

"You interrogated Mr. Norris?" Lord Craythorne exclaimed.

"Oh, it is a very subtle thing, and I assure you he did not know that is what it was," Lydia said quickly.

"I do not refer to the possibility of you alerting them," Lord Craythorne said, "but to the fact that if you are correct, these men are quite dangerous, and Deverell, for one, has a vicious temper and would have no remorse about eliminating anyone who threatens him. You should not have taken that chance."

"I thank you for your concern," Lydia said. She meant it, too; Lord Craythorne's intensity of speech matched his emotions, though they were still muted, and the fact that he experienced such concern told her he was not, in fact, secretly mad. "I am always careful, I promise, and you need not worry for me. Though I have said this to Mr.

Rutledge, and he never heeds that advice." She was babbling, she knew, but Lord Craythorne's emotional self-mastery unsettled her, as if her Discernment had failed her.

"You have powerful protectors who would be quite angry were I to permit you to come to harm," Mr. Rutledge said, with a concealed amusement that said he did not fear Clemency or Colin's retribution. "Tell me of this interrogation. I presume Mr. Norris was left believing you were merely an innocent young woman, unacquainted with guile?"

"You presume correctly, sir." Lydia focused on the corner where the bookcases met so as to avoid Lord Craythorne's gaze. "Mr. Norris is the weak link in their conspiracy, I believe, as he was quick to brag of his connections, and I observed him speaking too freely—at least, Lord Deverell's irritation at him told me Mr. Norris was not as careful in public as he should have been. I suspect I would not have gained as much information from Lord Deverell."

Quickly, she summed up what Mr. Norris had revealed and the conclusions she had drawn. "I do not know if the Prince Regent's attendance at Lord Deverell's house party means anything important," she concluded, "but it may not matter, as I daresay Mr. Norris' hope is a vain one."

She risked a glance at Lord Craythorne and discovered he and Mr. Rutledge were regarding one another closely. Mr. Rutledge looked grim. Lord Craythorne's expression was still neutral, though Lydia Discerned the tight hold he had on his frustration.

"Do you have someone with access to that house party?" Lord Craythorne said.

"Possibly," Mr. Rutledge replied. "It is the involvement of the Prince Regent that worries me. An attempt on the king's life might include one on the regency." Mr. Rutledge turned his gaze on Lydia, startling her. "Your information is most useful. Do not take it as a criticism when I say it leaves me with a dozen possibilities to investigate."

"Oh, I am not offended, I quite see how what I learned is just the beginning," Lydia said.

"I may be able to narrow down those possibilities," Mrs. Rutledge said. She rarely spoke when Lydia met with Mr. Rutledge, but the woman was a powerful Extraordinary Seer whose presence at these meetings was not just that of a duenna to protect Lydia's reputation. "But it will take some days." She rested a hand on her rounded belly. "I must be careful not to overexert."

"I should think so," Mr. Rutledge said, pretending to scowl. Lydia was always embarrassed when she Discerned his feelings of tenderness toward his wife. Though she was not unfamiliar with love in all its many expressions, Mr. Rutledge's stern and powerful demeanor seemed so at odds with such emotion Lydia felt like an eavesdropper, and not the interesting and exciting kind.

"And what am I to do?" she asked, hoping to shift Mr. Rutledge's emotions into something less intimate.

"You have already accomplished quite enough," Mr. Rutledge said. "None of those dozen possibilities I have to investigate are the sort an innocent young woman might reasonably be involved in."

"Oh," Lydia said, disappointed. "But surely—"

"*No*, Miss Wescott." Mr. Rutledge's sternness concealed genuine concern. "Your desire to help is laudable, but I cannot permit you to risk yourself. You are far too valuable as you are."

"I will see what I can learn from the Prince Regent," Lord Craythorne said. "Though I doubt I am so circumspect as you, Miss Wescott." He smiled, but his amusement was directed as much inward as it was toward Lydia.

"You would not be so foolish as to approach the Prince Regent so directly," Lydia said without considering her words. Then she stammered, "That is, I do not know what your connection is, and perhaps it is not foolishness—"

"I take your meaning, Miss Wescott." Lord Craythorne's amusement deepened. "Never fear, our relationship is as amicable as the Prince Regent deems possible. It helps that he respects his fellow Scorchers and heeds their words with perhaps too much easiness."

"Then you are a Scorcher, my lord?" Lydia's gaze swept swiftly over him again. She knew few Scorchers, but they were said to be as erratic in their speech and comportment as rumor said Extraordinary Discerners were. But Lord Craythorne showed nothing of such tendencies.

"I am. It is not a talent I trade on, save for how it gains me the

Prince Regent's ear." The amusement vanished as if it had never been. Before Lydia could stupidly comment on it, Lord Craythorne rose and said to Mr. Rutledge, "Report to me in three days' time—or is that not enough, ma'am?" He directed his final words at Mrs. Rutledge.

"I shall know something by then," Mrs. Rutledge said, again passing a hand over her belly.

"What of Varley?" Mr. Rutledge said, rising to tower over Lord Craythorne.

"What of him?" Lord Craythorne's expression was once more neutral, but the mention of Varley, whoever he was, sent a red spike of annoyance through him, and his voice deepened, giving Lydia the impression of someone preparing to deliver a verbal thrashing.

"He has once more made an effort to interfere with my organization. I have no need of the kind of thugs he employs, nor of their hamfisted attempts to gain information." Mr. Rutledge's annoyance was even greater than Lord Craythorne's.

"I see." Lord Craythorne shook his head slowly. "Leave him to me. And notify me if you experience any more interference. He does not have the authority to act unilaterally."

"Would that his lack of authority mattered," Mr. Rutledge said sourly. "Thank you, your Grace."

"I should extend my thanks to you, instead." Lord Craythorne turned to face Lydia and said, "I did not know what to expect from you, Miss Wescott. Rutledge's reports could not convey the reality."

"Most people say that about me," Lydia said, flustered at the directness of his gaze. "That I am not to be expected."

"And do you agree?"

The question caught her off-guard. "I," she began, blinked a few times to banish memories, and added, "I never know what to expect of myself, so perhaps that is an accurate assessment."

Lord Craythorne smiled. "I hope to meet you again," he said, and let himself out.

"Miss Wescott, are you well?" Mrs. Rutledge exclaimed.

Lydia realized she had slumped into the corner of the sofa. She felt as if she had been released from a tremendous, invisible tension, and yet she had not been conscious of it until it was gone. "I am very well," she said, straightening. "It is just that Lord Craythorne is over-powering."

Mr. Rutledge laughed. "I will not tell him you felt so," he said. "He does not need any more compliments to feed his self-love."

"I did not mean it as a compliment," Lydia replied automatically, then blushed when both Mr. and Mrs. Rutledge laughed heartily.

"Well, *that* I might tell him," Mr. Rutledge said. "No, do not look so, I would not be so ungracious," he added as Lydia began to protest. "The Duke of Craythorne has enough sycophants trailing him it is a wonder he is not insufferable."

A duke. Lydia blushed to think how informally and incorrectly she had addressed him as "my lord." To cover her embarrassment, she asked, "What does it mean that he is a member of your oversight committee? I believed you to report to the Prince Regent, or the House of Lords."

Mr. Rutledge resumed his seat beside his wife and took one of her hands in his massive one. "I have extensive experience in investigating threats to important or powerful entities," he said. "The East India Company, and the Bank of England, to name two. The House of Lords enlisted me to develop an organization that would counter threats to the British government. Unfortunately for them, I am very good at what I do, and some members of Parliament became afraid I might use my organization to either control them or attempt to overthrow them."

"Ridiculous notions," Mrs. Rutledge scoffed.

"Not all that ridiculous, as I...but that is irrelevant." Mr. Rutledge patted her hand absently. "The House of Lords decided I needed a keeper, and intended to put me under the charge of one of their own. When they could not decide on that one, their oversight turned into a committee of three. It has proved to be a mixed blessing as, on the one hand, I have a much clearer line of command, but on the other, I am at least nominally under the control of three men whose abilities and desires are somewhat erratic."

"But not Lord Craythorne," Lydia said.

"Not Lord Craythorne. He listens to what I have to say and provides a buffer between my organization and the other two committee members. Lord Varley, in particular, has a habit of attempting to take control of parts of my organization, or giving his own people the aegis of what I have built for his own purposes. And you, Miss Wescott, did not hear me say that."

Lydia nodded, suppressing a smile. "I am very good at keeping secrets," she said, "particularly the ones I have not heard."

CHAPTER 4

IN WHICH A PLEASANT FAMILY INTERLUDE IS INTERRUPTED BY AN UNUSUAL REQUEST

The drawing room of Emeraude House, or rather, the primary drawing room, for there were three, was the most comfortable room Lydia had ever seen. In an objective sense, this should not be true, as knickknacks and small china figurines filled its shelves and tables to overflowing, and Lydia was not fond of such trifles. They reminded her of her mother, and that was not a memory she wished to dwell on ever. Colin's house on Hanover Square, where they had lived before his marriage, had been cozier despite smelling of metal and machine oil due to Colin's passion for mechanicals.

But this drawing room, with its oversized hearth and many comfortable chairs and sofas and divans, never failed to make Lydia feel as if she were truly home. She loved the paintings on the walls, not portraits but landscapes of places she had never visited; it was as if she might step through their frames into distant reaches of England or France or farther afield in Europe. And, of course, there was the pianoforte and her own harp, poised ready for her to play whenever she chose. During the day, many windows brightened the room; by night, lamps and candles cast a warmer, golden glow over the furnishings. Lydia found herself in this room more often than not, day or night.

This morning, the entire family was gathered: Colin and Clemency seated by the fire, talking quietly of romantic matters, as Lydia perceived from their heightened emotions; Clemency's sister Prudence playing sonatas in the corner, oblivious to the world; Clemency's young brother Gawain reading near the pianoforte; and the Dowager Countess, Emmeline, preening herself before a hand mirror.

Emmeline's general feelings of pleasure, for she was always light-hearted and given to amusements, were tempered by the slight pain she felt as she Shaped her face to more closely suit her current ideal of beauty. Lydia liked Emmeline despite the fact that she was rather shallow. She had a kind heart and never experienced any emotion more terrible than mild annoyance.

Emmeline abruptly set her mirror aside and stood. "I regret I must leave you all, but I am engaged to pay calls with Lady Maria Swann," she said. "It will be very dull, but I do not wish to hurt her feelings by telling her so."

"That is very kind of you," Clemency said. "And have you plans for this evening?"

The faintest pink tinged Emmeline's cheeks. "The theatre, with Mr. Cameron."

Lydia Discerned Clemency's hidden pleasure and amusement, but her sister-in-law said, "I hope you both enjoy yourselves, then."

Emmeline left the room, and Clemency exchanged glances with Colin. "Mr. Cameron again," Colin said.

"Yes, she seems quite partial to him," Clemency replied. "I have not—"

The door opened, and Slater entered with his silver salver. "I beg your pardon for the interruption," he said, "but Miss Wescott has received a message."

Lydia rose to accept the envelope Slater offered her. Her heart beat faster for a moment. Another assignment, only two days after the last. But her name on the front of the small sealed envelope was in an unfamiliar hand, definitely not Mr. Rutledge's confident script. Curious, she broke the seal and extracted the single folded sheet from within.

The same fine handwriting covered the paper on one side, the lines clear and uncrossed. *Miss Wescott,* the letter began:

I have been engaged in Dream these many months, and of late, all my Dreams have pointed to you—or, rather, to a young woman of your description. I have only just put your name to that description, and address you now on a matter of some delicacy.

The purpose of my Dream was to procure relief for my grandfather, whose situation is known to all. Why the results should indicate I must bring you to meet him, I do not understand, but in my experience Dream does not fail. I hope it means that one such as yourself, untroubled by madness, may know of some treatment that will succeed where Extraordinary Shapers and doctors have failed.

I do not know why you conceal your Extraordinary Discerner's talent, but I assure you I respect your desire for secrecy, however motivated. I hope your need to remain anonymous in your talent will not prevent you joining me at Windsor Castle in three days' time.

I await your reply with much anticipation,

HRH the Princess Charlotte, Seer

"Lydia?" Colin said. "What is the matter? You appear close to fainting." He hurried to stand close beside her, one large hand on her elbow.

Lydia shook her head. "It is merely a surprise," she said, and handed him Princess Charlotte's letter.

Colin's grip on her elbow tightened as he read. "Astounding," he said. "This is—Princess Charlotte asks Lydia to attend upon the king, in the hope that she might know some way of easing his madness."

Prudence gasped. "But that is impossible. Is it not? For if it *was* possible, they would have done such a thing before now."

"I agree," Clemency said. "Lydia is not the only Extraordinary Discerner who has mastered her talent."

"But there are only a few of us in England who have," Lydia said. "Mr. Rutledge says I am the most competent of all of those, and the least erratic and fragile in my person. Perhaps no one has approached one of us on the king's behalf because they believe there is no point. And her Highness writes that it is Dream that drives her request—that must surely be unusual, as I doubt there are many Seers Dreaming of the king's condition."

"You will help, surely," Gawain said.

He sounded so certain Lydia replied, "But there is nothing I can do. I cannot stop the king's madness. I cannot give him the self-control I learned with such difficulty."

"But you have compassion, and you know it might have been you in his position," Gawain persisted. "Everyone believes his Majesty's madness is permanent, and I daresay no one is still looking for a cure except her Highness. Suppose you were to ease his suffering? It is worth seeing him, at least."

Lydia took the letter from Colin and read it again. "I believe Princess Charlotte is, not desperate, perhaps, but grasping at any possibility. And it is true, I feel such pity for anyone overwhelmed by Discernment. I believe I will accept her invitation." The idea satisfied her. She recalled Mr. Rutledge telling her she could be of no use in his hunt for potential regicides; he had meant well, but the memory still stung. This was a kind of assistance he could not tell her to reject. And to be of help to the king himself...!

Colin's jaw was set tight. "And if his Majesty's disordered senses overwhelm you?"

"I do not believe that is likely." It was the one thing Lydia was confident of, her ability to distinguish between herself and a single madman. "But if I am in danger, I will retreat and give my apologies. I am always careful, you know that, Colin."

"Forgive me wishing to protect you," Colin said. "I remember too well how you looked when you left Magdalen. I swore you would never endure that again."

Lydia put her hand on his arm and smiled. "And you have kept that promise. Besides, it is not as if I am in danger of being confined in an asylum."

"No." Colin sighed. "One might almost see this as a required service to your country."

"Let us not imagine that," Clemency said with a shudder. "Rumors that Extraordinaries will be required to perform civil service in place of their War Office years, now that the war is over, have not been entirely countered. Imagine one's life given over to using one's talent solely at the direction of others."

"It will not happen," Colin said. But his grip tightened on Lydia's elbow again, as if he did not believe his own assertion.

THREE DAYS LATER, LYDIA AGAIN SAT IN EMERAUDE HOUSE'S MAIN drawing room, waiting. She had dressed carefully in her nicest day gown, not because she wished to impress anyone—she did not believe Princess Charlotte would see even her best finery as comparable to her own attire, and of course the king would not care if she came dressed in sackcloth—but because it suited her self-esteem. She might not be of high rank, but she was as deserving of respect as anyone. And, she privately told herself, it was a princess who was her supplicant, and that gave her consequence few aspired to.

The door opened, and Colin entered. He, too, was dressed in his finest frock coat and wore knee breeches rather than pantaloons. "You look very fine," he told her. "I, on the other hand, feel very foolish. I believe I was born to the wrong place in society, as I much prefer workman's garb to this frippery."

"It is not frippery," Clemency said, entering after him, "and you look very handsome. I hope none of Princess Charlotte's ladies in waiting take a fancy to you. It would be so embarrassing if I were forced to fight one of them for your affections."

"Your attempt to put me at ease has succeeded, my dear." Colin took his wife's hand and pressed it to his lips. "Though I feel no trepidation at encountering those of noble birth. My concern is all for Lydia. I am by no means as sanguine about your meeting the king in his madness as you are."

"I promise there is no danger," Lydia said. It was true, he did worry, as did Clemency, though to a lesser degree. She tried not to resent them for it. Their emotions rose from love for her, after all—and yet she disliked being treated like thin glass. "If I were surrounded by a hundred madmen, that might be hazardous, but you know that will not happen again."

Colin sighed. "Yes. I know." He extended an arm to Lydia. "Let us go, then."

Lydia stepped close and arranged her arms around Colin's neck. Colin clasped her about the waist, lifted her as easily as if she weighed nothing, and—

light, drifting, falling through an airless space—

they were in an enclosed space with a low ceiling and white-painted walls, no bigger than five feet on a side. White lamps with frosted glass glowed, illuminating the painting on one wall of a stylized lion fighting a unicorn. The tiny room was warmer than the drawing room and smelled strongly of wax and sweat, making Lydia's nose wrinkle involuntarily.

Colin released her and rapped on one of the walls, which proved instead to be a door with no handle, so cleverly set into the wall Lydia almost did not detect it. Immediately, a man's voice came to them, muffled by the door. "Who goes there?"

"I have the way of it, and none shall bar," Colin replied.

The door opened outward, and a man dressed in the livery of the Royal Guard beckoned to them to exit. Lydia emerged into a larger room into which the Bounding chamber they had just left had clearly been added as an afterthought. It looked like a giant crate fitted into one corner of the room, much less ornate than its surroundings. Lydia surveyed the extensive gilding of the walls and where the walls met the ceiling and imagined how much gold that would be if one peeled all of it off. A cupful? A bucket's worth?

"Who is meeting you, sir?" the guard said. He ignored Lydia entirely, focusing on Colin. Lydia wondered if he disregarded her because she was small, because she was young, or because she was female. His emotions showed the beige placidity of someone doing a boring, common task. In her opinion, he ought to be more suspicious. Being small, young, and female did not make one harmless. Suppose she were a Scorcher, or a Coercer?

"Lady Harrisfurd," Colin said. "We are to wait in the annex, according to my instructions."

The guard nodded once. He snapped his fingers without looking around. Lydia realized there were other guards present, their uniforms, like Colin's interrogator's, ornate enough that she had overlooked them in her examination of the equally ornate room. One of the guards stepped forward in response to his superior's summons.

"You will escort the gentleman and the lady to the annex," the first guard said. "Remain with them until Lady Harrisfurd arrives."

The second guard gave a curt nod and marched away. Colin followed immediately, with Lydia a few steps behind. In that order, they looked like a truncated procession, she thought, or like a comet with a very short tail, as the guard was taller than Colin and Colin was taller than she. She continued to trail behind, wishing to give herself more time to observe the castle.

She had grown up listening to Colin's stories of knights and princesses and sieges of castles, and to her a castle was all old stone and drafty passages and narrow windows for shooting arrows through. Windsor Castle looked more like a mansion, though it would be the most elegant, ornate mansion ever conceived. The gilding in the guard post continued down the long hall and extended to the frames of the portraits hanging on the walls, staring down at Lydia. Her estimate of the quantity of gold leaf went from a bucket to a vat.

She cast glances at the portraits, none of whose subjects she recognized. She knew little of painting, or of any kind of art besides music, and these did not impress her—dark, sour faces wearing clothing that must have cost a fortune. She wondered whether the people were still alive, and what they thought of their images preserved for posterity.

Windows taller than Lydia set into the wall opposite the portraits revealed the pearly grey sky. Rain was coming, and Lydia was grateful that Bounding made it possible to traverse the twenty-plus miles from London to Windsor in the space of a breath. She did not love travel, and loved even less the notion of riding in a carriage all day with the rain beating down on the roof.

When they reached the end of the long hall, the guard opened a door that looked tiny by comparison to the size of the hall and gestured to them to enter. The room beyond was as small as the door, though still much larger than the Bounding chamber, and was painted a deep red. Few furnishings adorned the room, though it was as gilded as everything else; there was nothing but four gilded chairs with red cushions, the door they had entered by, and a matching door opposite the first.

Colin stopped a few feet inside and stood casually, looking as if castles and gilding were a part of his everyday experience. Lydia Discerned that his calmness was not pretended, and that most of his discomfort was a matter of anticipation. The guard was as blandly beige as his superior. The streaks of red that would mean an alertness to the possibility of violence did not pulse through him. Lydia had already evolved three ways she might use his indifference against him. She would never act on those notions, of course, but suppose she *were* a dangerous person? Really, these guards should be disciplined.

Less than a minute passed before the other door opened and a lady entered. Lydia knew immediately she was a lady and not merely a woman; her gown was of fine silk, her jewels expensive-looking, and her hair arranged so perfectly Lydia almost touched her own short blonde hair to assure herself it had not been disordered by Bounding, though of course that was impossible.

The lady smiled at Lydia, but in an absent manner, and this combined with her secret ennui told Lydia this lady believed herself well above Lydia socially. It also suggested that she did not know who Lydia was, or at least did not know her talent, and that relieved Lydia's mind, because Princess Charlotte had kept her secret at least to this extent.

"Good afternoon," the lady said. "I am Lady Harrisfurd. You are Miss Wescott?" She sounded politely interested, which amused Lydia as it was at odds with her continuing emotion of boredom.

Lydia curtseyed. "I am she."

"Please accompany me. Your companion may wait here." Lady Harrisfurd turned a polite look on Colin. "I shall see that refreshments are provided."

Colin bowed. Lydia bit her lip to keep from laughing at how amusing he found Lady Harrisfurd's languid politeness, though he concealed his emotions well. "I thank you for your consideration, my lady," he said. Lydia suspected he was wondering whether Lady Harris-furd would be genuinely polite if she knew she addressed the Earl of Ashford.

Lydia followed Lady Harrisfurd through the door and walked beside her down a series of long corridors, all of them gilt-bedecked. There were more portraits, and some statuary, and a pendulum clock with a case big enough for Lydia to stand inside, but Lydia was not overwhelmed by the magnificence. To her, it seemed very cold, not at all welcoming the way Emeraude House did. She could not imagine anyone liking living here.

Presently, Lady Harrisfurd, who had said nothing as they walked, opened a door beneath a painting of hounds baying after a fox and led Lydia inside, immediately dropping into a deep curtsey. Lydia swiftly did the same, but less gracefully as she had not been prepared for it. "Your Highness," Lady Harrisfurd said, "this is Miss Wescott. Miss Wescott, her Highness the Princess Charlotte."

CHAPTER 5

IN WHICH THE DEVASTATING NATURE OF DISCERNMENT IS DISCUSSED

"Rise, please," said the woman who now stood from where she had been seated on a green-upholstered sofa. Lydia's general impression of the entire room was of green—green-paneled walls flanked by gilded moldings, emerald cushions on gilded chairs, carpets figured in mauve and yellow on green backgrounds. Had these been emotions and not architecture, Lydia would have called the room the embodiment of romantic love.

She straightened, managing not to lose her balance, and examined Princess Charlotte. She knew the princess was nearly her own age, just turned twenty, but she had not realized that claims of Princess Charlotte's beauty were not so exaggerated as she always assumed. The princess had a finely shaped nose and a mouth not spoiled by pettiness, and her hair was arranged prettily, without the touch of artifice Lady Harrisfurd's had.

"Miss Wescott, thank you for joining me," Princess Charlotte said. "Lady Harrisfurd, you are excused."

Lady Harrisfurd's boredom was now tinged with curiosity, but she left the room with no more reply than another respectful curtsey.

Princess Charlotte waited for the door to close before smiling at Lydia and waving at the sofa. "Please be seated. I fear I cannot be formal with you, as you have been the subject of so many of my Dreams in recent weeks—oh, but that sounds rather predatory, does it not? I apologize. I have been told all my life that I should learn to think before I speak, which is so very difficult."

"I understand," Lydia said, then blushed, for she had spoken without thinking herself. "I mean, it is only that for an Extraordinary Discerner, the world is laid bare, and we—at least, I—feel an intimacy that makes it difficult for me to maintain formality as well."

"You see? Already I believe I have done the right thing in sending for you." Princess Charlotte clasped Lydia's hand briefly. Her emotions were a muddle of hope and fear and damped excitement that made Lydia's head whirl before she made herself focus.

"My grandfather...he was always so fond of me," the princess continued. Her eyes shone with unshed tears. "I remember him fondly, as well—I apologize, that sounds as if he were already gone, but in a sense, that is how it feels." She extracted a handkerchief from her sleeve and dabbed at her eyes. "And yet there are moments when he knows me, and I hoped, perhaps, you might offer some solution. Forgive my bluntness, but you do not seem at all mad."

"I am not, but I was once," Lydia said. "The condition came and went by turns while I lived in an asylum for those whose minds are afflicted. It is how I gained control, you see, by being constantly in a state of confusion. But it seems that has not been the case for his Majesty."

"No, sadly. At first, we believed his episodes would be infrequent and treatable, but as his talent grew in power, his madness increased. And now..." Princess Charlotte's voice trailed off.

"I should not give you false hope," Lydia said when it was clear the princess was done speaking. "I cannot guarantee I know anything that will help the king. But perhaps—may I ask some questions?"

The princess nodded and blotted her eyes again.

"Do you know what his Majesty's range of talent is? How far away he can Discern?"

"I fear not. His range increased over time—we believe it is one reason he is now driven mad by his talent." Princess Charlotte looked thoughtful. "Before he was incapacitated, Grandfather established that his range was some five hundred yards. That was twenty-five years ago."

Stunned, Lydia blurted out, "My own range is only fifty feet. I cannot imagine being exposed to so many emotions. He would never be free from Discerning at least a few people." She had considered, once, whether her own condition might have been helped by isolation, by being far from anyone whose emotions might impinge on her. Clearly, that would be impossible for the king.

"You said he has moments of lucidity," she forged on. "Have you noticed anything those periods have in common?"

Princess Charlotte shook her head. "We have tried altering his diet, altering his environment, and the doctors and Extraordinary Shapers have given him every treatment known to medicine. When he is clear-headed, it is in response to no stimulus they can identify."

"May I speak with him?" Lydia felt increasingly certain there was nothing she could do, but she did not like to come all this way and leave Princess Charlotte with nothing.

"I hoped you might. I understand there may be nothing—no." The princess tilted her chin in a gesture of defiance. "My Dream is never wrong, and I know there is a reason it put you here on this day. You may not be able to cure my grandfather, but I am certain you can do *something.*"

Her certainty struck Lydia a nearly palpable blow, blue-green and so strong Lydia closed a fist to keep herself anchored to the present. "I will do what I can," she heard herself say, her words seeming to come from some distant land.

Princess Charlotte took Lydia through a different door than the one she had entered by, down more long, gilded corridors, carpeted thickly so their footsteps were entirely muffled. They passed rooms whose doors were flung wide, revealing more sitting rooms, a dining room Lydia estimated could seat more than fifty, rooms lined with cushioned chairs, and a music room arranged as if in readiness for a performance. Lydia could not imagine the king in his madness caring about music—unless music soothed him. She had not thought to ask how his madness manifested. Well, she would learn that for herself, soon enough.

The farther they walked, the less opulent the halls and chambers became. They were still more ornate than anything Lydia had ever seen, and they were not dingy or in disrepair, but there were fewer furnishings, fewer chairs, as if not as many people were expected to use them. The lamps glowed as brightly as ever, which relieved Lydia's mind. Her imagination had begun to throw up fanciful notions of dim rooms full of silent people, memories of Magdalen she suppressed that refused to stay entirely dormant.

There were people present, though she saw none of them, merely Discerned their emotions. None of them roiled with anxiety or anger; some displayed the beige or pale blue of individuals doing tedious or routine tasks, a few felt irritation, and one or two pulsed with green desire, pale and mild such as one experienced when one loved one's work. Lydia had not Discerned anyone except the guards when they entered, and she guessed "annex" was meant literally, that she and Princess Charlotte were outside the central building of the castle.

Then she Discerned someone new, someone she instantly identified as the king. It could be no one else. Though the individual was in general as blandly content as everyone around him, other emotions shot through him, lasting barely long enough for Lydia to recognize them as fear and anger, love and lust, jealousy and sorrow.

"What is wrong?" Princess Charlotte asked.

Lydia realized she had come to a stop. "I can Discern his Majesty from here," she said. Her voice came out as a near-whisper, and she swallowed and added, more loudly, "His natural emotions are a tangle."

"What does that mean?"

Lydia shook her head. She was almost certain it meant there was no hope for King George, but she did not like to say so when she had not even seen him face to face. "I cannot say," she said, perfectly truthfully. "Pray, let me speak to him."

She again followed Princess Charlotte, who now entered a small room Lydia instinctively identified as an antechamber. It had no furnishings, and to her surprise was not slathered in gilt. In fact, the whiteness of its walls and the creamy ivory of its carpet made it appear to have been bleached. Two men dressed in courtier's clothing waited there, one beside each of the two doors. They bowed deeply to the princess, but said nothing. One of the men opened his door, the one opposite where Lydia and the princess had entered, and bowed again.

The room beyond was a comfortably appointed chamber, the first place Lydia had seen in the castle that appealed to her. Two windows without drapes let in brilliant sunlight, giving the impression of summer beyond the windows instead of a rather chilly spring day. A pair of matched sofas upholstered in gold-shot scarlet brocade flanked the windows, taking advantage of the light, and several chairs with cushions matching the sofas stood against the walls. Men and women, one wearing the black cap of a female Extraordinary Shaper, sat or stood throughout the room.

A console table to the left of the windows held a bowl of fresh fruit, oranges and bananas that must have been Bounded from far away. The scent of the oranges reminded Lydia of the first day she had been free of Magdalen, how Colin had found her an orange as a treat.

With that memory in mind, she bowed to the man seated on one of the sofas. "Your Majesty," she said. "My name is Lydia Wescott, and I am an Extraordinary Discerner like yourself—or, not exactly, you are much more powerful than I, but we have the same talent, both of us."

The King faced her, though he was not looking at her, instead gazing past her ear. "Charlotte," he said. "My dearest wife."

A pang of grief shot through Princess Charlotte. "It is I, Charlotte, your granddaughter," she said. Her voice shook as if she were controlling tears. "Charlotte, Grandfather. Remember?"

"Charlotte," the King said. "Dear Charlotte. Such a dear child. She knows to call me Grandfather, though she is but two years of age." His gaze fixed on Lydia, sharply acute. "You are empty. Void. How do you experience no emotion?"

Startled, Lydia said, "No, it is that my natural emotions are not as strong as the ones I Discern. What else do you sense within me, your Majesty?"

The King touched his forehead. "Do not presume," he said angrily. "I—" In a flash, his grief washed over Lydia just as his demeanor changed, and he said, "No, why is Charlotte not here? She is gone, gone forever!"

"Calm yourself, your Majesty," the Extraordinary Shaper said. "Queen Charlotte will visit you today."

Lydia turned on the woman. "That is a lie," she said without thinking. "How can you—"

Someone took her by the arm and drew her away to a corner. "The Queen never comes, but the King does not know it," a courtier said. His face was flushed, and his annoyance with Lydia swept over her. "He will not remember thirty seconds from now what we tell him, and that lie is all we know to calm him. Do not interfere."

Lydia jerked her arm out of his grasp. "It is cruel," she said. "He still feels everything. You give him hope, and it is unfulfilled, and he may not remember the facts, but he certainly feels the grief of loss."

"And what more should we do?" the man retorted. "You are an Extraordinary Discerner, and not mad—what secret do you know, and why have you not shared it with your King?"

"Miss Wescott is here by my invitation, Lord Welsch," Princess Charlotte said. "Do not presume. Miss Wescott, is there..."

Lydia looked past Lord Welsch at the King, who now sat on the sofa, staring out the window. He was calm, for once, but even as Lydia became aware of this, grief once more filled him, and he bowed his head and wept like a child. Grief suffused Lydia, and she realized it was her own natural emotion reacting to his. She closed her eyes and suppressed her emotions, embracing his grief as distinct from her own. She would not give in to madness.

The grief passed, and the King leapt to his feet and shouted furiously at the air, wordless, angry cries that broke Lydia out of her fugue. Two courtiers, both tall and broad-shouldered, approached him warily, their hands held ready to restrain him. But his anger passed as abruptly as it had appeared, and the King resumed his seat. His gaze fell on Princess Charlotte, and he smiled broadly.

"Ah, my dear," he exclaimed. "Sit. Tell me of your affianced husband. When is the wedding to be held? I wish to attend."

Princess Charlotte sat opposite the King, slowly. "Leopold is a dear, and I declare we shall be very happy," she said. "The official announcement is tomorrow."

"Wonderful!" The King glanced at Lydia, then looked at her more closely. "You are an Extraordinary Discerner, are you not? There are so few of us." He beckoned to Lydia. "I am not mad, you know. I realize they believe so, but it is passing madness. I am quite well."

Lydia, disconcerted, sat next to Princess Charlotte. "I was mad, once. I remember."

"Then you know I should not—"

The King's eyes lost focus, and a brilliant smile transformed his face. "Glorious, glorious news, I have a son!" he shouted. "They said it was a daughter, but it was a mistake. That fool, not determining the truth—and Charlotte is well, we are all so happy!"

He leaped to his feet and danced around the room, an awkward, loose-limbed cavorting. Lydia watched him, her mouth open. His joy was such a beautiful, multicolored rush she almost wished to dance with him, but that would make her look mad as well.

"You see," Princess Charlotte said.

"I do," Lydia replied.

"His lucidity—can nothing be done to extend the length of those periods?" Princess Charlotte clasped her hands tightly in her lap.

Lydia hesitated. The King's emotions flickered so rapidly through him she was becoming dizzy. "His emotions are linked to his memories," she said. "He feels joy, and his mind believes he is once more experiencing a moment in the past that brought him joy. Or he feels anger, or sorrow, or a dozen other emotions. But he is only rarely calm enough to be anchored in the present, and even then so much time passes between moments of lucidity—I am not sure how to explain." Lydia bit her lip in thought.

"Imagine a sleep that lasts a hundred years," she finally said. "Suppose you were to fall asleep this evening and wake a hundred years from now. To you, those hundred years would be nothing, and yet the world will have rolled on without you. Now imagine his Majesty's madness as lengthy sleeps. He becomes lucid and believes only a moment has passed, but really it has been two weeks, or three, or more. He asked about your Highness's engagement because it was the last thing you told him, when he was lucid before, yes?"

Princess Charlotte nodded. "But I still do not understand."

Lydia let out a deep breath. "He is already lost in the past, regardless of whether the madness brought on by his Extraordinary Discernment can be cured. Which, I regret to say, I do not believe is possible. His mind is shattered, his natural emotions run riot, and now it is his own emotions that torture him and not those of others. I truly regret having to tell you this."

"I see." Princess Charlotte wiped her eyes. "I cannot believe Dream has failed me so completely. I was so sure..."

"Perhaps I came to reveal the truth. You should not endure having false hope." Lydia took the Princess's hand. "And you know he loves you, deep within. These emotions, these moments of madness—those are not truly who he is. They are a mask he is forced to wear. You should not believe that anything he says—"

The King roared and swept the bowl of fruit off the console table to land with a clatter on the carpet. Oranges and bananas rolled or bounced in every direction, and the courtiers, all except the Extraordinary Shaper, bent to collect them.

"Or anything he does is truly him," Lydia continued.

The Princess nodded again. "Thank you. You have reassured me, and perhaps you are correct that that is all my Dream promised. Pray, permit me to escort you back. It is your brother who waits to Bound you home, is it not?"

"Yes, but he does not see it as a burden," Lydia said before remembering that Princess Charlotte's momentary concern at making Colin wait was not obvious to anyone but her. But the Princess did not comment, merely cast one last look at her grandfather before ushering Lydia out the door.

They did not speak as they retraced their path. Princess Charlotte was lost in a melancholy reverie Lydia wished she could shut out. She could not stop Discerning her emotions, but she could focus on her own true emotions until her companion's were distant and not troubling. The effort felt like grasping wet sand that oozed away from her, so weak and impalpable were her natural emotions.

She recalled what the King had said, how he had called her a void. She had never considered herself so, but on reflection, she realized how close to the truth it was. She could not afford to indulge her natural emotions when they were what tangled with those she

Discerned, bringing her to the brink of madness. Suppressing her own emotions when the emotions of others threatened her was her only choice. A void could not be overwhelmed.

This time, there were a few other people in the halls with them, mostly servants preparing the midday meal, as well as another Extraordinary Shaper, this one male, who passed them going the other way. Lydia, intent on her own emotional condition, barely noticed him, but she became gradually aware of something niggling at her awareness, some emotion that did not belong.

She stopped and turned. The Extraordinary Shaper had reached the far end of the hall and turned out of sight, but he had not yet moved beyond her range. Unlike the others, he felt anticipation, nervous excitement, and beneath all that, rich, red malice.

"Who was that?" she demanded.

Princess Charlotte, who had continued on a few paces, stopped as well. "One of Grandfather's doctors, I assume. I fear I did not notice him. Why?"

"Because he intends to kill the King," Lydia said, and broke into a run.

CHAPTER 6

IN WHICH LYDIA TAKES A STAND, AND RECEIVES AN UNEXPECTED OFFER

L ydia ran as fast as her skirts would permit back the way they had come. She stumbled as she came to the corner, caught herself, and sped onward. Behind her, Princess Charlotte called her name, her puzzlement a clear orange-gold note supplanting her melancholy. Ahead, the antechamber door swung shut on the Extraordinary Shaper. The door was no barrier to Lydia's Discernment; his malice and glee at having got this far was like a blow to the face.

"Stop that man!" she shouted, though there was no one to hear. She pelted toward the door, pushing herself faster and cursing the skirts tangling her legs. Staggering to a halt, she wrenched at the handle and jerked the door open.

The room was empty save for the two attendants at either door. "Who was that Shaper?" Lydia demanded. The man by the entrance was too surprised to stop her, but in the time it took Lydia to cross the antechamber, the second man had recovered and stepped into her path to bar her way. "Let me pass," Lydia said.

"Why have you returned?" the man said, not moving. "And unaccompanied? I cannot permit you entrance."

Lydia had never wished so much to be a Coercer, to make him fear her. She still Discerned the Extraordinary Shaper's malice. By the placidity of the King's courtiers, he had not yet taken action. But as an Extraordinary Shaper could kill with a touch, that state of affairs would not persist long.

In desperation, she stepped closer to the attendant and, drawing on Colin's instruction for her own defense against an attacker, drove her knee up between the man's legs. He let out a strangled sound somewhere between a moan and a scream and folded, clutching himself. Lydia pushed on his shoulders to move him more rapidly out of the way and flung the door open.

Her abrupt entrance stopped the King's courtiers where they stood or sat throughout the room. Lydia's gaze fixed on the malevolent Extraordinary Shaper, who with his colleague stood near the window. Their conversation broke off mid-sentence. The female Extraordinary Shaper's puzzlement matched the rapidly-approaching Princess Charlotte's. The male Extraordinary Shaper's malicious glee faltered. He took a few steps toward the King.

"Stop there," Lydia commanded. "You will not touch him."

"This woman is deranged," the Shaper said calmly, and continued to approach the King, now with his hand outstretched. "Someone remove her."

"I am an Extraordinary Discerner, and I know you intend harm to his Majesty." Lydia swiftly put herself between the Shaper and the King, who was lost in grief once more and sobbed loudly behind her.

"What nonsense is this?" the female Extraordinary Shaper exclaimed.

"Deranged indeed," the Shaper said. "I will calm her, and she can be investigated. No doubt it is she who wishes the King harm."

Too late Lydia saw her danger. If that Extraordinary Shaper touched her skin, he would kill her. Stop her heart, cause blood to clot in her brain, paralyze her lungs—it might be anything, and he would be free to attack the King before anyone stopped him. No one else had reacted to the drama playing out before them, though their rising confusion threatened to overwhelm Lydia. The female Extraordinary Shaper was not confused; instead Lydia Discerned her puzzlement attendant upon a situation that makes no sense.

Lydia took a step back, then another, until she was pressed against the King's legs, which were drawn up beneath him where he lay curled weeping on the sofa. "I have Discerned this man's intent to kill the King, and I insist you restrain him," she said, though in her heart she knew it was pointless. The Shaper assassin could kill anyone who approached him, and who among these stupid, uncaring people would sacrifice their lives for a mad king who would never know the truth of their sacrifice?

The Shaper assassin stepped closer, and now he smiled, a nasty, self-satisfied smile that chilled Lydia with its malice, echoing the wickedness suffusing him. He was close enough no one else saw his expression. "A fine effort," he whispered, "but you have failed." He extended one hand again. In a louder voice, he said, "I will simply calm you, my dear, your wits are disordered."

Then his eyes widened, and his hand stiffened, and in the next moment he pitched forward, falling into Lydia and forcing her back as well. They both ended sprawled against the sofa, next to the King, who sat up, blinked, and said, "I will not endure your reprobate follies longer, George."

The female Extraordinary Shaper removed her hand from the back of the assassin's neck and hauled him off Lydia to lie on the floor. "I believe he should be immobilized while I sort this out," she said. "You are uninjured?"

"Yes," Lydia said, though her stomach was sore from where the man's elbow had struck her. "Thank you."

"Explain yourself, please. You claim he intends to hurt the King?" The woman's puzzlement did not change, but it was joined by a murky brown worry.

"You did the right thing," Lydia assured her, responding to her emotions rather than her words. "He is filled with malice, and...it is difficult to explain, except that he wishes to hurt, and I am certain he intends to kill his Majesty. My Discernment does not fail me."

"Miss Wescott, what is this?" Princess Charlotte entered, prompting everyone but Lydia and the female Shaper to bow. "A threat to the King, but how?"

Lydia opened her mouth to explain yet again, but surprise and fear flashed suddenly through the female Shaper, and the woman dropped to her knees beside the assassin. Foam flecked the man's lips, and his body trembled as if he suffered terrible convulsions his paralyzed muscles could not fully express. The female Shaper snatched up his hand and closed her eyes, but a moment later she released him. "He is dead," she said. "Suicide."

Princess Charlotte gasped. "Why should Dr. Mervyn commit suicide? For that matter, why did you attack him, Dr. Coulter?" She turned and knelt beside King George, who had returned to a placid, unseeing state. "Grandfather, are you hurt?"

"Miss Wescott claims Dr. Mervyn intended to kill his Majesty," the female Shaper, Dr. Coulter, said. "As impossible as that may seem, I believe she is telling the truth. I can imagine no other reason for him to induce suicide after being subdued."

"But—" Princess Charlotte rose, slowly, keeping hold of the King's unresisting hand. "Dr. Coulter, I still do not understand. Dr. Mervyn has attended on the King in his illness for many months. If he truly did intend my grandfather's death, he might have acted at any time." Her speech slowed as she said these final words, and she turned an astonished gaze on Lydia. "Except my Dream brought you here at this time."

"Someone must remove this body," Dr. Coulter said, her emotions steadying into steely confidence. "And—but I do not know what should happen next. If Dr. Mervyn was bribed, or suborned, or blackmailed, his masters must be discovered."

"Your Highness," Lydia said, "you must send for Mr. Alexander Rutledge. He has—that is, he knows what must be done, though perhaps I should not have said that..." Lydia's head ached with the buffeting of more than a dozen rampant emotions. "Contact him," she added, but her voice sounded weak, and she found she was seated next to the King, her vision blurry.

"Sit there, and I will summon your brother to remove you," Princess Caroline said. "It is not your talent that troubles you?"

Lydia shook her head. "Not in the way you mean, I am not in danger of going mad, it is only that everyone is so bright." She was almost certain that did not make sense, but her clouded vision gave everyone a radiant aura that swayed with them. She clung to the fact that they were all still coherent to her Discernment and closed her eyes.

It was easier to stay conscious when she perceived nothing but emotions. The courtiers were a jumble of fear and confusion and relief, probably relief that the King had not been killed while they were in attendance on him and might be blamed. Dr. Coulter remained puzzled, but that was overlaid by calm certainty that the danger had passed. Princess Charlotte remained more puzzled still, but her relief, a blue-green wave that suffused Lydia, was greater even than the courtiers'. The King's rapidly changing emotions did not alter, for which Lydia was grateful. He would not suffer for having nearly been killed.

The door opened, and shut, and opened again, and courtiers began to move in and out of Lydia's Discernment. After a time, she Discerned Colin's approach. At least, she guessed no one but Colin would experience that tangle of anger and fear caught up in irritation. She was familiar with his reaction to what he considered foolishness on the part of those interfering in his business.

Presently, the door opened once more, and Colin exclaimed, "Lydia!"

"I am well and I am not overwhelmed, and you need not fear for me," she immediately replied, but when she opened her eyes, dizziness struck her again, and she decided she should not rise.

She heard someone kneel beside her, and Colin said, "You are ill. Do not lie to me."

"I am dizzy because it is loud." Lydia risked peeking at him and was relieved when his face did not shake or dance about. "I should return home."

"Miss Wescott." Princess Charlotte spoke from somewhere nearby. "Miss Wescott, this country owes you a great debt. *I* owe you much. My intent in Dreaming was to protect the King, and I believed its answer was you because you are also an Extraordinary Discerner. I see now that my Dream extended further than my limited understanding could penetrate. Had you not been here, my grandfather would likely either be injured or dead. Thank you."

Lydia did not like being thanked. It made her feel as if she, paradoxically, owed the thanker some consideration for her gratitude. But she could hardly be rude to the Princess. "I am glad I was near enough."

"This Mr. Rutledge," Dr. Coulter said. "He is someone of importance?"

Uncertainty filled Lydia. Mr. Rutledge's work was confidential, yes, but surely he must be informed that this assassination attempt had occurred? Lydia's head ached too much for reasoned thought. "No, he is—that is, I know he will know whom to talk to," she stammered.

"I will see to it," Princess Charlotte said. "Please, rest now, and again, I thank you."

Before Lydia could stand, Colin swept her up into his arms, and in the space of a breath they had left the warm, slightly stuffy confines of the King's room for the cooler air of Emeraude House's Bounding chamber. Colin set her down gently and put an arm around her shoulders to steady her, but the dizziness was already passing. She let out a deep sigh. "Thank you, I am mostly recovered."

"I should hope so," Colin said. "The King was nearly killed? You must explain everything, Lydia, because all I know is that I was summoned by her Highness, and then there was her extraordinary declaration of thanks to you for preventing his Majesty's death. What intrigue have you stumbled into?"

Lydia shook her head and pushed open the Bounding chamber door. "There was an assassin," she said, "an Extraordinary Shaper who had previously attended the King, at least that is my understanding. I Discerned his intent and I—" She shuddered at the sudden realization of how close she had come to death herself.

"Then you were right about those conspirators at Lord Ormerod's ball," Colin said.

In all the furor and her dizziness, Lydia had not connected her earlier discovery with this assassination attempt. "Oh, my," she said, stopping on the threshold. "I knew I was right in what I learned from Mr. Norris, but I did not believe—it is an astonishing coincidence that I should brush up against two conspiracies to kill the King."

"Not so astonishing, if I understood Princess Charlotte correctly," Colin said. "Seers often meditate on a subject in order to induce

Dreams related to it. If she Dreamed with the intent of finding something that would help the King, there is no reason she might not have Dreamed of someone who could Discern the intent of an assassin."

"But it still does not make sense," Lydia insisted. "Why should she not instead Dream of the assassin himself? Suppose I had not agreed to meet with her?"

"But you did," Colin said, "and the assassin was stopped. No one understands the mechanics of Dream. I am not convinced it is reasonable, when talking of Dream, to insist that it make sense according to our limited human understanding." He put a hand on her shoulder and propelled her gently forward. "You should lie down. I know, you were not overwhelmed, but you did become faint, and twenty minutes' rest usually benefits you in that condition."

"You are correct, and I believe I will do so." Lydia clasped his hand briefly. "Thank you for not giving in to your desire to protect me from myself."

Colin laughed. "You Discerned that, did you? I am accustomed to having no secrets from you, but I am still grateful for your discretion in not constantly reminding me of that fact."

Safely in her bedroom, Lydia lay on her bed and closed her eyes. She was never so aware of her body as when she had a bout of dizziness, of how her lungs drew in and expelled air smoothly, how her heart beat a steady rhythm, how her skin tingled with its exposure to the cool air of the bedroom. She had taken to wearing convenables, supportive undergarments not as uncomfortable or rigid as stays, and could not imagine ever going back, particularly as she would not have been able to rest so comfortably in stays.

The morning's excitement had not wearied her, but she did feel a strange anticipatory tension, as if the assassination attempt had been only the first of many thrilling events she would experience. She hoped that was not truly the case. Facing down that Extraordinary Shaper, knowing one touch from him would mean her end, had not frightened her at the time, but now that the moment was past and she had leisure to contemplate the day's events, she could not believe she had had such courage. She would perhaps not tell her family that detail. It would only frighten them as well, and to no purpose, since she was safe.

She let herself dwell on the emotions of those within her range. Clemency was either not at home or was in some distant part of the house; likely she and Gawain were out Flying. She had to guess at the identities of the others, none of whom were as readily matched to their emotions as Clemency. None stood out; they were all placid beige or blue or pale green, except for one whose heightened emotions showed yellow. That might be Colin, if he was still agitated over the events at Windsor Castle.

Lydia herself felt no great fear or excitement over what had passed. Entertaining deep or violent emotions unsettled her. They were too easily tangled with others' similar emotions, and she intended never to be overwhelmed again. Instead, she recalled what she had Discerned of the King's emotions. The fact that he was plagued by his natural emotions rather than those inflicted on him by others only confirmed Lydia's resolve not to dwell on her feelings. That way lay madness.

She lay quietly on her bed for much longer than twenty minutes, drifting from emotion to emotion, until the door opened and Clemency said, "Are you asleep, Lydia?"

"I am not." Lydia opened her eyes, but did not sit up. "I was merely enjoying the quiet."

"Well, you have callers—Lydia, is what Colin tells me true? You foiled an assassination attempt against the King?"

Clemency was more surprised than worried, Lydia noted, but then Clemency never thought twice about endangering herself in the cause of protecting others. "What callers?" she asked.

"It is Mr. Rutledge and the Duke of Craythorne, the latter of whom I never imagined I would see in my house." Clemency came fully into the room, letting the door swing shut behind her. "He is known to be rather reclusive, but I presume if he is in Mr. Rutledge's company, his reclusiveness must hide something else. Is that why they are here— because of your actions? Tell me, Lydia!"

Lydia sighed and sat up. "It is true, one of the King's Extraordinary Shaper doctors attempted to kill him, but I Discerned his intent in time. Did Mr. Rutledge say anything?" She had not exactly forgotten that Mr. Rutledge was likely to call on her, or summon her, but she had not permitted herself to dwell on the possibility, either. It was not that she feared him so much as she was not certain she had done right in revealing his name to the Princess.

"He said only that he wished to speak with you, and requested my presence. Which I would have insisted on anyway. Oh, Lydia, your hair is such a tangle!" Clemency Moved Lydia's hairbrush to her hand and gave Lydia a gentle nudge with her Moving in the direction of the dressing table. "Here, I will help. Mr. Rutledge will simply have to wait."

"And the Duke of Craythorne?" Lydia said, smiling at Clemency's air of firm resolve.

"He must wait as well. I daresay it will be good for him." Clemency swiftly tidied Lydia's short, fine hair and pinned it neatly. Lydia watched, not her own reflection, but Clemency's, and not for the first time envied Clemency's thick, ash-blonde hair, coiled neatly around her head. They had cut Lydia's hair when she entered Magdalen, and it grew so slowly it was barely more than shoulder length now. Long enough to pin, but not much more.

Clemency set the brush down. "I confess I would have insisted on joining you for this meeting even were you not in need of a chaperon. My curiosity is nigh to overflowing."

"No, it is not," Lydia said. "You know I will tell you what I can anyway, and you are convinced you will learn the truth soon, so curiosity is a mere idle fancy."

Clemency laughed. "Too true. You would not be a comfortable companion for an habitual liar."

"Or I would make such a person become truthful, and be a force for good in the world," Lydia replied, joining her sister-in-law's laughter.

When they descended, she saw immediately that Clemency had struck another blow in her ongoing battle with Mr. Rutledge. The two were not enemies, but were not precisely friends, and Clemency believed she must keep Mr. Rutledge from, as she put it, walking all over Lydia and Clemency herself. Clemency took her, not to the comfortable drawing room, but to a smaller drawing room usually used only as a second cloakroom on nights when Colin and Clemency or Emmeline entertained. One look at Mr. Rutledge as he greeted Clemency told Lydia he knew what Clemency intended and was amused rather than offended.

The Duke did not immediately join them when Lydia and Clemency entered, being occupied by looking at a painting hung opposite the door. Lydia Discerned Clemency's mingled annoyance and embarrassment and guessed it had to do with the painting, which was not of high quality, rather than Lord Craythorne's snub.

"Miss Wescott," Mr. Rutledge said. "I was surprised to receive a royal summons to Windsor today. Quite the coincidence, you visiting the castle at precisely the right time to stop an assassin."

"I do not know how much coincidence it was, since I was there in response to Princess Charlotte's Dream," Lydia replied. "Did she not tell you?"

"Her Highness has been remarkably forthcoming," Mr. Rutledge said. "As has Dr. Coulter. The doctor informed me that Dr. Mervyn, the would-be assassin, was not expected today, and had been absent many days prior when he *was* expected. Neither she nor Princess Charlotte could explain his sudden change of heart."

"Apparently sudden," Lord Craythorne said, turning away from the painting. His voice was as warm and mellow as Lydia remembered. "We have no idea how long Dr. Mervyn planned this attack."

Mr. Rutledge nodded in acknowledgment of this correction. "What we do know," he said, "is that Dr. Mervyn did not act alone. He was the instrument of a greater conspiracy."

"Now, that does seem a coincidence," Clemency said. "That Lydia should happen upon one conspiracy and then thwart another."

"Not a coincidence. My investigation had already turned up a connection between the doctor and Lord Deverell and his conspirators. I believe it was Dr. Mervyn's assassination attempt you, Miss Wescott, overheard Deverell and Norris discussing at the ball." Mr. Rutledge leaned forward and rested his hands on his knees. "I anticipate being able to arrest Lord Deverell and Mr. Norris and all their friends very soon."

"Then it is over," Lydia said. She did not believe it was over, because Mr. Rutledge's emotions had an edge to them that Lydia perceived as dissatisfaction, and Lord Craythorne, though his emotions were still muted, nevertheless was suffused with a not-quite-excited anticipation. But she could not imagine what else might be unresolved.

"Not quite." Mr. Rutledge glanced at Lord Craythorne, who had stopped looking at the painting and now strolled, apparently placidly, to take a seat opposite Lydia. "Lord Deverell also did not act alone. He has ties to another group, one with far more interest in seeing the King dead. And *that* group, I have no immediate way of countering."

"But you have some idea. I can tell." Lydia closed one hand over the arm of the sofa, gripping it tightly. Mr. Rutledge was deep in the grip of an emotion she saw regularly in him, an odd mix of eagerness and resolve and passion that had nothing to do with love and everything to do with his attachment to his vocation.

"The Libertymen are American dissidents," Mr. Rutledge said. "A group of individuals who resent the colonies' continued rule by their hated overlords and who seek freedom from it. If they have not started a second Colonial Conflict, it is only because their numbers are too few to successfully win a war. In the past, they have struck at our government, directly and indirectly, with varying degrees of success."

"They have tried other assassination attempts?" Clemency asked.

"No, this was the first attempt on the King's life." Mr. Rutledge's fists clenched. "But the Libertymen have attacked our shipping, destroyed government property here and in the colonies—they do what they can to stir up trouble, hoping their fellow colonists will blame England rather than them for any privations they suffer as a result."

"Not just colonists," Lord Craythorne said. "There are Englishmen who agree with them, sympathizers who believe we should give America her freedom immediately rather than at a time when the slavery issue has been resolved. Lord Deverell and Mr. Norris are representative of that faction. They provide material support, money, and political backing. Without them, this rebellion would wither and die."

"In any case, I am certain the masterminds behind this plot are in

America. However, my organization does not extend that far." Mr. Rutledge's emotions were now more frustrated than eager. "And I do not have the remit to recruit agents in the colonies."

"I believed you were responsible for countering threats to our government, though," Lydia said. "Does this not qualify?"

"Parliament, in its great wisdom, has decreed I operate solely within the bounds of our fair isle," Mr. Rutledge said sourly. "More fear that I will use my power to overthrow them."

"On the other hand," Lord Craythorne said, "I am under no such prohibition. I intend to carry on Rutledge's investigation myself."

"You, my lord?" Lydia's surprise made her forget the proper form of address for a duke. "I mean—you are qualified to do so, your Grace?"

Lord Craythorne's anticipation turned into amusement. "I have a few valuable skills," he said. "And I will not be alone. In fact, Miss Wescott, I intend you to join me."

CHAPTER 7

IN WHICH LYDIA ACCEPTS AN INVITATION TO ENTER THE LION'S DEN

"**I**?" Lydia exclaimed.

Lord Craythorne's amusement grew. "Indeed. You have proved your talent is powerful and versatile, and I believe you will serve very well."

"Miss Wescott is not a tool," Clemency said. The curiosity with which she had been listening gave way to anger. "I will not permit you to use her so."

"You cannot permit or deny anything on my behalf, Clemency," Lydia reminded her, though she was grateful to have Clemency argue on her behalf. Lord Craythorne's proposition had stunned her. It was one thing to attend balls and parties, passively gathering information for Mr. Rutledge's use, and another to travel to another continent and do...what, exactly?

"It is true, you are your own woman," Mr. Rutledge said. "But I cannot agree that this is a good idea."

"Why not?" Lord Craythorne said. "Miss Wescott will be in no more danger than she is now—much less than she was facing that assassin. Which I commend you for, by the way," he added, inclining his head politely in Lydia's direction.

"You propose to go into the lion's den," Mr. Rutledge said. Lydia noted again his complete lack of deference to one who was his social superior. "You do not know who is a member of this secret organization—"

"Hence my interest in having Miss Wescott's aid in discovering them," Lord Craythorne said smoothly.

"And without that knowledge, anyone who is a member has the advantage of you," Mr. Rutledge continued as if Lord Craythorne had not spoken. "Since they have shown repeatedly their ruthlessness in the pursuit of their goals, you have no guarantee they will not attack even someone so apparently harmless as Miss Wescott."

Lydia's heart warmed at the word "apparently." She said, "But surely Lord Craythorne does not intend to announce publicly his intentions. They are unlikely to suspect him."

"Exactly, Miss Wescott." Lord Craythorne faced Mr. Rutledge, his demeanor exactly matching his calm certainty. "I have arranged a royal appointment as liaison to the viceroyalty, which gives me the authority to pursue enemies of our government overseas. My official position will be as representative of the House of Lords, assigned to oversee the transition of power as Viceroy Madison retires from his office."

"That does not sound as if my permission is desired or necessary," Mr. Rutledge said, his voice low and threatening.

"I of course respect your opinion," Lord Craythorne said, unmoved by the threat, "but, as you say, your remit ends at our shores. I am the only one who can pursue these men. I should think you would applaud this solution."

Mr. Rutledge shot a glance at Lydia. "It is not your involvement I deplore. Miss Wescott—"

"Mr. Rutledge, I appreciate your concern," Lydia interrupted. "But I do not believe Lord Craythorne would have proposed this if he believed there were any chance I would be in danger. I would be doing the same things I do now, and you do not fear for my safety when you request my help, do you?"

Mr. Rutledge's eyes narrowed. "Lady Ashford, you have been silent," he said. "What do you say to this mad scheme?"

Clemency's initial anger had faded. "Miss Wescott is an Extraordinary, and free to enter into contracts of her own accord, which in a sense, this is. I dislike sending her into danger, but I also recognize that she is not a child, and not weak. If she chooses to accept Lord Craythorne's proposal, I will support her."

"It cost you much to say that," Lydia blurted out.

Clemency gave a wry smile. "It did. But you are always saying that we should not overprotect you, and I am trying to abide by that request."

Lydia impulsively took Clemency's hand. "Thank you."

Clemency shook her head ruefully. "I do not look forward to telling Colin of your decision. There will be an eruption before he becomes resigned."

"Then I may count on your assistance, Miss Wescott?" Lord Craythorne's anticipation had become more placid, tinged with satisfaction at having won his point.

"You may, your Grace," Lydia replied. "When do we go? Immediately?"

Lord Craythorne chuckled. "It will be another week or more. There is much to be done—including arranging for a companion for you."

"And an excuse for why the Duke of Craythorne travels with a young, unmarried lady in his entourage," Mr. Rutledge said. He still felt annoyed, but his annoyance was tempered by concern for Lydia. Such emotions surprised and pleased her. His regard reminded her of Colin's frequent sharp emotions regarding her safety and protection. Her father had died when she was twelve years old, and had not been very fatherly, having been jealous of his children for having talent when he had none, but Mr. Rutledge's regard was much as she believed a father ought to feel for his child.

"Leave that to me," Lord Craythorne said. He rose and bowed to Clemency and Lydia. "I shall send you word of our proposed departure, as well as the story we shall tell the world of our purpose in America."

"Thank you, your Grace," Lydia said.

Mr. Rutledge rose as well. "And I will set about apprehending our English conspirators. That, at least, I have authority to do." He scowled, but his heart was not in it.

Impulsively, Lydia said, "You are a dear to worry so, and I hope I do not give you more cause for concern than is reasonable."

Mr. Rutledge's eyebrows raised in surprise. "I am not a dear," he said, but his lips twitched as he controlled a smile. "You are an impertinent minx, and I hope you will give the Duke much cause for concern, as you put it. It will do him good."

"I have often been told I should not be so proud," Lord Craythorne said blandly. "I prefer to see it as being confident."

"You are confident, but you do not see that as having anything to do with who you are," Lydia said. "It is quite surprising in one of your rank."

Lord Craythorne's eyes widened. Mr. Rutledge clapped him heartily on the back. "And so it begins," he said. "Miss Wescott, Lady Ashford, good day."

When the men were gone, Clemency flung her head back and groaned. Lydia, who knew Clemency felt no strong negative emotion, said merely, "What is it?"

"Mr. Rutledge exhausts me," Clemency said. "Do you know, he asked me to Fly by night in a particular part of south London and bring him any criminal I apprehended?"

"And did you?"

Clemency nodded. "I approve of his efforts, and if we may work together, I see no reason not to turn my search for criminals to his needs. It makes me feel less of a criminal myself, having at least a little official permission."

"You are not a criminal!" Lydia exclaimed.

"Only because there is no law preventing a private citizen from protecting herself and others against crime." Clemency stretched inelegantly and stood. "I anticipate a day when Mr. Rutledge, or his successor, creates an organization dedicated to stopping criminals and requires all who wish to do so to belong to it. I am not sure what I would do in those circumstances. But enough dire talk! Let us dress for dinner, and you will conjure a way to tell Colin what you propose that will not make him explode with indignation that you did not consult him first."

"He is not so selfish as that."

"That was by way of being hyperbole." Clemency smiled and pulled Lydia to her feet. "I believe half his objections are old habit, and the other half are his way of showing he loves you."

"I know his emotions, and that knowledge resigns me to the explosion," Lydia said.

GREY SKIES PERSISTED FOR SEVERAL DAYS, MAKING LYDIA FEEL AS IF the heavens had not given over their worry about the King's safety. She roamed Emeraude House in search of employment, sometimes playing harp or pianoforte for hours, sometimes reading for half an hour at a time before becoming impatient. Eventually she took her embroidery hoop to the dining room, which faced the front of the house and had large windows to let in the light, and settled in to sew and Discern the emotions of those who passed on the street outside. It was an entertainment of last resort, as few people felt anything but beige-green intent regarding their destinations, but she enjoyed making up stories about those whose emotions were more exciting.

Needlework soothed her spirits as reading did not. So much was possible when one sewed; one's thoughts were free to rove as one's body was not, and Lydia liked her own imaginings better than those of a novel writer or essayist. And there was also the satisfaction of seeing a scene come to life through needle and fine colored wool. Lydia was particularly fond of stitching flowers, how delicately they could be shaded until they appeared ready to leap off the cloth.

She bit off the end of her thread—such an unrefined gesture, but it was faster than using the scissors—and examined the pattern, purple pansies on a golden background, slippers for Prudence for her upcoming birthday. The deep, rich purple was one of her favorite colors, and she used it often.

Outside, two people entered the range of Lydia's Discernment. Lydia kept her head lowered, amusing herself by speculating without seeing their physical forms. They were both moderately angry, though one's anger was mixed with sadness. They might be two lovers in a spat, arguing some minor point, or business partners disagreeing over the direction their latest investment should take. That did not explain the sadness, though. Perhaps one of the lovers imagined the argument indicated the end of their relationship. Or one partner might believe the other disregarded his opinions.

Lydia sighed happily and threaded her needle, this time with white for the tiny knots at the center of the pansy. She did so enjoy seeing others' secrets.

She looked up at Slater's entrance. "A message for me?" she said, observing the silver salver.

"Indeed, miss."

Slater felt no annoyance, no boredom, but impulsively Lydia said, "Does it never disturb you that your employment is the same thing, over and over again? Suppose you might do something different?"

Slater's emotions did not change. "Serving this household is what I do, miss. I do not regret my choice of employment."

"I would be terribly bored," Lydia said.

Slater's lips twitched in a smile. "Then it is fortunate you are not a butler, miss." He lowered the salver, and in a lower voice added, "You would not say so if you knew of our lives below stairs, miss. I assure you there is nothing boring about service to this family."

Lydia's eyes widened. "I love gossip. Tell me more, Slater!"

Slater fixed her with a disapproving glare, but she sensed his amusement and was not put off by his expression. "I do not gossip, miss, and you should not wish for it, as I might gossip about *you*."

Lydia laughed. "I appreciate your circumspect attitude. Thank you."

Slater nodded and withdrew.

Lydia opened the note, which was merely a folded piece of paper, not sealed.

My dear Miss Wescott,

Forgive my impertinence in writing to you, but as our relationship is both formal and a matter of business, I hope you will excuse it. I wish to introduce you to my mother, who has chosen to accompany me to America and is in need of a young companion—or at least, that is the story we shall give the world. I ask that you join us at my home this afternoon at one o'clock so that the Dowager

Duchess may know you better. Please send word if this is agreeable to you, and I look forward to speaking with you again.

Craythorne

Lydia read the message twice. The Dowager Duchess of Craythorne? She had not realized Lord Craythorne was married—or was he a widower, that he had not immediately suggested she travel as his wife's companion? The idea of the proud and self-confident duke having family of any kind seemed strange, though of course everyone had family. She guessed Lord Craythorne must have told his mother the truth about her involvement—or had he decided not to reveal her talent, even to her? In that case, she could not imagine what reason he had given for proposing Lydia as a companion to Lady Craythorne.

She folded the paper and tucked it into her workbag, which she had embroidered with butterflies of green and purple. Threads of real gold winked dully in the grey light. Her two encounters with Lord Craythorne had given her the impression of someone strong-willed and determined on his own path, someone who also was willing to be proven wrong. If his mother was the same, that might prove entertaining, as strong-willed people rarely could stop themselves clashing with other strong-willed people. Lydia looked forward to meeting Lady Craythorne.

She rode unaccompanied in Clemency's carriage later that day, enjoying the unexpected sunshine and spring-like warmth. All of London appeared to have taken to the streets in response to the unseasonably warm weather, and the pleasure of so many over the fine day washed over Lydia like being engulfed in a sea of buttercups, mingled here and there with red anger and green passion and, most beautifully, the pure blue of blissful peace. Never did her talent give her so much happiness as on days like this.

The Duke of Craythorne's town residence was on the fashionable side of Mayfair, on a street where every mansion had its own unique character. Emeraude House, while beautiful and large, nevertheless shared its general appearance with its neighbors. Craythorne House, by contrast, stood out boldly, its pale stone brighter than the darker stone of its neighbors as if someone scrubbed the façade daily. Ranks of tall windows marked each floor, including one row of oval windows across the third floor that Lydia judged she could step through without ducking. Though the day was bright, most of the windows were lit from within, enhancing the whiteness of the stone.

Lydia examined the door as the carriage pulled up to it. Unlike the rest of the mansions on this street, tall, fat pillars flanked the double door, which was of oak stained dark cherry red. It stood out from the white stone like a portal to a hidden kingdom of fairy folk, though they would be stocky, stolid fairies rather than anything ethereal. She shook her head to clear it. It was the rush of emotion that set her to thinking such fanciful notions. She had no desire to appear frivolous or air-headed in front of Lady Craythorne.

A fan-shaped window filled with delicate iron traceries surmounted the door, enhancing its portal-like appearance. Lydia rang the bell and waited, shivering inside her wool pelisse. The brightness and warmth of the sun did not stop a chill wind from blowing, lightly but constantly, and ruffling her skirts.

The door opened, and a portly man dressed in a plain but formal black suit bowed her inside without comment. Lydia handed him her pelisse absently, her attention focused on the bright foyer lit by a dazzling chandelier to a whiteness even greater than the house's exterior. Its walls were uninterrupted by paintings, and no flowers graced the two pedestals flanking the one door to the left, which was of a dark ruddy color matching the front door. Ahead, narrow stairs rose to the first floor, while the hall continued deeper into the house.

The butler bowed again, and indicated that she should follow him. His continuing silence did not disturb Lydia, who sensed his placidity and the faint hum of curiosity threaded through it, likely about her. That Lord Craythorne, who was himself so self-possessed, should employ servants of a similar nature did not surprise her at all.

They ascended the stairs, which were uncarpeted—Lydia could not imagine any carpet that would not look gaudy in this pristine environment—and proceeded to yet another door, which the butler opened. "Miss Wescott, your ladyship," the butler said. His voice was unusually high-pitched for someone of his size, and it startled Lydia enough that she passed through the door without being aware of her movement.

The room beyond was as white and imposing as the foyer, filled with sofas upholstered similarly brightly and chairs with cushions worked in white and gold on cream-colored backgrounds. White lilacs too early for the season filled the air with their strong floral scent. She had been wrong about carpets being a mistake here; the carpet covering the floor was pure white and unmarked by footprints. In passing, Lydia reflected that this, more than anything, declared the Craythorne wealth. All this she perceived in a glance, taking it in for future analysis. When she came to herself, the door was closed, and she faced the Dowager Duchess of Craythorne.

She guessed Lady Craythorne to be in her sixties, but her face was not deeply lined and her dark hair was only just threaded with white. The regularity of her features gave her the kind of beauty age cannot rob anyone of, but Lydia did not like how the corners of her mouth curved in a permanent frown. Her eyebrows, perfectly plucked and shaped, also drew down over the bridge of her nose in a disapproving way. She was not angry, but she was awash with irritated resentment and, more deeply, a sense of disappointment Lydia did not understand. Whether the resentment was directed at Lydia or at Lord Craythorne, Lydia could not know without an interrogation.

Lady Craythorne regarded Lydia steadily, assessing her from head to toe. Belatedly, Lydia curtseyed and said, "Lady Craythorne, thank you for the invitation."

Lady Craythorne's frown deepened. "It was my son's invitation, as I'm sure you're aware," she said. Her voice was level, unemotional, but her irritation rose higher.

"You would not have agreed to meet me had you been unwilling," Lydia said. She had made up her mind to be direct with this formidable lady, as she knew demure politeness would only make Lady Craythorne despise her.

"Do not think to toad-eat me," Lady Craythorne said, but surprise joined her emotions of irritation and resentment. "Lord Craythorne made it clear what he expected." She rose from her chair and advanced on Lydia, who was surprised at how tall she was, surely almost as tall as her son. Lydia held her ground and refused to be intimidated even when Lady Craythorne loomed over her.

"So," Lady Craythorne said. "An Extraordinary Discerner. You don't appear mad."

"I am not, Lady Craythorne." Lydia did not rise to the bait.

Lady Craythorne's mouth curved in an unpleasant smile. "And you know when others lie. What an uncomfortable talent."

"Only for those who lie, Lady Craythorne," Lydia replied coolly. She was beginning to question her prior assessment of *Lord* Craythorne, whom she had judged well-mannered and not arrogant if a trifle overconfident. That he might have such a mother and yet not have partaken of her unpleasant traits seemed unlikely.

"I see." Lady Craythorne turned and paced to the window, which illuminated the room clearly. "And I am to accept you as my young companion. Oliver must be mad to propose such a thing."

"Then he has told you of my true purpose in accompanying you to America."

"He has given me some nonsense about requiring your services." Lady Craythorne sniffed. "What services, I wonder."

"I suggest you do not try to discomfit me with innuendo," Lydia retorted, stung despite her knowledge that Lady Craythorne did not actually believe what she had just suggested. "You know Lord Craythorne has not made me his doxy, and you are resentful of being asked to dissemble in any way."

Lady Craythorne turned on her. "Do not tell me how I feel," she snapped. "I will not be lectured by someone of your age and station."

"Then do not suggest I am lacking in morals," Lydia replied. She ignored the flash of memory of her mother shouting similar accusations. "Lord Craythorne wishes me to help discover those who would attack our government. That is all."

"Lord Craythorne should not have taken this on himself," Lady Craythorne said, but less heatedly. "He has a station in life to uphold."

"Perhaps that is so," Lydia said. "But I cannot dictate his actions." She refrained from adding *and neither should you.*

Annoyance surged through the Dowager Duchess and was supplanted by a distracted curiosity. "I beg your pardon, I am being addressed," she said, and tilted her head back in the attitude of a Speaker receiving a Spoken communication.

Lydia stood quietly, observing both Lady Craythorne's demeanor and her emotions. Whoever was Speaking to her conveyed nothing of excitement or even of great import, based on what Lydia Discerned. It annoyed her slightly that Lady Craythorne would be so discourteous as to interrupt their conversation, but it was clear Lady Craythorne had used the interruption to give herself a moment to recover.

Lady Craythorne abruptly lowered her head and returned to her chair. "Sit," she said ungraciously, waving at the sofa across from her. Lydia sat. "Tell me of your family. You are a gentleman's daughter?"

"My father, Edwin Wescott, was a gentleman of good repute. He passed away when I was twelve years of age." Lydia had never sorrowed over his death, unless it was sorrow that she did not have proper sensibilities to mourn her own father. "My brother married Lady Ashford and took her title. He is now Earl of Ashford."

"I read of the marriage. I did not realize you were of that family." Lady Craythorne's mood was settling into something less antagonistic, though her irritation had not diminished. "And your mother?"

"My mother is Caroline Wescott. I have not seen her in more than four years." Lydia ignored the pang that always struck her at mention of her mother.

"Indeed."

Lydia braced herself for further inquiry, but Lady Craythorne did not pursue the question. "What skills have you?" she said instead.

"I am quite musical," Lydia said. "I play the pianoforte, the harp, and the flute, though I am only a middling singer. I am skilled with fine needlework. My drawings are passable and their subjects are at least recognizable, but I have never been fond of painting watercolors. My sister-in-law says I have a pleasant voice for reading, but I find the practice boring after half an hour."

"Have you been educated?"

"I fear my education has been limited. My father did not believe girls needed such, so what I know, I taught myself. History and geography interested me, mathematics and poetry did not. I speak enough French to translate what I read, but not enough to carry on a conversation in that language." The conversation had become more of an interrogation, but Lydia still did not fear the Dowager Duchess.

The door opened, startling Lydia. She had been so focused on the conversation she had not paid attention to Lord Craythorne's approach. His emotions remained as muted as ever, rousing her curiosity as to how he had come to possess such self-control—though, having met his mother, Lydia had a suspicion as to the answer.

"Your Grace," he said, addressing Lady Craythorne with unnatural formality. "I apologize for my tardiness. I take it Miss Wescott has been introduced to you."

"If one may call it that, when she simply entered this room and addressed me," Lady Craythorne said. Her irritation surged, tainted now by bitterness. "You should have been present."

"Again, I apologize," Lord Craythorne said. His calm demeanor matched his emotions perfectly. "I hope Miss Wescott will suit." He took a seat next to Lydia, and the scent of his soap, clean and fresh, briefly overrode the floral perfume suffusing the air.

"I have no need of a young companion, Oliver," Lady Craythorne said. "And I dislike being made to accept such simply to meet your whims."

"You would be doing me a favor, true." Lord Craythorne turned to Lydia. "I believe this arrangement will satisfy propriety, as well as giving you added concealment. No one will suspect Lady Craythorne's companion of ulterior motives."

Lydia had been Discerning Lady Craythorne's abrupt change in mood from anger to a calculating deliberation. "I will be a mystery, right enough," she said absently. "If Lady Craythorne approves."

"Well, such underhanded, sneaking behavior is of course abhorrent to me," Lady Craythorne said, casting her gaze demurely down. "But I suppose it is what I must do for the sake of my country."

Suspicion tinged Lord Craythorne's emotions. "And what do you expect from me in return?" His hand, resting on his knee, curled into a loose fist, making the signet ring glint as it shifted.

Lady Craythorne smiled. "Lord and Lady Fanshawe have made their home in America."

The flash of annoyance that shot through Lord Craythorne startled Lydia, but it did not show on his face. "I suppose that has meaning to me?" His voice deepened in a way Lydia now believed reflected that annoyance.

"Lady Dorothea would be pleased to see you again," Lady Craythorne said. "And now I come to think on it, Miss Adams was most charmed by your company. She, too, resides in America half the year—this half, in fact."

"I see," Lord Craythorne said. The annoyance returned, and this time he frowned. "This is your price?"

"It is for your own good, Oliver," Lady Craythorne said. "I wish only for your happiness."

"Of course you do. Miss Wescott, are you in agreement?"

Lydia, who had been caught up in Lady Craythorne's unexpected remorse for which Lydia found no reason, replied, "I believe Lady Craythorne does wish for your happiness, yes."

Lord Craythorne chuckled. "I meant, do you agree to accompany Lady Craythorne to America? You will have to pose as her companion, and that will constrain your time, but we will see to it you have access to those whom I intend to investigate."

Lydia blushed at her mistake. "Oh! Of course, Lord Craythorne. Being Lady Craythorne's companion will be my pleasure." How fortunate, she reflected, that no one could Discern the lies she herself told.

CHAPTER 8

IN WHICH LYDIA ARRIVES IN AMERICA AND MAKES A DECISION

The following day, Lydia received another message, this one from the Dowager Duchess of Craythorne. She read it, then went in search of Colin. She found her brother in his study, intent on assembling yet another timing device. Lydia was familiar with his quest for a mechanism that would permit someone to set an alarm for a given time; she had helped him turn all his failures into music boxes.

Calling the room a study was inappropriate, given that Colin had gutted it of desk and chairs and bookcases to install his own furnishings. Now it held two tables, one drawn up before the window to take advantage of the natural light, a larger one in the center of the room beneath the lamp. Where the bookcases had been now stood a series of tall cabinets with many small drawers, filled with bits of essential machinery. The one thing Colin had kept was an enormous globe in a frame. He said spinning it soothed him, but Lydia suspected he enjoyed looking for out-of-the-way places he might someday Bound to.

Colin did not look up when she entered. "One moment," he said, his voice distant the way it got when he was engrossed in a complex manipulation. Lydia loved his emotions at these moments, how his excitement was honed to a sharp edge she believed meant intellectual pleasure. It made all her nerves tingle pleasantly.

There was a snap, and Colin's pleasure spiked with annoyance. He tossed down the tiny tool in his hand and said, "That is the last brace I have on hand, and now it is broken, which means a delay. I believe I have solved the problem of timing, Lydia."

"Which makes any delay worse," Lydia said. "Well, now you are unoccupied and may listen to my news. I am to leave for America in four days' time."

Colin's brow furrowed. "So soon?"

"I am so pleased you are resigned to my adventure." Lydia smiled cheerfully. "I am growing rather fond of the notion myself. So many new places to see."

"You do not enjoy travel," Colin pointed out. He wiped his hands on a dirty cloth and rose. "You prefer to make your nest, so to speak, and then not leave it. Even if you may be Bounded to your destination, that does not prevent you grousing over the time spent in transit."

"Very well, it is not the travel that draws me, it is the chance to be of use to Mr. Rutledge and Lord Craythorne." Lydia idly spun the globe and trailed a finger across its spinning surface. "The travel is a necessary evil. And it is not true that I grouse about Bounding. I am very grateful for it. Imagine making this journey by ship. It would be so tedious."

"Indeed." Colin put his large hand on the globe, stopping it so Lydia's finger fell on the coast of North Africa. "I should not fear for you. This journey, and this assignment, are nothing dangerous. You may even enjoy your time in the colonies."

"It is possible, but unlikely, given that I shall be tethered to Lady Craythorne much of the time." Lydia shrugged. "She is unusual. I should not draw conclusions based on one encounter, but her manner and irritation with her son are at odds with her innermost emotions."

Colin half-sat on the edge of the table. "And how is that?"

"I should not say. But—she both wishes Lord Craythorne to marry, and feels regretful about the possibility. And yet she does not appear to be the sort of mama who would like to keep her son tied to her apron strings all his life. I do not understand it."

"Proximity will give you a chance to ferret out her secrets. Something I know you enjoy." Colin pushed off from the table and embraced Lydia quickly, then released her. "I should Bound to the colonies with you, so as to learn the signature of the place you will be staying. Then I might retrieve you if that becomes necessary."

Lydia quashed her annoyance at her brother's overprotectiveness. "That is kind, but unnecessary, and you know you wish to do so for your own sake and not mine. I will be well, never fear."

"I know." Colin picked up something from the table. "Go. You ladies all require days and days to pack for an extended stay. You should warn your maid—have you informed Ellery of this trip?"

"I have not, and I am ashamed of myself for simply assuming everything will take care of itself." Lydia spun the globe again, but did not stay to see it come to a halt.

She was nearly to the stairs when sorrow washed over her, the terrible pain of loss. She stopped, her own natural fear warring with someone else's grief. Memories of being caught up and overwhelmed by another person's sorrow flooded through her, and for a moment, she heard the cries of the mad and the desperate. She realized she gripped the newel of the stairs, clutching it as if she might drown without its support.

She closed her eyes and breathed in and out, not too deeply, but in a regular pattern, in for the count of three, then out again for the same length of time. This sorrow was not her own. She was not sad; she felt nothing, emptiness, a void. This sadness belonged to another. She would not let it take her.

Slowly, she climbed the stairs. The one she Discerned might be Ellery, she believed, because the person was near Lydia's rooms. For a moment, she considered walking away, retreating until the grieving person was beyond her range. Then she cursed her cowardice. She would not permit herself to be overwhelmed.

She pushed the door open and said, "Ellery? What is wrong?"

She Discerned that Ellery was in the dressing room, but Ellery did not answer. Lydia crossed the bedroom to the dressing room door. "Ellery? Maud? I know you are upset."

She heard a loud sniff, and then Ellery emerged from the darkness of the dressing room. Her eyes were red, her lips trembled, and she said, "It's nothing for you to trouble yourself over, miss."

"Ellery, you know I Discern your sadness. Do not tell me it is nothing I should fret about." The effort of maintaining herself against Ellery's emotions dizzied Lydia. She put a hand on the maid's shoulder, as much to steady herself as to comfort her, and added, "Is it your young man?"

Ellery's eyes filled with tears. "Oh, miss," she sobbed. "Miss, he has found another young woman he likes better than me. Miss, what am I to do?"

Cautiously, Lydia assessed Ellery's emotions and was relieved to find no evidence that Ellery's sorrow was deeper than mere grief at being cast off. At least Ellery was not in an expectant state.

"It is a terrible thing to love someone who does not return your regard," she said, letting Ellery's shifting emotions guide her words. "So much the worse when he claimed to have loved you once."

"I cannot believe I was so foolish," Ellery said. "He must have lied, miss, because if he truly loved me, he would not have been drawn to this other girl, yes?"

"In my experience," Lydia said, uncomfortably aware that her experience was drawn almost entirely from Discerning others and not from personal knowledge, "men enjoy novelty, and unless they make a deep connection, it is nothing for them to leave one woman behind for another who is new and interesting. But, Ellery, that does not mean their loves are not genuine while they last. You should not feel foolish for believing him."

"I would almost rather he had lied," Ellery said in a low voice. "It is terrible to know I could not inspire lasting devotion in someone."

"That is not your fault, it is his," Lydia insisted. "Oh, how I wish I had met him! I might have spared you this heartache."

Ellery wiped her eyes, and discomfort joined sorrow. "I should not speak so informally, miss. I apologize for burdening you with my troubles."

"It is no burden, and I wish you would always feel so free," Lydia said. "An Extraordinary Discerner sees so much of others' intimate selves, it is like she is family to the whole world. And as we are to go to America soon, you are all I will have of my familiar world."

Ellery gasped. "America? Why—that is, may I ask why?"

"I am to accompany Lady Craythorne as her companion, and she is to manage her son Lord Craythorne's household as he fulfils his responsibilities in the colonies." Lydia was sincere in wishing Ellery to be her friend and not just her maid, but that did not extend to telling her the truth about Lydia's secret assignment. "I hope you do not mind. If such a trip is not pleasing to you—"

"No, miss, I would not like to leave your service." Ellery's sorrow was ebbing, tamped to a bearable level. "But—*America*. It is so far away, and I hear there are savages, and wild animals roaming the streets."

"The Iroquois are not savages, but their lives are not the same as ours," Lydia assured her. "And my understanding is that American cities are far from the frontier, so we need not prepare to defend against lions and bears."

Ellery looked unconvinced, but she nodded. "Then I will begin to pack your things," she said, and her sorrow faded a little more. "I imagine it will be an adventure!"

"An adventure indeed," Lydia said.

☙❧

FOUR DAYS LATER, LYDIA AND ELLERY, COLIN AND CLEMENCY waited in the hall outside Emeraude House's Bounding Chamber. The house's construction predated the appearance of talent, and none of its residents had ever needed a Bounding chamber, but now that Colin lived there, Clemency had insisted. So a little-used storage room had been cleared and painted white, a Bounding symbol created and registered, and now the family was accustomed to being able to return home in the space of a breath.

Ellery was quietly excited, which cheered Lydia. Pangs of sorrow still suffused her maid, but they were less frequent; activity and occupation had had a salutary effect on her emotions. Lydia herself was restless as she always was in the hours before a journey. Colin was right that she disliked leaving her comfortable home for something unknown that might not be as comfortable. She wished herself an hour into the future, when the unknown would be known and she might begin settling herself into a new home, however temporary.

The hall outside the Bounding chamber was narrow and felt even narrower with all four of them and Lydia and Ellery's luggage crammed into the space. Lydia observed Colin's anxiety and Clemency's more placid anticipation. Her brother's emotions were not as intense as she had feared; in fact, they were more resignation than anxiety, and that eased her heart.

"You are resigned to this," she told him. "That is good. I grow weary of being coddled."

Colin laughed. "You are in no danger of what I fear most, which is being overwhelmed, and I believe it is natural for a brother to be mildly concerned for his sister's physical safety in a foreign land."

"It is," Clemency said. "We have none of us ever been to the colonies. You will have to bring us thrilling tales of adventure."

"There are no bears in the streets," Ellery said, then flushed crimson with embarrassment at having addressed the Countess so informally.

"I am glad to hear it," Clemency said with a smile. "Lydia, if you have need of anything—"

"Lady Craythorne is a Speaker, and she will get word to you," Lydia said. "But I daresay they sell hairbrushes and pins in America."

"And now *I* am indulging in over-worry," Clemency said.

The Bounding chamber door opened, startling all of them in its abruptness, and a tall, well-built woman in Craythorne livery emerged. "Lady Ashford, Lord Ashford," she said, bowing. "Lord Craythorne's compliments, and I am here to convey Miss Wescott and her attendant."

Clemency, and then Colin, swept Lydia up in their embraces. "Fare well," Colin said. There was no time for more than that, as the Bounder then put her arm around Lydia's waist and lifted her. There was a breathless moment, and suddenly the air was warmer and drier and her surroundings brighter.

The woman set Lydia down, and she stepped away and glanced about her. Small white lanterns set into recesses in the walls glowed steadily behind frosted glass, lighting the little room clearly. On the wall facing Lydia, three interlocking squares, red, green, and gold, made a Bounding symbol unique to this room. She turned, looking for the door, but the Bounder had already opened it. "If you'll clear the Bounding chamber, I shall return immediately," the woman said.

Lydia hurried out of the room and shut the door behind her. She was in a narrow hall so similar in shape to the one she had left behind in Emeraude House she suffered a moment's dizziness. The emotions of two people waiting a short distance away anchored her, so different were they from Colin and Clemency.

The man had the lined face and grey hair of late middle age and wore the formal garb of a butler. The woman wore a black gown and cap and shoes that pained her, or so Lydia guessed from the pinched expression on her face and the discomfort that shot through her other emotions. Both the man and the woman were suffused with the pale blue placidity of someone doing a familiar duty, tinged with curiosity.

"Miss Wescott?" the man said.

Lydia nodded.

"I am Trask, the butler. I have been requested to greet you and make you comfortable. May I introduce Mrs. Pogue, the housekeeper."

Mrs. Pogue curtseyed, and her discomfort spiked briefly. "We hope—"

The Bounding chamber door opened, and Ellery appeared. Lydia Discerned her excitement and realized Ellery had never been Bounded before. To Mrs. Pogue, she said, "Thank you for your welcome. May I see my room? Or—I did not remember to ask if her Grace is here yet, for perhaps I should wait on her first?"

"Lord Craythorne and Lady Craythorne have not yet arrived," Trask said. "Mrs. Pogue will show you to your room."

Mrs. Pogue curtseyed briefly, not too low—she was not overawed by Lydia—and indicated that Lydia and Ellery should follow her. They passed a few more closed doors, behind which Lydia Discerned a few people moving about in an absent hum of mixed placidity and boredom and one whose annoyance verged on frustration, and then Mrs. Pogue opened the door at the end of the hall and gestured for Lydia to precede her.

The room beyond, large and bright, eased Lydia's vague discomfort at having been in such a confined space as the hall. Through windows flanking the double doors to the left, Lydia saw a bustling street and Discerned at the limits of her range many people thronging it. Rectangles of brilliant sunlight stretched across the floor, which was tiled in white squares more than a foot on each side. It was a brighter light than she had left behind in England, possibly because the weather was more clement, but the light also had the feel to it of morning. Lydia knew the sun reached England earlier than it did America, and that when it was three in the afternoon in London it was several hours earlier than that in the colonies, but that had not been real until this moment.

She had time enough to notice the green marble fireplace, the white mantel picked out with gold leaf, the frieze of dancing Greek maidens across the mantel's front, and a pair of French doors open on a vast dining room before Mrs. Pogue said, "If you'll follow me, your room is on the second floor, miss," and began ascending the stairs immediately to their right.

Mrs. Pogue's discomfort spiked with every step, and Lydia had to remind herself that no one was to know of her talent and that she could not ease Mrs. Pogue's pain regardless. She followed the housekeeper up the stairs, which rose to a small landing and turned back on themselves before ending at a hallway that extended left and right. Paintings of unfamiliar people hung at intervals along the hall above small round tables bearing winter flower arrangements that smelled dusty rather than sweet.

Mrs. Pogue did not hesitate, or offer to show Lydia the house; instead, she turned to the right and immediately made her way up a second staircase. Lydia glimpsed, through an open door beyond the staircase, walls papered in cream and pale gold and a matching divan, as well as the portrait of a lovely young woman, before she had to hurry after Mrs. Pogue.

The second floor was no less beautiful and ornate than the first, though all the doors were shut and the carpet was light blue rather than navy and maroon. Mrs. Pogue opened the second door from the stairs. "I hope you will find this comfortable, Miss Wescott," she said. "It is quite convenient to her Grace's rooms."

"Thank you," Lydia said. With Ellery trailing behind, she entered.

Her first impression was that "comfortable" was an understatement. Glossy mahogany furniture filled the room to bursting, carved and polished in a way that even Lydia, who was not accustomed to wealth, recognized as expensive. She walked forward and ran a hand across the counterpane and discovered it was velvet, cream-colored and thick. A dressing table and bench faced the bed, and another table, this one round with a pedestal foot, stood beneath the three large windows. Near the table, a bookcase with three shelves packed full of leatherbound volumes enticed the viewer to sit and read for hours. Lydia almost wished she were a more avid reader, it was all so perfect.

She looked out the center window on a garden, a broad sweep of lawn constrained by short walls that defined paths for strolling along. A much taller brick wall defined the limits of the garden, and beyond it, she saw more mansions, each of them unique in construction. Lydia had not seen so much privately held space since she was a child in Sussex. London certainly had nothing like it.

"Is there anything I might do for you, miss?"

Lydia Discerned someone approaching, probably a footman carrying her things. She turned and said, "No, Mrs. Pogue, thank you. It is a lovely room."

"I'll leave you to settle in, but someone will fetch you when her Grace arrives." Mrs. Pogue curtseyed again and then stepped aside for the footman with Lydia's trunk. In another moment, the trunk was settled, the footman and Mrs. Pogue were gone, and Lydia and Ellery were alone.

"I'll unpack now, miss," Ellery said. "It's so much brighter here, isn't it? I don't understand how it can be afternoon in London, and morning here, and yet it's still now in both places. How very odd."

"I agree." Lydia ran her finger across the book bindings and absently Discerned the members of the household. Her Discernment did not reach the street from here, but encompassed most of the house and, she believed, part of the beautiful garden.

Two new people popped into existence, one of them placid, the other sharply anticipatory. That must be Lord Craythorne and the Bounder who conveyed him from England. Lydia considered going downstairs to greet him, and then she wondered why she was so impatient. It was not as if Lord Craythorne intended to begin his investigation this minute, and they were not friends, merely colleagues.

She looked out at the garden again and had a moment's uncertainty. She should not be anxious, as she would not be doing anything she had not done a dozen times before: dance, converse, eavesdrop, and Discern. But despite her assurances to Colin, she knew this situation was different; the men and possibly women she would seek out were engaged in treasonous acts, and traitors did not hesitate to attack or kill to protect themselves and their cause. Lydia needed to be alert to the possibility that her investigations might endanger her.

She drew in a deep breath and let it out slowly so it misted on the cold glass. Caution was important, but it did not have to lead to cowardice. And she would never give in to fear.

CHAPTER 9

IN WHICH LYDIA EAVESDROPS, AND LEARNS THINGS OF INTEREST

Lydia had not guessed the city of Washington would resemble London so closely. The houses might have been constructed by the same architects; the shops with their newfangled plate glass windows displayed the same merchandise as was available from London's finest merchants. It was the smells that told her she was far from the great city. The stink of the Thames, an odor Lydia knew so well it tended to disappear from her awareness until the wind forcefully reminded her of it, was completely absent.

Instead, breezes brought the distant scent of a different river, a not entirely pleasant scent, but one that did not drill into the brain via the nostrils. They also carried the smell of animal waste and wood smoke, also fainter than that of London—but then, Washington was a smaller city, however modern in appearance.

She strolled along the sidewalk with Ellery as her companion, having no real purpose beyond exploration. As far as her Discernment went, Washington was as thronged with people as any major metropolis. She had to remind herself to pay attention to her surroundings, so distracted was she by the colorful hum of thousands going about their business. She considered it fortunate that they were not all possessed of strong, overwhelming emotions. Then she laughed at herself for even giving passing heed to that thought. Why should the American colonies be any different from Europe in their emotions? That was foolishness talking.

Ellery, on the other hand, was unusually apprehensive, though to all appearances she was calm enough. Lydia debated asking her about her fears, decided this was intrusive, and then changed her mind. "You need not fear," she said in a low voice. "I have seen no bears anywhere."

Ellery gasped, then giggled. "Oh, miss, I am not afraid of bears!"

"No, but you fear something. It cannot be the people, for none of them pay any heed to us, and I assure you they are all caught up in their own concerns." Lydia impulsively clasped her maid's hand. "If it is not the people, and not bears, what troubles you?"

Ellery shook her head. "It is not fear, precisely, as it is that I have never left London before, and I do not know what to expect. They have such strange accents, these people, and suppose that is not all that is different?"

"Likely there is much that is different, but they are still people, and they speak our language even though they do it oddly." Lydia caught sight of a tea shop across the street and added, "We will drink tea and pretend we are colonials, and you will see I am right."

Ellery held back when Lydia would have crossed the street. "Miss, I cannot drink tea with you. I—"

Lydia recollected herself with a start. "My apologies," she said. "It is that as an Extraordinary Discerner, I see so much of people's innermost selves I feel an intimacy that transcends issues of social rank. Could you not pretend, for this moment, that we are friends? For I am terribly thirsty, and I cannot permit you to stand in the corner and watch me drink tea."

Ellery's inner turmoil lasted a moment longer before settling back into apprehension, not quite as intense as before. "If you say, miss," she said.

Lydia considered that as they crossed the street to the tea shop. She knew Ellery considered herself beneath Lydia in terms of social rank, because of Lydia's talent if nothing else, but she thought of the young woman as a friend and wished Ellery felt the same. Aside from how Ellery was the first maid who had not left Lydia's service out of fear after less than a week, Lydia liked her openness and good cheer. They were much alike, in fact. And Lydia had not had a friend of her own age she was not related to in years.

The tea shop was smaller than the other shops on that street, but it was well-lit by the many large windows and felt at once cozy and open. It smelled deliciously of hot tea and sweet cakes, and Lydia whispered, "You see? This could almost be an English tea shop."

She and Ellery settled themselves near one of the windows, and in no time they were served refreshments by an apple-cheeked lady whose hair was as white as her cap. Lydia sipped her tea and pretended to watch the passersby. In truth, she was listening to the conversations around her. She loved eavesdropping; it was like an extension of Discernment, and the two combined meant she learned all manner of secrets she cherished.

Many of the tea shop's tables were occupied, most of them by women sitting in pairs or groups of three. Two young men sat near Lydia and Ellery, though they were intent on one another rather than on the attractive young women nearby, and a family sat on the opposite side of the shop from Lydia. The father's grumpy resentment revealed that he wished he was elsewhere; his wife and two adolescent daughters did not notice his mood, given how cheerful they all felt. Lydia could not make out their chatter, but she guessed it had something to do with gowns and bonnets, based on their gestures. That might explain the father's mood.

She turned her attention on a nearer table, one where sat three matrons dressed rather fussily in dark, sensible gowns trimmed with an abundance of ribbons that made them look much less sensible. The blonde woman was telling the other two, one brunette, the other a faded redhead whose hair would have been a bonfire in her youth, a complicated story in an urgent voice not low enough to escape Lydia's ears:

"...and I heard it from Mrs. Margolis herself that those soldiers demanded Mr. Lyman shelter them and feed them, and when he refused, they forced him out of his home, him and all his family, and took all his stores!"

The brunette gasped. "Surely not!"

"Do you expect anything less from these British oppressors?" the redhead demanded, in a voice even quieter than the blonde's. "The revolution is years in the past, and yet the British Army is still a present threat to all of us. So much for their claims to generosity and that so-called Declaration."

"Mr. Lyman has three daughters," the blonde said. Lydia waited for her to continue, but it seemed that one statement was meaningful in itself, for all three women nodded as if she had said something very profound.

"Miss?"

Lydia startled. "Ellery," she said. "I apologize, I was distracted."

"It's nothing, miss, just that I asked if you would like more tea." Ellery was eyeing her with some trepidation.

"Oh! Yes, I would, thank you." Lydia accepted another cup and poured a thin stream of milk into it, taking her time in order to conceal her interest in the women's conversation. But they had moved on already to talking of someone they all knew who had worn an inappropriately youthful gown to some public event. Lydia found such talk boring.

"I would like to find a stationer's after this," she told Ellery. "I have decided to keep a diary of my time here in America. Though it is likely to turn into a sketch journal, as all my previous diaries have."

"I can't imagine doing that myself, miss. I never know what to write." Ellery nibbled a cake, which shed fine crumbs across her plate.

"Neither do I, but I believe it will be a stimulating exercise." Lydia drank down her tea slowly, casting about for more interesting conversations. The two young men were not, unfortunately, talking of anything more profound than the one young man's parents and his financial expectations of them. The nearest women were Movers and were entertaining themselves with some game that involved Moving the salt cellar and tiny bud vase in intricate patterns.

The apple-cheeked shop owner appeared, and Lydia shook her head at the woman's offer of more refreshments. She took out her reticule to pay the woman, whose smile concealed embarrassment and a hint of anger Lydia could not explain. Almost she challenged the shop owner on it, but she remembered in time she was in America incognito. Making a guess, she said, "Prices in America are not the same as in England."

The woman's anger surged, but it was not directed at Lydia. "Taxes are high due to Napoleon's war," she said. "I have to charge what will let me earn a living."

"I hope you did not believe that was a criticism," Lydia said, pretending to embarrassment.

"Oh, no, of course not!" the woman exclaimed. "It is not as if you are to blame. No, I blame those in Parliament who believe they can extract every last drop of profit from their colonies. They—" She reddened. "Excuse me. I spoke out of turn. This is nothing for you to concern yourself with, a nice young lady like yourself."

Lydia smiled. "I understand. It does seem quite unfair, doesn't it? Thank you for the tea."

She reflected on that exchange once she and Ellery were on the street again. She knew so little of politics, she did not believe she should judge based on one interaction, but she could easily imagine Parliament imposing higher taxes on the colonies so they might not raise taxes at home and suffer the criticism and acrimony of the citizens. So much easier to ignore complaints when they happened a thousand miles away.

She surveyed the streets as they walked, searching for a stationer's sign. Again, she marveled at how closely the place resembled London, down to the scatterings of refuse in the streets. Well, Washington had been called New London until seventeen years ago, when the King had renamed it in honor of the Colonial Conflict's greatest hero. Perhaps the similarities were intentional.

Drifts of handbills lay across the streets and sidewalks, adding to the clutter. Lydia idly kicked at them as she passed, sending the papers sliding like dead leaves to and fro. These all seemed to be copies of the same handbill, tossed out in a profligate way. Impulsively, Lydia bent and retrieved one.

"Miss, what is it?" Ellery asked.

"Something political," Lydia said absently, her attention focused on reading. "It is a list of grievances against the government and a demand for colonial freedom and self-governance."

"But America lost the Colonial Conflict," Ellery said. "Was not that the end of it?"

"Not for everyone, apparently." Lydia reached the end of the badly-printed page. "It is signed 'John Steadfast.' I wonder if that is a real person."

"It must be a real person, or how else could that all have been written?" Ellery leaned over Lydia's shoulder to peer at the paper; she was some five inches taller than her mistress, but rarely stood tall enough to draw attention to that fact.

"I mean it might be a pseudonym, meant to conceal the writer's identity. This is inflammatory stuff." Lydia folded the handbill and tucked it into her reticule. Lord Craythorne probably already knew about this, but she wished to be useful nonetheless.

They found a stationer's two streets away, and Lydia purchased a small diary bound in glossy red leather, a penknife, and three pencils. As she was paying, surprise flashed through Ellery, and turned just as the young woman said, "Look there, miss!"

Ellery's attention had been caught by a trio of men strolling along the street, dressed in clothing Lydia had never seen before, soft leather trousers and shirts of a light brown color and head coverings adorned with three upright feathers and colorful beads. The men all had skin of a deep, ruddy brown, and their black hair was pulled back sharply and tied at the crown of their heads in a fanlike shape. The strong, chiseled bones of their faces gave them a fierce, regal appearance, as did their confident stride. "They are Iroquois," she said. "We should not stare."

"Everyone is staring," Ellery pointed out. Indeed, many people on the street outside not only stared at the men, they had stopped walking to do so. The Iroquois men did not appear to notice, but Lydia Discerned their chagrin and anger at being so obviously treated as outsiders. She felt sadness on their behalf. She herself disliked being treated differently for her talent, disliked how so many people thought nothing of whispering about her supposed madness when they knew she was an Extraordinary Discerner, and how much worse to have a difference people cared about that was readily visible?

"I believed they would dress as we do when they are among us," Ellery continued, whispering though the men were much too far away to hear. "But perhaps that is wrong, to expect them to conform to our customs?"

"I know little of the Iroquois save that they are a powerful nation that fought our armies to a standstill," Lydia whispered back. Then she came to herself and cleared her throat. The men had disappeared out of sight beyond the shop window and were nearly at the edge of her Discernment range. "It grows late. Let us return to the house."

It was even later than Lydia had realized, and by the time they returned, she had to hurry to dress so she would not be late to dinner. Ellery helped her silently, but Lydia knew she was merely tired from their expedition and not melancholy. As Lydia donned her pale pink evening gown, she remembered the family at the tea shop and their supposed conversation about clothing. As an Extraordinary, Lydia was permitted to wear colors and fabrics normally not allowed a young, unmarried woman, but even had she not wished to conceal her talent, she was not comfortable dressing in such rich apparel. People underestimated a young, delicate-looking woman in white muslin, and it suited Lydia to be underestimated.

She arrived downstairs in time for dinner to be announced. She and Lord Craythorne and the Dowager Duchess were the only ones dining, but then Lydia did not believe many of Lord Craythorne's staff had arrived yet. She knew he had men who handled his business under his direction, and she guessed this political appointment required more of the same, even though Lord Craythorne's primary purpose in Washington was clandestine.

She took her seat at Lord Craythorne's right hand, and immediately self-consciousness struck her at how Lady Craythorne sat at the far end of the table, even though it was her proper place. It was not a long table, but the seating arrangements reminded Lydia that they were not friends, because how much friendlier if they might all sit together? But Lady Craythorne was irritated over something Lydia did not know, and Lord Craythorne's calm demeanor concealed annoyance over something else—at least, Lydia hoped it was something else, for how terrible a meal would this be if mother and son were angry with each other and Lydia was caught in the middle?

"Your Grace," she said, "have you heard of a man called John Steadfast?"

Lord Craythorne's annoyance faded slightly, and curiosity took its place. "I have not. Is he someone of importance?"

"I am not sure. He is the author of a handbill—there were many of them, many copies of a single handbill, I mean—protesting British rule over America and citing many instances of brutality and oppression." Lydia picked up her spoon, but did not taste the clear broth ladled into her bowl. "I cannot even say if John Steadfast is a real name."

"Is this the proper topic of discussion for the dinner table, Miss Wescott?" Lady Craythorne said.

"As we have not introduced any other topics, I say Miss Wescott is daring to speak up at all, Mother." Lord Craythorne shrugged and began eating soup. After a few spoonfuls, he said, "My informants tell me there has been an increase in handbills and pamphlets distributed throughout the cities of America, with the greatest increase appearing here in Washington. I have not heard any particular names attached to them. I would have assumed anonymity to be more important."

"Why is that, your Grace?"

"Fear, mostly," Lord Craythorne said. He set his spoon aside. "There is a general sense that Britain intends to retaliate against anyone who threatens her rule, even the small supposed threat of publishing dissenting opinions on the subject of taxation, for example. That fear is unjustified, but fear is not always rational. And these Libertymen feed those fears with lies and exaggeration."

"Oliver, I insist you choose another subject, or I shall leave this room," Lady Craythorne said, dropping her spoon into her soup bowl so clear broth splashed onto the tablecloth. "Really, it is inappropriate to talk politics at the table."

"I apologize, Mother," Lord Craythorne said. He was not actually apologetic, not in his heart, but neither did his annoyance increase. What surprised Lydia was that *Lady* Craythorne's irritation became twined with regret that ached all through the Dowager Duchess. Lydia filled her mouth with soup so she would not question Lady Craythorne. She had seen that tangle of emotions several times before, and in every case it had indicated someone who had fallen into habits of speech they did not know how to reverse. As Lydia had classified the Dowager Duchess as one of those wealthy, pampered women who resented anyone who defied them in any way, this was a compelling mystery.

"Miss Wescott," Lord Craythorne said, and Lydia jerked out of her reverie. "How do you find Washington?"

"It is a lovely city, and I see why they called it New London," Lydia replied. "We saw Iroquois men, and ate cakes, and I find the place most congenial."

"Iroquois?" Lady Craythorne said. "I believed them to live much farther north."

"Their men frequently come to the city to trade," Lord Craythorne said. "I am told their women are never seen outside the Haudenosaunee nation."

"They afford their women so little freedom, then?" Lady Craythorne sounded curious rather than critical.

"I believe it is the other way around, and they do not trust Europeans to treat Iroquois women with respect." Lord Craythorne leaned back in his seat to permit the servant to remove his soup bowl. "Given our earliest interactions with the American natives, it is perhaps a not unjustified reaction."

Lydia remembered the emotions she had Discerned from the Iroquois men and had to agree. "They certainly were aware of how unlike us they are."

"I suppose that's true." Lord Craythorne waited for the dishes of the first remove to be set out. There were not many of them, and Lord Craythorne might almost have been a Discerner, because he said as if in response to Lydia's unspoken question, "I choose to eat simply when there are only the three of us. It seems less wasteful. I hope you are not offended."

"Offended?" That seemed an odd choice of words. "Of course not, your Grace. I agree with you, in fact."

"I do not," Lady Craythorne said. "You are forever neglecting the consequence that comes with your station." Again, regret throbbed through her. Lydia's curiosity sharpened painfully.

"If my consequence can be injured merely by my requesting fewer dishes be served at dinner, it is far too easily damaged." Lord Craythorne carved a slice of tender beef and offered it to Lydia. "Besides, I will always prefer three or four dishes prepared to perfection to a dozen middling offerings."

He said this with such assumed pomposity Lydia giggled. "You should warn your cook," she said, "or his feelings will be hurt."

"Irrelevant, as he would not dare complain to the Duke of Craythorne," the Duke said, intoning these words like a Shakespearean actor, his voice once more deep and mellow. Lydia laughed. "And your impertinence in laughing offends me. Off with your head!"

"I beg your pardon, your Grace," Lydia said, covering her mouth to control another laugh. "I should be more respectful of your dignity."

"*You* should be more respectful of your dignity, Oliver," Lady Craythorne said, but without rancor, merely resignation, as if this was not the first time Lord Craythorne had made himself ridiculous in public.

"This is a private meal, Mother, not the town hall." Lord Craythorne smiled at Lydia, the corners of his eyes crinkling in amusement. "I promise to comport myself with greater decorum at the investiture at the end of the week."

"Am I to attend?" Lydia hoped she did not sound as eager as she felt. She wished to be useful, not simply explore Washington and eavesdrop on random strangers.

"Not the investiture itself, but the ball that evening to celebrate it," Lord Craythorne said. "You will have ample opportunity to spy."

"That is a terrible word," Lady Craythorne said. "It suggests such underhanded behavior."

"Investigate?" Lydia said, though privately she enjoyed being referred to as a spy. It sounded daring and adventurous.

"Very well," Lord Craythorne said, sounding amused again. "Ample opportunity to investigate."

"I will do my best, your Grace," Lydia said.

CHAPTER 10

IN WHICH LYDIA ENTERS AMERICAN HIGH SOCIETY

T he gas lamps lighting the streets of Washington near the viceroy's palace rose at intervals so close there were no pools of shadow between them. If Lydia squinted, the lights ran together like a river, and she imagined the carriage sailing along the bright flood toward their destination.

Beside her, Lady Craythorne twitched her cloak closer over her maroon satin gown. Her mood was anticipatory, though not eager, and Lydia recognized the emotions connected to looking forward to a pleasant but not thrilling event. Lord Craythorne, seated opposite in the backward-facing seat, was suffused with excitement honed to a sharpness that reminded Lydia of Colin deep in the passion of intellectual fervor.

"You anticipate discovering things, your Grace?" she asked.

Lord Craythorne's gaze fixed on her. "Of course," he said. "But I do not expect the ringleaders of this American conspiracy to declare themselves openly, nor for them to readily give themselves away through their emotions. Tonight, you will be merely Lady Craythorne's young companion, newly out and eager to experience society. Anything you discover will be welcome but not expected."

"But I wish to be of use." She chose not to challenge him on the

difference between his emotions and his more rational words. Sometimes keeping secrets meant keeping them even from their owners.

"You will be. I simply wish for you not to expect this mystery to
crack wide open at our first encounter with the conspirators. For all we
know, none of the men attending tonight belong to that faction." Lord
Craythorne smiled, and his excitement became tinged with rueful self-
mockery. "Much as it would be pleasing to capture all of them in one
dramatic gesture."

"That would be terrible, to ruin the ball with such foolishness,"
Lady Craythorne said. "Mrs. Monroe would be devastated. You know
she has been unwell."

"Viceroy Monroe would be thrilled," Lord Craythorne said, his
smile widening. "And I imagine it would not hurt his popularity to
preside over the breaking of the Libertymen."

Lady Craythorne sniffed. "You will at least dance tonight. I am
certain Lady Dorothea will be there, as will Miss Adams and Miss
Tarleton."

The smile disappeared. "As you command, my lady."

Lydia knew Lord Craythorne was not angry at the suggestion he
dance, but Lady Craythorne said, "I have your best interests at heart,
Oliver. You should not remain unwed."

"I have experienced marital bliss, Mother. Forgive me for not being
eager to enter that state again." Lord Craythorne's sarcasm cut through
the air like a knife. Lydia barely heard his words, because guilt had
surged within him as well as within Lady Craythorne as he spoke, and
Lydia did not understand it. She wished devoutly to interrogate one or
both of them, because inappropriate guilt usually concealed the most
delicious of secrets.

To distract herself, she looked out the window to where the
viceroy's palace had just become visible in the distance. It was built in
the same European style as every other part of Washington, with high,
white walls and many large windows. Ionic columns framed the
portico, above which was a triangular frieze whose detail Lydia was too
distant to make out. The flat roof sloped only slightly, and a low railing
with hundreds of tiny balusters supporting it encircled the entire

surface. Lydia imagined Clemency Flying them both to the rooftop so she might walk across it, looking down on the guests.

The nearer they approached the palace, the more carriages joined them, until the road was so thronged with traffic everyone slowed to a crawl. Lydia heard their driver shout, a wordless cry that was echoed by two other voices nearby, and then the man called out, "*Make way for his Grace the Duke of Craythorne! Make way!*"

Lord Craythorne grimaced. "I cannot regret the use of my consequence to gain the advantage," he said. Their carriage gave a little jolt, and then they were moving again, not as fast as before but still faster than the snail's pace those around them were held to. "But in cases such as this, it seems a waste. We will arrive eventually, regardless of our speed."

"You sound as if consequence is a well that might run dry," Lydia said.

"An interesting notion, Miss Wescott." Lord Craythorne frowned. "And a not unlikely one. I know those among my peers who puff themselves up so frequently they are ridiculous, and their power to impress is therefore weakened. And yet I imagine many of those not of my social and political rank believe I can gain anything I wish by virtue of being Lord Craythorne, which is certainly not true."

"You command respect wherever you go, Oliver," Lady Craythorne said. "You should not disdain that."

"It is not disdainful to acknowledge that my privileges are not unlimited," Lord Craythorne replied. "And as Miss Wescott has pointed out to me, I am not so conceited as I might be, and I credit that realization."

Lydia blushed. "I have never called you conceited, your Grace."

"How fortunate," Lord Craythorne said. "You are among a rarefied crowd."

The carriage jerked to a halt, saving Lydia the embarrassment of a reply. Lord Craythorne in private was nothing like he had behaved in Mr. Rutledge's Lair, and she had thought him confident yet relaxed there. At the moment, he felt the contented satisfaction of having won his point, though she did not believe they had been arguing, and it was such a pleasant emotion she almost did not hear when he addressed her. She came to herself to discover he and Lady Craythorne had exited the carriage, and Lord Craythorne had extended his hand to her to assist her down. His grip was firm and steadying, and Lydia held tightly to it when the carriage steps shifted underfoot.

Lord Craythorne, in a low voice, said, "Remember, discovering the conspirators is not essential tonight." He was not looking at her, but at those guests near enough to possibly overhear his words. He transferred his grip from her hand to her elbow, and the warmth of his hand steadied her again, as if strength might flow from him to her.

"You do not trust my talent," Lydia said, momentarily disappointed.

Now he looked at her, his head tilted so the curve of his jaw had a strength that matched his intensity of feeling. "I trust your talent. However, Rutledge told me you are prone to wearing yourself out in pursuit of your assignment, and I will not have that. Overexert, and I will send you back to London."

Lydia gaped at him. "But—" She swallowed. "That is monstrously unfair."

"That I should send you home, or that you are not the only observant one?" Lord Craythorne smiled, his lips quirking wryly. "Rutledge gave me strict orders. Yes, laugh if you wish at the idea of *me* being given orders—"

"I did not laugh, your Grace."

"Perhaps you should have; it is an amusing notion." Lord Craythorne's smile disappeared. "You must learn what all of us have— that outrunning one's resources is the same as not using them properly. Now, dance. Enjoy yourself. We shall see what comes of it."

"Oliver," Lady Craythorne said, her voice a clear warning.

Lydia realized she and Lord Craythorne had been standing at the foot of the two steps leading up to the front door, and that other carriages had deposited guests beside them, guests who pretended not to stare. "I will, your Grace," she said, and turned to join Lady Craythorne.

Lights blazed from the open doorway, and as Lydia followed Lady Craythorne into the palace, she covertly gawked at the many crystal-studded chandeliers shedding a bright glow over the white walls.

Guests thronged the entrance hall, which was unexpectedly large and smelled faintly of the pink roses arranged in vases flanking all three doors and lining the far wall. Flowers blooming out of season had always struck Lydia as representative of true wealth.

A rich red strip of carpet stretched to left and right along the cross-hall that led deeper into the palace. Though other rooms opened off the entrance, most of the guests followed the carpet to the left, from which direction music could be heard. There did not seem to be a host or hostess to greet them, and Lydia supposed as this was a political function, the rules were not the same as those of society.

She floated along, buoyed by the crowd's emotions, which were not universally pleasant; many of the guests were happy and anticipatory, but the pleasure of more than a few was honed to that same intent excitement that characterized Lord Craythorne's emotions, and there were several who pulsed with the sort of anger that comes with having one's expectations dashed. Lydia resolved to encounter those men or women if she could, if only to satisfy her curiosity. And if some of them turned out to be secretly Libertymen, how much the better?

She did not realize Lord Craythorne had left them until she entered the ballroom, which was smaller than she had expected. When she turned, hoping to glimpse him in the direction she Discerned he had gone, the crowd was too thick and pressed her too closely for her to see anyone but the person immediately before her. Quickly, she drew close to Lady Craythorne, feeling unexpectedly timid surrounded by strangers. She had not realized she found Lord Craythorne's strong, confident presence so reassuring.

Lady Craythorne, immune to the intimidation of the crowd, sailed across the ballroom to greet a well-dressed, beautiful woman. "Mrs. Monroe," Lady Craythorne said. "How good to see you. I hope this means your health has improved?"

"Lady Craythorne, welcome," Mrs. Monroe said. "I consider it fortunate that my attacks have lessened somewhat in recent days. I have let my hostess duties fall sadly by the wayside these last few weeks."

Lydia, fascinated, Discerned Mrs. Monroe's emotions further. Most people who experienced chronic, debilitating pain showed that pain in muted emotions. But Mrs. Monroe showed no sign of such pain. In fact, Lydia could not tell from her observation that Mrs. Monroe was ill at all. Possibly her illness was all imaginary—except Lady Craythorne had behaved as if it was real, and Lydia's assessment of Lady Craythorne's character indicated that she had no patience for fools, particularly those who played on the sympathies of others.

In her distraction, she almost asked Mrs. Monroe what ailed her, but as she opened her mouth to speak, Lady Craythorne said, "My dear friend, may I introduce my young companion, Miss Wescott?"

Lydia came to herself and curtseyed. Mrs. Monroe clasped Lydia's hand briefly. "Welcome to America," she said. "How pleasant for you, Lavinia, to have such a lovely young person to keep you company."

Lady Craythorne's irritation swelled very briefly, not enough to offend Lydia, but her reply was perfectly polite. "It has been quite enjoyable, yes. I hope she will engage to dance often, you know how young people are about their pleasures!"

Lydia realized how foolish she had been. She had imagined herself walking through the ballroom, assessing those around her, but of course that would look ridiculous. She would have to dance. "It will be most pleasant, yes," she said, casting down her eyes demurely.

"Permit me to make introductions for you—no, there is James catching my eye, I should join him. Lady Craythorne, Miss Wescott, if you will excuse me?" Mrs. Monroe nodded as regally as a queen and walked to where a tall, attractive older man stood conversing with a cluster of other men, all of them shorter than he.

"The Viceroy is extremely popular," Lady Craythorne said, nodding at the tall man. "But poor Elizabeth really is so unwell much of the time, their daughter Eliza frequently acts as hostess." To Lydia's surprise, she offered her arm to her. "Perhaps we may find her; she knows everyone in Washington."

Suspicious, Lydia focused on Lady Craythorne's emotions, but found no secret desire to embarrass Lydia or ruin her investigation, just that general irritated resentment at being part of Lord Craythorne's ruse. Lady Craythorne, she reflected, was as much a mystery as her son.

They strolled through the crowd, with Lady Craythorne nodding or curtseying occasionally to women they passed but not stopping to converse. Lydia made note of those gentlemen and ladies whose emotions were tinged green with desire rather than yellow with more abstract pleasure and watched to see whom they approached. The moments when men and women came together and their mutual interest surged thrilled Lydia.

"Ah," Lady Craythorne said, and tugged Lydia in the direction of a woman who looked similar to the Viceroy, though she lacked his height. "Mrs. Hay," Lady Craythorne said, "how good to see you."

Mrs. Hay clasped Lady Craythorne's outstretched hand. "And you, Lady Craythorne. Will you introduce your companion?"

"This is Miss Wescott, and she accompanies me here while Lord Craythorne is engaged in business. I had hoped to press you for introductions on her behalf."

Lady Craythorne sounded close to indifferent, and her emotions matched her demeanor, but Lydia was surprised at Mrs. Hay's suspicion when Lady Craythorne mentioned her son. Mrs. Hay fixed her gaze narrowly on Lydia. "Naturally," she said. "I have not seen Lord Craythorne this evening."

"I am sure he is deeply engaged in conversation, though he ought to dance." Momentary annoyance filled Lady Craythorne. Mrs. Hay again looked at Lydia, and her suspicion grew. Lydia could not imagine why Mrs. Hay suspected her of an amorous relationship with Lord Craythorne, especially given how Lady Craythorne had introduced her. The idea was absurd. And yet the woman's emotions were unmistakable.

Lydia concealed her own annoyance and curtseyed. "Thank you, madame," she said. Inwardly, she considered saying something that would deflect that suspicion—but what would be the point? It was not as if Mrs. Hay's opinion mattered—though if she was, as Lady Craythorne had suggested, the premiere hostess in Washington, her opinion likely mattered a great deal. But in general, refuting rumor merely meant giving it strength, and Lydia could not stop Mrs. Hay from speculating privately or publicly.

Now the whirl became greater as Mrs. Hay steered Lydia toward gentlemen in frock coats and knee breeches, some of which were provincial in cut, others which might have done any English gentleman proud. She danced, and asked subtle questions, and even flirted a little. Partner after partner turned out to be innocuous, not concealing any secrets more dangerous than their interest in her—or in ladies they wished they were dancing with instead of her.

In one dance, she found herself near Lord Craythorne, who nodded but did not smile. Lydia watched his partner rather than him. The young lady was beautiful, with dark hair and dark brown eyes that set off her porcelain skin, and she was graceful, dipping and floating like a swan. Lydia observed the deep green of her emotions when she touched Lord Craythorne's hand and suppressed a giggle, because Lord Craythorne's emotions revealed nothing but indifference and a sort of weary resignation. Then she regretted her mirth. Suppose the young woman's attraction represented true feeling, and she was doomed to disappointment? But avarice threaded through the young woman's desire, and Lydia suspected the only thing she was in love with was the possibility of becoming the Duchess of Craythorne.

After that dance, Lydia went in search of refreshments, belatedly realizing she should have permitted her partner to fetch her punch. But the man's conversation had bored her, and she knew he had only asked her to dance out of a sense of obligation to Mrs. Hay, so she had been happy to bid him farewell at the end of two dances.

With cup in hand, she strolled around the ballroom, trying not to feel that she had failed. Lord Craythorne was correct; she should not expect the men she met tonight to be conspirators. There would be many events.

She was so absorbed in the emotions of the guests, letting them lift her up, that when she passed near a small knot of conversing men, she failed to see the man who stepped backward into her path until his elbow jostled her arm. Punch slopped over the edge of her cup and spattered her dress's hem. "Oh!" she gasped.

The man turned, startled. "I beg your pardon," he said. "How careless of me. I fear I did not see you. I did not hurt you, did I?"

"No, but I fear my gown cannot say the same," Lydia said, smiling so he would know she was not angry. "It is nothing a good sponging will not remedy."

"Still, I hope you will accept my apologies." The man bowed. "Adam Ruskin, at your service. May I fetch you another glass of punch?"

Lydia examined him closely. He appeared to be Lord Craythorne's age, or close to it, with handsomely styled sandy blond hair and hazel eyes that crinkled at the corners. He did feel remorse, though not as much as he professed. His companions had turned to see whom he spoke to, their mild curiosity twining with their general pleasure. "We have not been properly introduced," she said, concealing her discomfort at being the focus of so much male attention.

"You are English," Mr. Ruskin said. "We are not so formal in America as the mother country demands. Please, you must permit me to make amends."

"Very well, sir," Lydia said. She had known too many unhandsome spirits to be swayed by such a handsome face as Mr. Ruskin's, but his insistence on politeness he did not actually feel intrigued her. She accepted his offered arm.

"I have not seen you before," Mr. Ruskin said as they walked. "Are you new to Washington?"

"I am Lady Craythorne's companion, newly arrived. My name is Miss Wescott." Lydia did not Discern in Mr. Ruskin any amount of romantic interest in her, which relieved her mind even as it roused her curiosity further.

"Ah, Lady Craythorne. My wife has spoken of her. Her son Lord Craythorne is the representative of Parliament come to oversee the transfer of power, yes?"

Lydia relaxed. Having a wife did not mean a man might not cast his eyes in other women's direction, but his lack of attraction to Lydia made it more likely he was a devoted husband. "That is correct. I fear I know little of politics."

"But that should not be. Women can have a great influence on men in their political lives. One need only look at our former viceroy's wife, Mrs. Madison—she wielded great influence through her husband. Though as she is a Seer, perhaps that makes her unique." Mr. Ruskin took Lydia's nearly-empty glass and handed her another. "There, I have made amends."

"Thank you, sir." Lydia sipped, and added, "And you, sir—what is your role in the government?"

"I am the Secretary of the Interior," Mr. Ruskin said. He smiled at Lydia's confusion. "Those of us who maintain different departments within the colonial government are referred to as Secretary. The Secretary of the Interior manages land use and commerce between the colonies. It is as dull as it sounds, sadly."

"That is unfortunate," Lydia said. She was paying attention to Mr. Ruskin's emotional state and not giving much heed to her own words, so she was startled when he laughed, a merry sound that threaded through his less volatile emotions.

"I expected a young lady to protest that my employment is not dull at all," he said. "You are most unusual, Miss Wescott. Not interested in the polite lie?"

Lydia blushed. "I beg your pardon—"

"No, no, do not apologize, I dislike the polite lie myself." Mr. Ruskin bowed, his eyes twinkling. "May I have the pleasure of the next dance? I would like to continue our conversation."

He still felt no romantic interest in her, but Lydia said, "Will not Mrs. Ruskin object?"

"Mrs. Ruskin is currently dancing with the aide to the colonial Treasurer, who is an old friend to both of us. At these political gatherings, conversation, not courtship, is the rule. And I hope you do not believe me so crass as to impose upon a young lady who, I assume, is only just out?" Mr. Ruskin offered Lydia his hand.

Lydia hesitated only a moment before accepting it. "Many men would so impose, sir."

"Then you and I will enjoy our dance, and speak disdainfully of such men," Mr. Ruskin said.

Lydia was about to respond when unexpected anger flashed through her partner. She instinctively followed the line of his gaze to where a trio of men had just entered the ballroom. She glanced back at Mr. Ruskin, but his anger was gone as if it had never been. Lydia cast about for some way to inquire after the newcomers. Surely such a reaction meant something interesting.

"You must know much of Washington, then," she began. "I saw

handbills on my walk through the city that claimed the viceroy's government was not as even-handed as it should be. Handbills that demanded colonial self-governance. That cannot be true, can it?"

Surprise showed both on Mr. Ruskin's face and in his emotions. "Not so ignorant of politics, are you, Miss Wescott?"

Lydia blushed with frustration at having potentially overplayed her hand. She decided to see her mistake through. "Well, is it true?"

"There are those who wish the Colonial Conflict had ended differently, yes," Mr. Ruskin said. "They are in the minority, and no one of importance pays them any heed."

It was a lie.

CHAPTER 11

IN WHICH LYDIA DISCOVERS MANY THINGS, NOT ALL OF THEM USEFUL

Lydia controlled her expression, putting on the vapid look she wore when she wished to seem most innocent and harmless. "There were many handbills for people who are in the minority," she said.

"The smallest mouse may yet squeak loudly in defiance of the cat," Mr. Ruskin said. He glanced over Lydia's shoulder, and once more he pulsed with anger. She turned more rapidly in the dance than was required and noted the same trio of men. Cursing inwardly, she returned her attention to her partner.

"I hope that is the case, for I would not like to see this lovely city embattled again," she said with a smile. "It is much like London."

For some reason, that comment annoyed Mr. Ruskin, though again his emotions did not show in his demeanor. "It has its own unique character," he said.

They danced in silence for several moments, with Lydia frantically searching for some question that would turn the conversation toward the three men. They were among those whose emotions were keen-edged excitement rather than bright yellow pleasure, and every time Lydia caught sight of them, they were intently conversing with a new man or small group of men. Everyone they spoke to experienced that same excitement. Suppose they were plotting something, right here at the investiture ball!

She swiftly ran down the list of topics she knew that related to America and its society and government, and landed on one she had a genuine interest in. "I had expected to see more Africans here," she said when she and Mr. Ruskin clasped hands again. "Or—perhaps that is wrong to call them by such a general name. I know there are many nations in Africa."

"I know little of that continent, except what everyone knows of the Maasai warriors and how they used powerful Moving and Bounding talents to subjugate their neighbors," Mr. Ruskin said. "But you ask not about free blacks, but of those enslaved."

His tone of voice, and his emotions, were both those of an indulgent parent speaking to a precocious child, and Lydia blushed in mingled embarrassment and anger. "I suppose I do," she said. "I do not understand why anyone would consider himself entitled to enslave another, regardless of a difference in skin color."

To her surprise, this sally did not stir Mr. Ruskin's emotions. "A full explanation of the history of slavery is beyond me," he said, though he clearly meant he believed it was beyond Lydia's comprehension. "The trade in slaves began before the advent of talent, and there was a time shortly after that event when slaves possessing strong talents fought back against their oppressors, but that only meant the slave trade moved to encompass just those men and women who lacked talent and could not resist."

His casual recitation made Lydia ill. That anyone might consider someone lesser simply for lacking talent—Mr. Ruskin was correct; it was beyond her comprehension. "And the American colonists fought to defend their right to continue to enslave others," she said.

She had spoken sharply without realizing how at odds her words and tone were with the simpering maiden she wished to appear. Mr. Ruskin looked at her with suspicion, but when he spoke, it was with the same placidity as before. "The slavery issue is complex in some ways and simple in others. It is true, there are many Americans for whom its continuance is a prominent concern, but slavery was not the only reason those men rose up against England." Again, his emotions pulsed with anger briefly.

Lydia widened her eyes and tilted her head to appear vacuous. "But I still do not understand—I believed there to be many slaves in America, yet I have seen practically no one of black skin in Washington."

Mr. Ruskin's anger ebbed. "That is because there are few of that description living here. Now that England has made the buying and selling of slaves illegal, one sees slaves—those born to that state—only in the Southern colonies, on the great plantations."

"But that does not explain away those who are free. They must live somewhere."

"Many of those find homes farther north, or in the Iroquois Confederacy." Again Mr. Ruskin's anger flashed, an identical emotion to what he had experienced in seeing those three men. "They prefer not to risk being misidentified as runaway slaves."

"I imagine many slaves must attempt to flee." Lydia hoped the answer to that was "yes."

"It is not exactly a commonplace, but it happens. There are many free blacks who use their talents, particularly Bounding, to assist in such escapes." Mr. Ruskin's demeanor again was so placid he might have been commenting on the weather.

"If they may no longer purchase slaves, slave owners must be angry at the loss of some of their livelihood." Lydia tilted her head again as if an idea had only just occurred to her. "Perhaps *they* are the source of those handbills!"

Unexpected amusement ran through Mr. Ruskin, but he merely smiled. "Slave owners are more likely to riot. Handbills require a delicacy they lack."

"A riot? How dreadful!"

"You need not fear, Miss Wescott." Mr. Ruskin's amusement was still greater than she believed was justified. "These rumors of unrest are nothing more than that."

That was another lie. Lydia could not tell, however, what the lie concealed. Did Mr. Ruskin mean the rumors were true, or did he mean they were not rumors of unrest, but something more dangerous?

She opened her mouth to ask another question, and the music

ended, and Mr. Ruskin bowed. Frustrated, Lydia curtseyed and smiled sweetly at Mr. Ruskin. "Thank you, sir, and I appreciate your willingness to instruct me."

"Perhaps, if Mrs. Ruskin calls on Lady Craythorne, you will be present. I am certain my wife will enjoy meeting you. Until then—good evening, Miss Wescott." He bowed again, more shallowly, and walked away.

Lydia waited for the space of two breaths before following him, leaving enough space between them that it was not apparent that was what she was doing. Mr. Ruskin was, in fact, moving in the direction of the three men whose presence made him angry and was not concealing his interest. Lydia's heart beat faster with excitement. This interaction must be of interest.

She slowed her steps when Mr. Ruskin joined the three and observed with her natural and Discernment senses. Mr. Ruskin looked and felt angry, his shoulders tense, his brow furrowed like thunder. Embarrassment and chagrin suffused one of the men, as if he was conscious of chastisement. The other two were angry, an anger twined with belligerence, the emotion of a defiant child caught snitching pastries. Casually, Lydia changed her path so it would take her past the men and listened for their words. They were difficult to make out, as the din had grown considerably in the last hour.

"...invited. You...reject such...?"

That was the oldest of the strangers, a grey-haired man who was slim and short and yet carried himself with the confidence of someone ten inches taller. No trace of the uncertainty creeping into his emotions showed in his demeanor.

Mr. Ruskin towered over the man, his anger and irritation rising. "...innocence. I saw...you dare...posturing fool...?"

The grey-haired man still did not flinch. "...exaggerate...reassure those...does not mean...lost."

The other belligerent stranger, a red-headed youth as tall and strapping as the grey-haired man was not, cut in with a forcefulness that revealed his impatience with the conversation and made his companions attempt to hush him. "...should act...enemies are in...would take nothing to eliminate...skulking in shadows."

"Suggitt, you fool," Mr. Ruskin said, his voice momentarily rising above the noise of the crowd. He jerked as if surprised at how loudly he had spoken, and murmured something else too quietly for Lydia to make out however she strained to hear. Whatever it was quelled the young man into sulky silence. Mr. Ruskin then said, "I insist you leave—"

"Miss Wescott!"

Lydia jerked in surprise. "Mrs. Hay! I beg your pardon, I did not hear you."

"The noise is quite astonishing, is it not?" Mrs. Hay laughed. "Mrs. Madison, my predecessor—or rather my mother's, I meant as she was previously the premiere hostess in Washington—at any rate, she would call this a rare success based on the clamor alone." She took Lydia's arm and drew her away from Mr. Ruskin. "I wish to introduce you to other young women of your age. You will wish to make friends, I am certain."

Lydia wished for nothing less at that moment than to make friends. Behind her, the four men's emotions receded as she walked away, but did not lessen in intensity. Eavesdropping had not told her enough, but she could weave what she had heard into a satisfying story. The antagonism of the three men suggested animosity toward those in attendance, and Mr. Ruskin intended them to leave. She wondered about the man, Suggitt, who had spoken of eliminating enemies; suppose he meant to attack the Viceroy? But Mr. Ruskin had not been afraid or suffused with the excitement that presaged violence, and surely he would act to stop anyone who tried to kill the Viceroy? It was something to tell Lord Craythorne, at any rate.

"Here we are," Mrs. Hay said cheerfully, coming to a halt before a small group of young women. To Lydia's Discernment, the young women were not pleased at Mrs. Hay's interruption, but they had good manners and did not show their dissatisfaction. "Lady Dorothea, Miss Harcourt, Miss Adams, may I introduce Miss Wescott? She is companion to Lady Craythorne and newly arrived in Washington. I hope you will make her welcome."

"Certainly," Lady Dorothea said. Lydia recognized her as the young woman she had seen Lord Craythorne dancing with, the one whose green ambition aimed at becoming Lady Craythorne. She and Miss Harcourt and Miss Adams were all very lovely, and they dressed fashionably, but what caught Lydia's attention was how their emotions all heightened when Mrs. Hay mentioned the Dowager Duchess. They felt curiosity, and intent excitement, and, very faintly, the ugly tangle of green twined with red that meant jealousy.

Mrs. Hay patted Lydia's arm. "Do enjoy yourselves," she said, and sailed away into the crowd.

Lady Dorothea smiled. It was not a very friendly smile and verged on a sneer. "Lady Craythorne's companion," she said. "How very interesting. She is a lovely woman."

"I agree," Lydia said. She had already taken Lady Dorothea in dislike: she was spiteful, disdainful of other women, and rapacious in her desire for a title. And Lady Dorothea disliked Lady Craythorne, which angered Lydia. Then she was surprised at her anger. She and Lady Craythorne were not friends, but Lydia respected her, and she found she did not like anyone speaking ill of her, even if it was only in the form of Lady Dorothea lying about her true feelings.

"I have never been to England," Miss Harcourt said. "Is it very different from America?"

"In some ways, yes, but Washington resembles London closely." Lydia liked Miss Harcourt much better; she was genuinely interested in Lydia's opinions, and her jealousy was a less active thing than Lady Dorothea's. She decided to make a test and added, "Lord Craythorne certainly believes so."

Jealousy surged through all three women, which amused Lydia. Well, it was not as if she did not know Lord Craythorne was a highly desirable catch. Less amusing was the intensity of Lady Dorothea's jealousy. Where the other two were mildly jealous in an abstract way, suggesting that they saw Lord Craythorne as one of many potential mates, Lady Dorothea experienced the bitter anger of one who has laid claim to a prize and will defend it against all comers. It annoyed Lydia on Lord Craythorne's behalf. She wished she could tell Lady Dorothea of her prize's indifference to her, but even if she could have revealed her talent, that would be too cruel to do even to such a selfish person as Lady Dorothea.

"You are close to his Grace?" Lady Dorothea said, poorly concealing her jealousy.

"Not I," Lydia said. "He is quite busy with political matters, and I am merely her Grace's companion, so we have little in common."

The answer soothed Lady Dorothea's emotions. "Of course. I suppose her Grace will not remain long, not if she has the delights of London to return to. I cannot imagine anyone wishing to remain in the colonies longer than necessary."

Now Lady Dorothea's bitterness was inward turned, mingled with regret and chagrin and resentment that sent a brief wave of nausea over Lydia with its intensity. Lady Dorothea's words embarrassed Miss Adams and Miss Harcourt, who exchanged glances that said they wished they dared challenge her. Lydia, making a guess about the birthplaces of each young woman, said, "Oh, Washington is actually very like London, and I believe anyone with knowledge of both would be hard pressed to choose one over the other."

This made Miss Adams and Miss Harcourt brighten. Miss Adams said, "My family spends half the year abroad, and I admire London, but Washington is a fine place to call home."

"I suppose," Lady Dorothea said, with a disdainful air that told Lydia she intended to regain control over the conversation. "I anticipate the day when I may have a true London season."

"And I have seen Iroquois men," Lydia said, ignoring this. "Their appearances are striking."

"They are a proud people," Lady Dorothea said, "and we do not see them often." For once, her emotions were not disdainful. "My father Lord Fanshawe says they dislike coming this far south, as it keeps them from their homelands."

"My father does business with the Haudenosaunee—that is their name for themselves," Miss Harcourt said. "Their men are so very handsome!"

Miss Adams let out a gasp. "You cannot imagine marrying an Iroquois man? They are so different from us!"

"One need not consider marriage to admire," Miss Harcourt said with an impish smile. "Besides, there is no fear of that. My father says no Iroquois would ever consider marrying one not of their race. They pride themselves on maintaining their traditions, which no outsider will understand."

"There are far too many attractive Englishmen one might wed to give any space to fancies over those who are unsuited," Lady Dorothea said, again with that air of disdain. "Though I daresay I shall not find a match until I am in London. My parents wish for me to marry someone whose interests lie far from America."

Lydia Discerned Miss Adams' rush of resentment and courage a scant second before Miss Adams said, "And that is why you preened yourself in front of Lord Craythorne, is it?"

"When his Grace chooses to dance with me, I shall make the most of it," Lady Dorothea said, raising her chin high. "He was most complimentary."

"He was complimentary to me, as well," Miss Harcourt said. "You should not pride yourself on a conquest you have not yet made."

The desire to set them both straight battered at Lydia's heart. She chose to say, "Lord Craythorne is always gracious, in my experience."

"Is that so?" Lady Dorothea said with another not-very-nice smile. Lydia was beginning to wonder why the other young ladies called her 'friend,' though perhaps they did not and merely stood together out of social niceties. "Lady Craythorne has invited Mama and me to call upon her tomorrow, and I am certain Lord Craythorne will be present to again be...gracious."

"Then it is a pity you cannot marry his mother," Miss Harcourt snapped, and flounced off toward the line of dancers.

Lydia bit her lip to control a laugh at Lady Dorothea's astonished chagrin. She said to Miss Adams, "Perhaps you will call upon me as well? I should like to be better acquainted with the ladies of Washington, particularly those my age."

"I would like that very much, and I believe my mother will enjoy meeting you," Miss Adams said.

"Then we shall all be very friendly together," Lady Dorothea said, somewhat sourly. "Excuse me, I see my mother calling." She, too, walked away. Lydia saw no one in that direction summoning her.

"I do not like to speak ill of anyone, particularly those I have only just met," she said to Miss Adams, "but is Lady Dorothea always so...prickly?"

Miss Adams stepped closer and lowered her voice. "Lord Fanshawe's finances are known to be in a sorry state," she murmured. "Lady Dorothea seems conscious of the need to marry well. Personally, I believe that would be a terrible state in which to seek marriage, but it is hard for me to remain in charity with her when she makes friendship so difficult."

Some of Lydia's annoyance with Lady Dorothea faded. She herself had always been grateful that she need not marry to maintain her family's fortunes, since she could not picture herself marrying at all, and the idea of having to attract a wealthy and titled husband made her uncomfortable. But she agreed with Miss Adams that Lady Dorothea's pride and snobbery made it difficult to sympathize with her fully.

She Discerned the approach of two people whose pleasure was mingled with faint desire, and glanced casually around, observing the crowd. Indeed, two men approached, both intent on Lydia and Miss Adams. Miss Adams smiled and blushed when she noticed them, and her jealousy disappeared entirely. "Mr. Cavanaugh," she said when the two were near enough for conversation.

The shorter and handsomer of the men addressed Miss Adams with a smile. "Miss Adams. I had quite given up hope of seeing you this evening. Perhaps you will introduce us to your friend?"

"Of course. Miss Wescott, these are Mr. Cavanaugh and Mr. Harvey. Gentlemen, Miss Wescott, who is newly arrived from London." Miss Adams' entire attention was focused on Mr. Cavanaugh.

Both men bowed politely. Mr. Harvey said, "Here from London? I was born in Sussex and lived for many years in London, though it has been some time since I visited. May I ask the pleasure of this dance, Miss Wescott? And perhaps you will tell me stories of our homeland." He offered Lydia his arm, and smiled in a way that made him seem nearly handsome.

Lydia Discerned Mr. Cavanaugh's satisfaction in Mr. Harvey's offer and managed not to laugh at how neatly he had achieved his objective of extricating Miss Adams from her companion without slighting Lydia. "I would enjoy that very much, Mr. Harvey," she said.

Mr. Harvey might not be as attractive as Mr. Cavanaugh, but he was an excellent dancer, good enough that Lydia for once was not annoyed at having to dance. With half her attention, she conversed with him, and with the other half continued to assess those in attendance. But it was growing late, and everyone's emotions grew muted with weariness, some of it physical, some of it the weariness that comes from sustaining a strong emotion for a long period of time. She no longer saw the trio of men Mr. Ruskin had been interested in, and their peculiar emotions no longer stood out from the crowd. Disheartened, she concluded there was no more to be learned that evening.

As their dance drew to a close, Mr. Harvey said, "Do you intend to attend the poetry reading at Mrs. Harcourt's home next Monday? It is sure to be a popular event."

"I had not heard of it," Lydia replied. "Whose poetry?"

"That is why I believe it will be of interest to you. Some of Washington's most promising poets will read from their works. It is an opportunity to discover the next great talent. I am certain Lady Craythorne has received an invitation."

"Then I will attend," Lydia said. Inwardly, she groaned. She was not much for reading in general, and poetry did not command her attention. But as Lady Craythorne's companion, she likely had no choice.

"Excellent," Mr. Harvey said. "Then I will—oh, that is one of our poets! I had not expected to see him here, as this is not his usual crowd. Come, I will make introductions. He is a splendid fellow, with the most interesting conversation." Without waiting for Lydia's assent, he drew her along after him toward a tall, thin man with long hair that curled in tight ringlets around his face like a girl's. He was looking away from them, toward the drawing room adjacent to the ballroom that was being used for cards, and Lydia slowed, dragging at Mr. Harvey's arm, for the man's powerful anger was like being struck in the face.

Mr. Harvey, of course, noticed nothing, and he hailed the man when they were yet some distance away, drawing his attention from the card-room. "Sabot! It is good to see you. May I introduce you to Miss

Wescott? She is Lady Craythorne's companion and newly arrived from England. Miss Wescott, Mr. Sabot."

Mr. Sabot turned indifferent eyes on Lydia. He was older than she had guessed based on his youthful hair, quite middle-aged, but with an intensity about him that would have suited someone her own age. She swallowed and managed a polite smile, though his anger battered at her like a powerful tide. "Mr. Sabot, Mr. Harvey tells me you are a poet."

"I am," Mr. Sabot said. "And you accompany one of the oppressors. How young you are, to be so used."

"Sabot, be polite," Mr. Harvey warned. "Now is not the time for political agitation. This is the investiture ball."

"A time to celebrate the failure of the American people to achieve self-governance. We gave up too readily." Mr. Sabot clenched both fists, and Lydia eyed him warily, in case his anger led him to forget himself.

"I do not understand why you are here," she said in her most demure, puzzled voice. "If you are not a supporter of the Viceroy, surely you are not welcome?"

Mr. Harvey made a sputtering, choking sound. Mr. Sabot's gaze focused on Lydia more intently. "I am a supporter of America," he said. "I wish only the best for my country. We did not win the war, but that does not mean the oppressors do not need to hear from America's advocates. Why, it was Mr. Jay and Mr. Madison who penned the Declaration of the Rights of Man that the English king signed—two Americans who stood up to the oppressors—"

"Miss Wescott is not interested in talk of oppressors," Mr. Harvey said. "You make her uncomfortable. Sabot, will you read your poetry at Mrs. Harcourt's soiree?"

Mr. Sabot blinked. "Of course. Miss Wescott, I consider it my duty to use my gift to inform others of the dangers facing us. There is a second revolution coming—"

"Yes, yes, and the people will rise up and be slaughtered," Mr. Harvey said, sounding bored. Then horror flooded through him. "I beg your pardon, Miss Wescott, I should not have said anything so horrid. Please forgive me."

"Of course," Lydia said absently. She was engrossed in studying Mr. Sabot's emotions and barely heeded her companion. Anger, yes, but it was not directed at anyone; it was the sort of generalized anger that marked a zealot, or a revolutionary. But she instinctively believed Mr. Sabot was not the man she had hoped to find. That type of anger did not lend itself well to coherent planning. Rather, it usually indicated a person who liked to rail at the world over supposed slights, but who would shy from taking action to correct those slights.

On the other hand, Mr. Sabot might easily be a tool of those with clearer heads. And while Mr. Harvey's emotions showed he believed Mr. Sabot to be a harmless crank, Lydia supposed it was possible Mr. Sabot might have connections to those who were not at all harmless.

"I would very much like to hear your poetry, Mr. Sabot," she said, interrupting the beginnings of speech from Mr. Harvey. "Or perhaps buy a volume? You are published, are you not?"

"Of course, and my work is available at all reputable booksellers." Mr. Sabot's anger eased. Now it was tinged with pride. "If you attend the soiree, I would be happy to sign my book for you."

"That sounds marvelous." Lydia curtseyed. "I beg your pardon, but it is growing late, and I must see if Lady Craythorne needs me. Thank you for the dance, Mr. Harvey, and for the conversation, Mr. Sabot."

She hurried away before either man could speak further. Excitement welled up within her until it began to twine with the excitement of the other guests and she had to suppress her feelings to keep from becoming overwhelmed. Mr. Sabot was almost certainly not a Libertyman; he was too obvious in his fervor, and the Libertymen would see him as a liability in their desire for secrecy. But he might be a link to those who were. She hoped Lady Craythorne was not one of those women who thought nothing of dancing and conversing until dawn, for she did not believe she could contain herself that long.

CHAPTER 12

IN WHICH A DISCUSSION OF CURRENT EVENTS TURNS INTO INSTRUCTION IN LITERARY APPRECIATION

Despite the late evening—they did not return to the mansion until after three o'clock—Lydia woke at ten the next morning invigorated. She had not spoken to Lord Craythorne about her discoveries on the ride home, conscious of Lady Craythorne's presence, though the Dowager Duchess had dozed off some minutes before they arrived and they might have spoken freely. But Lord Craythorne, too, had remained silent, his emotions muted by weariness almost to imperceptibility. Lydia had been content to wait for the morrow.

Now, she rose and dressed quickly and descended to the breakfast-room, where a light meal under covers had been laid. She was not fond of heavy food in the morning, certainly not before noon, but she had tea and toast and managed to eat daintily despite being the only person dining. Then she went in search of Lord Craythorne.

She had explored the house in the first few days after her arrival, and, making a guess, she went upstairs to the library. She had been pleasantly surprised by its light, airy ambience, having expected something more like Mr. Rutledge's Lair, windowless and full of oak bookcases that could crush a man beneath them were they to fall over. But this library was on the corner of the northern ell of the house, and tall windows broke the line of the bookcases on the northern and western walls so that indirect sunlight illuminated the room without damaging the books the way direct rays would.

Out the northern windows, the hedge bordering the estate and the rooftops of the neighboring mansion were visible; to the west, the long, curving drive through the front garden to the door stretched all the way to the street, and occasionally carriages or horses could be seen passing to and fro. Lydia liked the contrast between the placidity of the hedges and the movement of the street. She also liked the maps that hung on the walls above the windows and to the left and right of the door, framed in gilt as if they were masterpieces of art. They were not contemporary maps, but showed instead ancient lands and distorted coastlines from before the time Extraordinary Movers could Fly to map geography more accurately.

Lord Craythorne was not there. Lydia considered her options and decided she wished to spend time in this room regardless. Possibly Lord Craythorne had not risen yet, and she should not roam the house searching for him like she might a lost puppy.

She examined the shelves, something she had not yet done. Not being much of a reader, she had only been interested in the books for how they made the room smell. The richness of leather, bold and strong, competed with the fainter but more pervasive smell of paper. Lydia liked the scent, especially as it combined with the smell of sandalwood that came from nowhere she could detect. This time, however, she was curious about what the owners of the mansion—the previous owners, as Lord Craythorne had purchased the place sight unseen before arriving in Washington—had thought worthy of inclusion in their collection.

Many of the books had very dull titles impressed upon their spines: *Agricultural Findings 1803-1804,* or *Collected Works* of men whose names Lydia did not recognize. But there were also newer books that looked like novels, and histories, and atlases, which Lydia liked nearly as much as globes.

With both hands, she removed an oversized folio and carried it to the table in the center of the room. There was no title on the spine or cover, but when she opened it at random, she gasped. Watercolors of birds filled both pages, so detailed she could imagine them lifting away from the book and fluttering around the ceiling or bumping against the windows. Each was hand-labeled in Latin and English. She touched the drawing of *Erithacus rubecula*, English robin, tracing the line of the bird's head and neck.

"What is it you have found?"

Lord Craythorne's voice startled Lydia, who had been so engrossed in the pictures she had not been aware of his approach. Her gasp elicited a chuckle from him. "My apologies. I assumed you are always aware of others' presence."

"I am, most often, but you are as imperceptible as a shadow," Lydia said, "and one does not know a shadow is present except by looking." She considered her words, and added, "That is either wise or hopelessly inane, and I cannot tell which."

"I would call it 'mysterious,'" Lord Craythorne said. He came more fully into the library and let the door swing most of the way shut behind him. The clean scent of his soap mingled pleasantly with the smell of leather and paper. "You perceive the world so unusually. What about me makes me a shadow?"

Lydia sank into the nearest chair. "I may not explain it well. People never think to conceal or control the emotions they feel, only their expression. So people who are angry, or happy, or, well, anything—those emotions are bright and powerful even if the people do not shout or cheer. But some men and women have that control, so their emotions are muted, and you are one such."

"That is not at all confusing." Lord Craythorne sat opposite Lydia, across the table, and loosely interlaced his fingers to rest on the table top.

"I imagine that is because I did not try to convey how those emotions feel to me." Lydia turned a few pages, expecting to see more birds. Instead, watercolor drawings of spotted cats as vivid as the birds covered the two-page spread. Across the top of the left-hand page were the words *Panthera onca*. "Who painted these?" she exclaimed.

Lord Craythorne leaned forward to look at the pages upside-down. "Remarkable," he said, curiosity rising within him. "The family who owned this place fell on hard times and sold the house and most of its contents to me. They did not take any of the books, or at least I assume so from how there are no gaps on the shelves, and if they left something like this behind, they must have been desperate. May I?"

At Lydia's nod, he spun the book around to face him and began turning pages. "I do not recognize the style, but these were originally loose pages in a portfolio, hand-bound. I wonder who the artist is, or was. Someone well-traveled, obviously. The jaguar was drawn from life, and the elephant."

"You know something of art?" Lydia asked.

"Something. Not much. My father was the connoisseur. You should visit Craythorne Hall when we return—the house is full of my father's art collection."

"I would like that, though I fear much of it would be wasted on me. I am not very educated." Lydia realized she was slouching and sat up straighter.

"Mother told me you were self-taught. That requires dedication. I believe it would not take much to educate you, if you chose." Lord Craythorne rotated the book back to face Lydia. "This room is beautiful. I find it comfortable, do you?" He leaned back in his chair. In the indirect light, his curls were darker than usual, and the dimness gave his face an unexpected angularity that increased his satirical appearance, though his emotions were peaceful.

Lydia nodded. "I am not much for reading, but this room feels welcoming anyway. As if it knows itself, and does not need others to appreciate it to be confident in who it is."

Lord Craythorne laughed. "What a remarkable way to put things—and yet I agree completely." He settled into his chair more deeply as if emphasizing his words. "So, Miss Wescott. Did you break the Libertymen's secret? Learn their ringleaders' identities?"

He was joking, with no scorn nor ridicule, so Lydia replied, straight-facedly, "Of course, your Grace. I danced with their chief, who fell madly in love with me, and he told me secrets of where they would attack and where they meet to plot their nefarious doings. He also proposed marriage, but of course I could not accept so hasty a proposal. I apologize if that was not enough."

Lord Craythorne's smile broadened as she spoke until she reached the marriage proposal, at which he laughed and slapped his knee. "Miss Wescott, you are a marvel. Naturally you should never accept marriage proposals from hardened villains. Such men rarely represent good marital prospects."

"Oh, that is a relief," Lydia said, "as I feared I had lost more opportunities to gain information through my future husband."

"We will survive," Lord Craythorne said, still chuckling. "I did warn you there might be little to learn last night."

"I know, and you were right, in that I learned nothing of great import," Lydia said, sobering, "but there are things I believe you should know."

She told him about Mr. Ruskin, and his lie about the importance of the handbills, and his encounter with the three angry men. "He called one of them Suggitt," she said, "and I believe they were in opposition to the Viceroy, for he insisted they leave. I did not see whether they actually did." She would not tell Lord Craythorne about the young ladies and their interest in him. That would either embarrass him, or puff him up, and neither of those outcomes satisfied her.

"Suggitt," Lord Craythorne said. "There is a Thomas Suggitt among the Southern representatives to the American Parliament, but he was not in attendance. It might have been his son, of whom I have heard little, but all of it is unflattering. Young Abel Suggitt is often in company with Jarrett Hughes, and *he* is prominent among those who wish for the colonies' freedom."

"So he might be a Libertyman?"

"Might be, but he is careful not to speak sedition—at least not where anyone in power can hear." Lord Craythorne's brow creased in thought. "If Suggitt and Hughes were among those men, they were not the only ones in attendance intent on criticizing the Viceroy and the English government. I heard more than a few murmurs opposing Mr. Monroe as the new Viceroy."

Lydia frowned as well. "I believed him to be quite popular."

"He is, but there are many who believe he was installed as a British puppet. This despite the fact that the accords reached after the Colonial Conflict decreed that all Viceroys should be American born, to satisfy those who objected to the obvious 'oppression' inherent in an

English lord ruling over colonials." Lord Craythorne's expression soured further.

"Then what of the handbills?" Lydia asked. "I read one, and while I am not experienced at dissecting rhetoric, it truly did not seem dangerous. Merely filled with complaints that echo those of the colonists who started the Conflict."

"I don't know, but I intend to find out. Starting with identifying this 'John Steadfast.' And while it is true that most political rhetoric serves as a stopcock to ease or control public emotions, hidden among the harmless diatribes may be tinder for a fire." Lord Craythorne rubbed his chin thoughtfully. "Curious," he said.

"What is curious, your Grace?"

"You." Lord Craythorne's eyes narrowed. "I have been conversing with you the way I would a man who is my peer, and you have neither said nor done anything to indicate this conversation makes you uncomfortable. My mother would call your behavior unfeminine."

Again, Lydia detected no censure in his emotions, but she blushed anyway. "I prefer plain speaking," she said, "and I do not see why such speech should be solely the province of men. What do *you* call it, your Grace?"

"Refreshing," Lord Craythorne said. "But in a sense, my behavior has been inappropriate."

"You *did* leave the door open, your Grace," Lydia said. "It is not as if we are both entirely lost to decency."

"Inappropriate in that I would not speak this way to any other lady of my acquaintance," Lord Craythorne said. "My mother would definitely not approve."

"Then we shall not tell her," Lydia said, lifting her chin defiantly. "I prefer not to be treated as a fragile flower, your Grace, because I was many long years in developing what strength I have. And you are interesting because you are not arrogant even though you might be."

Lord Craythorne smiled. "A tremendous compliment, Miss Wescott." He rose. "I have business to be about, unless you have more information to share?"

"No, I fear it is only many engagements and visits and soirees in my future." Lydia sighed. "And poetry readings."

"Poetry readings? Your expression tells me you see such as equivalent to a visit from the hangman, intent on dragging you to your doom. What poetry readings?"

Lydia, startled at how Lord Craythorne's emotions had sharpened keenly at this new topic, stammered, "It...it is something Mrs. Harcourt does—do you know her, or Miss Harcourt? No, of course you know Miss Harcourt—she, Mrs. Harcourt, that is, hosts readings by rising new voices in American poetry, and I have been invited. Except I have no ear for poetry, and it is all tedious paeans to flowers and clouds and such silliness."

Lord Craythorne's mood heightened as she spoke, not growing angry so much as indignant, and he squared his broad shoulders as if preparing for a fight. "Miss Wescott," he said, in an even, deep tone at odds with his emotions, "I now see why you consider yourself improperly educated. No ear for poetry? Flowers and clouds? You cast me quite into despair."

"You are not in despair," Lydia blurted out in her confusion, "you are amused and horrified in equal parts, and you are also astounded that anyone could be as ignorant of literature as I."

Lord Craythorne stared at her in amazement. Then he laughed, a deep, merry sound that eased Lydia's confusion. "You are the very picture of an innocent maiden," he said, "and then you come out with comments as incisive as that, and I must reevaluate you all over again."

He crossed the room to a bookcase on the northern wall and ran his long fingers over the spines, his lips moving soundlessly. Finally, he settled on something he liked and pulled a small, fat volume off the shelf. Returning to Lydia's side, he said, "Here. Read these. You will have to decide for yourself if they are silliness."

Lydia turned the book over in her hands. *The Poems of John Donne* was printed on the spine, and an ornate geometric shape was impressed on the front cover. "I believed John Donne wrote essays. There was one about not being an island that my father liked to quote."

"He wrote many things, but his is some of the finest poetry our country has produced." Lord Craythorne tapped the cover with one elegant finger. "I believe even you will find it appealing."

Lydia grimaced, which made Lord Craythorne laugh again, his eyes crinkling at the corners. "There, you are already softening," he said, "because if you truly found my assignment distasteful, you would have smiled and curtseyed and said, 'Of course, your Grace.' You see I am nearly a Discerner myself when it comes to your moods."

"I suppose it is only fair that I be as transparent to you as you are to me, if we are to work together," Lydia said. "And because I respect you, I will warn you that it is when you feel the deep satisfaction you currently experience that you are most in danger, because you are prone to granting wishes in that state. If I wanted something from you, I would need only to maneuver you into self-satisfaction and then ask for a favor."

"That is not true, for I—" Lord Craythorne began. His expression changed, became introspective. "How have I never noticed this before?"

"Because giving makes you happy, and it enhances that self-satisfied state," Lydia explained. "But it is something that might be manipulated, so you should take care to be conscious of it."

Unexpected anger flashed through Lord Craythorne, followed by that same guilt she had noticed the previous evening when he and Lady Craythorne had discussed marriage. "I should," Lord Craythorne said, without any of the amusement he had felt earlier. "I thank you for the warning, Miss Wescott. You might have kept that knowledge to yourself, and used it to your benefit."

"I could not, not and call myself your friend," Lydia said absently, caught up in examining his odd blend of emotions.

"Are we friends?"

The words cut through Lydia's absorption. "I," she began, startled, then paused to consider. "I do not know if we are friends yet," she said, "but I believe we are on a way to becoming so. I hope that is not forward of me."

"I have so few friends, I will not reject one simply because it is an unconventional friendship." Lord Craythorne extended a hand to Lydia. "I am impertinent in offering you my hand, Miss Wescott, but I feel inspired to seal this momentous occasion with a handshake."

Lydia accepted his hand immediately. His grip was firm and confident, and she liked how his skin was slightly rougher than hers, not callused, but not the smooth softness of someone accustomed to idleness. Its texture helped her distinguish between the two of them. "You have few friends, your Grace?"

Lord Craythorne released her. "I have many acquaintances, among them several dozen whom I can call 'friend' without stretching the definition all out of true. But I find it difficult to maintain closeness with most of them, for one reason or another. Many of them, I fear, watch me to see if I will become erratic and unstable like most Scorchers. Some of them are more interested in my generosity than in myself. A few I trust with my life."

"You maintain self-control so you will not be a typical Scorcher," Lydia said, understanding dawning. "It is why your emotions are muted. I see."

"I will take your assurance that that is so," Lord Craythorne said, and some of his amusement returned. "I have never embraced my talent, as I find it unpleasant. For me, using it has always been a matter of controlling my impulses and my temper. A Scorcher in a rage is a dangerous thing."

"I know," Lydia said. "I have seen it, and it was terrifying."

"That sounds like a story worth hearing," Lord Craythorne said. "But I will not inquire now, so as to give us something to talk about in future." He tapped the John Donne book. "We will discuss this later— and I will accompany you to the poetry reading, that I may guide your understanding further."

"How very generous, your Grace," Lydia said.

"Sarcasm ill befits you, Miss Wescott," Lord Craythorne said with a smile.

CHAPTER 13

IN WHICH MR. SABOT GIVES AWAY MORE THAN HE INTENDS

Mrs. Harcourt's home was not beautiful either inside or out. Its exterior was bland and white, with a few token columns pretending to grandeur that merely drew attention to the poor disposition of the doors and windows. The halls were crowded with indifferent portraits of people Lydia guessed were Harcourt ancestors and pedestal tables displaying objets d'art with no theme to their selection. And the salon to which Lydia and Lady Craythorne and Lord Craythorne were ushered, while large and brilliantly lit, was muffled by a thick carpet and heavy drapes that settled a hush over the room Lydia believed would silence even the most clear-spoken orator.

But what preoccupied Lydia as she entered the salon was the question of where all the chairs came from.

It was not a question she had ever considered before, nor did she know why it had occurred to her to wonder about it now. She surveyed the many chairs arranged in rows facing the far end of the room, where the readers would stand. They all matched, as far as she could tell, and their cushions of satiny cream and gold brocade were also all identical. And yet, from the sofas and small tables pushed back against the walls, poetry readings were not this room's primary purpose. So where did the chairs all live when not in use? They ought to hire out to different families, and show thrift.

"Hire out? I beg your pardon, Miss Wescott, but whatever do you mean?"

Lydia jumped. She had not meant to say that last sentence out loud. "It was idle fancy, that is all," she told the Dowager Duchess. "Mere foolishness."

"You ought to watch your words, Miss Wescott," Lady Craythorne said. "I am sure you do not wish to be believed an air-dreamer."

To Lydia's surprise, Lady Craythorne was genuinely concerned rather than censorious. "No, that is true, your Grace," she stammered, "and I appreciate your care."

"There are worse things to be considered," Lord Craythorne said. He escorted both ladies to seats not too near the front or the rear.

"But you are different," Lydia began, then realized there were other guests within hearing and decided not to continue that comment about the difference between Lord Craythorne's public and private personae.

Lord Craythorne's eyebrows raised, but his gaze flicked to the nearest guest, a small, elderly woman wearing enough jewels to suit the richest dowager, and he, too, said nothing.

Lydia settled herself on her cushion and folded her hands in her lap. The chair was tall enough her feet almost did not touch the floor, but she stilled her legs so they would not swing like a child's and Discerned the room's occupants.

They had arrived early, Lord Craythorne being a great believer in claiming the best seats for any performance for which he did not possess a private box, and only ten other people were present. Nine of them were filled with varying degrees of calm blue tranquility laced with yellow threads of pleasant anticipation; the tenth man was nothing but bored. Lydia watched that man with her natural vision for several moments. He concealed his boredom well, as he was in conversation with Mrs. Harcourt and seemed fully engaged. Lydia decided she liked him, if only because he shared her opinion of poetry readings.

She glanced sideways at Lord Craythorne. Light from the many candles gilded his curls and gave attractive definition to the angles of his face, but despite his apparent calm, he surveyed the room with mild distaste. Apparently she was not the only one who found Mrs. Harcourt's home uncongenial.

She felt slightly guilty at this, as it was criticism even if it was unvoiced, and it was not as if she had a home of her own to hold up as a comparison. The idea set off a sharp pang of sadness in her chest. She instantly quashed it. Emeraude House might not belong to her, but it was home, and it was unimportant whether she owned her own property.

But, having considered this, she could not stop following the idea to its conclusion. She was unlikely to marry, and would be Colin and Clemency's dependent relation all her life, and she had never given any more contemplation to that than she had the question of where all the chairs came from. She did not know whether the idea pleased her or distressed her, but she was distressed over not knowing. That distressed emotion rose, suffocating her, and once more she squelched it. She did not need her natural feelings overwhelming her in public.

She wished the room were not so bare, that she might distract herself by looking at paintings or other art. Instead, as she gazed around the room, she saw Miss Harcourt, standing near the front of the ranks of chairs. She was gowned beautifully in white muslin with a simple strand of pearls, and her hair looked very pretty—and every whit of her attention was focused on Lord Craythorne.

Lydia examined the young lady's emotions. Miss Harcourt had positioned herself where Lord Craythorne could not help but see her. The clear green of attraction was predominant, though she did not overtly notice Lord Craythorne, and mingled with it was bright yellow excitement and anticipation, sharper than anyone else's. Lydia glanced at the Duke, whose placid emotions had remained smooth since leaving his mansion. His gaze passed over Miss Harcourt without stopping, and Lydia Discerned not the smallest spike of interest.

Sympathy for Miss Harcourt welled up within Lydia. She had met the young lady only once, and had not made a strong attachment, but if Miss Harcourt truly did care for Lord Craythorne, how sad if he remained indifferent to her! Making a decision, she said, "Miss Harcourt looks very well tonight, do you not agree?"

Lord Craythorne regarded Miss Harcourt, whose excitement surged even as she continued to pretend inattention. "I fear I know little of female fashion," he said, "though I agree the style of her hair suits her."

"We met at the investiture ball," Lydia continued, "and she seemed a very nice young lady."

"Nice enough." Lord Craythorne turned his attention on Lydia. "Though I wish she had not set her sights on me. I dislike being fawned over."

He spoke quietly enough Lydia did not believe his words went farther than her own ears, and she replied quietly as well. "Set her sights on you? You make her sound lacking in natural affection. How do you know her interest is not genuine?"

Lord Craythorne's lips quirked in a smile almost as faint as his voice. "I assure you, Miss Wescott, when one is an unmarried man of wealth and rank, one is constantly alert to the efforts of women interested in making a marital attachment. Miss Harcourt is not subtle in her bid for my affections."

"One might call your speech arrogant, your Grace." Lydia did not know why his words offended her on Miss Harcourt's behalf. Miss Harcourt was not her friend, was nothing more to Lydia than a young woman of similar birth and status.

The smile vanished. "I believed you knew me better than that," Lord Craythorne said. He looked away from her, apparently indifferent, but sorrow flashed through him.

The emotion was unexpected, and lasted for barely a second, but it struck Lydia to the heart. She had not known until that moment that they truly were friends, and it hurt her to know she had caused her friend pain. She blushed. "It is not—I do not mean to call you arrogant, just that such a response might be considered so—oh, pray forgive me, I shall never speak again!"

For a moment, Lord Craythorne did not speak. Then he turned his gaze on her again. "Miss Wescott," he said, "I should beg your forgiveness. I harbor no ill will toward Miss Harcourt, but neither do I feel anything warmer toward her. Does it help at all to know that I am quite certain is it Mrs. Harcourt who has inspired in her daughter the desire to attach the Duke of Craythorne?"

Lydia's gaze shot to Mrs. Harcourt, who now stood in the doorway to greet her guests. She appeared as blandly pleased as everyone, but as she surveyed the room, every time her gaze lit on Lord Craythorne, her pale blue placidity turned teal with avarice. "You are correct," she said, "at least, I believe her emotions reveal that truth. Please forgive my misplaced criticism."

"There is nothing to forgive. I cannot—"

"They are beginning," Lady Craythorne said. "Hush, now. I wish to hear."

Lydia again composed herself and crushed her embarrassment to where it would not trouble her. She wished she could forget how she had censured Lord Craythorne. Of course it was none of her business how he responded to the young ladies who found him attractive. And he was likely correct that many of them found his wealth and title more attractive than himself, however handsome he was. She could not imagine being in such a position, being courted for something that had nothing to do with who one truly was.

She made herself listen to Mrs. Harcourt's introduction of the first poet, though she missed the lady's name. That this was a woman and not a man surprised her, though of course women could be poets. She had simply assumed that because Mr. Sabot was male, all of Mrs. Harcourt's discoveries were also male.

The poetess was an excellent reader, but Lydia found her poetry tepid, and her mind wandered. She had begun reading the book of John Donne's poetry, and this poetess's work suffered badly by comparison. Lydia did not believe she would ever become fond of poetry for its own sake, but Mr. Donne's words affected her deeply at times.

The poetess finished, and Lydia joined in the applause. It was not robust applause, and she wondered if that meant she was not the only unimpressed listener. But she made no critical comment. Having an opinion was all very well, but when one was uneducated as she, one did not air one's opinion where others might make mock of it.

The next poet Mrs. Harcourt introduced was Mr. Reginald Sabot.

This time, there was scattered applause before Mr. Sabot began, and a stirring among the guests that matched the heightened feelings of anticipation. Mr. Sabot did not bow to acknowledge the applause. He had tied his curls back from his face in a very old-fashioned style that only needed white powder to complete the look, but his frock coat and knee breeches were modern, if not cut of the finest fabrics.

Lydia paid closer attention to Mr. Sabot's reading than she had to the poetess's, though this was easy as Lydia believed Mr. Sabot to be the superior poet. Certainly, his verse was more interesting both in structure as well as in content, and Lydia listened intently to the story in verse of the shepherd lad and the wolves on the moor.

She was not so intent on the poem that she was unaware of Lord Craythorne's growing disquiet. The sharpness of his intellectual curiosity might be expected, but twined with that was suspicion that deepened the longer Mr. Sabot read. Lydia could not imagine what about Mr. Sabot or his poetry might produce such a reaction, so she set her curiosity aside until she might task Lord Craythorne about his suspicion later.

She applauded wholeheartedly with the others when Mr. Sabot finished. He did bow that time, accepting their accolades with a smile that was as smug as his emotions. Lydia did not mind that he gloated in his heart. People with artistic talent generally deserved at least a little gloating when their works were well received.

Three other middling poets read, and Lydia decided Mr. Sabot was the unofficial winner of the laurels that evening. As the final poet made his bow, Lydia rose with the others. Lord Craythorne bent to speak in her ear. "Have you become a lover of poetry, Miss Wescott?"

"I fear not, not if this was representative," Lydia said absently. Then she gasped when Lord Craythorne chuckled. "Oh! That was rude. I should not be critical, I know so little of literature, but it seemed to me Mr. Sabot's was the best, and perhaps the others suffered by comparison."

Lord Craythorne's suspicions, which had been in abeyance, roused again. "Perhaps," he said.

Lydia longed to interrogate Lord Craythorne on the spot. "Shall we speak to him?" she asked instead. "He did promise to sign my book."

Lord Craythorne looked surprised. "Your book? Do not tell me you purchased his book of poetry? *You*, Miss Wescott?" His lips twitched as if he was suppressing a smile.

Lydia refused to blush. "I was curious. I have never met a real poet before, and as your friend Mr. Donne is long since passed away, Mr. Sabot seemed my only opportunity."

"Well said, Miss Wescott. And I find myself interested in speaking to the poet as well. Mother—" Lord Craythorne looked back, but Lady Craythorne had walked away to converse with their hostess. "Very well, if you will permit me?"

Lydia accepted the Duke's arm and let him break a path for them through the crowd. Mr. Sabot was surrounded by guests, though he was not overwhelmed by the clamor; in fact, his sense of preening pleasure was great enough that Lydia enjoyed floating along with it.

Lord Craythorne had no compunctions about forcing his way through the crowd. "Mr. Sabot," he said when they were near enough. "Congratulations. You are quite popular."

Mr. Sabot experienced only a moment's confusion, that of being addressed by someone one has never met, and then his eye fell on Lydia and the confusion cleared. "Lord Craythorne," he said, not bowing. "I did not realize you would accompany Miss Wescott. Are you a lover of verse?"

"I am, and I welcome the opportunity to hear a new voice such as yours." Lord Craythorne's suspicion and keen interest rose higher. "I fear I have little experience with American poetry."

"Of course not." Mr. Sabot's disdain, which overcame his pleasure like a red tide, showed very little in his demeanor. "The English have little use for American provincials and their literature."

"That is sadly true in many instances, but I like to believe I honor literary genius, whatever its source. Your Phillis Wheatley, for example." Lord Craythorne's emotions did not alter. If he perceived Mr. Sabot's rudeness, it did not disturb him in the least. But his voice was deeper now, and Lydia knew him well enough to recognize when he was intent upon a problem.

"She was skilled, yes, but her works were divisive," Mr. Sabot said.

"She should have put all her efforts into supporting her country rather than harping on anti-slavery themes."

The mood of the crowd nearest Mr. Sabot shifted instantly. Lydia shivered at the intensity of the resentment about a third of the guests felt, twining through their more surface emotions of pleasure or interest. She had never heard of this poetess, but she resolved to seek out her works as soon as possible, if so many men and women disliked hearing Mr. Sabot criticize her.

Still Lord Craythorne did not react. "Miss Wescott tells me you offered to sign her book of your poetry," he said. "Though I suppose you must have no pen and ink handy—"

"I carry a fountain pen against such need," Mr. Sabot interrupted. He reached within his coat and withdrew a pen cased in brown wood with an attractive swirling pattern, a thing Lydia had only ever heard of as the fountain pen's invention was of very recent date. Lydia could not look at Lord Craythorne, whose sudden intense amusement washed over her. She herself wished she might laugh at Mr. Sabot's conceitedness. Faintly, she felt embarrassed at having called Lord Craythorne arrogant, if this was what true arrogance looked like.

She removed Mr. Sabot's volume of poetry from her reticule and handed it over. Mr. Sabot awkwardly juggled pen and book and managed not to drop either. Swiftly, he wrote a few lines inside the book and waved it about to dry the ink before returning it to Lydia. "I have great hopes for the rising generation, if they are all so intent on bettering themselves as you are, Miss Wescott," he said.

Lydia curtseyed. "Thank you, Mr. Sabot, and congratulations on your success."

"Indeed," Lord Craythorne said. Intent suspicion suffused him once more. "Miss Wescott, I believe Lady Craythorne requires your attendance. Mr. Sabot, good evening." He put a hand on Lydia's elbow and squeezed, gently, warning her not to react.

Lord Craythorne steered Lydia away so rapidly she protested, in a low voice, "This is not a race, surely?"

"I wish not to remain in that man's presence longer. And I will not explain, as you have Discerned my emotions. But more than that will have to wait upon our return." Lord Craythorne said all this quickly and in a voice matching hers.

To his mother, Lord Craythorne said only, "Are you ready to leave?"

"Goodness, Oliver," Lady Craythorne said, surprised and slightly annoyed. Then her emotions quieted, and she added, "If it is your wish, I am not opposed."

Lydia regarded Lady Craythorne's emotions as they bade their hostess goodnight, barely noticing Mrs. Harcourt's continuing avarice when she contemplated Lord Craythorne. The Dowager Duchess felt unexpectedly weary, with all her pleasure and curiosity over Lord Craythorne's haste dampened in color and intensity. In the carriage, she said to Lydia, "I hope you enjoyed yourself. You appeared interested in Mr. Sabot's work."

"He seems very talented, though of course I know little of poetry," Lydia replied. "And he signed my book. I did not realize that was something writers did." She removed the book from her reticule and opened it, but the light was too dim for her to make out more than that Mr. Sabot had written three lines.

"A true gift, that," Lord Craythorne said. He sounded as amused as he felt, but that strong thread of suspicion still ran deep within his emotions. Lydia glanced at Lady Craythorne and decided not to press him on it in his mother's presence. Then she felt mildly guilty at excluding Lady Craythorne, which was ridiculous—she was not one of Mr. Rutledge's people, not a member of Lord Craythorne's committee, and she likely did not feel excluded at all.

When they arrived at the mansion, Lord Craythorne stopped Lydia before she could retire to her bedroom. "I would like to see that book," he said.

Puzzled, Lydia handed it over. Lord Craythorne opened it and read what Mr. Sabot had written. A surge of elated satisfaction swept over him. "What is it?" Lydia asked.

"Something important," Lord Craythorne said. "Join me in the library. I would like your insight."

That made Lydia proud. Even Colin, who loved her dearly, never treated her as an equal, and that Lord Craythorne, politically powerful and intelligent, gave her that respect filled her with satisfaction.

In the library, Lord Craythorne seated himself with great deliberation. "Read that inscription," he told Lydia.

Lydia opened the book and read aloud: "'*To Miss Wescott, in the hope that liberation and vigilance may yet be your watchwords, Reginald Sabot.*' Is that a usual sort of inscription to a young lady? It sounds priggish, like the chastisement of a schoolteacher."

"I cannot say whether it is what Mr. Sabot always writes in the books of young ladies with whom he is barely acquainted," Lord Craythorne said. "But that is not what strikes me. Does anything about that stir your recollection?"

Lydia shook her head. "Not at all."

"It does mine," Lord Craythorne said grimly. "The phrase 'liberation and vigilance' is prominent in the handbills written and distributed by our old friend John Steadfast."

Lydia gasped. "Then—but no. Mr. Sabot need not be John Steadfast. He might only be an admirer."

"True, but that is not all." Lord Craythorne extended his hand for the book of poetry. "I have read many of the various handbills produced by John Steadfast, enough that I am surprised I have not gone blind. In his poetry he read tonight, in addition to the facile analogy that cast Parliament as wolves preying on an innocent shepherd lad, Mr. Sabot used other phrases that predominate throughout those handbills. If he is merely an imitator, he is an avid one. And I do not judge Mr. Sabot the kind of poet who imitates anyone. It would be counter to his principles."

Lydia clasped her hands in her lap. "Then what are we to do? Or—perhaps it is not 'we,' forgive my presumption—"

"It is very much 'we,'" Lord Craythorne said. "I intend to question Mr. Sabot, and you will be present to judge whether or not he lies and what the lies conceal, if possible."

Excitement surged through Lydia. "I will? Oh, thank you, your Grace!"

Lord Craythorne laughed. "No one has ever thanked me for giving them work before."

"But I came to America to be useful, and this is the right kind of usefulness." Lydia gripped her hands more tightly so she would not leap from her chair in her eagerness. "You wish to learn what 'John Steadfast' knows, and what his sedition conceals?"

"With luck, I may discover his compatriots, for I judge they are the true danger." Lord Craythorne rose. "Now, off with you. It will take some doing to maneuver Mr. Sabot into the right position, and sleeplessness will do neither of us any good."

Lydia nodded, but she knew sleep would be long in coming.

CHAPTER 14

IN WHICH THERE IS A GREAT DEAL OF FEMININE DISCOURSE

Lydia's restless night, rather than inducing her to sleep late, made her rouse when the sun cleared the horizon, illuminating her east-facing bedchamber fully. She lay still for a few moments, blinking up at the canopy of rose damask that draped her bed, then sat up, disordering the bed linens, and rang for Ellery.

"No, I do not wish for toast and chocolate, I am too restless to eat just yet," she told her maid when Ellery appeared. Then she examined Ellery more closely. Ellery's clothes were as neat as always, her cap settled just so on her brown curls, and the excitement that suffused her maid showed nowhere in her face. But Lydia knew instantly what was different.

"You have a beau!" she exclaimed. "How perfectly delightful!"

Instantly, Ellery's emotions shifted toward guilt and embarrassment, and Lydia blushed. "I beg your pardon, that was extremely thoughtless of me. I should never comment on another's emotional state. That is what my mother always said, that it was like revealing secrets, and revealing secrets is most unbecoming a young lady. Pray, forgive me. I spoke out of turn."

Ellery was redder than Lydia guessed herself to be. "No, miss, or at least yes, you are nearly correct. It is simply that nothing has been declared, and I do not call him my beau because he is not. Not yet."

"And that is why I should speak more circumspectly," Lydia declared. "My Discernment does not lie, but it does not always perceive the details that make for truth. I Discerned within you only the happiness that comes when one begins to fall in love, and I made an assumption in my joy for you."

"Thank you, miss, I'm sure I don't deserve your kindness—"

"Never mind that. You are honest, and sweet-natured, and of course you deserve every happiness." Lydia sprang back onto her bed and settled her legs beneath her. "And after your young man in England treated you so shabbily, too. Will you tell me his name? The one who is not your beau yet, of course, not the horrid man in England."

Ellery giggled. "It is James the footman," she said. "He and I have spoken many times—oh, but perhaps you will say it is improper, as I am a lady's maid and he is merely a footman—but, miss, he aspires to be much more, and I cannot believe it is wrong to form an attachment with someone as well-spoken and ambitious as he!"

"My brother married well above his station, so I am not so rigid in my attitudes about what is appropriate in romance," Lydia said. "James is the one with dark hair, the tallest of the footmen, is he not?"

Ellery nodded. "He is handsome, but he is also kind, and respectful of me—and I am certain he holds the warmest regard for me, but he has not spoken, and suppose I am wrong? I was wrong about Charles, back in England."

"That is possible, but you cannot let fear govern you. Trust your good sense, and all will be well. And you may thank the horrid Charles for showing you an example of what kind of man *not* to give your heart to. I assume James is nothing like."

"He is not, miss." Ellery sighed. "He gives me pretty compliments, but not in an overwrought way—they are all romantic, and that means something, yes?"

"I have no experience with romance myself," Lydia said, "and for me, compliments are always overwrought in the sense that I know the true feelings of the giver, and many men are insincere in what they tell ladies. But I understand your meaning."

"No experience with romance?" Ellery exclaimed. "But I believed
—" She shut her mouth abruptly, and her emotions shifted again,
further toward embarrassment.

"You believed what?" Lydia asked.

Ellery blushed again. "You and Lord Craythorne are often in one
another's company."

"Lord Craythorne?" Lydia exclaimed. "There is no romance
between us."

"Forgive me, I should not speculate. I simply believed, with him a
widower, and in need of a wife, and you so close to him—forgive my
impertinence!"

Stunned, Lydia could not at first respond. She and Lord Craythorne
were friends, of course, and she admired him, and of course he was
quite handsome, but she had never perceived any warmer emotion
than friendship when he spoke to her. "I understand," she managed.
"But we are nothing but friends and associates. I hope you have not
voiced this suspicion to anyone else."

Ellery's eyes widened. "Of course not, miss! I do not spread your
business abroad, not at all!"

"Thank you." Lydia stood and crossed the floor to her dressing
room. "I wonder," she said absently as she searched through her
wardrobe for an appropriate day gown, "whether anyone else has
made that supposition. I cannot believe it did not occur to me,
between Lady Dorothea's jealousy and Mrs. Harcourt's
maneuverings."

"It is common knowledge that Lord Craythorne is here in search of
a wife," Ellery said. "Of course I do not gossip, but I listen to what is
said in case it will be of help to you. There is much talk below stairs of
the young ladies Lady Craythorne intends to introduce Lord
Craythorne to. She made his first match, you know."

"I did not know." Lydia loved gossip so long as it did not involve
herself. "She arranged the marriage?"

"The first Lady Craythorne, Lord Craythorne's late wife, I mean,
she was the Dowager Duchess's second cousin once removed." Ellery
helped Lydia don her chosen gown and briskly shifted Lydia's hair
away from the neckline. "Many of the servants here, the ones who

came from Lord Craythorne's English household, knew her, and Mrs. Pogue likes to talk."

"I shall have to remember not to confide anything in Mrs. Pogue unless I wish it spread far and wide." Lydia sat at her dressing table while Ellery combed and pinned her hair. "Did she say how the first Lady Craythorne died?"

"Complications in childbirth. Both she and the babe perished. It was quite sad, though I regret to say Mrs. Pogue told me this with barely hidden glee. I believe she is the sort of woman who relishes tragedy so long as it is not hers. Though possibly she did not like Lady Craythorne much. I understand Lady Craythorne and Lord Craythorne did not have an amicable relationship."

Lydia recalled what she had sensed in both Lord Craythorne and the Dowager Duchess when the subject of Lord Craythorne's marriage had arisen. Not sadness, not relief at being free of an unsatisfactory liaison, but guilt. Guilt did not make sense. Lydia resolved to pursue the mystery—quietly, of course, and discreetly.

But pursuing the mystery had to wait, as Lydia discovered when she went down to breakfast that Lord Craythorne had left on an errand and had not said when he would return. Lydia wandered the mansion, feeling rather bored, until Lady Craythorne rose at noon and summoned her to attend on her.

Lady Craythorne had claimed one of the two upper drawing rooms for her own use, and Lydia found her there, seated on a pink and white striped divan embroidered with dark pink roses. Lydia cast an expert eye over the needlework and was impressed by the deft work. The entire drawing room bore the mark of a single person's taste, and that taste ran to pink roses and white-painted wood. Even the carpet was figured with white and pink roses, their outlines blurry with age.

"Miss Wescott," Lady Craythorne said. "I shall have callers today, and I wish you to join me for their visits. You are well-spoken, but it is my judgment your manners could use some polish, and observing the well-bred is an excellent way to gain such."

That did not sound like a pleasant way to spend the afternoon, but it was not as if Lydia could refuse, not with Lord Craythorne unavailable to provide her an excuse. "Of course, your Grace," she said, curt-seying politely. "May I ask who your callers will be?"

"Lady Fanshawe and Lady Dorothea," Lady Craythorne said, "Mrs. Ruskin, Mrs. Adams and Miss Miranda Adams, and I believe Mrs. Trenton of my reticulum intends to call, but her sciatica has been plaguing her and it is possible she is unable. I hope you and the young ladies will become acquainted. Miss Adams and Lady Dorothea are models to which you should aspire."

"Yes, your Grace," Lydia said. Lady Craythorne spoke those last words with such disdain Lydia would have felt angry and insulted were she not capable of Discerning the emotion that lay beneath. Once again, that unexpected tangle of regret and remorse Lydia had Discerned at dinner their first night in Washington, the one that suggested her words did not truly reflect her emotions, flooded Lady Craythorne. Lydia did not know what she should say. If Lady Craythorne did, in her heart, wish not to be so abrasive and cutting in her speech, perhaps being challenged on her behavior might jolt her out of the habit. On the other hand, if Lydia were to do so, suppose Lady Craythorne became defensive and antagonistic to protect herself? That would be worse than doing nothing.

"It is kind of you to consider me," she said instead.

Lady Craythorne's remorse deepened, and her lips twisted in a scowl. "You are at least nominally in my charge, and I must appear to do my duty. I still find deception abhorrent, but Oliver has convinced me of the need for it." She settled herself more comfortably. "Perhaps you will choose a book to read aloud until my guests arrive."

"Of course, Lady Craythorne." Lydia decided she would not task Lady Craythorne with her emotions just yet. Instead, she resolved to be polite and even friendly to the Dowager Duchess. Perhaps a greater closeness would afford Lydia the opportunity to address Lady Craythorne's remorse, and maybe even resolve it.

There was a small bookcase beside the western windows, painted white as all the other furniture was, and Lydia scanned its shelves for something interesting. Unfortunately, all the books were of the sort her mother would call "improving literature," which to Lydia meant the same as "tedious and moralizing." She finally settled on a book by

Hannah More as being slightly less tedious than the others and returned to sit in a chair across from Lady Craythorne. As Lydia read, Lady Craythorne's mood eased, and her remorse faded until only a pale blue calmness remained.

The door opened, and Trask entered. "Lady Fanshawe, Lady Dorothea Elliott," he said, and a handsome middle-aged matron entered the room, followed by Lady Dorothea, who looked even prettier in daylight than she had by the light of hundreds of candles. Lydia rose when Lady Craythorne did and waited, her thumb marking her place, as the Dowager Duchess greeted her guests.

"Lady Fanshawe, how good to see you, and Lady Dorothea, you look very well—come, sit, and be comfortable. Lady Fanshawe, have you met my companion Miss Wescott?" Lady Craythorne's words came, not quite in a rush, but more quickly than was typical. That, combined with how her emotions became slightly agitated, told Lydia she was uncomfortable at deceiving these ladies about Lydia's relationship to her, though she had not said anything close to a lie.

"Trask, I am expecting Mrs. Adams and Mrs. Ruskin, if you would show them up when they arrive?" Lady Craythorne continued. "And send someone with refreshments. Lady Fanshawe, I hope you are well?"

"As well as might be expected in the colonies," Lady Fanshawe said. Her voice was not unpleasant, but her tone was disdainful, and unlike Lady Craythorne, her emotions matched her tone. "I had hoped for a London season this year for dear Dorothea, but alas, Lord Fanshawe's responsibilities keep him here." Bitterness joined disdain, but Lydia was preoccupied with how chagrined her mother's words made Lady Dorothea, as if Lady Fanshawe had said something embarrassingly personal.

"Next year, perhaps. Lady Dorothea is still young." Lady Craythorne looked up as the door opened again, admitting three women, among them Miss Adams. "Oh, ladies, please join us! I do so enjoy company. Mrs. Adams, Miss Adams, Mrs. Ruskin, this is my companion, Miss Wescott."

Lydia made her curtseys while she silently assessed the newcomers. Miss Adams's pleasure and mild interest was centered on Lydia, which cheered her as she had liked Miss Adams when they had spoken at the ball and wished to know her better. Mrs. Adams was tall and thin and sat as if her back pained her. But Lydia reserved her longest scrutiny for Mrs. Ruskin, recalling her conversation with Mr. Ruskin; her brief acquaintance with that gentleman made her curious about his wife.

Unlike the other women, Mrs. Ruskin's emotions were strong and clearly coherent, very like Clemency's always were. Mrs. Ruskin was bathed in deep satisfaction beneath her surface pleasure, a combination of emotions that few people ever felt. It indicated someone secure in her own identity, someone confident and certain. Lydia liked this emotion, because such people rarely let other emotions disturb their inner peace.

The conversation had gone on without Lydia noticing, and she came to herself when Mrs. Adams said, "Miss Wescott, are you enjoying your time in America?"

"Oh, yes," Lydia said. "Washington is quite lovely, and I have met so many interesting people. They have all been very kind."

"Mr. Ruskin said he made your acquaintance at the investiture ball," Mrs. Ruskin said. "He spoke highly of you, which is remarkable as Mr. Ruskin rarely takes to anyone who is not a mature man interested in politics."

All the women laughed at Mrs. Ruskin's droll delivery of that line. "I declare Mr. Adams is the same," Mrs. Adams said. "Though of course he feels compelled to restore our good name, ever since his cousin John with his wife Abigail—but that is disturbing talk, and I wish to hear none of it, particularly not from myself!"

That had sounded like a promising line of gossip, and Lydia wished to know more of this reprobate cousin, but the conversation had already moved on to talk of gowns and the jewels Lady Fanshawe had recently received from Lord Fanshawe, subjects Lydia had no interest in.

"Miss Wescott." Miss Adams shifted in her seat, drawing slightly away from her mother. "Miss Harcourt said you attended the poetry reading—did you enjoy Mrs. Darracott's verse?"

Lydia guessed this was the name of the poetess whose poetry she had found lackluster. "It was interesting," she lied. "I fear I do not know enough about poetry to judge its quality."

"Mrs. Darracott is quite well known in Washington," Lady Dorothea said. Lydia realized that all three of them sat to one side of the older ladies and wondered if that had been intentional on Lady Craythorne's part. She was surprised to find Lady Dorothea so pleasant. Recalling Miss Adams' words about Lady Dorothea's need to find a suitable husband, Lydia felt a flash of sympathy for her.

"Of course, Mr. Sabot is feted everywhere," Lady Dorothea continued. "He is definitely someone of talent."

"Though his subject matter is occasionally inappropriate for young ladies—at least, that is what Father says," Miss Adams said. By the sly guilt that accompanied her words, Lydia guessed Miss Adams had done some secret reading of the inappropriate poetry.

"Lord Craythorne is appalled at my lack of literary appreciation," she said. "He insisted I read John Donne, and I daresay he would develop an entire curriculum were he not otherwise occupied."

The mood instantly shifted. Lady Dorothea's jealousy burst into being fully formed, casting Miss Adams' less volatile emotion into the shade. "You must be close, to have such discourse," Lady Dorothea said.

Lydia considered her options and decided on mollification. "I believe he sees his mother's companion as someone in need of guidance, and has been kind enough to offer his advice and direction in my studies. He is very busy, and I see him rarely."

Lady Dorothea's jealousy waned noticeably. "He is a fine man whom I admire," she said, "and you should appreciate his attention." She spoke as disdainfully as Lady Craythorne ever had.

Miss Adams opened her mouth, but whatever she might have said was lost in the arrival of the tea tray and an assortment of cakes, bringing the two small groups back together. Lydia took advantage of the interruption to shift away from Lady Dorothea. If Lydia's unsubtle hinting was not enough for the prickly young woman to give over her jealousy, there was nothing else she could do. She wished Lady Dorothea had not come, for she would have liked to speak with Miss Adams further.

"Miss Wescott," Mrs. Ruskin said, "tell us of your family. Is it true your brother is the new Earl of Ashford?"

"It is, Mrs. Ruskin," Lydia replied. "He married Lady Ashford some three months ago."

"I am very interested in all the news from England. That was quite the event." Mrs. Ruskin sipped tea and added, "How did it come about? It seems the stuff of fairy tales, the proud but poor young man winning the hand of the great lady."

Lydia Discerned Mrs. Ruskin's emotions and decided she meant no insult. "My brother is a maker of mechanical wonders, and Cle—Lady Ashford took an interest in them, and then she took an interest in him," she dissembled, as the details of Colin and Clemency's romance were in part a secret. And none of that was truly a lie, just not the entire truth. "And as Lady Ashford is a Countess in her own right as well as an Extraordinary, she elevated her husband to her own rank."

"Truly romantic," Mrs. Adams sighed. "One wishes the same for one's own daughters—that they will find love, that is."

"Love rarely survives the realities of life," Lady Fanshawe said, darting a glance at her daughter. "One must look to practicalities. One cannot live on love alone, and marrying someone without at least some estate and income is simply foolishness."

"I suspect we disagree as to how much estate and income is essential," Mrs. Adams said, her voice sharpening with her emotions.

"How fortunate if one finds both," Mrs. Ruskin said swiftly.

"Indeed," Lady Craythorne said. "And, of course, one must be worthy to attract the right sort of man. I have always encouraged Oliver to consider carefully his choice in marriage. The late Lady Craythorne was charming and accomplished, and I am certain he appreciated that."

Now everyone in the room was in a heightened state. Lady Dorothea and Miss Adams were jealous as well as embarrassed by their respective mothers. Lady Fanshawe and Mrs. Adams's anger burned hot and red within them. Lady Craythorne was agitated at the turn the conversation had taken, and she also was filled with that same inappropriate guilt she felt whenever the late Duchess of Craythorne was mentioned. Even Mrs. Ruskin, otherwise still supremely self-confident, showed an orange-brown concern at how antagonistic the conversation had become. It was enough to make Lydia's head whirl. She made herself breathe calmly and focused on the teapot to give herself stability.

"Miss Wescott, are you well?" Mrs. Ruskin asked.

Lydia realized she had closed her eyes and guessed she had been swaying in her seat as she sometimes did when she was close to being overwhelmed. "I felt dizzy for a moment," she said, truthfully. "It is nothing. It passes quickly."

"You must lie back," Mrs. Ruskin said. "Miss Adams, will you change seats? There, Miss Wescott, I am persuaded a little tea will do you good."

Lydia sipped tea and enjoyed how its warmth spread through her body. "I am well, you need not be concerned," she said, though in truth it was the lessening of emotions as everyone focused on her that eased her dizziness.

"You are so small and slight, and this room is so warm, it is no wonder you are easily overcome," Mrs. Adams said.

"I suppose," Lydia said. "May I have another cake? And, Lady Fanshawe, I believe you were about to tell us of Lord Fanshawe's proposed trip to England."

For once, Lady Craythorne felt nothing but relief. "Yes, indeed," she said as if grasping for an innocuous line of conversation. "Lord Fanshawe has business interests in London?"

Lydia let the words wash over her. No one would guess she was an Extraordinary Discerner from her moment of weakness, not when her apparent frailty made for a better explanation. But for a moment, she had been overcome as if she were in danger, as if these five women posed a threat. It was nonsense, brought on by her knowledge that no one knew the truth, but it discomfited her nonetheless.

The ladies stayed for another half an hour, at the end of which time Lydia had listened and Discerned enough to draw a number of conclusions. Lady Fanshawe was indeed committed to finding a rich husband for Lady Dorothea; Lady Dorothea had set her sights on Lord Craythorne. Miss Adams' jealousy over Lord Craythorne was tepid, almost a rote emotion, if there was such a thing, and she did not realize her heart was already given elsewhere, probably to that Mr. Cavanaugh Lydia had met at the dance. Lydia suspected she pursued Lord Craythorne to please her mother, not realizing her mother truly did believe her daughter should marry for love and not money.

Mrs. Ruskin continued to interest Lydia in both her emotions and her kind demeanor and easy manners. When she commented on the fine needlework displayed in the drawing room, Lydia responded eagerly and discovered in Mrs. Ruskin a fellow practitioner of the art. This led to Mrs. Ruskin saying, as she rose to leave, "I hope you will call on me, Miss Wescott. I have a great many works of embroidery at my home I would enjoy showing you."

"I would like that very much, Mrs. Ruskin," Lydia said with a curtsey.

Miss Adams, too, expressed an interest in pursuing a friendship, though she was shyer about it. Lydia finally had to take the initiative. "I have heard there is a very fine museum of American textiles here in Washington," she said. "Perhaps you and Lady Dorothea might join me there one day?"

Lady Dorothea was too well-bred to show the disdain that filled her. But to Lydia's surprise, she said, "That would be pleasant. We must arrange a time," rather than declining the offer outright. Miss Adams, on the other hand, accepted with a relief that told Lydia she was not good at making friends unless someone else extended the hand of friendship first.

When the ladies were gone, Lady Craythorne said, "You conducted yourself very well."

"I hope I satisfied you," Lydia said, too weary to curb her tongue.

"Do not be impudent," Lady Craythorne said. "When someone compliments your behavior, you should accept with humility."

"I am certain you know best, Lady Craythorne." This time, Lydia managed a semblance of politeness.

Lady Craythorne was not fooled. "Do not imagine I will endure your taunts," she said hotly. "You may be here under Oliver's aegis, but that does not mean you should not give me respect. I am your guardian, and your behavior reflects on me. I am grateful you did not display this rudeness in front of my guests, for I should have been forced to take notice."

Once more, remorse filled the Dowager Duchess, and once more Lydia was uncertain what action to take. She was increasingly convinced that the lady would be happier if she no longer spoke so rashly, but she did not know if she was the one to correct her.

The opportunity was taken out of her hands when Lady Craythorne rose, saying, "I hope you will consider my advice, and behave with better decorum. I have only your best interests at heart." Before Lydia could respond, she swept out of the drawing room and shut the door with a bang behind her.

Lydia composed herself. The house was still full of people and their emotions, but most were distant and placid enough not to trouble her. Then she left the room and walked across the house to the library. That it had become a refuge surprised her, given her lack of interest in reading, but refuge it was.

The room was unusually dark, and she lit a few lamps hanging ready on the wall to brighten it. Then she sat at the central table thinking of nothing much for some time, until she perceived the approach of Lord Craythorne. His emotions were as identifiable as Clemency's, though in the other direction, as his were muted where hers were strong and clear, and she always recognized him whenever he was within her range. At the moment, unexpected agitation suffused him, as well as the sharp anticipation of an intellectual challenge.

She sat up to face the door some few seconds before he opened it. "Ah, good," he said. "I hoped I might find you here."

"What is the matter?"

She liked that Lord Craythorne never said anything inane about how she knew his emotions. Instead, he said, "How would you like to interrogate a revolutionary?"

CHAPTER 15

IN WHICH LYDIA DISCERNS SOME EXTREMELY UNWELCOME EMOTIONS

"I? Do you mean Mr. Sabot? He is not here now, is he?" Lydia exclaimed.

Lord Craythorne laughed, and his agitation faded. "I must apologize for misleading you. Yes, I mean Mr. Sabot, but I do not intend to tie the man to a chair while you badger him with questions."

He came fully into the room and drew out the chair opposite Lydia, who resumed her seat a moment later. "I arranged to meet Mr. Sabot 'accidentally' at his club today to test the waters, so to speak. Mr. Sabot's arrogance and self-importance worked against him, and I am now convinced he has some connection to the Libertymen. However, it became clear as we conversed that he is also suspicious of anyone in power bringing up politics with him."

"He believes you will try to trick him," Lydia said.

Lord Craythorne tapped the side of his nose twice, making his signet ring flash. "Precisely so, Miss Wescott. Which means we will need another approach. He will never suspect anything underhanded of an attractive young lady who hangs on his every word, and he will certainly not imagine that his emotions will betray him. Rutledge told me you can Discern lies; is that correct?"

"Yes, your Grace, but I cannot explain how it works, so please do not ask for details."

"I will not. Your word is enough for me." Lord Craythorne ran one hand through his curls, bringing them back into a semblance of order. "I will tell you what to ask and what information we need, but the rest must be up to you. Do I ask too much?"

It was a little daunting, but Lydia would never admit to uncertainty. Lord Craythorne might send her back to England if he believed she was incapable. "No, your Grace, with your guidance I am certain I can manage it."

Lord Craythorne's lips curved up on one side in a rueful smile. "Then why do I feel," he said, "as if Rutledge would have me eviscerated if he knew what I propose?"

"Mr. Rutledge is kind and considerate, and he worries for my well-being," Lydia said, "but I am stronger than he knows. Still, we shall not tell him until it is all over and there is no chance of him stopping us, shall we?"

"I am in full agreement, Miss Wescott." Lord Craythorne pushed back from the table and stood, resting one well-shaped hand on the table top. "I must find Mother and inform her of the impromptu party I have organized for this evening. I suggest you stay here until the explosion is over."

"Surely her Grace will not be angry?"

"Her Grace enjoys social gatherings, but she prefers to be the one who plans them and prefers even more to be given plenty of notice of the ones she does not plan. Once she overcomes that initial reaction, I predict she will take the reins and behave as if this gathering was her idea from the start."

Lord Craythorne's smile grew more sincere, and the deep satisfaction characteristic of him when things went his way permeated his mood. Lydia impulsively said, "Lady Craythorne is a fine hostess, so I imagine you do not feel the lack of a wife."

Again, Lord Craythorne's emotions became guilty, almost furtive. "I have not had much luck in marriage," he said. "My late wife was also a fine hostess, however, and I am grateful Mother was willing to step into that role on my behalf."

"I heard your wife died, and your child." Lydia did not know where this was coming from; her sense that she should not disturb a friend's memories was being shouted down by the part of her that wished to know the tragic details. "You must have been devastated."

"I was," Lord Craythorne said, and Lydia nearly fell off her chair in her astonishment at hearing the lie. She gripped the armrest with one hand and maintained a placid expression. If Lord Craythorne were an Extraordinary Discerner, her shock and dismay would have stunned him.

"I suppose if I had had such a loss, I should be reluctant to marry again as well," she managed.

Lord Craythorne's guilt became twined with the kind of relief that arises when a guilty person sees a chance to escape punishment, as if her words had been a lifeline. "Naturally," he said, "when one feels a deep attachment, one has difficulty replacing it. But I must marry again someday, if only to perpetuate the line."

"That does seem rather cold, to marry simply for dynastic reasons," Lydia said.

Now the guilt and relief were a horrid tangle of confusion joined by sadness, all those emotions so entwined Lydia was dizzied again. She closed her hand even tighter on the armrest. Lord Craythorne did not seem to notice her distress; he did not even attempt to control his emotions, as if he had forgotten about her talent. Perhaps he believed she would make nothing of what she Discerned. Or, less likely, he believed his emotions too muted for her to Discern. In any case, she did not wish to reveal what she had learned.

Lord Craythorne's eyes were distant, looking past Lydia at the northern windows. The light from the nearest lamp illuminated his face sharply, giving him the appearance of a beautifully carved statue, and turned the tips of his eyelashes gold. "The idea is not displeasing," he said. "If one does not love, it hardly matters whom one marries. I realize that sounds hopelessly unromantic."

"It is sensible, particularly for someone in your position," Lydia said. "I myself do not intend to marry, so I do not put much stock in romance."

"I imagine an Extraordinary Discerner sees too much of human nature to willingly put herself in another's power, as is necessary for love." Lord Craythorne abruptly focused on Lydia. "The party begins at eight o'clock this evening. We will meet before that to discuss what you will ask. Thank you for your willingness to help."

"Thank *you*, your Grace, for trusting me enough to ask," Lydia said.

When he was gone, she released her death grip on the chair and made herself breathe evenly until the dizziness faded. She had not expected Lord Craythorne to lie about his feelings for his late wife, and that lie enhanced the importance of the guilt he felt when he spoke of her. Whatever he might say, he had not loved the late Lady Craythorne, and worse, he was relieved to be rid of her.

And it was not at all impossible to consider whether he might have had a hand in her death.

It was a ridiculous, Gothic notion, but Lydia could not help contemplating it. Lord Craythorne seemed friendly, but a core of steel lay hidden beneath the façade, a core that let him stand up to the over-powering Mr. Rutledge and enhanced the rock-hard certainty that in other men Lydia would call conceit. He was not the sort of man who would long endure the company of someone abhorrent to him. And, having seen him outmaneuver Mr. Rutledge, she did not doubt Lord Craythorne had the intelligence and cleverness to manage a murder. Even Ellery's information that Lady Craythorne and her child had died in childbirth might have been a manipulation, or even a lie.

Lydia shook her head violently. Being capable of murder did not mean one was inclined to it, and she did not believe she could be fooled as to someone's essential nature. This was all melodrama and speculation, and she refused to dwell on it. But for the rest of the afternoon, she could not rid herself of the notion.

❦

SHE ENTERED THE DRAWING ROOM WELL BEFORE THE OTHER GUESTS, having dressed quickly in her impatience and then being too eager for the evening to begin to wait patiently in her room until the appropriate time. Servants were still bustling about, rearranging furniture under Lady Craythorne's imperious direction. She turned at Lydia's entrance, and her generalized irritation flowered into annoyance. But she gave no outward sign of her mood.

Lydia reviewed possible conversational gambits as she crossed the room to stand next to Lady Craythorne. Most, she discarded as sounding sycophantic; others she believed were too antagonistic. She finally settled on a simple "Good evening, Lady Craythorne."

"I suppose," Lady Craythorne replied. "I would have preferred a quiet night in."

That was a lie, but it was rooted in annoyance, and Lydia did not mind the bitterness directed her way. "I am sure Lord Craythorne did not intend to disrupt your evening's plans, not intentionally."

"I am not accustomed to rearranging my life to suit Oliver's political maneuverings. James, move those vases to the mantel, they seem precariously placed on that table," she added, addressing one of the footmen. Lydia examined him closely. He was quite handsome and well formed, and he bowed politely to Lady Craythorne before removing two bud vases to where they would not be jostled by a crowd. Lydia saw very well why Ellery had been drawn to him.

"May I ask, then—why did you come with him to America?" Lydia asked.

Lady Craythorne turned a suspicious eye on her. "More impertinences?"

"I do not mean the question as such, but do not answer if it is private. It is simply that you do not seem fond of politics yourself, and I assume you have a busy life in London, so what prompted you to join Lord Craythorne here?" Lydia's tongue began to run away with her, and she stopped her babbling.

The annoyance faded slightly, replaced by the guilt Lydia now associated with mention of the late Lady Craythorne. "Oliver needs someone to manage his household, and naturally I could not permit him to live under the same roof as an unmarried young lady to whom he is not related. And, of course, I have many friends in America, members of my reticulum whom I rarely see."

"That was very generous of you," Lydia said, "and for my part, I am grateful that you were willing to grant me the protection of your presence. I should not have been able to do this otherwise." She was conscious of James and another footman near enough to overhear, and spoke circumspectly.

Lady Craythorne regarded her with an expression Lydia would have called suspicious had she not known Lady Craythorne felt no such thing. "I admit you are not what I believed at first," she said. "When Oliver proposed this odd arrangement, I imagined someone forward and lacking in propriety."

Lydia nodded. "I see why you would believe that."

"You lack refinement, but perhaps that is to be expected," Lady Craythorne continued, "and as you show every intention of remedying that lack, I suppose I should not criticize beyond what you need in order to improve."

Lydia bit back a sharp reply. Lady Craythorne had not meant to be insulting. "Thank you," she said instead.

Lady Craythorne looked her up and down. "You look very well tonight."

Lydia smoothed her skirts. She wore pale pink muslin, a color that enhanced her fair skin and light blonde hair, and her gown was of a conventional, modest style. Around her neck, she wore the simple gold chain Colin and Clemency had bought for her in Spain while they were on their wedding trip. Her mirror told her she looked the very picture of an innocent maiden, possibly one who was not terribly bright. "Thank you. Your necklace is lovely."

Lady Craythorne rested her fingertips on the row of rubies and diamonds circling her throat. "It is a family heirloom. I am fond of it."

Footsteps in the hall made them both turn, and Lydia curtseyed to the approaching Lord Craythorne, who bowed to each lady in turn. "All is in readiness," he said. "The guests will arrive shortly, and I anticipate a pleasant evening of cards and conversation."

"I hope no one believes there is anything underhanded about this evening," Lady Craythorne said. "Such short notice."

Lydia wished she could hush the Dowager Duchess. James again stood close enough to hear. But doing so would look even more suspicious than Lady Craythorne's words had sounded. So she said only, "It is an evening with friends, and no one will see anything odd about that."

"Precisely," Lord Craythorne said. "And I sent invitations to the ladies you suggested, Mother. They will be the perfect addition to our party."

Lady Craythorne frowned. "You presume too much sometimes, Oliver. Now, please excuse me, I will greet our guests."

When she was out of sight, Lydia said, "She means well."

"I question that assertion," Lord Craythorne said.

Lydia had spoken to ease the hurt caused by his mother's harsh words, and his dismissal annoyed her even as she knew it rose from those same feelings. "I would not lie to you," she said, "and she wishes only for your happiness. She simply does not know how to produce it."

Lord Craythorne shot her a sharp glance. "I forgot, for a moment, that you—" His gaze flicked to the nearby footman, and Lydia saw him recollect the need for secrecy. "Forgive me. Lady Craythorne and I have a long history of misunderstanding each other."

Lydia recalled her own mother and had to squelch the fear and pain such memories always roused. "There is no pain quite like the pain inflicted by love," she said.

"That is very wise, and also very sad," Lord Craythorne said. He turned his head as the sound of the front door opening reached them, and Lydia caught the faintest hint of his usual clean scent. "You are prepared?"

"I am, your Grace." Now that the moment was here, Lydia felt no anxiety, only a pleasant eagerness. All her assignments for Mr. Rutledge had, she hoped, prepared her for this.

She took a seat where she would not be the first thing anyone entering would see and folded her hands in her lap. They did not tremble, but she had a deep desire to be *doing*, to accost Mr. Sabot and wring his secrets from him. In a genteel and surreptitious manner, of course.

The pedestal table next to her right elbow held four china figurines that had escaped Lady Craythorne's frenzy of reorganization. Lydia picked up one and examined it. It was a curly-haired youth whose head was bowed as he looked down at the dog by his side, a frolicking Irish setter. The artist had painted the figure delicately in pastels which made it look faded from a thousand years in a tropical sun. Lydia preferred bright, robust colors.

She looked at the face more closely and was struck by how it resembled Lord Craythorne—a younger Lord Craythorne, naturally, but the aquiline nose and curly brown hair were the same. Curious, she reached for a different figurine, but she did not recognize the young woman depicted. It occurred to her that she did not know if Lady Craythorne had more children than just her son. She resolved to remember this question for some time when she needed an amicable conversation with Lady Craythorne. She hoped the conversation would be amicable. Perhaps Lady Craythorne disliked her children, or they were all dead, or—

"Miss Wescott, how good to see you."

Lydia startled and nearly dropped the two figurines. She had not been paying any heed to those around her, and this person's approach was a surprise. "Mrs. Ruskin," she said, setting the figures aside and rising to greet the lady. "I am glad to see you again."

"Lady Craythorne hosts the loveliest gatherings, and I was pleased to attend." Mrs. Ruskin smiled at Lydia in a friendly way. "Do you play whist, or euchre? I am in search of a partner."

Lydia's desire to please this lady, whom she had taken a liking to, fought with her knowledge that she should remain free to speak to Mr. Sabot. "I fear I am terrible at cards, and would make a poor partner. But I appreciate the invitation."

"Ah, that is as well, for I am a keen player and dislike losing. Mr. Ruskin is quite in despair over my rapacity for whist." Mrs. Ruskin laughed. "Perhaps Lady Craythorne will agree to partner with me, though she is busy being the hostess."

Lydia looked up as Mr. Ruskin stopped beside his wife. "Miss Wescott, good evening. I hope you continue to enjoy your stay in Washington."

"I do, sir, thank you." Lydia swiftly assessed the room with her Discernment. Now that she was paying attention, she had Discerned the arrival of others, most of them eager for an evening's amusement. A few were blandly beige, and Lydia suspected spouses who were present as reluctant companions for their wives or husbands. She did not sense Mr. Sabot, who was a sullen mass of dark red anger when he was not preening like a peacock, but it was early yet.

"Have you pursued your interest in politics, Miss Wescott?" Mr. Ruskin asked with a smile that invited Lydia to laugh with him at the droll question.

"No, Mr. Ruskin, I have decided politics is not to my taste," she said. "I have been reading poetry of late, educating myself."

Mr. Ruskin's eyes widened in pretended astonishment. "Educating? Mrs. Ruskin, have you ever seen anyone who looks less like a bluestocking than this young lady?"

"I must say I have not," Mrs. Ruskin said, her lips twitching with amusement. "But reading poetry hardly makes one a scholar. Perhaps your assessment is too harsh."

"I must agree. I have of yet read only Mr. Donne's poetry and that of Mr. Sabot, and I believe I have far to go before I can consider myself truly educated," Lydia said.

"Mr. Sabot is quite talented, or so I hear." Mr. Ruskin removed his snuff box from within his frock coat and took a pinch. The box was of figured enamel picked out with real gold and studded here and there with tiny gems, red and green. Mr. Ruskin noticed Lydia's interest and offered it to her. "Of course you will have no interest in its contents, but I consider its materials and craftsmanship very fine, if you would care to look."

Lydia ran her fingers over the gold traceries before handing it back to its owner. "I agree, it is quite beautiful."

"There, I see Mrs. Abelard seating herself at the card table, and that is my cue to join," Mrs. Ruskin said. "Pray, excuse me."

"And what a coincidence, that we have been talking of the man and he appears," Mr. Ruskin said, nodding at the doorway. Lydia had already noted Mr. Sabot's approach, or at least someone she presumed to be Mr. Sabot, for how awful if more than one man felt such anger and disdain for his fellows! Her heart sped faster for a few beats until she told herself to remain calm.

"I hope it is not our words that summoned him here, as if we were Bounders capable of turning our talent on others," she said with an airy laugh. "Imagine if such a thing were true. One could never speak of one's enemies without bringing them into one's presence!"

"An interesting notion, Miss Wescott," Mr. Ruskin said.

His general sense of unfocused pleasure sharpened, and Lydia's heart sank. She had said something too clever. Mr. Ruskin was not suspicious of her—what was there to suspect her of?—but he now clearly believed there was more to her than appearances suggested, and he might watch her too closely.

She let out another brainless laugh. "I am glad I have no enemies, for being pulled hither and yon does not appeal to me, don't you agree, Mr. Ruskin?"

That inanity soothed Mr. Ruskin, and Lydia Discerned amusement in him. "Well," he said, "as Mr. Sabot is here, perhaps you should speak with him. He will be *most* interested in hearing your opinion of his verse."

Lydia widened her eyes and let her mouth fall open in an O of surprise. "I, speak to him? Surely not. I would not know what to say."

"Tell him your honest feelings about his poetry. All writers enjoy talking about their work." Mr. Ruskin's wicked amusement deepened, and Lydia maintained her innocent expression through sheer willpower. So, he believed she would make a fool of herself, either by pandering to Mr. Sabot's self-love with compliments or by angering him with uninformed criticisms. Her earlier liking for him dissolved.

"Then I shall," she declared. "Pray, excuse me, Mr. Ruskin."

She did not wait to see him bow, but took three determined strides in Mr. Sabot's direction before remembering her instructions and slowing her pace. She should not be aggressive in dealing with her prey. More sedately, she walked to where Mr. Sabot stood just inside the doorway, off to one side where no one entering would bump into him. He wore his hair loose around his face as he had the night of the investiture ball, and his clothing was somewhat more well-cut than it had been before, but his expression was the same: chin held high and eyes half-lidded in haughty disdain for those around him. Lydia could not imagine why he had accepted Lord Craythorne's invitation, but he had, and now was her moment.

Mr. Sabot did not notice Lydia's approach, so intent was he on the group gathered at the card tables. Lydia curtseyed and, with her eyes demurely cast down, said, "Good evening, Mr. Sabot, I am so glad to see you again. I hoped to speak with you about your poetry."

She glanced up through her lashes in time to see the poet smile and hear him say, "Your attentions are flattering, and you will find me *most* attentive, I assure you, Miss Wescott."

Horrified, Lydia Discerned his emotions shift from haughtiness to the rich deep green of physical lust.

CHAPTER 16

IN WHICH AN
INTERROGATION ENDS
UNSATISFACTORILY

She could not explain it. Mr. Sabot had not displayed any sort of romantic interest in her the two times they had spoken before. Yet now his emotions of desire were unmistakable. Lydia concealed her revulsion and said, "Oh, but I do not wish to monopolize your time, sir. Perhaps this is the wrong—"

"Nonsense," Mr. Sabot said. "I will always have time for *you*, Miss Wescott. You need not fear offending me." He smiled, and his expression, the eyes half-lidded in a sensual manner, the lips slightly pursed, revealed his attraction nearly as well as his emotions did.

Lydia considered running—no, not running, but extricating herself as gracefully as possible from the encounter. She had no idea what had happened, but Mr. Sabot's attention was like hands crawling across her body, and it sickened her. But she had a duty. She was not actually a simpering miss; she was an Extraordinary Discerner with an assignment to interrogate this man, and she would not permit his unwelcome attentions to prevent her accomplishing it. And, if she was careful, she might use this new development to her advantage.

So she smiled, and tilted her head so as to appear more innocent, and said, "I wished to ask you about what you wrote in my book—your book—oh, I am so muddled! The book of your poetry that you so kindly inscribed to me. 'Liberation and vigilance,' such inspiring words. But I fear I do not fully understand their meaning in reference to me."

Pride elbowed its way into Mr. Sabot's romantic desires. "It is my hope for all, but particularly for such as yourself, Miss Wescott—a young person who cares about the future and is eager for instruction. Liberation from archaic notions. Vigilance in maintaining one's freedom. The two together are at the heart of any revolution."

Lydia widened her eyes. "Revolution? But I believed the Colonial Conflict was over. Surely *you* are no revolutionary, not with how much you respect the current government."

Contempt joined pride and made passion retreat further. "I do not respect our Viceroy, who is a tool of the English and no true American. I realize you are English yourself, but surely you can see how unjust our treatment has been at the hands of King George and his government. I feel certain your sensibilities are keenly aware of how right it is that America be given self-governance. Your interest in my poetry reveals that."

That sounded like an excellent opening. "You write poems in favor of American freedom? Perhaps I am less intelligent than I believed, for I have read your book twice now, and none of the poems were about politics."

To her chagrin, this comment swung Mr. Sabot's emotions back toward romance. He smiled, a rather sensual smile, and said, "I would not be so foolish as to air my opinions where the Viceroy's men might read them and imprison me. But there are more types of writing than poetry. Perhaps you will permit me to show you other of my work?"

Lydia, astounded that Mr. Sabot believed she would ever wish to meet privately with him, steered the conversation elsewhere by saying, "Do you mean handbills? You must be so clever to write those. I have seen many produced by the man called John Steadfast and found them *so* thrilling and inspiring!" She clasped her hands melodramatically at chest height and sighed.

She had a guess as to what Mr. Sabot might say next, so she was not astonished when he stepped nearer, lowered his head, and whispered in her ear, "It is a great secret, but I believe I may tell you that *I* am John Steadfast."

Lydia let out a gasp that was the perfect response, based on Mr. Sabot's gratification and smugness. "*You*, Mr. Sabot? But then, why do you not use your real name?"

"For my protection," Mr. Sabot said. He looked past Lydia's ear with an expression he meant to indicate noble suffering, but it only made him look as if he had passed wind and wished no one to realize it. "This government, with its pandering to England, is not kind to those who show their commitment to their true country. I dare not reveal myself or my confederates."

Lydia almost leaped on that revelation. In time, she Discerned Mr. Sabot's flash of uncomfortable guilt at having mentioned confederates. So she said, "You are so brave, Mr. Sabot. I am sure I could never do what you do."

For a moment, she feared she had oversold herself. Suspicion touched Mr. Sabot's emotions. Hating herself for the necessity, she glanced up at the man through her lashes the way she had seen many, many women do when they wished to entice a man.

It worked. Mr. Sabot's emotions again shifted toward desire. "It is for the sake of young ladies like yourself that I dare what I do," he said.

"I can almost picture it, you writing in secret—but someone must know, if your work is published as handbills," Lydia said, hoping it sounded like casual curiosity. "The printer, at least."

"There are many of us who share the same goals. It is not so dangerous." Mr. Sabot clearly hoped she would believe it was terribly dangerous despite his words.

Lydia treated him to a dazzling smile. "So many writers, all working in secret—it is most thrilling."

"Not all of us are writers," Mr. Sabot said. "We labor in many occupations. Will you take a turn about the room with me? You would no doubt like refreshment."

Lydia did not take his arm. "I cannot credit that you keep this all secret, Mr. Sabot. I have heard the old saying 'two can keep a secret if one of them is dead'—so gruesome, and yet it rings true, does it not?"

"We take precautions to ensure no one man knows enough to betray his fellows inadvertently. Of course, none of us would willingly give their identities away. I hope you do not intend to finesse such information out of me, Miss Wescott!" Mr. Sabot laughed.

Lydia joined in his laughter. "*Me*, Mr. Sabot? Why, whatever would I do with that information? Although..." She gave him another shy glance. "I wish I might learn more of your cause. You quite inspire me to do more with my time than sew and pay calls."

"There are many women among my confederates, all of whom are staunch patriots," Mr. Sabot said. "You might be surprised to discover that some of them are known to you."

Lydia's heart leaped. She did not need to pretend to excitement as she said, "Mr. Sabot! Truly? Oh, but now you must tell me!"

That had been too much. Mr. Sabot shook his head. "No, I have been indiscreet."

"No, of course you have not," Lydia quickly said. "You have been most circumspect, and I admire you. Not like Mr. Suggitt."

A complex whirl of emotions struck Mr. Sabot, surprise and suspicion and guilt and anger. Dizziness threatened to overwhelm Lydia, but she drew in a deep breath and added, "I have heard him brag about his connections, and how he is deep in the confidences of those in power, but I believe he simply preens himself to attract the attention of young ladies."

"Abel Suggitt is no revolutionary," Mr. Sabot lied.

"He could not possibly be! His friend Mr. Hughes is far too respectable to permit such an association." Lydia was coming to the end of the names she knew who might be Mr. Sabot's confederates. She did not know if this would do any good; for all she knew, Lord Craythorne already knew the truth about Mr. Hughes and Mr. Suggitt. But Mr. Sabot's emotions had started shifting toward the romantic again, and she did not feel entirely in control of this interrogation.

"Oh, Mr. Hughes is of an old Southern family. He has his problems with the Viceroy's government, but he would never strike against it." That was another lie.

"But..." Lydia's lips curved in a frown, and she furrowed her brow the tiniest bit. "I know *you* would never take part in violence, but you make it sound as if there are those sympathetic to your cause who would." It was risky to speak so forthrightly, but Lydia did not believe she had learned much of anything. She would not let this man escape her.

"No one I know, naturally." It was not exactly a lie, but uncertainty washed over Mr. Sabot's other emotions, as if he questioned his own veracity. "But I do know of those with fewer scruples than I."

Inwardly, Lydia raged at herself for not being cleverer. "Pray, do not tell me, I am fair quivering at the horrid notion," she said. "I can imagine those men attempting to burn the Viceroy's palace, or attacking the Treasury—it is so distressing."

"You need not fear, Miss Wescott, you are in no danger," Mr. Sabot said soothingly. Once more, his desires rose to the top of his conflicting emotions. "I can promise no harm will come to you."

His utter certainty made Lydia once more suspicious. Unfortunately, she saw no way to compel him to speak of his confederates' plans. Another, more disturbing thought occurred to her: perhaps Mr. Sabot was not so important to the Libertymen, but he puffed himself up to be more important than he was. All of this might have been nothing more than his attempt to woo an attractive young lady. Lydia had never felt so discouraged.

She realized Mr. Sabot had spoken again and said, "I beg your pardon, I was distracted by my thoughts."

"I asked if you would walk with me," Mr. Sabot said, once more offering his arm. Lydia regarded it with the revulsion she would otherwise reserve for a slime-covered worm, though she permitted none of her emotions to show. She could not conjure a single excuse to avoid taking it.

She smiled, and said, "Of course, Mr. Sabot."

As they strolled, Lydia ran over possibilities in her mind. Mr. Sabot was likely to stick close to her all evening if he was attracted to her, which would give her opportunities to redeem herself. But when she considered what else she might ask, she came up blank. She decided she would see where the evening led. Eventually, Mr. Sabot would have to leave, and she could try to forget the crawling feeling his regard gave her.

"I must admit," Mr. Sabot said after a moment, "I did not realize you were so moved by my work. One does not expect young ladies of your age to be so mature in their tastes."

"I do not know whether or not I am mature. I simply know what I like," Lydia said absently. That was inane even for the starry-eyed girl she was pretending to be, so she added, "It is most flattering that you give me your attention. There are so many other people here you might converse with."

"Oh, but when Lord Craythorne told me you had particularly asked after me, I felt it incumbent upon me to satisfy your interest," Mr. Sabot said.

His rushing green desires made it clear to Lydia what kind of satisfaction he had in mind, but Lydia had caught hold of two words that nearly brought her to a halt. "Lord Craythorne?" she said. "What did he tell you?"

Mr. Sabot did not appear to hear the edge in Lydia's voice, or if he did, he attributed it to a different emotion than rising suspicion. "You need not worry," he said. "I feel the warmest admiration for you, Miss Wescott, and I can see by your maidenly blush that you are unfamiliar with the deeper emotions."

Whatever crimson reddened Lydia's cheeks bore no resemblance to anything maidenly. Lord Craythorne had enticed Mr. Sabot to his house by the promise that Lydia would not only be there, but was deeply interested in speaking with the poet. Lydia saw the conversation as clearly as if she had been present. Lord Craythorne had suggested Lydia was attracted to Mr. Sabot; Mr. Sabot, in the way of some men, was flattered by Lydia's supposed attraction and decided he reciprocated her feelings. Lydia did not care that Lord Craythorne's actions were likely innocent. She would have strong words with him the next time they were alone.

"Mr. Sabot," she began, "I—"

"You need say nothing," Mr. Sabot said. He rested his hand caressingly on hers where it lay on his arm. "I understand completely. But we know little of one another, and there will yet be time to remedy that lack."

Now Lydia was sick as well as furious. She suppressed those

emotions so she would not be overwhelmed. This was a horrid misunderstanding, but she could extricate herself.

"Oh, Miss Adams!" she exclaimed, and let go of Mr. Sabot's arm. "How delightful to see you! Mr. Sabot, I must speak with Miss Adams —you do not mind, surely?—we will speak again later, and you can tell me of your latest poem." She sank down onto the sofa next to a startled Miss Adams and clasped the young woman's hand briefly in her own.

Once again Mr. Sabot was a tangle of emotions, anger and lust and confusion, but confusion won out. "Miss Wescott," he said, bowed, and walked away.

Miss Adams, too, was confused, but did not show it. "Miss Wescott, good evening," she said. "I did not realize you were so friendly with Mr. Sabot. My mother says he is not at all the sort of man she wishes me to be acquainted with, which naturally makes me most keen on meeting him." She giggled, a merry sound that cheered Lydia.

"We discussed his poetry, that is all," she lied.

"Well, he seemed *very* intent on you." Miss Adams glanced after the retreating Mr. Sabot. "I hope he does not harbor a secret interest, because he is far too old to contemplate marriage with someone our age! More than forty, or I miss my guess!"

Lydia managed a smile.

"It was kind of Lady Craythorne to include me in her invitation," Miss Adams continued. "I had hoped to speak with you further. Do you play cards?"

"I am terrible at all games of chance," Lydia said. "Particularly those that require skill. I can never remember what cards have been played."

"I am sure that is not true. I should teach you one of my favorites, but not here, for Papa says poker is a vulgar game not suited to young ladies." Miss Adams appeared thoughtful. "I realize now how many things I do because I have been told not to. That is a marvelously contrarian attitude to have, and I hope—" She blushed pink and would say no more.

Lydia, watching desire and hope rise within Miss Adams, said, "I see. There is someone you wish to impress. A young man, perhaps?"

"I cannot—that is, Mr. Cavanaugh is quite attractive, but then so are many men." Miss Adams blushed harder.

"I believed you to have an interest in Lord Craythorne," Lydia pressed.

Miss Adams glanced in Lord Craythorne's direction. He stood beside the hearth, deep in conversation with a man Lydia did not know. "Oh, I imagine every woman has an interest in Lord Craythorne. That is a terrible thing to say, but it is true. He is attractive, but his manners are so cold, and one always has the sense he is comparing one to some unattainable ideal, possibly his memory of his late wife. But Mr. Cavanaugh—"

"I remember meeting him at the ball," Lydia said. "He seemed quite attentive to you."

"That is nothing, he is attentive—"

Lydia cut her off. "No, I am certain of it. I observed him in conversation with other ladies, and his attentions to you were much warmer." She felt no shame in lying about the source of her information. Discernment was much more accurate than reading people's expressions.

"You believe so?" Miss Adams' hope was nearly a tangible thing.

"I do," Lydia said, "and you must be sure he knows you return his affections. It is a terrible thing for two people to permit fear to come between them. I daresay, if he has not been more direct, it is because he does not know how serious your interest is."

Miss Adams nodded slowly. "Yes," she said, "yes, I see what you mean. You are so wise, Miss Wescott."

"I am only wise about others. For myself, I never know what I am doing," Lydia said. She gave her words only half her attention, because someone was approaching the drawing room—someone whose agitation was so intense Lydia was sure anyone might detect it in his expression and manners. So she watched the door, waiting.

The person was running, and in only seconds he appeared in the doorway. It was a young man dressed very plainly, not in knee breeches but in common laborer's trousers, and his breathing was heavy from his run. He paused only for a moment, then hurried straight to Lord Craythorne's side. Lord Craythorne had noticed his arrival and turned from his conversational partner to speak to the young man. Lydia was too far from them, and the noise of conversation was too loud, for her to hear their words, but the young man bent his head close to Lord Craythorne's and spoke at length. Whatever he said caused Lord Craythorne to react first with surprise, then anger, and finally with that determined excitement honed to a fine edge that represented an intent to act.

"Miss Wescott, are you well?"

Lydia realized she had missed what Miss Adams had said. "I feel dizzy," she said.

"That is right, you are sometimes light-headed in company," Miss Adams said. "You must sit back, and I will bring you tea." She rose and walked away.

Lydia looked back at Lord Craythorne, but he was already in motion, headed for the door. She wished with all her heart she might go after him, and not only because she still owed him a tongue-lashing for encouraging Mr. Sabot to feel lust for her. Whatever news he had received was surely exciting.

Taking advantage of Miss Adams' absence, she Discerned the emotions of everyone in the room. Mr. Sabot was not the only one filled with desire; a couple at the whist table were engaged in more than just card play, though they were discreet about their involvement. There was likely good gossip there, but Lydia did not care about it at the moment.

Most people had not noticed Lord Craythorne's departure and continued in their pleasure or bland contentment. Lady Craythorne was the exception. She sat glaring at the doorway as if preparing to fling daggers at Lord Craythorne when he returned. Lydia considered going to her, but there would be no point, and Lady Craythorne's dark mood meant she would likely just snap at Lydia regardless of what Lydia said or did.

Miss Adams returned with a cup of tea she handed to Lydia. Lydia sipped and realized as her head cleared that dizziness had not been entirely a lie. "Thank you," she said.

"Of course," Miss Adams replied. "Goodness, did Lord Craythorne leave?"

"I suppose." Lydia sipped again. The tea was very good.

"I see Lord and Lady Fanshawe did not attend. Do you suppose they were invited, and chose not to come, or were not invited at all?"

"I don't know." Lydia reflected how nice it was that Lady Dorothea was not there. She was sympathetic toward the prickly, proud young woman, but she did not believe her sympathy could stand in the face of Lady Dorothea flinging herself at Lord Craythorne.

She continued to follow Lord Craythorne's progress and was surprised to find he had gone only as far as the front door, where he had been met by someone whose agitation was greater than his. Someone had brought news, dire news, and it gave Lydia an almost physical pain to not be present to hear it.

Then Lord Craythorne returned through the house, heading back to the drawing room. Lydia finished her tea and hoped she did not look as eager as she felt. She lowered cup and saucer to her lap just as Lord Craythorne appeared in the doorway. His curls were disordered, and he was breathing more heavily than before, as if he had run through the house instead of walking rapidly as Lydia had Discerned.

"Ladies and gentlemen, please do not be alarmed, but you must be our guests for longer than you anticipated," he said. "I fear the Viceroy's palace is under attack."

CHAPTER 17

IN WHICH INFORMATION IS SHARED

asps, and a few feminine shrieks, brought all the low-voiced conversations to a halt. Lady Craythorne rose and approached her son. "The Viceroy's palace is less than a mile from here," she said. "Are we in danger?"

"Not to my knowledge, but my informants tell me the streets are overrun by those fleeing the fire—"

Exclamations rose up throughout the room. "Fire?" said Mr. Ruskin. His anger overrode his concern. "Who dares burn the palace?"

Lord Craythorne hesitated only a moment. When he spoke, he sounded intent but not distressed, but his right hand curled into a loose fist. "Reports say the palace is under siege by Iroquois attackers."

A lady near the whist table let out a shriek and collapsed, rather dramatically, Lydia thought, considering that she was not unconscious and merely wished to draw attention to her sensibilities. Two men rushed to her side, supporting her. Beside Lydia, Miss Adams was pale, and her fear coursed through her so sharply Lydia impulsively took her hand.

"Do not fear, we are safe here," she said. "Truly we are. Lord Craythorne would not lie to us."

"I know, it is just—an Iroquois attack. How terrible," Miss Adams said. "We have been at peace with them for years, but of course that is no guarantee of perpetual amity. One sees them in the streets, or speaks with them in public, and it is easy to forget they are not like us."

Lydia nodded, already forgetting the young woman's fear in her attention to others' emotions. Lord Craythorne was not afraid; he was as angry as Mr. Ruskin, though his anger was muted as all his emotions were. It was also tinged with suspicion.

"I repeat—we are safe here," he said, raising his voice over the clamor. "The Army has already been dispatched, and the fire is being contained. I have sent messengers to return with word of the Viceroy's safety. Do not be alarmed." He looked directly at Lydia as he spoke, his eyes fierce with unspoken meaning, as if he were an Extraordinary Speaker to send his thoughts into her mind.

Lydia did not at first understand his meaning. Then she made herself consider the matter logically. If there truly was no danger, there was no point in alarming the guests; Lord Craythorne should have refrained from saying anything. Unless saying something was the point.

Lydia swiftly assessed the room. Fear was predominant, followed closely by confusion. Mr. Ruskin was angry, and to a lesser extent, so was Mrs. Ruskin. Lady Craythorne was annoyed, probably at the disruption of "her" party.

And a deep, wicked satisfaction twinned with the exultance of vindication suffused Mr. Sabot's emotions.

"I beg your pardon, please excuse me," Lydia gabbled out, releasing Miss Adams' hand and rising. No one paid her any heed as she crossed the room to Mr. Sabot's side. "Oh, Mr. Sabot, this is too dreadful!" she exclaimed. "Are we truly in no danger?"

"Miss Wescott," Mr. Sabot said, his emotions sliding back toward lust. "You need not fear. Those savages cannot stand against the Army, however I may despise General Fotheringham and his ungovernable troops."

That had been a lie, but his statement was complex enough Lydia could not tell where exactly the lie was. "But the Iroquois are fierce warriors, I have heard," she essayed.

"The fiercest. But they lack the weapons the Army put to such good use against American citizens, curse them." Mr. Sabot smiled. "They will be defeated."

Still, the lie eluded Lydia. "I believed the Iroquois to be, not allies, precisely, but not enemies. Why would they attack?"

"Who knows why savages do what they do? Perhaps the Iroquois were offended by some slight." Mr. Sabot took Lydia's hand and held it caressingly. "Truly, you should not fear, Miss Wescott."

Lydia retrieved her hand with as little force as she could manage and did not grimace at Mr. Sabot's touch. She understood now what knowledge he was concealing. "I shall take your assurance to heart, sir," she said. "Thank you. Please excuse me, I should see to Miss Adams."

She walked away before Mr. Sabot touched her again. So. Mr. Sabot knew whoever was attacking the Viceroy's palace, they were not Iroquois. But she did not doubt the reports brought to Lord Craythorne. Which meant the attackers were disguised as Iroquois, and only Libertymen would have cause to conceal their attacks in such a way.

She Discerned the others in the house again. The fear was abating, though one or two of the women were filled with the kind of excitement twined with fear that marked anticipation of some dreadful event. They likely wished for an attack on the mansion, though Lydia could not tell what they hoped to gain by it. Mr. and Mrs. Ruskin stood near the door, speaking in low voices Lydia could not make out. Mr. Ruskin was angry, and determined on action; Mrs. Ruskin's emotions had calmed, and she appeared to be attempting to extend that calm to her husband.

Lydia wished she dared approach Lord Craythorne, but that would look odd, so she contented herself with observing him from a distance. The poorly-dressed man had returned, and the two of them were having a conversation as intense as the Ruskins', though Lord Craythorne was not angry at all; his emotions were sharp and focused on solving a problem. Then he left the room in company with the man, and this time he went to the front door and then passed out of her range.

She returned to her seat beside Miss Adams, whose fear had faded somewhat as her curiosity rose. "Whyever did you speak to Mr. Sabot?" she asked.

Too late Lydia realized how that must have looked to anyone who cared to watch. She stumbled over an answer she hoped made sense. "I...Mr. Sabot told me he had connections at the Viceroy's palace, and I wished to know what he made of the attack."

"That is peculiar," Miss Adams said, her curiosity rising rather than waning. "Your association with Mr. Sabot is stronger than I realized." Her nose wrinkled as if she smelled something bad. "You do not feel an attachment, do you? Because it almost seemed as if you went to him for reassurance."

"No!" Lydia exclaimed with enough force that those nearest turned to look at her. She blushed, and said, "No, of course not. He is far too old, and—well, I do not—his poetry is interesting, that is all, and I am so curious about this attack, I thought only to learn what he knows. That is all, truly."

Miss Adams did not seem convinced, but she was too well-bred to press Lydia for more. "I wonder that you did not approach Lord Craythorne instead."

"Oh, he is far too preoccupied with the matter—you see, he is gone again." Lydia searched the room for unusual emotions, but found nothing, which was a disappointment. After Mr. Sabot's declaration that there were women among the Libertymen, and that Lydia knew some of them, she had hoped to catch one or perhaps more of the ladies present in guilt or exultation. But no one felt anything but curiosity or fear or anxiety now, and the conversations Lydia overheard were all speculation on what might have caused the Iroquois to attack.

Now that the initial shock was past, Lydia considered what she had learned from Mr. Sabot, and discouragement settled over her. Surely all that questioning had resulted in nothing Lord Craythorne did not already know. He had trusted her talent, and she and her talent had failed. If only she could have made Mr. Sabot give up the names of his confederates!

"Miss Wescott, are you well? You do not feel faint?" Miss Adams' inquiry sounded as if it came from far away, though Lydia did not feel ill or faint. Inwardly, she chastised herself for permitting her disquiet to show.

"I am well," she said, "merely concerned for those at the Viceroy's palace who are in danger. Surely there are soldiers on guard there?"

"There are, but it is not a large force. Mr. Cavanaugh—" Miss Adams blushed, hesitated, then forged on— "Mr. Cavanaugh is attached to the Treasury, and he makes frequent visits to the palace. He always says the soldiers are cautious, and examine him closely every time he arrives, though they all know him by sight now. They surely must have protected Mr. Monroe."

"How I wish we had more news!" Lydia exclaimed.

At that moment, Lady Craythorne entered the room, surprising Lydia, who had not noticed her absence. She truly was a terrible agent, if she even dared call herself that. Lady Craythorne cleared her throat in a delicate way and said, "Let us enjoy more refreshments, and not dwell on such horrid doings! Miss Wescott, may I prevail upon you to play for us? And perhaps Miss Adams will sing, if you will accompany her."

Lydia and Miss Adams exchanged glances. Miss Adams' relief at having occupation displaced the last of her fear and curiosity. "I would be pleased to, Lady Craythorne," she said.

"As would I," Lydia said.

A few moments' discussion at the pianoforte produced agreement on a song, and Lydia settled herself on the stool and flexed her fingers. Miss Adams was not nervous, not even the mild anxiety most people experienced on preparing to perform in front of an audience, and after the first few bars she sailed confidently into the song with her chin held high. Her voice was high and sweet, but without the breathiness many amateur sopranos of her range had. Lydia's admiration for the young woman grew.

The song was a familiar one, and Lydia idly Discerned the mood of the crowd as she played. If Lady Craythorne had intended their performance to soothe nerves disordered by Lord Craythorne's announcement, she had succeeded brilliantly; though emotions still varied widely, the general mood was one of pale blue peacefulness, threaded through with satisfaction and occasionally romantic inclinations. Of those, Mr. Sabot's were the strongest, and as his attention was fully on Lydia, she had no trouble guessing the object of his passion. The idea made her queasy, and her irritation with Lord Craythorne grew. How *dare* he make her nothing more than a lure for his quarry?

She and Miss Adams played and sang three songs before Lord Craythorne returned, alone this time. "Ladies and gentlemen, I am happy to say the threat is over," he said.

Murmurs rose up, and peaceful reverie gave way to relief and some hints of curiosity here and there. Lord Craythorne raised a hand for silence and got it. "The palace is safe, though the fire did some small damage. The attackers were routed, and the Army has secured this area of the city against their return."

"Their return?" a robust middle-aged man said. "Craythorne, what do you mean? Need we fear more attacks by those savages?"

Lydia Discerned Lord Craythorne's annoyance clearly, but the Duke did not say anything more irritated than, "Mr. Lynch, there will be no Iroquois attacks tonight," in a way Lydia immediately perceived as completely truthful as well as avoiding the whole truth. Her heart fell further. So he already knew that the so-called Iroquois attackers were nothing of the sort. She might as well not have bothered.

"I am glad to hear the crisis is over," Lady Craythorne said, sounding calm despite her secret annoyance at her event being disrupted. "But I am certain there is nothing more I can provide by way of entertainment that will outdo this excitement!"

Nervous laughter sounded throughout the room, and people began rising from their seats. All of them understood Lady Craythorne's veiled invitation to leave. To Lydia's surprise, none of them were resentful of being evicted. In fact, most of them were eager to be gone. Lydia suspected they either wished to go in search of more gossipy information, or wished to spread such gossip themselves despite the hour.

"Thank you for playing for me," Miss Adams said. "You are so talented."

"As are you," Lydia said. "We made an excellent partnership."

Miss Adams giggled. "Shall we still meet at the museum as planned?"

"Yes, indeed." Lydia found she looked forward to the outing more than she had when she had impulsively proposed it. "And perhaps Lady Dorothea will join us—though she did not strike me as one much for museums."

"She will not wish to be left out." Miss Adams' mirth disappeared. "I wish she did not make it so difficult to be her friend. She was much more congenial last year, before she—" She stopped speaking, embarrassed, but Lydia guessed what she had meant: that last year marked the beginning of Lady Dorothea's interest in Lord Craythorne.

"I hope she will join us, then," Lydia said, and clasped Miss Adams' hand in farewell.

She moved from the piano stool to the sofa she had previously occupied and waited quietly for all the guests to leave. When she Discerned no one left in the mansion except Lord Craythorne, Lady Craythorne, and the servants, she rose and left the drawing room, ascending the stairs and walking at a measured, calm pace to the library.

She paced the circumference of the room, reading a title here and there, until she Discerned Lord Craythorne's approach. He was moving at a normal pace, not hurrying or dawdling, and his emotions were not tinged with great urgency, as if he already knew she had not learned anything he did not already know. She pushed aside discouragement and took a seat at the table facing the door.

When Lord Craythorne entered, Lydia was poised to speak, but his unexpected emotional weariness combined with his tired appearance stilled her tongue. Lord Craythorne closed the door most of the way, then stood with his shoulders sagging and his head bowed so his curls caught the light. "I sincerely hope you learned something from Mr. Sabot," he said, "for I have reached the end of what I can easily do."

Lydia's despondency deepened. "I learned things, but now I do not know if they are useful. He confirmed that he is John Steadfast, but perhaps you know this already—"

"Suspected," Lord Craythorne said. "That is, in fact, useful knowledge, as I may now turn more resources toward following him. What else?"

"Ah," Lydia said, reaching into memory. "He said he has many confederates, among them Mr. Abel Suggitt and Mr. Hughes, and that there were women as well as men. He claimed some of them are women I am acquainted with. I regret so much being unable to give you names!"

Lord Craythorne's head lifted slowly. "Suggitt and Hughes are enough. Either of them has the resources to mount an attack such as we saw tonight."

"Then you know they were not truly Iroquois who attacked the Viceroy's palace."

Lord Craythorne scowled. He pulled out the chair opposite Lydia's and sank heavily into it. "Someone certainly intended we believe it. Someone who has a very low opinion of our native neighbors. The men who attempted to destroy the Viceroy's palace dressed in feathers and rough furs the way Europeans believe the Iroquois dress, and they behaved with wild abandon such as savages would. It was a ridiculous display, but it has done much damage, as members of the American Parliament have already called for a strong response to this 'native assault.' Only my assertions, and the word of several others in Mr. Monroe's confidences, stopped them from sending the Army against the Six Nations Confederacy this very night."

"Then the Libertymen's purpose was to start a war?" Lydia asked.

"I think not," Lord Craythorne said. "It is more likely they wished Mr. Monroe's government to be distracted so they might strike another blow elsewhere. I believe I have forestalled them so far, but the fact that they were able to make such an attack disturbs me. In absolute terms, the attackers were few, but there were still some forty or fifty of them, and when one considers that for every attacker, there are likely dozens more who were not among that group, well..." He spread his hands wide as if indicating defeat. "Was there more?"

Lydia considered. "Mr. Sabot knew of the attack, and was not surprised when you announced it. He also assured me that I was in no danger from the Libertymen, which tells me he knew the attack would be confined to the Viceroy's palace. He said they take precautions so no one man knows enough to betray the others, but I believe he knows more than he should. A real interrogation would reveal much, but perhaps that would give the game away."

"It would," Lord Craythorne said. "But, as I said, I will have him followed more closely, and with luck he will reveal more than he wishes. Suggitt and Hughes, too. I am glad you understood my meaning in announcing the attack."

"Yes, but no one else felt guilt or triumph over it, and I am quite cast down that I did not learn at least a few more identities," Lydia said, scowling.

"You have done enough. And eventually I will be free to capture one or all of these men, and you will interrogate them more directly." Lord Craythorne smiled, his eyes distant as if in appreciation of some happy future. "That is excellent work for one night. I hope you had at least some pleasure, as well."

Lydia remembered the other thing she had discovered. "Not as much as some," she said. "Tell me, your Grace, did you tell Mr. Sabot explicitly that I doted on him, or was it a more subtle revelation?"

Lord Craythorne sat up, startled. "Did I what?"

"Mr. Sabot did not have the least bit of romantic interest in me on our previous encounters." Lydia sat forward, fixing Lord Craythorne with a fierce glare. "And yet tonight, your Grace, he felt the deepest attraction to me—and he believed I returned his interest. *I* have not spoken to him since the poetry reading, therefore I must lay his remarkable change of heart at your door. So I repeat—what exactly did you say to Mr. Sabot that convinced him I was ready to fall into his arms?"

Lord Craythorne's look of astonished dismay was nothing compared to the wild tangle of emotion that rose up within him: surprise, chagrin, horror, and an inexplicable flash of anger, all for once strong and unmuted, battered at Lydia. She held her ground, continuing to glare, though his reaction had done much to mollify her. They sat in silence for a moment or two as Lord Craythorne struggled to master his initial reaction.

Finally, he said, "Miss Wescott, I offer my deepest apologies. I thought to offer Mr. Sabot enticement to attend because he was not enthusiastic at my invitation. I realize now how my comments must have looked—oh, and I believe I even said you wished wholeheartedly to speak with him." Now his emotions showed nothing but penitence and embarrassment. "Did he impose greatly upon you?"

"No more than I could manage," Lydia said. "Though I admit it was unpleasant. I cannot understand why a man of his age might believe a woman of mine would wish—oh, but that is indelicate, I apologize."

Lord Craythorne smiled, and Lydia Discerned rueful amusement taking the place of embarrassment. "I completely agree, and you need not apologize to me, Miss Wescott. I am the one who spoke rashly." He slapped one hand on the tabletop as if in emphasis. "Well, we have learned things, and Lady Craythorne is speaking to me again—"

"She stopped speaking to you?"

"She was not happy at having her party interrupted, and I realize the ridiculousness of her emotion, given that the interruption was unplanned and the party was not actually hers. But she has Spoken to her many friends in her reticulum, and I believe being able to pass on information about the attack has eased her anger."

Lydia, alert to Lord Craythorne's changing mood, said, "What disturbs you?"

Lord Craythorne eyed Lydia narrowly. "I know Rutledge would chastise you for commenting on my emotional state when I have not given you leave."

"Mr. Rutledge is not here, and it is much better I not permit you to keep secrets, you know. And it is not as if I will tell anyone that Lady Craythorne's reticulum worries you."

With a chuckle, Lord Craythorne said, "As I am a gentleman, I will not point out all the logical flaws in that argument." More seriously, he added, "All the ladies you know in Washington are known to my mother as well, and many of them are in her Speaker's reticulum. I am concerned that she may have close contact with some of the Libertymen."

"You do not believe she is in danger?" Lydia exclaimed.

"Not danger, precisely, but—no, it is unworthy of me to harbor such distrust." Lord Craythorne sighed.

"You mean you believe Lady Craythorne may give away secrets," Lydia persisted.

"Not intentionally. But as my mother is not deep in my confidences

—could not be, as she has no official position—she will not always know what should be held secret. At least we need not fear she will give away your talent."

Lydia nodded. "Someone is coming," she said, noting the approach of someone whose general calmness was spiked through with excitement.

Presently, the door swung open, and James the footman said, "Your Grace, you asked me to confirm all the ground floor entrances are secured."

"Indeed. Thank you, James."

James bowed and retreated, not before casting a curious eye at Lydia. Lydia regarded him steadily in return, but he felt nothing more than mild curiosity, no lascivious suspicion and no speculation on Lydia's presence alone with the Duke.

Lord Craythorne sighed again. "Off with you," he said with a tired smile that made his eyes crinkle at the corners. "You have done yeoman's work tonight, and I thank you."

His words set off a wave of tiredness that ran through her whole body, though it could not be later than eleven o'clock. "I wish I might have done more."

"Be satisfied with what you have learned. I am." Lord Craythorne bowed. Lydia curtseyed in return and left as he settled himself back in his chair. Why he did not follow his own advice, Lydia did not know, but she was too weary to wonder much about it.

CHAPTER 18

IN WHICH LYDIA UNEXPECTEDLY MAKES FRIENDS

L ydia paced between glass-topped display cabinets, by turns awed and delighted at what she saw. "I cannot believe," she said to Miss Adams, "that this was tucked away within the museum's walls. The examples of native dress are beautiful, but *this*—" She stopped in front of a case no bigger than a hatbox, wherein lay gleaming earrings of silver coiled in tight spirals, depending from slim wires shaped like fishhooks.

"I believed it was what interested you when you proposed this visit," Miss Adams replied. "Lady Dorothea, only look. These earrings are from China."

Lady Dorothea strolled over to join them. "Impressive," she said, "especially since I cannot see how that hook, with its fat spirals on both ends, could possibly fit through a pierced earlobe."

The others looked more closely. "Do you know, I believe you are right," Lydia said. "How curious."

"I am fond of the enamel ones," Lady Dorothea said, gesturing to a nearby case. Lydia had seen them already; elongated silver trumpets and oval rubies, cabochon cut, hung from the colorful enameled lion's head attached to the hook. The enamel looked dusty, but the colors hinted at how vibrant they had once been.

Their guide, a small, tidy man with an unfashionable but neat mustache, cleared his throat delicately. "You ladies may be interested in this," he said, leading them to another case. Inside lay a wire loop Lydia believed to be a necklace, though it scarcely resembled the chain link necklaces of Europe. Fifteen wide silver rings studded with flattened silver beads were threaded along the wire.

"This was given by Martin Cotterell to his wife, Lady Susan," the guide said. "All the items you see here belonged to Lady Susan before her death in 1795. Mr. Cotterell was a Bounder with an avid interest in the Orient, and he made his wife many gifts of the treasures he purchased from the Chinese. They had no children, and after her death Mr. Cotterell presented her collection to the museum."

"He might have given it to the British Museum, where it would have been more widely appreciated," Lady Dorothea said.

"Mr. Cotterell was a staunch patriot, and he wished for America to develop its culture independent of the mother country." The guide's tone and emotions cooled. "If you will excuse me, I see Mr. and Mrs. Smoot have arrived, and I should see to their needs."

When he had walked out of earshot, Miss Adams said, "We are merely young women of no consequence, or so he believes. Suppose we used our innocent appearances to conceal our true identities as thieves?" She giggled. "I daresay we would be extremely successful!"

"You have the oddest imaginings, Miss Adams," Lady Dorothea said without rancor. "Though I admit now I am considering how one might steal some of these without being noticed."

"My brother had thefts from his collection of mechanicals, one where a visitor hid an object beneath a false stomach and simply walked out the door," Lydia said. "But he did not protect his mechanicals under glass. Perhaps he should have."

"How thrilling, and how horrid!" Miss Adams exclaimed. "I did not know your brother invented mechanicals—or is that wrong, and he merely collects them?"

"No, he is an inventor, though he also possesses mechanicals created by others. We used to live above the collection, but now that he is Earl of Ashford, it is located somewhere more secure than our house on Hanover Square was." Lydia leaned closer to examine the rings. "Do you suppose these were meant for money? I have heard the natives of India wear belts of gold or copper rings that are both decorative and used as coin."

"One might say we Europeans do that as well." Lady Dorothea touched one of her pearl drop earrings, making it tremble. "Sell our jewels when we are in need of money."

"I have heard of women—the demimonde, not women of culture—enticing men to give them jewels so they might have resources when those men lose interest," Miss Adams said in a hushed voice. Her emotions were tinged with nervousness and daring at voicing such an indelicate notion.

"Their lives must be so uncertain." Lydia said. She did not like the dark mood coming off Lady Dorothea, who had said nothing in response, but whose emotions were the oddest mix of frustration tinged with grey-black despair that unsettled Lydia. It was a terrible emotion to feel as well as being one that might potentially overwhelm an Extraordinary Discerner.

"I believe we have seen all there is to see," she continued. "Lady Dorothea, Miss Adams, shall we find a tea shop? I am rather hungry, and I believe it is past three o'clock."

Lady Dorothea's mood lightened only slightly, but she did not refuse the invitation.

James the footman waited at the museum door, impervious to the chill. Lady Craythorne had insisted he accompany them. "Suppose the Iroquois attack again?" she had said. "You cannot wander around Washington with no protection." Lydia, unable to explain why such an attack was impossible, had given in.

Now he bowed politely, just as if he was not bored and annoyed at having stood outside even though that had been his choice. "Will you return to the mansion, ladies?" he asked.

Lydia cast an eye on the skies. Clouds had darkened the sun and the temperature had dropped dramatically, causing her to huddle deeper into her pelisse. "I believe we should return to Lord Craythorne's house," she told the others. "It is closer than the nearest tea shop, and we will be quite comfortable there."

"Thank you for the kind offer. I should like that very much, don't you agree, Lady Dorothea?" Miss Adams said. "We should hurry. Rain is coming."

They did hurry, walking rapidly along the sidewalk beneath bare-branched trees just showing small, pale green buds. The tree limbs quivered when the wind gusted, making the trees seem to shiver in the cold as the young women did. Lydia smelled rain, a pleasant enough smell when one would not be caught in it, and walked faster.

The first drops had spattered them when they rounded the corner onto the long, curved drive that led to the mansion's front door. Its windows glowed with warm light Lydia imagined she could feel radiating into the chilly air. Miss Adams let out a squeak and ran for the door as the rain began falling harder, and Lydia and Lady Dorothea followed close behind. James quickly outpaced them and had the door open by the time they reached it.

The three ladies hurtled through the door and let it bang shut behind them. For a moment, as they stood panting in the foyer, pleasure suffused Lady Dorothea, but in moments the dark mood descended again. To her surprise, Lydia felt, not irritation, but compassion for the young woman. Something troubled her, and Lydia wished she could discover what it was.

"James, we will use the small drawing room," she told him. "Would you take our wet things, and then send one of the maids with tea? Thank you."

James bowed and smiled. His smile was so attractive, Lydia reflected, and now that they were inside, he was no longer resentful of the cold. She hoped for Ellery's sake his feelings for her matched his lovely smile.

"The small drawing room is this way," Lydia said, leading them up the stairs to the smallish room opposite Lady Craythorne's chosen space. It was colder than the other drawing room, having a smaller chimney that did not draw as well as it might and a northern view that did not welcome the sun's direct rays, but it was beautiful and Lydia never minded the chill. "How fortunate that we reached this place in time," she said, removing her bonnet. "And now we must have tea and cakes, because no one could expect us to go out in *that*." She nodded at the windows, where rain now beat hard against the glass and the wind made a low, droning hum as it thrashed the tree branches.

Lady Dorothea and Miss Adams seated themselves, and Lydia took a moment to build up the fire. By the time the tea came, she was much warmer and felt comfortable enough to essay a question. "Lady Dorothea," she said, "you have been so quiet. Does something trouble you?"

"No, nothing," Lady Dorothea said, so quickly it was clear even to a non-Discerner it was a lie. Then she added, "Nothing of consequence, anyway. Miss Adams, how does your mother?"

Miss Adams darted a glance at Lydia with her eyebrows raised. "She is very well," she said, "but that is not what interests you, is it?"

"I have said there is nothing wrong," Lady Dorothea snapped.

Lydia hesitated. She was certain, if she pressed in the wrong way, Lady Dorothea would walk out the door into the storm and never speak to either of them again. But that dark mood troubled her with its intensity and the pain it gave Lady Dorothea.

Before she could speak, Miss Adams said, "Family is a complicated thing. My mother, thank you for asking after her, wishes me to make a fine match. And I believed she meant a wealthy one. But when I confessed to her my interest in someone not very wealthy, and not titled, she was so pleased for me. I did not understand her, but now I believe I do."

"How fortunate," Lady Dorothea snarled. "And how foolish. How do you expect to be happy if you are poor? Love cannot prevent starvation."

Now the despair was mingled with such terrible sorrow Lydia wished she could flee. Memories of dark nights in Magdalen tried to drag her into Lady Dorothea's grey-black despair, and she desperately pushed them aside, focusing on the calm beige dullness of the two servants passing nearby to keep herself anchored to the present.

Miss Adams regarded Lady Dorothea calmly, as if she were an Extraordinary Discerner herself and knew Lady Dorothea's anger was directed at herself and not at Miss Adams. "I did not say poor," she said quietly, "but I imagine in your position, 'not wealthy' might as well mean 'impoverished.'"

Lady Dorothea closed her eyes. Her pain and despair faded enough that Lydia regained control of herself. She told Lady Dorothea, "We will say nothing to anyone, but I believe it will do you good to speak."

Lady Dorothea, her eyes still closed, bowed her head. "It is so shameful," she said. She looked first at Lydia, then at Miss Adams. "I believe it is no secret that I am on the hunt for a wealthy husband. 'That rapacious Lady Dorothea,' they whisper where they believe I cannot hear. But I must. We will be ruined utterly if I do not."

"That is a terrible burden to bear," Miss Adams said. "Is there no other way?"

Lady Dorothea shook her head. "My father—our family's fortune was lost in a series of failed trading ventures—oh, I do not know why I am telling you this! If you speak of it to anyone—"

"We will say nothing," Lydia repeated, and Miss Adams nodded assent. "And that is why you are interested in Lord Craythorne."

"He will do as well as anyone," Lady Dorothea said bitterly. "Though I begin to imagine he is an impossibility. He is so cold in his manners, so lacking in sensibility."

Lydia would never had described Lord Craythorne so, even had she not been fond of him, but she recalled watching him dance and Discerning his indifference and admitted he could appear cold. "I believe you remind him of his late wife," she said, and immediately regretted her rash words. She had spoken out of a sudden realization that came from putting several facts together in the right way, and had not considered to whom she spoke.

Both Lady Dorothea and Miss Adams sat upright in sudden interest and curiosity. "Is that so?" Lady Dorothea said. "Has he said so?"

"No, not at all," Lydia stammered. "Not—it is entirely my conjecture, pray do not give it any heed."

"I have heard there was something odd about the death of Lady Craythorne," Miss Adams said in a hushed, confiding voice. "Lord Craythorne may not wish for any reminders. And you *do* resemble her slightly. She was also dark-haired and dark-eyed."

"No," Lydia protested, "no, that is not—"

"I heard Lord Craythorne married Lady Craythorne for her

money," Lady Dorothea said, "and that he disliked her. They were rarely in the same city at the same time."

"How do you know that?" Lydia exclaimed, interested despite herself.

"It was common knowledge when we lived in London five years ago." Lady Dorothea's dark mood was nearly gone, replaced by that sharp, intent excitement that characterized interest in a subject. "His fortune is why my father considered him an acceptable match for me. It was substantially augmented by Lady Craythorne's dowry."

"*I* heard he attended one of the Prince Regent's parties the day after Lady Craythorne's death," Miss Adams said, "just as if he were not in mourning."

"That cannot be true," Lady Dorothea said. "He would not be so lost to propriety."

"Perhaps, and perhaps not," Miss Adams persisted. "But he never showed the least bit of sadness over losing his wife and child. That is what my mother says, and she is one of the Dowager Duchess's reticulum and would know."

Lydia wished she could deny that Lady Craythorne would gossip about her own son, but she was by no means convinced of that. "This is all speculation," she said.

"Well, what do *you* believe? You live in his house," Miss Adams said.

Lydia hesitated. "I cannot believe he is so hardened as that," she said. "But I believe it is true that he and the late Lady Craythorne were not fond of one another. Even so, that is not the same as suspecting him of evil behavior."

Both Lady Dorothea and Miss Adams looked at her in astonishment. "Evil behavior?" Lady Dorothea said. "You mean...he might have had something to do with Lady Craythorne's death?"

Now Lydia cursed herself for a fool. "Of course not! I meant, well, that he did not care for her, and perhaps that means he was glad she was gone—oh, no, I do not mean that either!"

But Lady Dorothea was filled with suspicion, and Miss Adams was filled with horror. "Of course you do not," Miss Adams lied. "That is the stuff novels are made of, and no real person would act so."

"That is exactly right," Lydia said.

"Perhaps it is for the best I cannot attach Lord Craythorne," Lady Dorothea mused. "I suppose I shall have to turn my search elsewhere."

"That is the saddest thing I have ever heard," Lydia said, leaping on this change of topic. "Why can your father not settle his affairs some other way? Some way that does not require you to sacrifice yourself?"

Lady Dorothea shrugged. "It is not as if I love anyone," she said, "and if I must marry, it might as well be for a fortune and a title." She made a face. "Though it is Mother who wishes for the title. She is so proud of being Lady Fanshawe, as if she were born to the viscounty and not married into it."

Her comments reminded Lydia strongly of what Lord Craythorne had said about marriage, and she nearly remarked on it before she remembered she wished to direct the conversation away from him. "There is nothing wrong with choosing how one wishes to marry, but you seem unhappy with your fate."

"I do not wish to marry at all," Lady Dorothea said. "I would like to travel the world and have adventures before settling down. But there is no money for that, either."

"I would prefer to stay at home and have excitement come to me," Miss Adams said. "One need not travel far to experience dramatic— well, such as that Iroquois attack on the Viceroy's palace!"

"We were none of us there, fortunately, so how are we to know how dramatic it was?" Lady Dorothea shrugged. "It might have been more terrifying than exciting."

"Likely you are right," Miss Adams said, subsiding. "I have heard from Mr. Cavanaugh—"

"Mr. Cavanaugh?" Lydia said, arching one eyebrow in a trick she had learned from watching Colin.

Miss Adams blushed, and her emotions shifted dramatically toward the romantic. "Mr. Cavanaugh was there in the Viceroy's palace during the attack, and he said it was nothing so awful, mostly commotion and noise and fire. I suspect he intended me not to be afraid—oh, but he was so brave!"

"I would love to see Egypt, and Persia," Lady Dorothea said. "But I suppose you would not be satisfied with those destinations unless you could be attacked by pirates en route." She smiled teasingly as she said this, and the smile so transformed her face Lydia was astonished that it was the same woman.

"Pirates are tedious. Bandits attacking a caravan, that would be something." Miss Adams turned to Lydia. "What of you, Miss Wescott? Your brother is a Bounder; have you seen many exotic places?"

"I prefer both to stay at home *and* remain adventure-free," Lydia said. The memory of lying curled on her bed in Magdalen intruded briefly and then was gone. "My brother says I like to build my nest and never venture out of it."

"Then what prompted you to travel with Lady Craythorne?" Miss Adams asked.

The unexpected question caught her off guard, and she stammered, "I, well, it was for my health, I suppose. And I believed perhaps staying in my nest would not help me—that is, I wished to meet new people."

"Of course," Lady Dorothea said, but she was suspicious again. Lydia did not know what in all of that sounded suspicious. Well. All of it, based on how muddled it was. She noted the presence of someone outside the door and hoped he would enter, to be a distraction to Lady Dorothea. But the person, who by his sharply intent emotions was a servant on an important errand, moved on.

"My mother says Lady Craythorne speaks well of you, when she Speaks to her reticulum," Miss Adams said.

"That is kind of her. I did not believe she considered me well suited." Lydia's mind was still partly on the servants and partly on her previous words. Surely they did not give away her secret? Of course not. But they might make someone like Lady Dorothea believe there was something mysterious about her attendance on Lady Craythorne. With luck, Lady Dorothea would not pry.

"*My* mother was surprised Lady Craythorne wished for a companion," Lady Dorothea said. Her suspicion had not faded, and she gazed at Lydia with uncomfortable directness. "She has never had one before."

Lydia began to make up a story, realized she could not remember what she had already said only seconds before, and said, "I do not know what prompted her, but I am grateful for her consideration."

"Yes, because it means we met you, and that pleases me," Miss Adams said with her usual giggle. "Do you know when Lord Craythorne returns to England?"

"No, but Lady Craythorne suggests it will be some time," Lydia said, grateful to Miss Adams for once more changing the subject. "I am glad of it. There is so much to see here."

"Yes, but I would like to hear more of London," Lady Dorothea said, without the haughty disdain Lydia now expected. "A true London Season would help me tremendously. You must tell us what it is like, Miss Wescott."

"I will," Lydia said, "but I wish you would call me Lydia. I believe we are fast becoming friends." It was an impulse that came from she knew not where, but for the first time in her life, she felt a connection that had nothing to do with Discernment. She had Colin, and she had Clemency and her family, but she had never had friends before, and the thought shook her with its intensity before she shrugged the feeling aside. Friends. It was the sort of thing a normal young lady would have. She was never going to be truly normal, but this might help her come close.

CHAPTER 19

IN WHICH LYDIA MAKES A RASH ACCUSATION, AND A NEW ACCORD IS REACHED

Lydia knew something had changed the moment she walked downstairs that evening and Lord Craythorne came within her range. His heightened emotions of suppressed excitement and anticipation filled Lydia with curiosity. But when she entered the drawing room where Lord Craythorne and the Dowager Duchess waited, he said nothing, and his expression gave away none of his feelings. This deepened Lydia's curiosity, because if his emotions meant anything innocuous, he would have spoken. It had to have something to do with the Libertymen.

Supper, therefore, felt strained, at least to Lydia. Lady Craythorne showed no sign of noticing Lord Craythorne's emotional state, though as he controlled himself well, Lydia did not believe that made Lady Craythorne unobservant. The Dowager Duchess was more affable than usual, speaking freely of her reticulum and even complimenting Lydia once or twice. She was so cheerful Lydia said, "You are in excellent spirits, your Grace."

"You should not comment on what you Discern," Lady Craythorne said, but without anger. Lydia reflexively Discerned the room and its surroundings, for fear a servant might have been within earshot of that careless remark, but she sensed no one close enough to hear, or so she hoped.

"Mother," Lord Craythorne said in a warning tone.

Lady Craythorne frowned, but embarrassment tinged her emotions. "Miss Wescott continues to improve," she said, "and I believe she appreciates correction."

"Thank you, your Grace," Lydia said, refusing to be drawn into a pointless argument over her behavior and manners and how they did or did not please Lady Craythorne. "I appreciate your guidance."

Lord Craythorne eyed her with suspicion, as if she had been too affable, but said only, "If Miss Wescott is satisfied, I will not criticize."

"That is good, Oliver, because Miss Wescott's behavior is not your business." Lady Craythorne delivered this statement in a pleasant tone that blunted her harsh words. "And speaking of behavior, I am glad you were able to join us this evening. I take it Mr. Monroe does not need you tonight?"

"The threat of Iroquois attack has been resolved." Lord Craythorne applied himself to his beef as if his emotions had not just sharpened into anger at having to lie about the previous night's events. "The representative of the Onondaga claims no affiliation with those who attempted to destroy the Viceroy's palace and assures Mr. Monroe those involved, if apprehended, will be punished according to Haudenosaunee law."

"I should hope so," Lady Craythorne said. "How dreadful. They should be more conscious of dissident elements within their confederacy."

Lord Craythorne did not respond. Lydia wondered if the Iroquois Nations had been informed of the truth, that their people were not responsible for the purported Iroquois attack. She could not imagine why they would not be, and yet Lord Craythorne's words and emotions suggested it was not the case, and suggested further that he did not agree with that decision.

Searching for a less fraught topic of conversation, she said, "Lady Dorothea and Miss Adams and I viewed Mr. Cotterell's collection of Chinese jewelry today. It is so beautiful. I know nothing of Chinese art, but I feel I should remedy that lack if only I knew how."

"Does this mean you consider yourself an expert on English poetry, then? You are prepared to move on with your education?" Lord Craythorne arched his eyebrows in a way that, combined with his sly smile, gave him a satirical appearance.

His amusement made Lydia laugh. "I will admit to being wrong about poetry being nothing but flowers and nymphs and silliness," she said. "But some of what Mr. Donne writes makes no sense to me. 'Go and catch a falling star,/Get with child a mandrake root'—that one sounded like a collection of impossibilities, and one that was rather disdainful of women's fidelity."

"Very true, Miss Wescott." Lord Craythorne laid down his fork and leaned forward, intent on Lydia.

"It sounds almost indecent," Lady Craythorne said. Lydia paid her no mind; the Dowager Duchess had made the protest for form's sake and not because she was offended.

"That one is intended as a love poem," Lord Craythorne continued. "What do you make of that?"

Lydia considered. "Thwarted love, or betrayal, are powerful emotions. To me, it seemed as if the poet had been betrayed by his love and had decided that meant all women were fickle. Which is ridiculous."

"You call John Donne's poem ridiculous?" Lord Craythorne still looked nothing more than intent upon her, but bitterness rose up within him, bitterness and resentment, as if she had in disdaining the poem disdained him as well.

Lydia made an impatient gesture. "No, it reflects the belief of many men and women, and it is quite powerful in doing so. I mean that it is ridiculous to permit one bad experience to define every other experience one might have. How incredibly short-sighted."

Guilt surged to tangle with the bitterness suffusing Lord Craythorne, surprising Lydia, because despite knowing of Lord Craythorne's guilt over his dead wife, she had not imagined he saw any parallels to his experience with Mr. Donne's poem. She almost challenged him, but remembered Lady Craythorne's chastisement and heard more distantly the voice of her mother berating her and subsided.

"What, you would not have men learn from their mistakes?" Lord Craythorne asked, his tone light and amused in contrast to his raging emotions. "Suppose the man in the poem had trusted deeply in the woman who was inconstant—should he not be wary in future?"

"This is not wariness, it is bull-headed prejudice," Lydia countered. "And worse, the man in the poem tells all other men that *their* experiences with women will always be as awful as his. It is unfair to impress one's own biases on everyone else."

"Sharply spoken, Miss Wescott." Lord Craythorne's guilt had deepened to anger as she spoke, but he smiled as pleasantly as ever. "I see you have given the matter much consideration."

Lydia Discerned the approach of servants to clear the dishes for the second remove and could not remind him that she had seen love and failed love manifested in a thousand different ways. "But there were poems that spoke of love more delightfully," she said, hoping to distract him. "There was one in which the poet compared his love to a bewitching angler's bait—oh, that does not sound delightful, but it was subtle and beautiful, how he wrote of being captivated by her." She closed her eyes and recalled the final verse, and repeated it aloud:

For thee, thou need'st no such deceit,
For thou thyself art thine own bait;
That fish, that is not catched thereby,
Alas, is wiser far than I.

Lord Craythorne chuckled. "I had forgotten that one. You did not believe the poet was resentful of his love's bewitching charms?"

Lydia considered this. "That interpretation did not occur to me. In fact, I felt rather that his 'alas' in the final line was uttered with a rueful amusement at his own ensnarement."

"Insightful. Your tastes are remarkably refined for someone who protests dislike of poetry."

"Pray, do not throw my ignorance in my face, your Grace," Lydia said, blushing.

"I meant no such insult. I honor you for being willing to change your opinion." Lord Craythorne's emotions were ebbing, which eased Lydia's heart. For once, she did not wish to pry into his past, not when his reaction had been so alarming.

When the meal was over, Lady Craythorne rose and said, "Miss Wescott, I should like very much for you to play for me this evening. I feel the need for something calming."

Lydia did not point out that Lady Craythorne's emotions were already peaceful. "Of course, Lady Craythorne."

"I fear Miss Wescott will be otherwise occupied," Lord Craythorne said. "I have need of her assistance." His emotions were once more keenly anticipatory, and Lydia's curiosity roused again.

Lady Craythorne frowned. "This is most inappropriate, Oliver."

"It is why I am here, Lady Craythorne," Lydia said. "It is not as if we are conducting an illicit affair under everyone's noses."

The frown deepened. "Do not make light of social mores, Miss Wescott. You should be as conscious of your reputation as I am—more so, even."

"I am, your Grace, and I appreciate your concern. But I cannot be of use to Lord Craythorne if we cannot speak privately." It surprised Lydia to find she did not resent Lady Craythorne's interference. She saw clearly that it arose not from spite or sanctimony but from genuine concern—concern Lady Craythorne was incapable of expressing in any way but criticism.

"And I have no intention of compromising Miss Wescott," Lord Craythorne said. "You need not fear, Mother."

Lady Craythorne sniffed and left the dining room without another word.

"I fear Lady Craythorne has always been concerned with appearances over substance," Lord Craythorne said in a low voice. "Shall we adjourn to the library?"

"She means well," Lydia said as they crossed the foyer to the stairs. It was a chilly night, and someone had lit a fire in the hearth that radiated warmth throughout the foyer. Lydia shivered nevertheless. Lady Craythorne had not said anything in response to Lord Craythorne's assurances, but Lydia had perceived her guilt, the same guilt that attended any mention of Lord Craythorne's late wife, and she did not understand it.

She considered what she knew as she walked with Lord Craythorne to the library. Son and mother both had guilt associated with the late

Lady Craythorne's death. There were mysterious circumstances surrounding the event. Lord Craythorne was widely known to have disliked his wife. And for all his affability toward Lydia, she had seen his cold, hard demeanor, had watched him stand up to the formidable Mr. Rutledge, and had just perceived his unexpected anger. She was sure Lord Craythorne was capable of anything if it meant achieving his goal.

She covertly examined Lord Craythorne with her eyes and her Discernment. People's villainy was never written on their faces, regardless of what the more sensational novels claimed. And unless they were contemplating their evil actions, their villainy did not show in their emotions, either. Lord Craythorne did not give the appearance of someone who had murdered his wife, but Lydia had known men and women whose natures were profoundly evil, and many of them felt no guilt or shame or remorse over the things they had done. That Lord Craythorne experienced guilt meant he was not one of those, but it also did not absolve him of murder.

Lydia bit her lip in thought. This was ridiculous. It was only in novels that men killed their wives and got away with it. Guilt might mean anything. But she resolved to discover the mystery behind Lord Craythorne's reaction, if only for her own peace of mind.

In the library, Lord Craythorne gestured for Lydia to have a seat. He ostentatiously left the door open a hand's breadth, making Lydia laugh. "Well, it is essential, Miss Wescott," he said, pretending to haughtiness.

"Of course, your Grace," Lydia replied in the same manner. "One should be aware of others' observation at all times."

"I hope that means you will Discern anyone who approaches," Lord Craythorne said, his amusement subsiding.

"I will, your Grace. That is a simple thing because I am always aware of those around me." Lydia folded her hands demurely in her lap. "Pray, tell me what excites you so."

Instead of sitting, Lord Craythorne paced in front of the northern windows. The sky beyond was a faded dark blue that faded to soft peach to the left, and the boundary hedge was a stark black line that moved in the heavy wind of the storm that rose once again. Lord

Craythorne clasped his hands behind his back as he paced, making his shoulders strain against the fine fabric of his coat. "My men's observation has paid off," he said. "They discovered illicit goods being moved through Mr. Hughes' warehouses, and captured a shipment of weapons as well as Mr. Hughes himself."

Lydia gasped. "That *is* good news, your Grace."

"It is a start. We have prevented arms from reinforcing the Libertymen's resources, and put an end to that source of supplies." There was no pleasure in Lord Craythorne's voice or emotions "But it is the only good news. Mr. Hughes, after capture, took his own life rather than permit himself to be questioned."

"That is horrid," Lydia said, feeling ill. "And now you have no way of learning the identities of more of his fellow Libertymen. Was Mr. Suggitt captured with him?"

"Mr. Suggitt has disappeared, and his father swears he does not know where his son has gone," Lord Craythorne said. "I wish you had been present for that encounter. I do not believe Thomas Suggitt knows of young Mr. Suggitt's connection to the Libertymen, but he is a canny politician of many years' standing, and such men lie as easily as breathing." He turned his back on Lydia and stared out the window. "But that is not the problem Mr. Hughes' suicide has given me. He could not have killed himself without help."

"Oh," Lydia said, not at first understanding the import of his words. Then realization struck. "One or more of your trusted men is a Libertyman, or a sympathizer."

"Precisely." Lord Craythorne bowed his head. "Someone who may have been passing information about our plans to our enemies all along."

"But it could not be someone very high in your confidences, your Grace, or Mr. Hughes would have been warned and would not have stayed to be captured."

"I know, and that is a small comfort. But I must root out the corruption in our ranks. I am trying to conjure a way to bring you into contact with them so you may identify the traitor or, heaven help us, traitors." Lord Craythorne resumed pacing. "Forgive me, but this would be easier if you were a man."

"I understand, your Grace."

Lydia watched him pace like a tiger on a leash for a few moments. He seemed to have forgotten her presence, for his emotions were a tightly focused blade of anger and intellectual passion wound around with keen anticipation. Finally, she said, "Your Grace?"

"Yes?" He did not stop pacing.

"How deep a groove do you intend to wear in the floorboards?"

Lord Craythorne pulled up sharply, surprised. Then he laughed, a rueful chuckle. "Pacing will not help, indeed," he said, and walked over to the table to sit opposite her. In that position, his demeanor was more open, his smile more sincere. "I am in dire need of distraction. Tell me something of your day. You visited the textiles museum?"

"Yes, and made friends, and gossiped merrily. But perhaps you do not approve of gossip."

He laughed again. "I have discovered gossip is the lifeblood of intelligence gathering. But I did not believe *you* approved. You always keep your own counsel."

"I love learning others' secrets, your Grace, and I love even more keeping them concealed in my heart." Lydia watched him carefully, but Discerned nothing that might indicate he believed she knew any of *his* secrets.

"Then you are remarkable among women," Lord Craythorne said. His smile remained pleasant, but bitter anger surged through him, strong enough that Lydia caught her breath. Lord Craythorne's smile vanished. "Pay me no heed," he commanded.

"Then you agree with the poet," Lydia said, ignoring this. "You hold all women to be faithless because of one woman's sins." It was a guess, but a guess founded on a dozen little revelations.

The familiar guilt returned, but the bitter anger remained, making Lord Craythorne seem to pulse red. "I have said you should not mind me, and you are rude to comment on my emotional state, which is no business of yours."

"Then I do not understand why you have always been so forthright and trusting of me," Lydia said. It was as if some force impelled her, causing words to spill over her lips in an uncontrollable flood. "Is it that—"

Lord Craythorne slammed a hand down on the table. "By God, woman, leave off battering me! You understand *nothing*, and if this is what you call keeping others' secrets, I have nothing but disdain for your honor—if indeed you have any."

Lydia sat frozen, staring at his fist on the table. "You are not angry with me," she whispered. "All your guilt and anger are directed at yourself." She stood, her hands shaking, and gripped the edge of the table to still them. His emotions raged, but she was not afraid. "Then you did not kill your wife, after all."

Immediately she cursed herself for a fool. If she was wrong, she was alone in the room with a murderer.

Lord Craythorne's eyes widened. He leaped to his feet. "Kill my—" His lips and cheeks were pale. "Of course I did not kill my wife! What kind of accusation is that?"

"You experience such guilt every time she is mentioned, you and Lady Craythorne," Lydia said. "You disliked your wife, and you showed no regret at her death. You are intelligent and clever enough to manage killing someone with no one being the wiser. But despite all that, you did not kill her, and I would apologize for harboring those suspicions if you did not make it so difficult for me to believe otherwise."

For a moment, fury so intense it staggered her swept over Lord Craythorne. His face reddened, and his jaw clenched so tight Lydia saw a muscle twitch. Sparks flared, and the tabletop burst into flame.

Lydia gasped and jerked her hands away before the fire burned them, shoving backward into her chair. Lord Craythorne stepped back, and for a moment surprise and shame overrode his anger. He tore off his frock coat and used it to beat the flames out, leaving behind the smell of scorched wool and burnt wood and melted lacquer.

Lydia stared at the Duke, telling herself silently that she was in no danger, that she need not fear, but his anger and shame filled her and roused her fears higher. Breathing heavily, she closed her eyes and willed herself calm. She was not afraid, she was not angry, she was a void, empty of emotion and unable to be overwhelmed.

Gradually, the anger ebbed, and Lydia recognized Lord Craythorne controlling his emotions. She opened her eyes and met his gaze. He looked haunted, his eyes wide, his breathing heavy. "I cannot believe I have done anything to encourage you to think so poorly of me," he said in a low voice. "I apologize for losing control of my talent."

That reminded her again of her foolishness. Lydia pushed aside her embarrassment and remaining fear and said, "Some of it was my imaginings, true. But your own emotions betrayed you."

"Guilt, you say?" Lord Craythorne let out a deep breath. "I did feel guilt at the memory of Clarissa. I was guilty of not mourning her death at all, nor the death of her child."

"*Her* child?" Lydia leaped on that. Again, part of her shrieked that she should not intrude so completely on someone else's privacy, but she could no more have stopped the storm raging outside than stop herself.

"How surprising," Lord Craythorne said, wearily resuming his seat. "I had not guessed *that* rumor had not spread." He sighed again, and this time Lydia recognized resignation, the sense of no longer striving to stop the inevitable. "I suppose, since you already believe me a monster, telling you the truth will not diminish me further in your eyes."

Lydia did not protest this statement, though it seemed unfair that he should exaggerate so. She was certain speaking now would stop his confidences entirely.

"It is true, I did not love my wife," Lord Craythorne said, his voice deep and quiet as if despite his words, he was confessing to some terrible sin. "Clarissa Denham was a distant cousin, someone of whom my mother approved. I had never been drawn to any of the women who angled to become Lady Craythorne, and Clarissa was beautiful and well-spoken and seemed interested in me for more than my wealth and title. I believed I needed to marry so as to produce an heir, and she would do as well as anyone." He let out a low, bitter laugh. "And now your opinion of me is no doubt lower than before."

That, Lydia could not permit to pass unchallenged. "You know I put no stock in romance, your Grace. I see nothing wrong with marrying for reasons other than love, if there is respect between you."

"You will have to judge for yourself if that is true." Lord Craythorne bowed his head and looked at his hands resting on the table, loosely clasped with the fingers entwined. The signet ring for once did not catch the light, as that side of him was in shadow. "It did not take long for Clarissa's true nature to be revealed. Every gentle behavior on her part, every tenderness, had been a sham intended to entice me into marrying her. Had she been indifferent to me from the beginning, I would not have minded, as I was indifferent to her, but her pretended affection was supplanted by disdain, and that I could not endure. We did not separate, but I spent more and more of my time away."

Lydia nodded, silently encouraging him to continue, but he said nothing as he struggled to master the emotions warring within him, anger and bitter resentment and humiliation twined with guilt.

"There came a time," he finally said, "when she approached me in affection, claiming to wish to mend what was broken between us. I am ashamed to say I believed her. Shortly thereafter, she told me she was with child, and after that she resumed her cold, disdainful manner, rejecting any overtures I made to unite us for the sake of the child. It did not take much intelligence to guess what had happened."

Lydia had seen it, too. "She was unfaithful, and the child was not yours, but she intended to make you believe otherwise."

"I could not discover the identity of her lover, and of course she would claim fidelity," Lord Craythorne said, "and I could not endure the scandal if I chose to cast her off. I hated the very sight of her, so I left—those whispers, the ones criticizing me for my coldness, those I could bear. I was in London when she neared her confinement at my country estate, and I was nowhere near when she gave birth to a stillborn son and died shortly after."

He shook his head slowly, and now terrible, aching guilt flooded through him. "I was so relieved at being rid of a terrible burden, and then I felt guilt at being glad of two deaths. How hardened must one be to feel so!"

"Not hardened," Lydia said. "You trusted, and were betrayed, and she put all the burden of the consequences of that betrayal on you."

"That is quite the reversal on your part," Lord Craythorne said bitterly. "Since moments ago you believed me a murderer."

Lydia blushed. "I admit I permitted my imagination to carry me away somewhat, but your emotions and your demeanor were such—no, I will only apologize for my suspicions, not justify them."

Lord Craythorne nodded. "They were not completely unfounded," he admitted, "at least, I can imagine what a Discerner would make of my guilt."

Lydia chose not to go into detail about the many elements of his character that had contributed to her wrong conclusion. "I see now why Mr. Donne's poem appeals to you," she said. "Betrayal makes one wary of being betrayed again. But it is perfectly ridiculous that you assume *every* woman is potentially like your late wife."

"I do not assume that," Lord Craythorne protested. "I have never treated you, for example, with less than respect."

"Very well, every woman who shows an interest in you," Lydia persisted. "They cannot all be potential adulteresses."

Lord Craythorne's eyes widened. Then he laughed. "Miss Wescott, that is the kind of indelicate talk my mother would reprimand you for."

"I can be far less delicate if I choose, your Grace," Lydia said. "And indelicacy is called for when someone is far gone in a delusion. You should not be so afraid."

"I, afraid?" Bewilderment rather than anger at her attack filled Lord Craythorne. "How is a reluctance to be betrayed a second time fear?"

"Because you remember the heartache you felt the first time, and you fear experiencing it again. But fear is no basis for making decisions, your Grace. Trust me. I know whereof I speak."

"I imagine you do," Lord Craythorne said. "But you cannot expect me to marry someone who I know feels only indifference or a rapacity for my title and fortune. Those are precisely the conditions that led to the previous disaster."

"You know I will not tell you to wait for true love," Lydia said. "But most women are faithful to their marriage vows even when they do not love. And—" She hesitated, then made a decision. "If it will ease your mind, I will Discern the emotions of the ladies you might court, and I will tell you which ones are well-disposed toward you."

Surprise shot through Lord Craythorne, and then he smiled and clasped Lydia's hand. His grip was warm, and firm, and the touch of his hand eased Lydia's heart. "You are a true friend to suggest it," he said, "but that would be a terrible intrusion into their privacy, much as I am tempted to accept."

"I do not believe in keeping secrets that hurt others, your Grace, and I see no reason those ladies should expect—"

"Thank you, but no." Lord Craythorne released her. "I fear you are correct, and I have fallen into self-indulgent ways of thinking. Of course it is wrong to attribute evil to others simply because they share characteristics with one who was venal and wanton."

"That is more reasonable, your Grace." Lord Craythorne's emotions were once more muted, and she gradually regained an aware-ness of everyone else in the house. She noted how close some of the servants were, and for a moment feared someone had overheard that conversation, but she Discerned only ordinary boredom and placidity mingled with a few who were keenly intent on an errand. She felt at peace herself, and was surprised to discover how unsettling believing Lord Craythorne was a murderer had been.

Impulsively, she added, "Perhaps you should study a poet other than Mr. Donne, so as to be guided to better behavior."

That elicited more laughter. "I see it is time you were introduced to Herrick and Marvell," Lord Craythorne said.

"So long as they do not write of flowers and rainbows and dancing sylphs, I will not mind," Lydia replied.

CHAPTER 20

IN WHICH THE LIMITS OF DISCERNMENT ARE TESTED

T he following morning, Ellery's cheerfulness was greater than usual, but Lydia held her tongue, recalling her earlier mistake regarding Ellery's feelings for James who was not yet her beau. She wished so much to join in her maid's happiness, perhaps share confidences, but she had made a resolution to be more circumspect. Sometimes keeping secrets was so difficult.

"Miss," Ellery said as she brushed Lydia's hair, "you must know how I feel." Her sense of subdued excitement and cheerfulness rose.

"I have said I should not comment, and I will not, except to say that your happiness satisfies me," Lydia said.

"I do not mind this time, miss, because I am so very happy I declare I might burst!" Ellery lowered the hairbrush. "James has all but told me he harbors a deep affection for me, possibly even love, and I— oh, miss, I believe I love him, too!"

"That is wonderful!" Lydia turned and clasped Ellery's hand, the one not holding the hairbrush. "I am so happy for you, except—what do you mean he has all but told you? Has he not yet spoken?"

"He is quite shy, and does not speak openly of matters near his heart." Ellery smiled, a somewhat misty, faraway expression. "But I see it in his eyes, and hear it in his voice when he tells me he would rather be with me than anyone else."

"Oh, I see." Lydia turned back so she was facing the mirror. Ellery still looked radiantly happy. "That does sound rather definitive. Well, I hope he gathers the courage to address you directly. How very satisfying to receive a declaration of love!"

"I believed you did not care for love, miss." Ellery resumed her brushing.

"I have yet to meet any man whose attraction to me is something more profound for me than physical," Lydia said. "And I am not certain I would not be overwhelmed by love of the romantic sort. Better for me to avoid the question entirely."

She remembered chastising Lord Craythorne for ascribing evil motives to every woman because of his wife's infidelity, and guilt briefly struck her. She was in the habit of dismissing all men because of the few who lusted after her, and how was that different from Lord Craythorne's behavior?

She regarded James closely when he brought a footstool to Lady Craythorne's drawing room an hour later. He was unexpectedly intent on his task, alert in a way Lydia did not believe such a simple thing required. Then she caught him glancing at her, and his interest sharpened. He felt no attraction to her, so it was not that kind of interest, but Lydia could not explain it.

She went on Discerning his emotions after he had made his bow and left. He remained intent on his tasks, which she found laudable—perhaps he was as ambitious as Ellery had said. And perhaps his interest in Lydia was an extension of his interest in her maid. It would be natural for him to be curious about the woman his love served. Lydia resolved to find a moment to speak to James and Discern his feelings for Ellery. Ellery was clever, but she had at least once given her heart to an unsuitable man, so her judgment might not be entirely sound where James was concerned. Lydia wished too much for Ellery's happiness to take chances.

That reminded her of her offer to Discern the emotions of the ladies Lord Craythorne might court. She saw nothing amiss in spying out their secret feelings when that might spare her friend some pain.

Still, he had refused, so she intended to honor his wishes. She was so glad Lady Dorothea had abandoned her goal of winning his hand in marriage—or was it only women's hands that could be won? In any case, she liked both Lady Dorothea and Lord Craythorne, and wished happiness for them, and she was convinced neither of them would be happy with one another.

She played for Lady Craythorne for a time, popular songs of love she had not guessed Lady Craythorne would care for. Her Grace sat at a table with a writing desk, by her emotions intent on writing ordinary letters of thanks or invitation. Lydia appreciated the peace of the morning. Lady Craythorne had not chastised her, or brought up once more the subject of Lydia's association with Lord Craythorne and how inappropriate it appeared. Lydia might almost believe they were friends, the sort of friends who could sit quietly together and not need to speak.

She Discerned the approach of the servant before Trask appeared in the doorway, bearing a folded note he offered to Lydia. Lydia stopped playing mid-phrase and took it from the salver.

"Whoever is writing to you, Miss Wescott?" Lady Craythorne asked.

"It is Mrs. Ruskin," Lydia replied. "She asks the pleasure of my company for tea this afternoon."

"*Your* company?" Lady Craythorne was surprised rather than affronted at being left out. "Why should Mrs. Ruskin single you out?"

"I believe this is in regards to the conversation we had the other day, when we spoke of needlework. Mrs. Ruskin is an accomplished needlewoman and promised to show me some of her art." Lydia folded the paper and set it on the pianoforte cabinet.

Lady Craythorne's surprise ebbed. "Then of course you must accept. Trask, one moment while Miss Wescott writes a response." She rose from the writing desk.

Lydia chose not to be annoyed at Lady Craythorne's presumption. It was not as if she had intended to refuse. In fact, Mrs. Ruskin's invitation excited her. She had liked the woman's forthrightness, and anticipated the possibility that they might become friends despite the difference in their ages.

She swiftly wrote a reply and handed it to Trask, who bowed and left the room. "Perhaps I should have asked if you might join us," she said.

"That would be extremely inappropriate," Lady Craythorne said sharply. "As if the Dowager Duchess of Craythorne need go begging for invitations!"

The dismissiveness of her words contrasted so starkly with the regret that filled her and was so much at odds with her true emotions that Lydia lost patience. She swiftly checked to see that no one was within earshot and said, "Your Grace, why must you speak so harshly when it is not what you truly feel?"

Surprise, and then anger, coursed through the Dowager Duchess. "You dare turn your talent on me, after all I have done to welcome you into this household? Such impertinence!"

"I dare because you are unhappy, and you do not know how to stop yourself speaking this way," Lydia said. "You do not wish to be cruel, but you have fallen into habits of speech you regret, and then you berate yourself privately for them. I wish I could help."

The anger faded, replaced by that deep regret Lydia had Discerned so frequently. But Lady Craythorne's lips were a thin, taut white line, and she glared at Lydia as if Lydia were her worst enemy. "I have not asked for your help," she said coldly, "and I refuse to be taught by a girl who knows nothing of the world. My emotions are my own business and none of yours."

"See, you are doing it now," Lydia said. She ought to stop, but she knew she was right, and that rightness compelled her to go on speaking. "I cannot help but perceive your regrets. Sometimes it is necessary to chastise others, and that is a satisfying emotion, so perhaps you—"

Lady Craythorne shot to her feet. "I will hear no more of your nonsense. Leave me at once, and do not return."

Lydia rose from the table and curtseyed. "I will leave," she said, "but I wish you would consider my words." She left the drawing room before Lady Craythorne could say anything else.

As she retreated to her bedchamber, she continued to Discern Lady Craythorne's emotions. Anger and frustration and sorrow tangled within the lady, filling Lydia with regret. She should not have pressed so hard. Lady Craythorne's emotions truly were none of her business. It surprised her to discover that most of her regret was tied to a desire to ease Lady Craythorne's pain. She had not realized she liked the Dowager Duchess so much. But the lady was in many ways like Lady Dorothea; both women were trapped by circumstances outside their control, and both responded by lashing out at those around them. Lydia could not help but be compassionate.

She spent the rest of the morning walking in the garden. The storm had passed, leaving the skies clear, and while the air was still chilly, it lacked the bite yesterday's wind had had. When she finally became uncomfortably cold, she retreated to the library and spent an hour paging through the book of watercolors, admiring the many creatures the unknown artist had drawn and colored so beautifully. Now that Lord Craythorne had pointed it out, she saw that the binding was hand-sewn and might easily be removed to separate the pages. It was tempting to do so, and perhaps choose one or two of her favorites to frame and hang in her bedroom. But she refrained. The book belonged to Lord Craythorne, not to her.

At three o'clock she admired the scenery as the driver steered the carriage through Washington's streets. They drove past mansions similar to Lord Craythorne's, all of them set well back from the street and guarded by hedges and gates. Lydia caught only glimpses of most of them. She had considered walking to Mrs. Ruskin's house, so as to see the mansions more closely, but it was far enough away that a walk would have taken most of an hour and caused her to return after dark.

She was aware of James, hanging on behind; his emotions were keenly anticipatory again, with a surprising intensity of emotion as if he were looking forward to a long-awaited treat. Lydia contemplated his emotions and wished he were within the carriage so she might interrogate him, though of course that would be inappropriate. Instead, she conjured stories to explain his emotional intensity. She hoped his anticipation related to seeing Ellery that evening. Perhaps he intended to finally declare his love! That would be truly satisfying.

The Ruskin home was smaller than Lord Craythorne's mansion, but still beautiful, built of red brick that made an attractive contrast to the white pillars fronting the door, also white, and the white gables overlooking the front garden. James assisted Lydia out and walked before her to knock on the door. They waited long enough that Lydia had almost decided to ask him about his emotions—obliquely, of course—but then the door opened, and a man dressed not as sprucely as Trask always appeared ushered Lydia inside.

She gave the butler her pelisse and was grateful to be rid of it, for the house was extremely warm, almost as warm as if this were a summer day rather than the end of March. It looked warm, as well, with walls painted a deep red and floorboards whose brown stain had a hint of red that matched the walls. An arrangement of dried flowers in a tall floor vase shifted in the breeze created by the door closing, drawing Lydia's eye; they were red poppies, their color only slightly dimmed from being dried, surrounded by pale stalks bearing tiny cream-colored flowers Lydia did not recognize. It was pretty, but in a formal, distant way, and Lydia was not sure she liked it.

The butler ushered her upstairs, where she soon was out of range of James' emotions. They had become curious as well as eager, but she was familiar with James' usual curiosity about new situations and hoped only that he might be given refreshment in the kitchen so at least some of his curiosity would be satisfied.

The first floor hallway was not so warm as the entrance, but still verged on uncomfortable. Portraits of men and women resembling Mr. Ruskin in the chin and forehead lined the hall on one side, their varying costumes reflecting changing fashions over the centuries. Lydia had not imagined colonial families extending quite so far back, but those families had come from England originally, and suppose their lineages were as long and storied as anyone who had remained in England? It was not at all unlikely.

The butler opened a door about halfway down the hall and bowed. "Mrs. Ruskin, Miss Wescott," he said in a low, gravelly voice.

Lydia entered and made her curtsey to Mrs. Ruskin, who was just standing from her seat near the fire. *This* room was positively an oven, with the fire burning hotly and the west-facing windows letting in warm sunlight while blocking the wind. Lydia's skin felt parched, and she refrained from inelegantly licking her lips to moisten them. But Mrs. Ruskin showed no sign of discomfort.

"Miss Wescott, how good of you to come," she said with a smile. "Pray have a seat, and be comfortable. I hope you remain well."

"I am well, thank you, Mrs. Ruskin," Lydia said. Mrs. Ruskin's eager anticipation was similar to James's, though beneath that Lydia Discerned the lady's usual self-satisfaction and confidence. "Thank you for inviting me."

"I so rarely find a kindred spirit in my chosen art." Mrs. Ruskin sat opposite Lydia and settled her skirts. "Many ladies are skilled with the needle, but few of them see embroidery as anything but a socially acceptable pastime, or an arrow in their quiver, so to speak. One of many ladylike pursuits one may boast of."

"I have noticed this myself," Lydia said. "I wish it were otherwise. I have seen gowns displayed in a museum in London, a collection of royal gowns, that is, and the needlework is quite fine—every bit as much a work of art as a painting or sculpture."

"I daresay no one perceives it as such because clothing is ultimately utilitarian, and not as overtly artistic." Mrs. Ruskin tugged on a bell rope near to hand. "But I admit I did not ask you here solely to discuss needlework, though that was my primary purpose. Let me call for tea, and I will share my other interest in speaking with you."

Lydia, curious, remained silent as Mrs. Ruskin spoke with the maid who answered the bell. Mrs. Ruskin did not seem to have anything sinister in mind, nor could Lydia imagine why she might do so. She showed no furtiveness the way she would if she meant to discuss something secret or forbidding, and again, Lydia could not guess what of that nature Mrs. Ruskin might be interested in.

The maid brought the tea tray, and Mrs. Ruskin poured for both herself and Lydia and invited Lydia to help herself to thinly-sliced sandwiches smaller than her palm. Lydia set her cup and saucer on the nearest low table and nibbled her food. Her curiosity had grown intense. "I beg your pardon," she said, "but you cannot expect me to eat when you are being so mysterious."

Mrs. Ruskin sipped her tea and watched the maid bustle about, arranging cakes. When the girl curtseyed and left the room, Mrs. Ruskin set aside her cup and said, "Have you no idea what I have in mind?"

"None at all, Mrs. Ruskin."

"That is very interesting." Mrs. Ruskin's eyes narrowed. "I believed an Extraordinary Discerner's talent encompassed knowing secrets."

Lydia dropped her sandwich onto her lap. "I beg your pardon?"

"You shouldn't fear, I will not tell, since you have done so much to conceal your talent." Mrs. Ruskin remained as intent as ever, her emotions fixed on discovering new knowledge. "I hoped you would confide in me now that I have shown I can keep a secret. Can you truly not tell what I am thinking?"

"I Discern emotions, not thoughts," Lydia said, reacting without thinking. "But—how do you know?"

"I fear not everyone in the Duke's household is as circumspect as they might be," Mrs. Ruskin said. "The information came to me in a roundabout way that surprised me. I cannot imagine why you would need to conceal your talent, though. It seems, forgive me, almost underhanded."

"I prefer my privacy, and I dislike being stared at," Lydia lied, grateful that Mrs. Ruskin could not perceive the lie. "Please, tell me who shared my secret with you."

"I understand," Mrs. Ruskin said. "Of course you would not like to be considered an oddity. Is it true you are capable of Discerning when someone lies, though? Because that, to me, seems a very useful ability."

"I can. Mrs. Ruskin, I must know who told you of my talent."

Mrs. Ruskin sipped her tea again. "The person revealed the truth accidentally, and I would not like that person to suffer for a mistake."

"Nevertheless." Lydia suppressed anger over this betrayal. She should not permit herself to be overwhelmed.

"Very well. It was your lady's maid, Maud Ellery." Mrs. Ruskin said this as calmly as if she had asked Lydia to pass the sandwiches.

"That is a lie," Lydia said instantly. "Why do you try to conceal things from me?"

Mrs. Ruskin smiled, and her self-satisfaction surged. "A test," she said. "I wished to see for myself what an Extraordinary Discerner is capable of."

"I am not a plaything, Mrs. Ruskin," Lydia said. She stood. "And I do not believe we have anything more to say to one another. Good day."

She turned to leave, and Mrs. Ruskin said, "Wait. Please."

Despite herself, Lydia paused. She eyed Mrs. Ruskin, who was the picture of a penitent woman, though she felt no such emotion. "What am I to wait for?"

"Please forgive my rudeness," Mrs. Ruskin said. "You are correct, I should not have treated you so shabbily, but it is true I am curious about your talent and its extent, because I have need of it—if it can do what I hope."

Lydia considered this. She did not like Mrs. Ruskin's continuing eagerness, which now seemed like that of someone who has a problem they wish another person to solve. But Mrs. Ruskin must be persuaded to keep Lydia's secret, and how better to persuade her than by putting her in Lydia's debt? "Very well, I will listen," she said.

"Thank you," Mrs. Ruskin said. "If you will step over to the lamp, I will explain my problem."

Lydia, puzzled, did as she was asked. The wall near the lamp was covered with palm-size portraits in gilded oval frames. "Do you see the painting of the young man in the center? The one with blond hair?" Mrs. Ruskin asked.

"I do," Lydia said. The young man was extremely attractive, with a well-shaped nose and chin and blue eyes the painter had captured perfectly.

"Please bring it to me," Mrs. Ruskin said.

Lydia unhooked the portrait from the wall and brought it back to where Mrs. Ruskin sat. Mrs. Ruskin accepted it and looked at it in silence for several moments. "This is my cousin Elwin," she said. "He is a dear boy, but has fallen in with the worst company. I fear he has given himself over to riotous living."

Lydia took a long drink of tea and cleared her throat. "I fail to see where I enter into your cousin's problem."

"I have heard ordinary Discerners can question someone while touching that person and Discern not only that they lie, but what the lie conceals. Am I correct that Extraordinary Discerners can do the same, but without the need for a touch?"

"That is true." Lydia wondered briefly if she ought to give this woman information, and then she decided that so long as Mrs. Ruskin knew the truth of her talent, there was no point dissembling about the rest of it.

"Elwin has been accused of stealing a valuable object by one of his so-called friends. He claims he is innocent of the theft, and I believe him. His sins are many, but he is not a thief." Mrs. Ruskin drew in a deep breath. "I hoped you might be able to identify the actual thief."

Lydia drank again to give herself a moment to consider. "I can prove that your cousin did not steal the object," she finally said, "but unless the real thief is within range of my Discernment, I cannot simply pluck that knowledge from the air. And as I prefer to remain anonymous, I am not certain how I can help you." Weariness flooded through her, as if Mrs. Ruskin's request were a physical and not an emotional burden.

Mrs. Ruskin dabbed at her eyes with her fingertips. "I see," she said, her voice choked with tears. "Then there is no hope for Elwin, no hope at all."

Uncomfortable, Lydia said, "There are many other possibilities. The law—" She stopped, arrested by her sense of Mrs. Ruskin's emotions. "You are not sad," she said. "You do not feel..." Her voice trailed off as dizziness struck her, and she swayed, dropping her teacup to spill across the carpet.

Mrs. Ruskin regarded her calmly. "You are not as fragile as you appear," she said, self-satisfaction surging through her. "Nor is your talent as refined as I had imagined. But after Mr. Hughes' death, we cannot take risks that you have not already discovered our secret."

"You lied to me," Lydia said. Her words came out hoarse, as if she had swallowed acid rather than tea. "It is impossible."

"I have always been an excellent liar," Mrs. Ruskin said, pride filling her as if she had accomplished something noble. "A Discerner I knew said I believed the lies I told so they were opaque to his Discernment when I chose them to be. It was the last thing he ever said."

Lydia gripped the armrest of the sofa to keep herself upright. Her tongue felt swollen to twice its normal size, and the room spun like a top around her. "What—" she mumbled. "What have you done?"

Mrs. Ruskin glanced at the portrait in her hand, then casually tossed it aside. "What I must," she said. "Perhaps you know nothing as yet, but Craythorne's meddling will put you in the way of discovering the truth, and now—but I see no reason to tell you more. Not when your knowledge will be irrelevant soon."

"Kill...me..." Lydia gasped.

"Killing you would be difficult to conceal," Mrs. Ruskin said. "No, I have something else in mind." She stood and loomed over Lydia, her body elongated by the spinning of the room. "Something more permanent."

Lydia sagged, unable to support her throbbing head any longer. The spinning had become undulating waves that made her wish she could vomit, but her body was too weak even for that. Mrs. Ruskin pulled the bell rope and then busied herself picking up the fallen teacup and setting it on the saucer. The waves were stronger now, and Lydia closed her eyes to stop them, but the motion was even worse when she was blind.

When she opened her eyes, James was there, bending over her. "James!" she exclaimed, or tried to; it came out in a garbled shout even she could not understand. "James, help me!"

James carefully picked her up, cradling her like a baby, and left the room. She relaxed, confident in James' ability to carry her away from this place. But he was calm—too calm, not agitated or angry or afraid as he should if he were taking her out of danger. Before this could fully terrify her, she heard Mrs. Ruskin say, "James, you know where to take her. Return immediately, and we..."

Lydia's dizziness redoubled, and then her eyes slid shut and she knew no more.

CHAPTER 21

IN WHICH THERE IS DESPAIR, AND HORROR, AND MADNESS

L ydia fell into a deep, troubled dream in which the world rocked and shivered so she was forced to crawl through a spiny black landscape whose needlelike thorns pierced her flesh. Part of her knew it was a dream, because her cries made no noise; the rest of her searched desperately for an exit.

She came to herself so gradually she did not at first know she was awake. The world continued to heave around her. A strong, sour smell filled her nostrils, and between that and the constant movement she felt ill. As she became conscious of the nausea, it surged, and she twisted away from the person holding her and vomited until she was wrung out and empty. She sagged, exhausted, and hands gripped her shoulders and pulled her back into the semi-reclining position she had been in.

Awareness that this was all wrong struck her, and Lydia tried to wrench free of the hands. They held her more tightly despite her struggles. Lydia's vision was clearing, and she blinked up at her captor. It was James.

"Let me go," she whispered, unable to speak more loudly. "James, what are you doing?"

James ignored her. Determination and, faintly, guilt permeated his emotions. Lydia was too frightened to be grateful the drug Mrs. Ruskin had fed her had not diminished her talent. "This is wrong. Release me," she whispered.

Still James ignored her. With a great effort, Lydia turned her head. They were in a carriage, and the jolting motion was that of wheels on a rough surface. She tried to free herself once more, but succeeded only in making herself ill again. She pushed aside fear and made herself Discern her surroundings. There was no one but James and the driver, whose emotions were the dull beige placidity of someone doing a boring but necessary task. No one who might help her.

She closed her eyes and refused to weep. If James meant to kill her —though Mrs. Ruskin had said her death would be inconvenient, and Lydia clung to the hope that this, too, had not been a lie—at any rate, if her death was in the offing, there was nothing she could do at the moment to prevent it. If Mrs. Ruskin had given James other instructions...well, Lydia could do nothing about that, either. She must listen, and observe, and wait for her moment. She would not give in to the fear that said her moment might never come.

The road grew rougher, and soon the carriage stopped. James rearranged his grip on Lydia, and she heard the carriage door open. In his moment of inattention, she wrenched herself out of his hands and threw herself at the open door.

She landed, not on the ground outside, but on the floor of the carriage, her weakened muscles betraying her in her bid for freedom. Her chin hit the floorboards hard enough to send pain pulsing through her head, and she bit her tongue and tasted blood. James, still suffused with nothing more potent than determination, scooped her up and carried her over his shoulder like a sack. His lack of pleasure or even interest in what he was doing frightened her more than anger or lasciviousness would have.

The skies were dark, not with clouds but with sunset, and a chill wind had risen and now ruffled Lydia's gown and hair. They were far from the city, as she Discerned no one near except James and the driver. As she became aware of this, and realized she was farther from help than she had guessed, people came within her range. Their emotions varied from bland beige disinterest to keen interest in a task to a low-grade annoyance as of people having a mild disagreement. Lydia counted them to distract from her fears: sixteen people.

Then she Discerned anger, sharp and red and vicious, and sadness, and deep black despair, more and more hearts given over to terrible emotions the farther James walked. Lydia found she had covered her ears as if emotion could be shut out as easily as sound. As the dark emotions swept over her, she fought to keep herself free of them, but their unrelenting horror battered at her until she screamed a soundless cry of terror.

And in that moment, she knew where James was taking her.

"No! *No!*" she screamed, though all that emerged from her lips was a whistling rattle. She struggled and fought, terror lending her strength. James ignored her attack, shrugging off her fists beating at his back and shoulders. She slammed her forehead against the side of his head in desperation. For a moment, anger sharpened within him, and he shook her like a kitten until she was too dizzy to move and became temporarily blind.

In that state, she heard a door open, and then they were indoors, out of the wind and cold. Lydia's vision cleared, but it did not matter; the room was windowless and unlit by lamp or lantern, and the scant illumination came from very far away. Lydia continued to scream, though she still made no other sound than the rattle. She tried to kick James, but he held her tighter than before. His heavy feet thumped the floorboards, which creaked beneath his weight.

Through the terrible anger and despair, Lydia Discerned the approach of some of the intent people. She twisted, trying to see them, and James struck her on the back of the head and said, "Stop that." Lydia's ears rang from the blow, and she subsided briefly, panting from her exertions.

"What have you brought us, young man?" said someone whose voice was as silky-smooth as Lydia's was not. "She appears to be in the throes of an hysterical fit."

"This letter will explain everything," James said. He slung Lydia off his shoulder and set her down, holding her beneath one arm so she did not collapse. Lydia's head lolled briefly, and then she regained her balance and examined her surroundings, or tried to; she was still dizzy, and she could barely hear over the ringing in her ears.

The silky-voiced man wore a dark frock coat over ordinary pantaloons. He and another man, this one very old and possessed of a thick mane of white hair, were reading a letter that elicited a range of emotions from each. Both were intent on the letter's contents, but the silky-voiced man was filled with exultation and wicked, sinister pleasure, while the white-haired man felt nothing but greed focused on the smaller piece of paper, a banker's draft, that he held.

"Very well," the silky-voiced man said. "She is clearly a danger to herself and others, and we will be sure to confine her safely."

Lydia tried to stand and found her legs would not support her. "No," she said, "this is a mistake, I am not mad!"

Her voice came out louder than a whisper this time, but the two men seemed not to have heard, though in fact satisfaction surged through both of them, an emotion that filled her with despair. She fought to suppress the emotion, but it was too late. Despair overwhelmed her, and with it came the terrible aching emptiness she had hoped never to feel again. When James again picked her up, she did not fight.

Another door opened, and James carried her through it, followed by the two men. More terrible emotions battered at her, fear and anger and misery, tearing her apart until she no longer remembered her name or her identity or anything else. People closed in around her, all of them angry or exasperated, and then their anger was hers, and she forgot everything but the pain.

Fury raged through her, an overwhelming desire to hurt others. She surged upright and was restrained by many hands holding her arms and shoulders, implacable and inescapable no matter how she fought. She threw back her head and screamed out her anger, the thin sound tearing at her throat, then kicked and thrashed until her foot connected with something hard but yielding. One of the men holding her cursed, and her anger sharpened briefly just before he struck her an open-handed blow to the face. The impact made her bite her tongue again, and she spat blood at the man.

The hands lifted her and carried her supine, struggling body down a long, dark hallway. The distant ceiling lay in blackness, untouched by the wanly-burning lanterns that glowed at long intervals along the hall. It might have been three feet away or thirty. More emotions swept over her, fear and anger and dreadful sorrow, passing in waves until her throat was hoarse again from screaming and her body ached from straining against the men's grip.

Hinges squealed, rusty metal grinding against metal, and the men carried her into an unlighted room whose walls her screams echoed off, revealing the room was barely big enough to hold all of them. They deposited her on a bed with a hard, lumpy mattress and held her down as some of them strapped her arms and legs to the frame. Then they were gone, and the door was shut, and she was alone in the darkness.

The anger had passed, replaced by a growing sorrow that began in her chest and spread outward. She breathed heavily, gasping for air that stung her tortured throat, and strained to see anything in the darkness. Her body ached, not just from exertion but from a terrible throbbing weariness. But the physical aches were nothing compared to the emptiness in her heart. She no longer remembered a time when this awful desolation had not filled her to overflowing. She could not even weep, and if she could have, it would not have eased her pain.

Memories crowded in, every horrid thing she had ever done, every mistake she had ever made. A strident voice, criticizing, chastising, demanding she leave because the voice could not bear the sight of her. That person must have done this, sent her to this madhouse. No, that was wrong—or was it? The voice faded in and out, and she could not tell if she heard it with ears or with memory. She no longer remembered what had brought her here.

Occasionally, she heard footsteps passing outside the door, quiet and slow. Aside from the footsteps, she could not tell if time was passing, here in the dark. No windows, no light coming from the door's outline; there was nothing but the endless misery. She imagined she slept for a time, because the pain stopped and then resumed as she jerked out of a deeper blackness. The restraints were unnecessary, because she could not move regardless.

As her memories once more intruded, her sorrow deepened into despair. She longed for oblivion, for freedom from the despair that filled her. If she could truly sleep—but sleep did not come for the asking, not for her. Sleep, or death, anything to free her. Restrained as she was, she could not take her own life.

She became gradually aware that her stomach ached with hunger, though it was a passing realization and not anything that mattered to her. The idea of food sickened her. With that thought, her gorge rose, and she turned her head as her body convulsed, bringing up nothing. When the heaving passed, she gasped for air, her whole body trembling. Her arms and legs ached from how her convulsions had wrenched them against her bonds.

Again, she heard footsteps, these louder and doubled. Two people, one walking normally, the other dragging his feet. A red spark kindled in the center of the emptiness, growing brighter until it filled all of her. The anger swept away the despair, burning through her like fire through dry grass. She strained against her bonds, arching her back, and screamed obscenities, threatening the people walking past with death if they did not release her. She heard nothing over the sound of her own voice, but when she stopped screaming, all was silent. The anger ebbed, replaced once more by despair.

Her wrists and ankles throbbed, but she did not care. Again, the desire for oblivion gripped her. She could not bear much more of this hollow void that pulled at her, whispering to her to fall into its depths. If only she were not tethered to this body, she might lose herself in the void.

After an eternity, footsteps approached again. They were more rapid and louder than before, and this time there were at least three people. She distantly heard voices murmuring dully as if speaking beneath water. Two of the voices sounded agitated, as if they were begging for something. Then she heard, more clearly, a third voice saying, "Open this door or I will burn it down."

The door ground open with that horrid squealing sound, letting in light that hurt her eyes. She squinted and made out three figures backlit by the lamps. She did not recognize any of them through her watery vision.

The same voice said, "Release her. Now."

Hands tugged at the restraints, loosing the buckles. She lay still, breathing shallowly, as a figure crouched beside the bed. "I cannot bear this," she whispered. The anger was returning, hot and vicious, and she tried to rise and found she could not, which infuriated her further.

The man picked her up and stood, cradling her like an infant. His touch was gentle, but rage overcame any pleasure it might have given her. "No!" she shrieked. The word came out thin and without any force behind it, making her throat hurt so badly she coughed and coughed. She battered at the man with both fists, but he did not respond, not even to grab her hands to prevent her doing it again.

Then they were in the hallway, and her new captor was striding rapidly past the few lanterns, making the light pulse in her eyes. The other two men bobbed about, stumbling to keep up. "Your Grace, you cannot—" said one, his voice high-pitched and quavering as if he was quite old. "She is ill, she requires treatment—"

"I question what treatment ever justifies strapping someone to a bed in a windowless, lightless room," her captor said. Anger surged through her again, and she fought to free herself, but the arms carrying her merely tightened.

"You are not qualified to make that judgment, your Grace," said a second voice, this one silky-smooth and reasonable-sounding. "This is a medical matter."

Her fury found expression in another scream. This time, no sound emerged, and her throat felt bathed in acid. She kicked and thrashed, and now her captor stopped and rearranged his grip on her, holding her so firmly she gave up trying to fight him.

"I have no interest in arguing with you," her captor said. "You locked an Extraordinary Discerner in a madhouse filled with those whose emotions are disordered and violent, and I am certain you were paid well to do so. I doubt this was the first time you have accepted money to confine someone who did not deserve it."

"That is a foul accusation," the silky-voiced man said. "And one you cannot prove."

"I would not count on that," her captor said. "I will see to it that this institution is turned upside down in pursuit of the truth. And if she does not recover, I will do everything in my power to see you both destroyed."

He resumed walking, his stride rapid. She listened, but did not hear the other two following. Anger still filled her, and she wished she had the strength to strike—but this man had taken her out of that place, and he did not deserve to be attacked.

The pulsing lights made her ill again, so she closed her eyes and envisioned herself smashing the lamps, imagined punching and throttling the man with the silky voice until he was as raw-throated as she. Far from soothing her, her imaginings roused her anger higher until she was sure she might have battered her captor despite her resolve if her stupid body were not so weak.

Two more doors opened, and she heard more voices, exclaiming and then screaming. The smell of smoke reached her nose, but when she opened her eyes, she saw no flame, just her captor's chest and the underside of his chin. He was dressed like a gentleman in frock coat and cravat, but his grip was that of someone accustomed to physical labor. She closed her eyes again. She believed she should know him, but she was too angry to remember small details like names.

Another door opened, and this time a cool, brisk wind blew across her face, ruffling her gown and her hair. Instinctively she opened her eyes, but beyond her captor she saw only blue skies. She tried to turn her head, but exhaustion made it impossible. The wind swept away whatever smells there were, preventing her from identifying her location that way, and even the building they had exited was visible only in glimpses of dark brick and a few small, miserly windows. The scent of her captor was all she smelled, crisp and clean, and although she did not know who held her, the familiarity of his scent gave her a moment's peace, as if despite everything, he meant her no harm.

Her captor sped his pace, and she closed her eyes against the jouncing. Then his grip on her slackened, and she tilted, and without thinking she grabbed the front of his frock coat to keep herself from falling. In the next moment, they were in shadow, and she opened her eyes to see the inside of a carriage.

Her captor said only, "Go," and the carriage jerked into motion. She fought him, still furious, but he held her tightly and said, "I apologize for the impropriety, but you are too weak to sit unaided."

She realized she was sprawled on his lap, and fury surged again, but once more she was too weak to fight. "I will kill you," she whispered, her throat aching. "I will tear you apart."

"I know," the man said. "Forgive me."

She did not understand his meaning, and in her anger she did not care.

CHAPTER 22

IN WHICH LORD CRAYTHORNE SUGGESTS AN UNEXPECTED SOLUTION TO AN IMPOSSIBLE SITUATION

Eventually, she opened her eyes in the hope she might see something that would tell her where they were. Her captor was not looking at her, she discovered, but out the window. Gradually, her anger ebbed, replaced in dizzying succession by waves of frustration and sadness and excitement and pleasure that tugged her in all directions like a dozen warring tides. The emotions fought within her, and finally she wept, sobbing for no reason she understood.

The man still said nothing, merely held her close, his hand cradling her head, as she clutched the front of his coat and buried her face in his chest. She inhaled the clean scent of his soap once more, and again memory hinted that she should know him, but even his embrace did not comfort her. Aching misery, not the dread emptiness but a terrible longing for peace, filled her. She felt as if she had lost something, but she did not know what, whether it was a treasured possession or a friendship or someone she loved who was now dead. Whatever she had lost, she was certain she would never find it again, and she would mourn its loss for the rest of her life.

The carriage came to an abrupt halt, but the man did not move. "Do you know yourself?" he asked.

She could not imagine what he meant. She had no self, no identity;

224

she was nothing but the sum of her emotions. The anger was returning, and she fought against it. She would rather be swallowed up in the
pain of terrible loss than hurt this man.

After another moment, the man gathered her into his arms and
carefully maneuvered her out of the carriage. She clung to him again,
tears running down her cheeks though she no longer wept so harshly as
she had before. The noise of a city came to her ears, the movement of
carriages and horses, the low murmur of voices. Another door opened,
and the man's boots rang out on tile. She heard a gasp, and then
running feet shod in softer shoes. The man's grip shifted, and his gait
changed, bobbing in a way that told her they were ascending stairs.

More footsteps, not quite running, and several more gasps. A
woman said, "What on earth—"

"Clear the house," the man said. "Everyone leaves, down to the
boot boy."

"Clear the—Oliver, have you gone mad?" The woman's voice was
tremulous and low, but she sounded appalled rather than confused.

The man let out a short, harsh laugh. "It is not my madness you
should be concerned with," he said. "I need this house empty. Get as
far from it as you can. I will tell you when you can return."

"Oliver, you cannot make such demands without an explanation."

The man stopped. "Mother, do as I say and I will explain later," he
said, his voice harsh.

She opened her eyes and saw both the man and the woman bending
over her, with more women hovering at the edge of her vision. The
woman looked horrified. The man's jaw was tight and his lips thin with
anger. Her anger rose again, and she whispered, "Kill you all."

The woman gasped and recoiled. The man did not wait for a
response, merely turned and strode down a hall that smelled distantly
of roses. Before she could move or attempt to struggle free again, he
wrenched a door open and slammed it closed behind both of them.

In the next moment, he deposited her on a bed, much softer than
the one she had recently occupied. She opened her eyes on a midnight-
blue canopy stretched across four posters, its folds tied back on one
side. She was no longer angry, but confusion and fear and annoyance
swept through her, and she found she was curled in a tight ball,

breathing raggedly and staring at her knees. She heard nothing from the man, but the door had not opened a second time, so she presumed he was still there, watching her.

Gradually, her breathing calmed, and the wild tangle of emotion that had disordered her senses dissipated. Her whole body ached as if she had been beaten, though she did not remember being struck, aside from that one blow to the face.

That blow to the face. She had been so angry, and she had kicked that person, and he had struck her. Why had she been so angry? She did not remember anything that might have caused her such fury.

She uncurled and lay on her back, staring up at the canopy. With half the curtains pulled across the bed, it was a comfortingly secure nest, not terrible and confining like that little room. She could not remember why they had put her there. Surely she had done nothing to warrant such treatment? She was—

In a flash, memory returned. She was Lydia Wescott. She was an Extraordinary Discerner. And she had been overwhelmed into madness by emotions she could not fight. She had lost her awareness of herself, and she might have stayed that way forever had she not been rescued.

With an effort, she rolled onto her side, facing away from the curtains. Lord Craythorne sat in a chair near the door, staring at his loosely clasped hands. "Are you well?" Lydia asked, her voice raspy.

Lord Craythorne's head rose, and he regarded Lydia with astonishment. "Am *I* well?" he exclaimed. "What kind of question is that, Miss Wescott? Are *you* well?"

Lydia considered her state. "I am myself again, which is like being well—better than being well. But I am uninjured, if that is what you mean."

"As it happens, I referred to your emotional state and your Discernment." Lord Craythorne's hands gripped one another more tightly. "But the question of whether or not you were physically abused is important, too, as it influences exactly how much hell I intend to rain down upon that institution. Forgive my language."

"They did not hurt me." Memories of lying bound and alone in the darkness tried to intrude, and she pushed them away, focusing instead on the softness of the blanket and the give of the mattress. "I realize now—you cleared the house. How did you know that would restore me?"

"I recalled what you told me once about your Discernment range, and I made a guess that isolation would free you of entanglement with others' emotions. Though I hoped one person's presence would not matter, as I did not believe you should be left alone."

"You do not distress me," Lydia said. "You are in control of your emotions to a remarkable extent."

Lord Craythorne bowed his head again. "Not always. I was furious when I found you in that state, and I am aware my anger affected you. I must ask your forgiveness for that, as well."

Lydia blushed, remembering the threats and obscenities she had poured out. "I believed I had better control than that. I am so afraid, now. I cannot live my life isolated from everyone else, and yet suppose I am unexpectedly overwhelmed again?"

"I have no answer for you," Lord Craythorne said. "You remain the strongest-willed person I have ever met, and yet your control, forgive me, is imperfect. Perhaps you need a different approach."

"What approach would that be?"

Lord Craythorne smiled wryly. "If I knew, I assure you I would tell you immediately." His smile faded. "I hope it does not distress you if I admit you frightened me. You were nothing like yourself."

"No. I was mad." Lydia considered her words and decided they were no threat to her sanity. "I was deliberately made so."

"Yes." Lord Craythorne's anger flared briefly. "I hope you know what happened to you, and why James Parker decided to abduct you, presumably on Mr. Ruskin's orders."

Lydia swallowed, winced at the pain in her throat, and pushed herself to a sitting position. "It was not him. It was Mrs. Ruskin."

Lord Craythorne shot upright. "*Mrs.* Ruskin?" For a moment, sheer surprise overrode all his other emotions.

Lydia nodded. "James was in her pay, though I do not know whether he entered this household as her man or was suborned. Mrs. Ruskin drugged me, and James took me to that madhouse." Memories, these free of anything but confusion, returned piece by piece, and she paused to knit them together. "Mrs. Ruskin knows I am an Extraordinary Discerner. She told me someone in this household had revealed the secret, but I cannot trust anything she said, because I was incapable of Discerning her lies."

"I believed that was impossible," Lord Craythorne said.

Lydia shook her head. "It is just extremely rare. Some men and women are possessed of a kind of madness that does not show in their behavior. They lie, and in that moment they believe the lie, and of course a Discerner cannot detect a lie the speaker believes to be true. Mrs. Ruskin is one such—it makes me ill to remember all the times I have spoken with her and believed her to be amiable and honest." She put her hands over her face and sighed. "I cannot even say I have been a fool, for there was no reason to suspect her."

"There was not," Lord Craythorne agreed. "But why would she want you incapacitated, possibly permanently? For if you had stayed there very long, you would have become incurably mad, is that not so?"

Lydia raised her head. "That would take many years, so do not believe what I perceive in you, that you might have come too late. And the truth is, I do not know for certain her reasons for wishing me hidden where no one might find me. But she said, first, that she could not count on me not discovering 'their' secret—she did not say who 'they' are—and, second, that your meddling would put me in the way of that discovery. So I can guess."

"Mrs. Ruskin must be one of the Libertymen," Lord Craythorne said. "Based on what we found at the Ruskin home, I believe Mr. Ruskin is as well." He rose and paced from the chair to the hearth, where he gripped the mantel with one hand and bowed his head to stare at the grate where a fire burned low. Firelight gilded his curls and the tips of his eyelashes. "And I merrily put you in their path. I have been a fool."

"Do not fall into that trap," Lydia said sharply. "We neither of us had any way of knowing where that danger lay. Women such as Mrs. Ruskin are terribly rare, and if they are clever, they do not give themselves away. This is not anything we could have predicted."

"You did not see what you looked like when I brought you out of that place," Lord Craythorne said. "I swore you would not be in danger, and I failed utterly—"

"Stop being tedious, your Grace," Lydia said. "Express your regret if you must, because you did not wish me to be harmed, but if you intend to wallow in self-pity, I will—" She paused, searching for an appropriate punishment. "I will subject you to the worst poetry I can find, and as I have no literary sensibilities, that will likely be quite vile poetry indeed."

Lord Craythorne raised his head, his eyes wide. Then he laughed, a short, curt sound that nevertheless eased Lydia's heart. "You fill me with dread, Miss Wescott," he said. "Very well. I apologize for failing to protect you, and that is the last I will say on the matter. Though had you suffered permanent damage—no. No more."

He resumed his seat near the door. "So, the Ruskins. They were not home when I arrived there, and I imagine that means they have left for good."

"Will you tell me what happened? Or, I suppose, what appears to have happened from your perspective? For there is much I do not understand."

Lord Craythorne let out that short, sharp laugh again. "Nor do I, but perhaps we might put our stories together and learn something we may act on." He ran a hand through his brown curls, disordering them. "Very well. The first anyone knew you were gone was at suppertime two nights ago, when you did not come downstairs. Your maid knew you had left to visit Mrs. Ruskin as planned, but nothing else. A little searching turned up the fact that James and the carriage had not returned."

"I forgot to ask after the driver. Was he a part of the scheme?"

"I fear not. The messenger I sent to the Ruskins' house inquiring after all of you was told by Mr. Ruskin that you had left an hour previously. But that messenger is one of my informants, and naturally suspicious, and those suspicions were roused when he saw the carriage you had taken still on the Ruskins' property. A little more investigating turned up the body of the driver, hidden behind the carriage house. My informant immediately reported in, and I collected several armed men and returned to the Ruskins' house in search of you and James.

We did not at that time suspect he was involved; rather, I believed him to be another victim."

Lydia's hand flew up to hold in a gasp of horror. "That poor driver."

"Yes, and that is another thing I will hold the Ruskins accountable for," Lord Craythorne said grimly. "At that time, we were informed that the Ruskins were not home. My men and I forced an entrance and challenged the remaining servants, who pleaded ignorance, but eventually one of the upstairs maids confessed to having seen James carry you out of the house, unconscious, and into one of the Ruskins' carriages. We learned the Ruskins and several of their servants departed shortly thereafter without revealing their destination."

"So not all of the servants were involved," Lydia said. "But how did you find me, if James was gone and the remaining servants knew nothing?"

"I enlisted one of the Seers at the Viceroy's palace to Dream of your location, and that Seer produced a drawing of the madhouse that I presented to everyone I met while at the palace. One of the Parliamentary aides recognized it and was able to direct me." Lord Craythorne's anger rose again, but he looked at Lydia and apparently saw her distress, for he controlled himself almost immediately. "You were there for over thirty-six hours."

"It felt like much longer, and like no time at all, if that makes sense." Lydia drew in a deep, calming breath and let it out slowly. "Poor Ellery."

"What is wrong with Ellery?"

"Oh, it is only that she trusted James, and I believe she loves him, and he may have—" A horrid thought struck her. "We still do not know who told Mrs. Ruskin about my talent. Suppose someone here is still her secret informant?"

"When you are fully recovered, we will question the staff, but I believe we will find that the culprit was James. Servants go everywhere, and even you cannot be aware of their presence at all times." Lord Craythorne tried vainly to tidy his hair. "James could not have been her man from the beginning. He came from my Derbyshire estate with the others and did not know Mrs. Ruskin before arriving in America. I am not sure whether that is better, or worse, but I am inclined to say it is irrelevant whether he was introduced into my household as a spy, or bought by Mrs. Ruskin later."

"I suppose that is true. Still, it is very hard on Maud—on Ellery, because suppose he only pretended to care for her so she would tell him things about me? Or—" Horror filled Lydia. "Mrs. Ruskin claimed Ellery was the informant, and I Discerned that as a lie—but she was capable of deceiving me, and—oh, your Grace, if Ellery—"

"We will learn that as well. Do not fear, Miss Wescott." Lord Craythorne cleared his throat. "I fear we have a worse problem."

"What could possibly be worse than harboring a spy and a traitor in our midst?"

Lord Craythorne's smile was lopsided, giving him a cynical appearance, but his slight discomfort, the sensation of facing an unpleasant task, tinged his otherwise intent emotions. "I was not circumspect in retrieving you. I should have driven you into the countryside, in search of an isolated place, but I could think only of taking you to safety here. So I made a very public spectacle of myself, and then of you, carrying you to and from the carriage in full daylight. Then, when I entered this house, I encountered—perhaps you do not recall, but I spoke to my mother, who was surrounded by several acquaintances, some of them Speakers, all of them ladies of distinction."

Lydia blushed again. "I must apologize to her as well. I would never threaten anyone with violence were I in my right mind."

"That is not the problem," Lord Craythorne said. "I am afraid all of them witnessed me carrying you, disheveled and in tears, to my bedchamber. Where I shut the door on both of us in a very decided manner, having ordered all of them to leave us alone in the house."

Lydia covered her mouth to contain a gasp. "Oh," she said, stupidly. Then she giggled. "Oh, that is not good." Her giggles became laughter, and then she was weeping uncontrollably through her mirth.

"Miss Wescott, please, do not weep," Lord Craythorne said. He sounded alarmed.

Lydia controlled herself with an effort and wiped her eyes. "No, I beg your pardon, it is just horrid and amusing all at once." She drew in a shuddering breath and let it out slowly. "I suppose we will have to explain."

Lord Craythorne did not look as if he shared her amusement. "This is not a thing we can explain away," he said. "Even if it did not appear that your virtue was compromised, explaining will mean revealing your talent to the world. I will, of course, not tell you what to do, but I understood secrecy about your talent was important to you."

Lydia, her mouth open to protest, closed it sharply. Of course it did not matter if she became known publicly as an Extraordinary Discerner, but that would be the end of her usefulness to Mr. Rutledge and to Lord Craythorne. And it was not their disappointment that mattered; she could not bear the thought of no longer being useful, no longer being able to sail through a crowd unnoticed.

"But the Dowager Duchess knows the truth," she stammered. "She knows you would not compromise any woman. She will convince her friends."

"Any explanation she or I give will be taken as proof of guilt," Lord Craythorne said. "You will be utterly ruined, and I will suffer the scandal of having abducted an innocent young woman and preyed upon her. Which I would happily endure if it meant protecting your reputation, but I fear that is impossible."

Lydia squeezed her eyes shut. "I am an Extraordinary, and my word is my bond," she said. "I can defend myself—but only if I reveal my secret." But she recalled what Clemency had endured when everyone believed she had been voluntarily intimate with a man to whom she was not married. Based on that, Lydia was not sure her assertion about her word was true.

Lord Craythorne nodded. "You see the difficulty."

"I do." Lydia opened her eyes. "I suppose we shall just have to endure the scandal."

"That is not the only possibility," Lord Craythorne said.

Hope surged through her. "You have realized some solution?"

"I have," Lord Craythorne said. "I might marry you."

CHAPTER 23

IN WHICH LYDIA CONFIRMS
WHO HER TRUE FRIENDS ARE

L ydia gasped. "Marry—"

"Marriage will redeem your supposedly tarnished virtue," Lord Craythorne said. "And, at the risk of sounding selfish, it will prevent my peers believing I ravished you, or at least will silence the loudest of the criticisms."

"But— your Grace, it is not as if we love each other!"

Lord Craythorne's wry smile embarrassed Lydia. "I believe we have established that love is not necessary for marriage. And at least you do not despise me, or so I believe."

Lydia shook her head. "It is impossible. Suppose we do this, and later you find another whom you *can* love? I would stand in your way."

"I consider that extremely unlikely, given my history." He rose and walked toward her. "Though, if you consider me repulsive—"

"Do not be ridiculous, your Grace! You are not repulsive."

Lord Craythorne stopped in front of her and extended a hand. "It will not be so terrible, will it? We are friends, and that is better than a love that might fade. And the more I consider the matter, the more convinced I am that we shall suit one another nicely."

Lydia regarded his outstretched hand, how well-shaped and masculine it was, the signet ring gleaming in the scant light from the window.

It was morning, she noted, and there was another storm coming, turning the light silver and grey. Thirty-six hours lost. "Your Grace," she said, "is this truly what you wish? For I cannot have you sacrifice—"

"It is no sacrifice at all, and I repeat, I would rather marry a friend I can respect than a woman who sees me as nothing more than the means to an end." Lord Craythorne's hand did not waver. "Though perhaps I should worry more about the sacrifice *you* will make, giving up your chance at a future love."

"You know I put no stock in romance, your Grace." Lydia hesitated a moment longer. Then she clasped his hand firmly. "I accept your proposal, and thank you for wishing to protect me. Please believe I do not hold my captivity against you."

"I would be irrational to believe so," Lord Craythorne said. He squeezed her hand lightly and released her. "Very well. Having settled that matter, there is more we must do. First, we must determine if there are any spies remaining in this household. Then I will set to work discovering where the Ruskins have fled to. Capturing them will deal a heavy blow to the Libertymen, following as it will upon the heels of Mr. Hughes' capture and death."

Lydia nodded and stood. "I will not be easy until I know I can trust those here. Particularly Ellery. But—I simply cannot understand how anyone might have learned of my talent! I have been most circumspect."

She turned sharply to face Lord Craythorne, who had returned to his seat by the door. "You have a suspicion."

Lord Craythorne's emotions shifted from suspicion to an odd mix of anger and bleak regret. "At least we know your talent is not diminished by your experience," he said. "There are only two possibilities. Either someone overheard something that gave the secret away, or someone who knew of the truth revealed it to another. You say there is no way anyone might have overheard. You and I have not spoken of it to anyone. That leaves only your maid and my mother."

"I cannot believe evil of either of them."

"Not evil, but carelessness. Mother Speaks frequently with the ladies of her reticulum, and she has told me Speaking carries with it an intimacy that makes sharing confidences pleasant. She would not have told Mrs. Ruskin directly, as Mrs. Ruskin is no Speaker, but gossip carries far—as I'm sure you know."

"And I wonder now if James did not single Ellery out intentionally to learn my secrets." Lydia paced the length of the bedchamber, not seeing her surroundings. "She claims she does not air my business in public, but confiding in one's love—she might not even have realized what she was giving away." She felt sick at heart.

Out of the corner of her eye, she saw someone approaching, but it turned out to be her reflection in a large mirror in a frame of gilded laurel leaves. She stared, aghast, at her appearance. Her hair was wildly tangled with loose pins clinging to a few strands. Her gown was filthy and in places shiny with grease. Her wrists were abraded and red from the straps that had bound her, and a bruise on her face where the man had struck her was a vivid purple. Reflexively she pushed a hank of hair out of her eyes. "I must clean myself up," she said. "I look like a madwoman."

"Should you be alone with Ellery, if she is, in fact, the one who betrayed you?"

"I do not fear her," Lydia said. A hopeful idea occurred to her. "If she is the one, she will know by now what has happened, and she will have fled rather than stay to be interrogated. I must go at once."

"Take care," Lord Craythorne warned. "I must go myself if I wish to set the search for the Ruskins in motion. I may leave discovering true loyalties to you?"

"Of course, your Grace." It eased her heart to be so trusted—better, to have her abilities so respected and her own self given responsibilities. A flash of pleasure shot through her at the idea that she was marrying someone who would not coddle her. Marriage. No, that was too strange to consider for the moment.

Lord Craythorne opened the door and bowed. "Thank you for accepting my proposal," he said. "I fear we cannot be married immediately, as I anticipate the search for the Libertymen to intensify. But I will publicize our engagement at once. And I suppose I must tell the household they may return—without implying anything untoward in our behavior or revealing your talent further."

"Thank you for your consideration, your Grace," Lydia said, and put a hand over her mouth to stifle a giggle. "Listen to us. We can do better than this tepid talk."

"Indeed." Lord Craythorne took her hand and kissed it, a feather-light touch that sent a thrill of pleasure through her. "Until later, then, and I will prepare a number of witty remarks you can respond to with equal wit and cleverness, astounding those who observe us."

"I appreciate your consideration," Lydia said.

She found, as she walked to the stairs leading to her room, that her ankles were sore enough to make ordinary exertion painful. By the time she opened her bedchamber door, she was limping. She was also, now that nothing else demanded her attention, very hungry. Pain and hunger warred with each other, but she reminded herself she could not simply walk into the kitchen and steal from the pantry. Food would have to wait until the servants returned.

The bedroom was empty, and she did not Discern anyone's presence nearby, but she remembered Lord Craythorne had cleared the house and was not surprised. She Discerned him moving away toward the front door and wondered what reason he would give for making them all leave. No doubt they would all believe she and he had been intimate regardless of his excuse. She found the idea did not disturb her. It was the price she paid for keeping the secret of her talent.

She removed her gown with some difficulty; it was of the War Office design Clemency preferred, able to be removed without assistance, but her wrists and arms hurt so she had difficulty raising them above her head and behind her back. The temptation to put on a nightgown and sleep for a year, real, untroubled sleep, was great, but in the end she donned a simple day gown over her convenables and sat at the dressing table to brush and pin her hair.

She became aware of people coming within her range of Discernment and lowered the brush as she focused on each. Their emotions varied, curiosity and concern and resentment, the last probably at having been evicted as they went about their duties. One felt heightened anger, and Lydia guessed that was Lady Craythorne, who had been so brusquely dismissed by her son in front of her friends. If Lady Craythorne had given Lydia's secret away, Lydia had no idea what she could do about that. It was not as if anyone, even Lord Craythorne, could punish her. And Lydia's heart ached at the idea that the Dowager Duchess might have betrayed her.

Someone was approaching rapidly, someone whose fear and remorse ran so deeply Lydia had to suppress her own fear at being once more overwhelmed. She set down the brush and rose just as the door opened and Ellery burst in. "Oh, miss," she exclaimed, "what happened to you? Your face! Where have you been these two days? Did Lord Craythorne abuse you?"

"Of course not," Lydia said sharply. "What are you afraid of?"

Ellery's emotions became tinged with embarrassment. "I wondered if you would believe I should have been here. He would not have dared...that is, if you had been accompanied, you would not have been vulnerable."

Lydia realized abruptly that Ellery had no idea what had actually happened to her. She had been so caught up in having been kidnapped, her secret revealed to her enemies, that she had not remembered that none of that had been made public. Only those involved in the scheme would know the truth. And Ellery clearly was not one of those, unless by coincidence she and Mrs. Ruskin shared the same vile facility with lies.

She reached around Ellery and shut the door. "Where was I said to be these past days?"

Ellery's fear spiked. "Lady Craythorne said you were visiting friends, but I did not know why you would visit anyone without me, so I did not believe...and James has been missing, and I heard whisperings —there were such terrible rumors—"

"That James and I had run off together," Lydia interrupted. Ellery blushed, and pain and misery flooded through her. "And now they will say that Lord Craythorne found us, and brought me back and ravished me, yes?"

"I would never believe that, miss, not even if Lady Craythorne herself said it was true." Tears shone in Ellery's eyes. "But—where is James, miss? Something dreadful must have happened if he is still gone!"

Nothing in the maid's demeanor or emotions showed her to be

lying. Relieved, Lydia sat in the chair near the bookcase and rested one elbow on the table. "Then you have not told anyone of my Extraordinary Discerner's talent," she said, deciding she would not take chances no matter what she Discerned in Ellery.

Ellery's mouth fell open. "Miss, of course not! Have I given you some idea that I am not trustworthy?"

Lydia shook her head. "Maud, sit there," she said, pointing to the dressing table bench. "I must tell you some dreadful things, and you will not be comfortable in your emotions, so I do not believe you should be uncomfortable in your person."

She told Ellery everything, only eliding the dreadful time in the madhouse when she had been lost. Ellery's lips whitened when Lydia revealed that James had been complicit in her kidnapping. "And I suspect he murdered the driver," Lydia said. "Maud, I so regret that you were taken in by him. Though I have no reason to believe he did not care for you."

Ellery wiped her eyes and shook her head. "I am not so certain. Miss, he was always asking questions about you, and telling me how he admired you—not in a romantic way, but how you had left your home to travel with Lady Craythorne and come to the colonies and such. I see now he wished for information he might sell." Tears threatened to spill over again. "And he never promised me anything, just hinted at— oh, I was so foolish!"

Lydia hurried to her side and put her arms around the weeping girl, ignoring how Ellery's sorrow dragged at her heart. "You believed him, and why should you not? You are so honest yourself, it does not occur to you that anyone else might not be as honest, and it is to their shame if they abuse your good nature, not yours. Hush, hush."

"I will never love again, never!"

"I hope that is not true. Maud, look at me." Lydia clasped Ellery's hands. "People can betray us, but that is no reason not to hope for better in the people we love. And perhaps we can turn James' perfidy to our advantage."

Ellery wiped her tear-reddened eyes. "How is that, miss?"

"He questioned you, but he could not have avoided revealing something of himself if he intended to make you care for him. What do you know of his associates? His usual haunts?"

"I don't—" Ellery stopped, looking thoughtful. "He sometimes spoke of friends he claimed were influential, friends who held positions of power, and how he intended to be more than a footman one day. And he mentioned a place they met—at least, that is what I assume, because he specifically said he was going there to meet with those influential friends."

"Then you remember this place?"

"It was something to do with a bird. Raven's Rest. That sounds like a tavern, or an inn, doesn't it, miss?"

"It does." Lydia hugged Ellery again. "You have been so helpful. I hope your heart will not remain broken for long. It is such a terrible feeling."

"I feel better knowing I may have helped you, miss." Ellery glanced away, and embarrassment suffused her. "But Lord Craythorne—"

"It is all right. Lord Craythorne and I are to be married." Saying the words again gave Lydia an odd, floating sensation, as if she were detached from her own body and drifting inches off the ground. It was not unpleasant, but it did make her feel briefly a stranger to herself.

Ellery's astonishment reflected itself in her wide eyes and slack mouth. "*Married?* But—miss, you did say nothing untoward happened between you, and you have said you harbor no romantic affection for the Duke, so why are you to marry?" She blushed again. "Pardon me, that was forward."

"You are my friend, Maud, and it is not forward for friends to have concern for one another." Impulsively, Lydia squeezed Ellery's hand. "Unfortunately, Lord Craythorne rescued me in such a public manner word of his actions has no doubt already spread wide, especially since members of Lady Craythorne's reticulum witnessed our return to this house. This is the only solution that will redeem my virtue and protect his honor."

"I understand." Ellery still sounded skeptical. "I suppose I truly am a starry-eyed dreamer, for marrying without love seems so cold to me —that is, for myself, because I do not mean to criticize your decision."

"I understand you. But Lord Craythorne says that he would rather marry a friend than a woman with mercenary intent, and I believe I agree with him." Lydia laughed. "It is a strange notion, though. I had intended never to marry, and now I am to be—oh, dear, Maud. Duchess of Craythorne. That is so odd." She laughed again. "Do you mind attending on a Duchess?"

"Of course not, miss." Ellery's dismay rose despite her words. "Though I am not elegant, or a Frenchwoman, and perhaps a Duchess ought have a lady's maid more in keeping with her station."

"Nonsense. I would rather you stay by me. My life will change enough without disrupting our friendship." Lydia rose and walked to the dressing table to examine her face in the mirror. "This will be hard to explain away," she said, gingerly prodding the bruise at its center and wincing.

"We can cover it with powder, and make it less obvious," Ellery offered.

"That will help. For now, though, I must speak to Lady Craythorne. I am almost certain she did not speak too freely to her reticulum, but I prefer to be entirely certain instead." Lydia smoothed her loose hair to fall forward, casting a shadow over her injured cheek. "See what you can find in the way of cosmetics and powder. I never guessed I might need the like."

"I will, miss." Ellery began tidying the dressing table. "I hope Lady Craythorne is innocent as you say."

"So do I," Lydia said.

She ran her quarry to ground in the large drawing room, the one she thought of as Lady Craythorne's territory. Quarry, territory...Lydia did not know when she had begun to think of herself as a hunter, but the image did not displease her. She already felt stronger, more capable, now that she had direction. The memory of being overwhelmed and lost inside the madhouse had faded, though she was sure it would resurface in the darkest hours of the night, and all that remained was a deep resolve to find those who had put her there and see them incapable of doing it again.

Lady Craythorne looked up when Lydia entered. She was seated on the pink roses divan, holding a book which she closed on her index finger to mark her place. "So," she said. "Oliver has spun me an unlikely tale. What have you to say?"

"Unlikely?" Lydia exclaimed. "Surely you do not believe your own son would lie to you!"

Lady Craythorne's gaze was steady and implacable. "It is the stuff of horrid novels, and not very believable regardless who tells it. As it happens, though, I did not disbelieve Oliver. I merely hoped you would do me the courtesy of filling in some necessary details."

"I think not," Lydia said, putting as much disdain into her expression and words as she could manage, as if she might make the Dowager Duchess a Discerner by will alone. "I feel no obligation to the woman whose carelessness revealed my talent to one who intended me permanent harm."

Lady Craythorne's lips tightened, but she showed no other sign of the anger and affronted pride that lashed through her. "How dare you accuse me of such a thing!" she said, her voice low and furious. "I never reveal a secret, Miss Wescott. Never. And you are a fool if you believe yourself entitled to lay blame for what happened to you at my feet."

Lydia walked forward until she was within arm's reach of Lady Craythorne. "You sound so guilty," she said, her full attention on Lady Craythorne's emotions. "I Discern that you are not, but anyone might believe otherwise. But your guilt attaches to something else, does it not? Something to do with the late Lady Craythorne?"

The Dowager Duchess looked away. "That is none of your business," she said. "Leave me at once."

"I don't believe I will." Lydia took a seat at the other end of the divan. "Lady Craythorne, you must realize I am the only person who knows your secret heart. I know the remorse and regret you feel at the sharpness with which you express yourself. I have never done anything to reveal your secrets, any more than you have revealed mine. Can we not come to a true understanding?"

Lady Craythorne continued to fix her attention on the opposite wall. "Why do you care?" she said, her voice even quieter than before so that only Lydia's keen hearing perceived it clearly. "I have never been friendly toward you. I know you take my improving instructions as meddling insults. Why would you wish things otherwise?"

"Because we will soon have a closer relationship than that of lady and companion," Lydia said. "Did not Lord Craythorne tell you everything that passed between us while we were alone in the house?"

Lady Craythorne turned, curious. "He told me he removed you from a madhouse and that he intended to find those responsible for sending you there."

Lydia briefly wished she had Lord Craythorne there to scold for leaving this announcement to her. "Lord Craythorne has offered me marriage, and I have accepted."

Astonishment flashed through the Dowager Duchess, but to Lydia's surprise it did not last long, being swiftly overridden by knowing comprehension. "I see. Then he is not lost to all decency as I feared." Lady Craythorne looked Lydia up and down, pausing only briefly at the bruise. "You will do, I suppose."

"Bridle your tongue, your Grace, or am I wrong, and you truly do prefer this...this façade of sneering superiority?" Lydia did not wish to bridle her own tongue after the ordeal she had endured.

To her surprise, Lady Craythorne smiled, somewhat bitterly, and her emotions soothed into resignation and regret. "I hoped to make him a better match than I did the first time," she said. "I should instead have sworn not to interfere. Looking back on his first marriage, I cannot believe I had the effrontery to try to guide his decision a second time. I meant no insult, and in truth, I spoke in mockery of myself just now."

Lydia settled back in her seat. "You meant well. In suggesting he marry Clarissa Denham, I mean."

"The road to Hell is paved with such phrases as 'I meant well,'" Lady Craythorne said. "But, yes. I knew Oliver had no strong attachment to any woman, and I believed he would be as happy with Lady Clarissa as with anyone. Then I watched her belittle and mock him where she believed no one would hear, and in time she no longer cared who knew of her indifference and spoke ill of him in public. And I could do nothing. When she died, I was glad of it. Glad, and relieved. I wish the child had lived, of course, but perhaps it is all for the best."

"Of course you were relieved," Lydia said. "Lord Craythorne was entangled with someone who intended him to be miserable, and you love your son and hated to see that woman's behavior. But you did not kill her. I doubt you even wished for her death. So I do not see why you should bear that guilt."

Lady Craythorne let out a single, sharp laugh. "For one who supposedly sees into the human heart, you are remarkably unaware of human frailties. I cannot forgive myself for encouraging the match, Miss Wescott. Had I not—"

"Lord Craythorne might have married another who was equally inappropriate," Lydia said promptly. "Or someone worse. You cannot know what might have been, Lady Craythorne. And, please—I wish you would stop berating yourself, and permitting that self-loathing to affect your dealings with people you love. No one benefits from that."

"I cannot," Lady Craythorne said. "It has been so long, and I am so accustomed to defending myself by speaking sharply...I fear it is too late for me."

"If you speak honestly to Lord Craythorne, I believe you will discover speaking your heart at other times becomes easier." Lydia shifted closer and put a hand on Lady Craythorne's wrist. "You wish more than anything to express your regret at your part in his horrid marriage, and I know very well how freeing it is when people apologize for their unintentional misdeeds."

Lady Craythorne shook her head, but she smiled. "I imagine you do." She rested her hand atop Lydia's. "Very well. I suppose, as you are to be my daughter, I should heed your requests."

Daughter. That, too, made Lydia feel untethered from reality. "I hope Lord Craythorne and I will suit," she said.

Lady Craythorne regarded her closely. "You do not seem very attached," she said. "I had suspected there were rather warmer sentiments between you than either of you admitted to."

"We are friends, and that is more than enough," Lydia said. "Though I suppose our friendliness might have appeared like romantic intimacy." The briefest pang of sorrow shot through her, too fast to disorder her senses, almost too fast for her to recognize what had prompted it. Lord Craythorne was right; they did not need love, because friendship was better and more lasting. But she could not help wondering, for that brief moment, whether they were wrong.

CHAPTER 24

IN WHICH A NEW DANGER ARISES

The day passed, and Lord Craythorne did not return. Lydia submitted to Ellery's attempts at concealing the marks on her face and was surprised at how successful they were. "You have missed your calling on the stage," she said. "Or, not on the stage, but behind the scenes—you understand me, yes?"

"I do, miss." Ellery dabbed Lydia's cheek with powder one final time and stood back. "Now, you must take care not to touch, because the makeup will rub off and your face will look smeared."

"I will remember." Lydia walked to the window and looked out over the garden. "I wish I knew what Lord Craythorne was doing. I cannot bear idleness when I might be a help to him."

"I hope he finds James," Ellery said, putting away the cosmetics in a neat little case. "I would like—no, I do not know what I would say to him. He likely does not care if he has made me angry, if he did not care about lying about his feelings. I do wish I had asked you to Discern his true emotions, miss!"

"It is what I offered to do for Lord Craythorne, but he refused," Lydia replied absently, with half her attention on the conversation and the rest of it preoccupied with Discerning the household. She would recognize Lord Craythorne's peculiarly muted emotions if he was within range, so she wished to remain alert for his approach.

"He refused, miss? But that could only help him, if he wished to avoid another marriage like the first." Ellery went into the dressing room. "I suppose it no longer matters, not if he is to wed you, miss."

"That is true." The mention of her engagement felt less odd than it had before. Perhaps, if she contemplated it long enough, it would become ordinary, an event no more surprising than a musical evening or a visit to a bookshop.

She cast her gaze over the garden, where long shadows stretched across the expanse of lawn like streaks of charcoal. Clouds massed on the eastern horizon, but the west remained clear of overcast, and the last light of the setting sun turned the sky peach and gold. Lord Craythorne was out there somewhere, with luck learning things that would mean the downfall of the Libertymen. Absurdly, she resented him, a feeling she told herself not to entertain. The Libertymen were serious business, and their capture was not for her amusement. Still, she wished to be out and doing, to send him to investigate the Raven's Rest, not to be trapped in this mansion preparing to go down to supper.

She and Lady Craythorne ate alone in the dining room that evening. Sometimes members of Lord Craythorne's party, or American dignitaries, or friends of Lady Craythorne's joined them, and then the mood was serious or stately or lively by turns. Tonight, though, neither spoke; Lydia was conscious of not having had a true restful sleep in nearly forty-eight hours, and Lady Craythorne's mood was subdued and thoughtful. Lydia was occasionally aware of the emotional startling that characterized someone attempting to Speak to Lady Craythorne, but the Dowager Duchess was never impolite enough to Speak at the dinner table.

Lydia realized she was drooping and made herself sit upright and enjoy her food. Perhaps it was as well Lord Craythorne had not called on her assistance, if she would only fall asleep during an interrogation.

Distantly, the front door slammed open and then shut. Weariness vanished, and Lydia half-rose from her chair. The person was not Lord Craythorne, unless the Duke was more animated in his emotions than usual, and whoever it was did not make straight for the dining room, but headed to Lord Craythorne's study.

"Who is it?" Lady Craythorne asked.

Lydia shook her head. "He is agitated and a little afraid, and I believe he does not know Lord Craythorne is gone. Now he is with someone—he has communicated his agitation and fear to that other person, and now—" She tilted her head as if that would bring the emotions she Discerned into better focus. "The agitation is spreading, like a contagion. It frightens me."

Lady Craythorne's incipient fear tinged her emotions as well. "Perhaps we should see what is amiss," she said, rising from her chair.

"Here, he is coming now," Lydia said, rising as well.

In the next moment, a stranger lurched through the dining room doorway. His clothing was filthy, as if he had rolled in the dirt before entering, and his hair was disordered. He breathed so heavily Lydia was moved to say, "Calm yourself before you fall unconscious, sir."

"I cannot stay, I must warn the others," the man said. "Lord Craythorne instructs Lady Craythorne and Miss Wescott—please say you are they, ladies, because I cannot exert myself much longer."

"What instructions from my son?" Lady Craythorne said.

"You are to leave for the Viceroy's palace immediately," the man gasped. "A mob has devastated the center of Washington and is coming this way, and this house is not defensible. Lord Craythorne says to take everyone to shelter in the palace."

"The Iroquois?" Lady Craythorne said with a glance at Lydia.

The man shook his head. "I do not know, and it does not matter, does it? Now, go—forgive my rudeness, but I must continue." He nodded briefly and was gone as quickly as he had appeared.

"He did not say how close the mob was," Lydia said. "And when I am able to Discern them, they will already be too close."

"Then we must go now," Lady Craythorne said. She rang the bell, and when Trask appeared, she said, "We are evacuating to the Viceroy's palace. Gather everyone. We leave no one behind."

Trask's placid demeanor perfectly concealed his extreme curiosity and agitation at these instructions. "You must leave at once, your Grace, and we will follow," he said. "What should we take?"

"There is nothing in this house that is worth losing a life to the mob," Lady Craythorne said. "But you will lock the doors—it is probably a pointless precaution, but one never knows—and see to it that no one is foolish enough to carry a burden that might delay them. Miss Wescott, please join me."

Lydia was already on her way out the door and up the stairs, calling for Ellery.

Two minutes later, she and Lady Craythorne, along with Ellery and Lady Craythorne's maid Bisset, were flying along the dark streets in the Craythorne carriage. The path was the same as they had taken to the investiture ball, and Lydia was struck by how normal the streets were, the lights still glowing brightly in a burning flood that swept the carriage along. It was difficult to believe in mobs on such a night.

But in the distance, out the carriage window, a sunset glow lit the horizon. The northern horizon.

Lydia gripped the seat and stared at the light. There must be hundreds of lamps or torches to be visible at that distance. Hundreds of men intent on violence. She wondered what had set them off, whether the Ruskins had learned of Lydia's removal from the madhouse and decided their plans could be delayed no longer, or whether this was completely unrelated violence, and realized it did not matter. A mob, once incited, could not be controlled, and this one would put Washington to the torch.

Not for the first time, she wished for an Extraordinary Coercer's talent. Such a talent *could* control a mob. Her own helplessness frustrated her. What good was it to sense anger if one had no way of soothing it? She never voiced these desires in front of Clemency, who had been violated by Napoleon's Coercion, but secretly, she hoped the rumors were true that Napoleon had been defeated by another Extraordinary Coercer. She applauded that man, whoever he was.

The carriage rounded a corner at speed, and Lydia, unprepared, was flung into Lady Craythorne's lap. "I beg your pardon," she said, righting herself.

"I hope the Viceroy's palace is a true refuge," Lady Craythorne said. "We might simply be exchanging one trap for another."

"It has fewer doors, and the windows are higher, so I believe it is more defensible than the mansion." Lydia craned her neck to look ahead at where the Viceroy's palace stood, all its windows blazing with light as if daring the mob to come after it. "But it is not large enough to shelter everyone in Washington."

Lady Craythorne did not reply; she had tilted her head back to Speak with someone. Lydia was not astonished to sense no fear in the Dowager Duchess. For all the lady's faults, she was not a coward. Lydia herself did not fear either. At last, something was happening. Perhaps that made her as adventurous as Miranda Adams, after all.

This time, there were no other carriages waiting in a line to deposit their passengers at the palace door. A single high-perch phaeton with enormous spindly wheels raced past them as they rattled up the drive and then was gone, disappeared into the night. Lydia observed the agitation of the driver, but could not tell if he was fleeing in fear or setting off on some mission, he moved so fast.

She accepted the driver's hand down, and it was such a common-place gesture she felt for a moment that they were here for nothing more exciting than a ball. Then she gave heed to the many people within the palace, all of them with emotions as heightened as the phaeton driver's, and had to collect herself to avoid being over-whelmed. Whatever danger neared, everyone here was aware of it.

Lady Craythorne shooed all of them inside as rapidly as if they were fleeing a rainstorm instead of a distant riot. Immediately, they were surrounded by three men whose surprise overrode their anxiety. All were dressed like clerks, or at least as Lydia imagined clerks would dress, and one of them was annoyed at the women's entrance. That one said, "Excuse me, but what are you doing here?" in a rather officious tone.

"I am Lady Craythorne, and Lord Craythorne instructed his house-hold to shelter here," Lady Craythorne said, sounding even more officious than he did. "Is he here?"

To Lydia's surprise, the man's manner immediately became respect-ful. She had judged him to be the sort who insisted on having the final say in everything that ever happened. "Lady Craythorne, of course," he said. "Pray, come with me. Lord Craythorne gave instructions before he left. You will join Mrs. Monroe in the family quarters." He shot a curious glance at Lydia, and she Discerned his curiosity and faint prurient regard, but he was too well bred to say anything about someone he suspected was Lord Craythorne's doxy, even though she was in the Dowager Duchess's train.

The man led them up stairs and around corners and down a long passage painted a brilliant white bearing portraits of stately men. Lydia was conscious of how little she knew about the Viceroy's palace and the American colonial government. She wished there were time to observe the portraits and learn the identities of their subjects. Surely those men had stories. But they were past that hall in an instant, and their guide was opening a door at the far end. "Mrs. Monroe, Lady Craythorne," he said.

Mrs. Monroe sat up from where she was reclining on a chaise longue. "Lavinia," she said in a husky voice. "It is too, too dreadful."

"If they have not Bounded us to safety, it cannot be very dreadful." Lady Craythorne knelt beside the chaise longue and took one of Mrs. Monroe's hands in hers. "You have had an episode recently, I can tell. Pray, what can I do for you?"

Mrs. Monroe smiled weakly. "Tell me what is happening. I fear the worst—and do not say that will make me worse, for I am never made ill by bad news, only my own weak body."

"We know only that a riot has devastated the heart of Washington, and the rioters are headed this way." Lady Craythorne was scanning the room as she spoke. "Bisset, bring me that footstool so I need not crouch on the floor."

The Frenchwoman nodded and carried the footstool over in silence. Lydia took the opportunity to draw Ellery over to one of the windows farthest from Mrs. Monroe. "I see the torches," she whispered, pointing. "They are nearer than before."

"And they are certainly approaching this place," Ellery said. "Miss, is it all right if I am afraid?"

"Of course, because I am afraid as well, but you should not let fear govern your actions." Lydia spoke only half the truth; she was not afraid for herself, but for Lord Craythorne, who might be somewhere out in the darkness, facing the mob.

She idly Discerned everyone within her range. The Viceroy's palace was larger than Lord Craythorne's mansion, and she was certain her Discernment could not cover the entire building, even were she standing at its center instead of on the farthest edge as she was now. People raced in and out, intent on their business, and more people ran about between the ground floor and the first. They made a knot in the west wing of the palace, where the agitation was greatest. Lydia Discerned three people whose emotions were focused rather than in turmoil. She hoped one of them was the Viceroy, and that he was a sensible man in a crisis.

She blinked back to awareness as she realized Ellery had addressed her. "I beg your pardon, Maud, did you say something?"

"Lady Craythorne asked—" Ellery whispered.

"I said," Lady Craythorne said, enunciating clearly as she would to someone with poor hearing, "would you play for us, Miss Wescott?"

"Oh!" Lydia regarded the small but elegant pianoforte in the corner. "Of course, Lady Craythorne, please excuse my inattention."

"You should not dwell on the mob's approach," Lady Craythorne said, not harshly. "We can do nothing about it. Mrs. Monroe would welcome a distraction."

"Of course," Lydia repeated.

The pianoforte was imperfectly tuned, and Lydia suspected its nearness to the windows where the prevailing winds blew had something to do with that. But she settled herself at her seat and began playing the same song with which she had accompanied Miranda Adams. She wondered where her friend was at that moment. Surely Miranda was safe, and Dorothea's parents lived well outside Washington proper. She worried nonetheless.

CHAPTER 25

IN WHICH VIOLENCE AND DESTRUCTION END IN AN UNEXPECTED DISCOVERY

After half an hour, she Discerned Lord Craythorne's approach, his muted emotions better than the sound of a voice to identify him. She made herself go on playing as if she had noticed nothing. For the first time, though, she considered revealing her talent. It was not as if it was shameful, and as useful as concealment was, there were so many things she might do if she was openly an Extraordinary Discerner. But her usefulness to Mr. Rutledge and Lord Craythorne was not yet over, and she wished to carry out those secret assignments more than she wished to publicly announce herself.

She did not raise her eyes from the keyboard when the door opened. Lord Craythorne said, "I am glad to see you here, Mother. What of the others?"

"They were behind us when we left." Lady Craythorne rose from her footstool and hurried to Lord Craythorne's side. "Oliver, what news? Is it the Iroquois?"

Lydia looked up just as Lord Craythorne's gaze swept over her. He looked calm, but even muted as his emotions usually were, his worry and excitement were palpable. "The mob is growing," he said. "It is not the Iroquois, but the Libertymen, and they will be here within the next half-hour."

"We should be Bounded to safety, then," Mrs. Monroe said.

"I fear that is impossible," Lord Craythorne said. "The violence is not confined to this city. We have news of similar riots in New York and Philadelphia as well as in many smaller cities. Unfortunately, the Bounders attached to the palace know of no signatures that are located in unthreatened places. This is currently the safest place to be in Washington."

"Many riots?" Lady Craythorne said. "That cannot be coincidence."

"It is not." Lord Craythorne crossed to the window and looked out at the increasing glow. "But I believe they acted prematurely, and that will be their downfall. Miss Wescott, will you join me for a moment?"

Lydia startled. "Of course, your Grace."

She followed Lord Craythorne into the hall, where he closed the door on Lady Craythorne saying, "Elizabeth, we must—" The distant noises of men running and doors slamming were louder now, and their intensity of emotion increased, but Lydia felt detached from all of it.

"The discovery of your kidnapping precipitated the attacks," Lord Craythorne said without preamble. "They were not as well coordinated as I'm sure the Libertymen wished. Even so, this qualifies as a major uprising, not just a riot."

Lydia gasped. "Do you mean war?"

"No one has sent demands or articles of war, possibly as a result of that lack of coordination." Lord Craythorne's muted emotions now showed frustration and anger. "But if they can succeed at destroying their targets, it will not matter that there is no official declaration."

"I hope you have cause for telling me this other than a desire to terrify me," Lydia said.

Lord Craythorne smiled. "You are not terrified, admit it."

"I am not, but perhaps that only shows a lack of imagination." Lydia smiled at Lord Craythorne's laughter. "There, you see, your Grace? It cannot be so terrible if we can still laugh."

"I laugh because running mad is frowned upon." Lord Craythorne sobered. "How much in danger are you from being overwhelmed by the mob?"

"None, actually. The anger of a mob has a peculiar quality to it that is easy to distinguish from myself." Lydia was less certain of this than she sounded, but she did not believe it was a lie. "Though that seems irrelevant, as I cannot leave."

"I wished mainly to determine whether you will need watching. No, I do not consider you a liability, do not make that face." Lord Craythorne gripped her hand for a moment, and his touch reassured her. "But having so recently seen you fall to madness, I prefer not to let it happen a second time if I can help it. I had thought to ask for your assistance, but I cannot see how you might help under these circumstances."

Lydia let out a deep, frustrated breath. "I am forced to agree."

"We must move you ladies to an interior room, one without windows," Lord Craythorne went on. Lydia was surprised to find his mood altered, his former bleak pessimism and anger more anticipatory of success. "The Army has been dispatched, and it will all be over soon, unless these ruffians are better armed than I imagine. And...thank you."

"Thank me? For what?" Lydia exclaimed.

"At the risk of sounding as sentimental as a daffodil-obsessed poet, I find speaking to you calms me." Lord Craythorne shook his head, but he was smiling. "Come, let us find you another place to stay, and then I must be off. I promise to return with news as soon as we have any."

"That is a very optimistic thing to say, your Grace. Much better than 'prepare for invasion,'" Lydia said, making him laugh again.

When they rejoined Lady Craythorne and Mrs. Monroe, Lydia found Mrs. Monroe eyed her with wary suspicion she could not explain. It was not tinged with condemnation for Lydia's inappropriate liaison in the hallway, but neither did Mrs. Monroe believe Lydia to be perfectly innocent of guile. And yet there was no way Mrs. Monroe could have guessed the secret of Lydia's talent. Lydia ignored this suspicion in favor of saying, "We must move somewhere more defensible, and Lord Craythorne will show us where to go."

The new room was an interior sitting room not as comfortable as the first. Mrs. Monroe immediately lay down upon a divan and closed her eyes. "I would like water, if that is possible."

"Of course, Elizabeth. Bisset, see to it. Ellery, perhaps you will accompany her." Lady Craythorne pulled a chair around to where she might sit near Mrs. Monroe's head. When the two maids were gone, she said, "I have told Mrs. Monroe about your engagement, Miss Wescott. Of course you would not do anything so improper as be alone with a man were you not engaged."

"Of course, and I realize that must have looked strange," Lydia said. "But our conversation was nothing very important. Just an instruction to see to it that all of us remain here for the duration."

"Like rats in a trap," Mrs. Monroe said, unexpectedly bitterly. "I suppose the first we will know of the fall of the palace is armed men bursting in upon us, bent on our deaths, or worse."

"Hush, Elizabeth, there is no reason to believe such a thing will happen." Lady Craythorne shot a meaningful glance at Lydia. She remained confident, but beneath that confidence was uncertainty. She obviously wished for Lydia's support.

Lydia took a chair nearby. "It is true, Lord Craythorne is extremely optimistic about our chances. He said the Army is on its way, and they are better armed than the mob. And this house is quite secure, with how it lacks windows on the ground floor."

"Secure, but none of Mr. Monroe's advisors are fighting men. We are doomed." Mrs. Monroe began to weep, a series of deep, choked sobs that sounded wrung out of her by force. Lydia closed her eyes against the rush of sorrow that now brought back more recent memories than of Magdalen.

For a moment, she resisted it. She imagined a wall within her that Mrs. Monroe's sadness dashed upon, a wall of stones too large to be moved by emotions. For a moment, the fancy worked; she Discerned Mrs. Monroe's violent emotions at a remove from herself, something she was aware of but did not feel. It was a strange, beautiful sensation.

In the next moment, as she was rejoicing in her solution, sorrow crept over her, seeping through cracks in her imaginary wall until it became an overpowering wave that threatened to sweep her away. Desperate, she told herself *you are separate, a void, this is not your sadness* and made herself breathe slowly until calmness filled her. Her heart ached at her failure, and she made herself ignore that ache, too. Suppressing her emotions seemed her only recourse.

"Hush, Elizabeth, we are not doomed," Lady Craythorne said,

clasping Mrs. Monroe's hands in hers. Lydia was impressed at how none of Lady Craythorne's irritation with her friend's despondency showed in her manner or voice. "We will have Miss Wescott read to us, or perhaps we will take turns reading, yes?"

Lydia was already at the room's one bookcase. It had been stocked by someone whose tastes ran to the bloodcurdling and dramatic, which would have been a relief had she been choosing solely for herself. But she knew Lady Craythorne well enough to realize she would not appreciate *The Mysteries of Udolpho*, however popular it was. So she selected a book of modern verse and returned to her seat to read aloud.

She heard very little of her own voice, preoccupied as she was with the emotions that pulsed and flowed over her: fear, determination, occasional anger, even less frequent satisfaction. That last emotion came from one of the three men she had originally observed in the west wing, and once more she hoped he was the Viceroy. Mr. Monroe's courage and leadership would matter more to these men than the Army, at least while the Army was not yet there.

She followed Lord Craythorne as a matter of course, Discerning his presence as he moved in and out of her range. It occurred to her to wonder, briefly, why his muted emotions were not drowned out, so to speak, by the more violent emotions of those surrounding him. He was always clearly perceptible to her Discernment. His presence soothed her as the poetry did not.

Ellery and Bisset returned while Lydia was reading, with water in a pitcher and a tray bearing glasses for the ladies. After a time, she handed the book to Lady Craythorne and sat quietly in a corner, not hearing the words as the Dowager Duchess took a turn reading. The emotions rushing through her had risen to a painful peak and were now predominantly fear, though determination still ran strong. Lydia once more made herself empty, suppressing her natural fear so nothing would overwhelm her, and waited for the mob.

It came suddenly, a surging horde of anger and self-righteous pleasure, passing into her Discernment range on the north and east sides of the palace. Lydia drew in an incautious breath and had to say, "It is nothing, I struck my ankle against the chair leg," when Mrs. Monroe commented on her exclamation.

There were so many of the rioters Lydia imagined she heard their shouts. Then she realized she did hear shouting, very faintly, and that Lady Craythorne had stopped reading mid-sentence. She opened her eyes and blinked away tears, not of sadness but of concentration. "It is well," she said, reassuring the others.

Bisset gasped and said something in rapid French of which Lydia caught only the words "fire" and "attack." Lady Craythorne replied in the same language, then added in English, "There is nothing more we can do. I shall continue reading."

Lydia closed her eyes again. With her eyes closed, the world was full of color that billowed as the emotions it represented did: jagged brown terror, or greenish-yellow determination, all of it surrounded by great clouds of hot, red anger. It was like watching a sea of watercolors, painted by someone who could not make up her mind as to the picture she intended so the paper blossomed, over and over, with color in abstract shapes.

She had briefly lost track of Lord Craythorne as he slipped outside her range to the west, but he reappeared at that moment on the northern side, so close to the mob she had to control a gasp of fear. More rioters pressed in, now on the south as well, and Lydia's frustration at merely watching grew until it nearly overwhelmed the other emotions. What point, she wondered again, to being able to see everything and do nothing?

Then Ellery was chafing her wrists and saying, "Miss, are you well? Miss, you fainted!"

Lydia again opened her eyes and discovered she was on the floor. She did not know what had happened, but the back of her head ached as if she had been struck, so it was possible she had forgotten to breathe in her intent concentration. "I am not ill, I simply grew dizzy," she said, and permitted Ellery to help her to a sofa to lie down. She immediately felt better, enough so that she said, "I imagine I just needed to rest."

"Yes, Miss Wescott, you should be careful, as frail as you are," Lady Craythorne said. She suspected that Lydia's fall had not been from faintness, but a familiar irritation told Lydia she disliked deceiving Mrs. Monroe about Lydia's talent.

"I will go on lying here, I believe," Lydia said, and turned her attention back to the mob. She heard their cries, and the crackle of fire, and between that and her sense of their anger and triumph, her own natural emotion of fear rose. Nearer to hand, someone addressed her, but she pretended to be asleep; she could not bear to stop attending to her Discernment, as if by doing so she abandoned Lord Craythorne and the defenders.

A rush of terror supplanted the rioters' anger. Lydia heard screams that seemed to make the terror echo, pulsing brighter and brighter until she feared she might fall unconscious again. Beneath the screams, the fire crackled—no, surely that was her imagination; if the fire were that loud, it would be in the room with them. She did not fear being overwhelmed, for the emotions she Discerned were completely unlike her own, but dizziness threatened to engulf her regardless.

She clung to her sense of Lord Craythorne's emotions like an anchor. He was so near the mob it terrified her. His anger was fierce and focused, but she could not imagine him fighting; would he wield a gun, or a saber, or use his fists? None of those suited the man she was coming to know.

She almost asked Lady Craythorne whether Lord Craythorne had any martial training when, in a single heart-stopping instant, she felt him go from anger to terror to surprise—and then his emotions faded entirely.

She was on her feet immediately, crying out, "No!"

"What is it, Miss Wescott?" Mrs. Monroe asked.

"Lord Craythorne," Lydia said, "he is—"

She saw and Discerned the fear filling Lady Craythorne at this declaration, saw Mrs. Monroe's confusion, and said, "I believed—I must have slept, I, well, I dreamed—how I could sleep through all this, I do not know—"

"Have some water, Miss Wescott, and calm yourself," Lady Craythorne said. She poured water herself and brought the glass to Lydia. As Lydia drank, she whispered, "What of my son?"

Lydia could not bring herself to reveal what she had Discerned. There were many reasons someone might disappear from her Discernment. It did not have to mean death. "I cannot say. Something happened, but—"

"Do you hear that?" Mrs. Monroe demanded. "The shouting is less than it was."

Lydia did not believe this was so. She Discerned no difference in the intensity of the emotions, though it was true the rioters feared more deeply than before. Then she Discerned the approach of others, these newcomers filled with intense determination only lightly laced with fear. "It must be the Army," she said, fixing Lady Craythorne with a look that said she was sure of her declaration. "They will stop those men."

"Lie down again, Miss Wescott," Lady Craythorne said, pushing on Lydia's shoulder. "We will soon know what has happened." She returned Lydia's look with one of her own that just as clearly said Lydia should determine what had happened to Lord Craythorne.

But everything was fading, not in intensity but in distance. She guessed the rioters had broken and were fleeing, because their places were being taken by the ones Lydia believed were soldiers. Those within the palace were excited and relieved rather than afraid. But she still did not perceive Lord Craythorne anywhere. Her heart beat so hard and fast it hurt her chest. She willed herself to Discern more fully, though Discernment did not work like that; she simply could not bear it if he was dead.

Then he was there, his emotions muted more than usual but still Discernable, somewhere outside the palace just inside the limit of her range. Lydia let out a deep, relieved breath. "He—" she began, realized Mrs. Monroe was listening, and converted that sentence to, "I am sure Lord Craythorne is well."

"Of course," Lady Craythorne said, relief surging through her.

Lydia continued to recline, just in case, but it seemed the riot really was over, based on the increasing relief and triumph and satisfaction filling the palace. She did not know how long the violence had lasted, and she did not care, because Lord Craythorne was finally approaching, and she was eager to learn the details. How eager she would have been had they lost—but that was ridiculous, as she would not have been alive to be eager had they lost. She realized her wild fancies were a result of too much strain and with only a twinge of guilt suppressed those emotions. She did not need to become overwhelmed now that everything was, if not over, at least close thereunto.

The door opened, and Lord Craythorne entered. Lady Craythorne gasped; his face and clothes were smudged with char, and his curls were wildly disordered. Lydia sat up and regarded him with eyes and with Discernment. She could make no sense of his emotions, which were a tangle of excitement and fear and a truly inexplicable confusion.

"Were you involved in the fight?" Lady Craythorne demanded. "Oliver, that is beyond rash. You should not have risked yourself."

"We were all at risk, Mother, and had I not fought—" Lord Craythorne's fist clenched. "That is irrelevant. The Army is here, the mob dispersed, and many of its members captured."

"That is good," Lydia said, "but you do not look satisfied."

Lord Craythorne turned his gaze on Lydia, and she suppressed a gasp, for his emotions surged, bleak and terrible as anything that had ever overwhelmed her in the asylum. "It is not about satisfaction," he said. "I cannot—" He closed his eyes and let out a deep breath. "I apologize for my cryptic words. Something has happened that I have no explanation for."

"Oliver, speak frankly," Lady Craythorne said, just as Lydia said, "You frighten me, your Grace. How horrid is it?"

"Not horrid, precisely," Lord Craythorne said. "It seems I have been wrong for years. I am not merely a Scorcher. I am, in fact, an Extraordinary."

CHAPTER 26

IN WHICH THERE IS MUCH DISCUSSION OF THE NATURE OF TALENT

Lady Craythorne stepped back, involuntarily, Lydia believed, as her Grace's emotions were incoherent confusion. "That is impossible," Lady Craythorne said. "Impossible. You are far too old to manifest an Extraordinary talent. You must be mistaken."

Lord Craythorne shook his head. "It is no mistake. In a moment of panic, I extinguished a fire. And then I went on doing it."

The room fell silent. Lydia's own astonishment was mirrored in the other women, all except Bisset, who Lydia did not believe spoke English as fluently as was needed to follow this conversation. Lord Craythorne was breathing heavily, as if he had run far and fast, but it seemed speaking his astonishing news had calmed him, for his fear and confusion had diminished. Lydia had so many questions she did not know where to begin. "What fire did you extinguish, your Grace?" she said, wishing desperately to ease his emotions.

Lord Craythorne turned his gaze on her in some relief. "The rioters had Scorchers of their own," he said, "and they attempted to set the palace on fire. Our defenders sought to identify and eliminate the Scorchers, but they were wary of our efforts and turned their talent on those who were most a threat. Which included me." He drew in a deep breath. "One minute, I was taking aim at one of these Scorchers, and the next minute, I was on fire."

"*Oliver!*" Lady Craythorne's voice rose a full octave in her horror.

Lord Craythorne did not react, merely continued, "And then I...it is so peculiar, I cannot explain what I did, except that I told the fire to go out and it did."

"But you have never been able to do this before, Oliver," Lady Craythorne insisted. "Perhaps there was another Extraordinary Scorcher—or you imagined it—"

Lord Craythorne plucked at his sleeve, which Lydia now realized was badly scorched in addition to being black with char. "No imagination could have done it, Mother. And I doubt another Extraordinary could have doused the fire burning me at exactly the moment I tried to extinguish it."

"You never use your talent," Lydia said, enlightenment dawning. "You actively avoid using it. You might have developed the Extraordinary talent years ago and never known it."

"That is precisely my supposition, Miss Wescott." Lord Craythorne drew in another breath. He turned to face the fire and stretched out a hand as if warming himself. In an instant, the fire was extinguished.

Lady Craythorne and Mrs. Monroe gasped. Lydia stepped forward to examine the hearth. No heat now radiated from the logs; they were dusted with pale grey ash and smelled of a fire long dead. "Oh, my," she said faintly. "I believed you, but that is not the same as seeing it done."

She turned to face Lord Craythorne, who regarded the logs with a grim expression. "Your Grace," she said, "why do you behave as if this is a death sentence? England will rejoice to know she has two Extraordinary Scorchers."

Lord Craythorne blinked as if she had startled him out of some distant dreamland. "I—it is simply that I feel I am a stranger to myself, Miss Wescott. So many years of denying my talent, and then to see it flower into a new and unexpected shape—it seems I must revisit my whole history."

"Surely not *all* your history," Lydia protested. "I am certain you were a sweet-tempered and biddable child."

Lord Craythorne let out a choked laugh. "I will leave it to Lady Craythorne to respond to that," he said.

"An Extraordinary," Mrs. Monroe said from where she was sitting up on the sofa. "What a strange..." A peculiar expression crossed her face, and her head twitched, snapping abruptly back. In the next moment, her whole body convulsed, jerking and writhing spasmodically. Only Lord Craythorne's swift movement to kneel by her side kept her from falling to the floor.

Lydia and Lady Craythorne hovered nearby until the seizure passed and Mrs. Monroe lay quietly in Lord Craythorne's arms. The Duke restored her to the sofa, but she was unconscious. "Thank you, Oliver, but please give way," Lady Craythorne said. "I do not know what is to be done for her when she has fits, but she will wake soon."

"Mr. Monroe has told me the Extraordinary Shaper Dr. Mansfield, who is attached to the palace, has never been able to do anything for Mrs. Monroe's condition. But there is another doctor who I believe tends to her." Lord Craythorne backed away to leave room for the Dowager Duchess to take his place. "I will send for him."

"But you have not said what happened," Lydia protested as Lord Craythorne walked to the door. "The mob is gone, yes, and...?"

Lord Craythorne regarded her calmly, an expression that did not reflect his emotions. His gaze flicked past her to Lady Craythorne, who was preoccupied with chafing Mrs. Monroe's wrists, and then to Ellery and Bisset, watching Mrs. Monroe carefully. "Come with me," he told Lydia in a low voice, and Lydia hurried past him out the door.

Once in the hallway, Lord Craythorne took Lydia by the elbow and set a rapid pace that had her occasionally hopping to keep up. "The mob has been dispersed, and the palace saved," he said, "but that is all the good news we have. Several of our men were killed before the Army arrived. That is bad enough, but worse from a political perspective is that none of the rioters we were able to arrest were anything but pawns. There was no sign of Suggitt or Ruskin."

Lydia cursed, and then blushed hard when Lord Craythorne laughed. "So indelicate, Miss Wescott. That is hardly the language I expect from you."

"I do try to curb my tongue, your Grace, but I fear extreme provocation is too much for my self-control."

"I forgive you your frailties." Lord Craythorne's amusement dwindled. "We have stopped a dire threat to the Viceroyalty and by extension England's government, but if we cannot find the ringleaders, I fear we only postpone the real threat."

Lydia stopped, grasping Lord Craythorne's grimy sleeve. "Oh! I intended to tell you, but there was no time—Maud knows of a place where James met with his cronies. If those were Mr. Ruskin and Mr. Suggitt, perhaps that is where the ringleaders went once the riot failed!"

Lord Craythorne stopped. "What place?"

"It is called the Raven's Rest. We guessed it might be a tavern, or an inn."

"I have never heard of it, but someone here will have." The Duke put a firm, comforting hand over Lydia's where it gripped his sleeve. "Come. We will find the doctor, and then I will set someone to investigating the Raven's Rest."

He drew her along rapidly in his wake, through the palace and into its west wing. More men thronged the rooms than before, some filled with satisfaction, others concerned, all of their emotions muted by tiredness. Lydia had lost track of the time, but she suspected it was well after midnight.

They ended up in a large, unfurnished room the twin of the ballroom Lydia had seen at the investiture ball. Men lay on the floor here and there in varying degrees of pain and fear Lydia had to work at ignoring, suppressing her own fears so she might not be overwhelmed. The idea of being overwhelmed in these conditions filled her with guilt and shame, as if she mocked the real pain these men experienced from their wounds by sharing it vicariously.

Lord Craythorne walked wide of the wounded men to where a short, round man with a white fringe of hair all around his balding scalp was just rising from his latest patient. A quiet conversation led to the doctor giving quick instructions to his assistants and making rapidly for the door. Lydia hesitated.

"Go with him," Lord Craythorne instructed her. "I will return once

I have settled the question of the Raven's Rest and sent someone to the mansion to see if it is intact. Mother will prefer to sleep in her own bed if she can."

"I hope Maud's information proves helpful. She was devastated to learn how James abused her trust."

"I assume this means you have proven her innocent of collusion." Lord Craythorne's voice lowered until his words could not be heard beyond the two of them.

"Her and Lady Craythorne both." Lydia almost told him of the conversation she had had with the Dowager Duchess, but realized in time that, first, it was the sort of conversation that should be kept confidential, and second, that she was delaying Lord Craythorne. "But —go, please, and return with good news!"

"Only you could possibly qualify the arrest of hardened traitors as good news," Lord Craythorne said with a wry smile. He gripped her hand briefly and strode away.

Lydia hurried back to the drawing room, though she kept a slower pace than Lord Craythorne had set, and arrived in time to see the doctor supporting Mrs. Monroe into a sitting position. "You must take to your bed as soon as possible, ma'am," he said in a creaky voice that sounded as if he needed a soothing drink to ease his throat. "No, do not attempt to walk. I will send someone."

"Do not tell James," Mrs. Monroe said, and for a moment Lydia believed she meant the treacherous one before she remembered the Viceroy's given name was also James. "He does not need another worry tonight. Tomorrow will be soon enough."

"Very well, ma'am." The doctor straightened. "Please stay with her until she can be moved, Lady Craythorne."

"Of course," Lady Craythorne said.

Lydia took a seat without saying anything and stared at the upholstery of the sofa, not wishing to meet Lady Craythorne's eyes and possibly start a conversation they should not have in front of Mrs. Monroe and Bisset. She Discerned Lady Craythorne's extreme curiosity and mild impatience and was amused at how those emotions matched her own. Perhaps she and the Dowager Duchess had more in common than she had realized.

They waited for perhaps five minutes before several large, uniformed men entered the drawing room. Two of them very respectfully lifted Mrs. Monroe into the cradle made by another pair's joined wrists, while the others bustled around in an attempt to look busy. Another man entered as they were all preparing to bustle out and said, "Lady Craythorne, the carriage is ready."

Lady Craythorne did not make any inane comments about whether that meant the mansion was secure for their return. She merely nodded at Lydia and followed the bustling men into the hall. Then there was much maneuvering and more bustle as Lady Craythorne bade Mrs. Monroe farewell and promised to return the following afternoon for a visit, and in short order Lydia found herself in the carriage, which was not Lord Craythorne's, bumping along the drive through the darkness.

She strained to see what damage the palace had sustained, but many of the interior lights were out, and although the skies had cleared, with the moon just past new there was little light beyond what burned at the main doors. She smelled no smoke nor char on the light breeze, so likely the fires had not done much damage—and if Lord Craythorne had been alert, he would have extinguished the fires before they could do even that.

An Extraordinary Scorcher. Lydia well understood the shock Lord Craythorne had experienced when the fire responded to his command. She recalled her own talent's awakening ten years before, how she had gradually grown in power and sensitivity until she had reached her current limits. That had been terrifying enough, but suppose instead she had woken one morning with her Discernment in full flower and the emotions of everyone near her battering at her?

She would never say it, because Lord Craythorne was her friend and she did not wish to criticize what he could not change, but she could not help wondering how his life would have been different had he not been so resentful and ashamed of his talent. Had he used it frequently, he would have discovered he was an Extraordinary years ago, and then...but it was impossible to know what might have been different, or even if he would have been happier.

Now that the danger was over, her body's weariness set in, and she nodded off and jerked awake more than once during the short drive. When the carriage finally came to a stop, she did not at first realize that meant she should exit, but Lady Craythorne got out, and that brought Lydia back to herself.

The mansion appeared untouched in the dim moonlight, and the doors were intact and still locked. Lydia bade Lady Craythorne good-night at the foot of the stairs and hoped Bisset's presence would be enough to prevent the Dowager Duchess questioning her. But she had only just achieved her room and put on her nightdress when someone knocked briskly on her door. With a nod, she sent Ellery to open it, and said, "Your Grace, please come in."

Lady Craythorne was still dressed in the gown she had worn all evening. She shut the door behind her and said, "What else did my son tell you?"

"We spoke—" Lydia hesitated, reviewing that conversation in memory. "It was of matters relating to why he is here in America, the true reason. I do not believe I should share the details. Forgive me."

Lady Craythorne waved a dismissive hand. "I have no interest in matters of politics, as I'm sure you know. What of this Extraordinary talent? It is impossible."

"We saw him extinguish a fire. It is hardly impossible. But I understand you—it happened so unexpectedly it is as if there must be some mistake."

"Exactly." Lady Craythorne took a seat without being invited and buried her face in her hands. "I do not believe I can endure any more shocks."

"That is precisely the sort of remark that ought to elicit something horrid to shock you further," Lydia said, straight-faced.

The Dowager Duchess chuckled, surprising Lydia, who had never heard the woman laugh. "It is with extreme difficulty I refrain from telling my reticulum the news of this development, but I believe Oliver would like privacy for as long as that is possible. Fortunately, almost everyone in my reticulum is in England and is currently asleep, so my eagerness is tempered."

She rose and straightened her skirts. "I thank you for your honesty," she said, and for a wonder she meant it. "I will Speak to Mrs.

Adams now, as she also evacuated during the riots. We will have much to tell one another—though I am not certain what she will be more surprised at, news of the palace under siege or news of my soon-to-be daughter." She smiled and let herself out. Lydia followed her progress until she entered the state of placidity tempered by pleasure that marked a Spoken conversation.

"She is not so unfriendly as I believed, if I may speak freely, miss," Ellery said from the doorway to the dressing room.

"I agree. She has simply fallen into habits of behavior she regrets, and I believe she wishes to be otherwise." Lydia climbed into bed and snuggled deep into the blankets. "I daresay I will sleep until noon, Maud. You should sleep, too."

"I will, miss." Ellery paused at the bedroom door. "You will tell me if aught happens with James, yes?"

"I certainly will. And if there is an opportunity for you to spit in his face, I promise to tell you that, as well!"

Ellery giggled and turned out the light.

❦

LYDIA WOKE TO THE WARM GOLDEN GLOW CHARACTERISTIC OF early afternoon. She lay in bed contemplating the nature of light. The light of dawn looked different from that of midmorning or afternoon, and the light of sunset looked different from all three, and yet it was all still light, capable of illuminating her surroundings. Things did not look markedly different, a different color or shape, in the afternoon than the morning. Though it was true the silks and wools of her needlework appeared different under different lights, and this was true of morning and evening sunshine as well as of lamplight and candles.

She stretched and rolled to where she could see the mantel clock. Just after one o'clock. She was sure Ellery had risen earlier, as she had told Lydia she became lethargic if she slept too long, and was grateful Ellery had chosen not to wake her. She already felt more rested than she had in days. The madhouse seemed weeks in the past.

She examined her cheek in the dressing table mirror. She had forgot to clean the makeup off her face before sleeping, and her face now had a smeared look to it, as if the bruise was the cosmetics and had been applied haphazardly across her fair skin. She prodded it briefly and was relieved that it did not hurt much, for all it remained livid.

Her stomach growled its hunger, and she pulled the bell rope. Food, then clothing—no, if Lord Craythorne had returned with news, she wished to be available to hear it. Clothing, then food downstairs.

Ellery, when she appeared, had no news of Lord Craythorne. "Though it is astonishing, miss, how everyone now has terrible things to say of James," she said as she helped Lydia dress. "The household servants claim to have never trusted him, and Mrs. Pogue says she spoke against hiring him, which is ridiculous because James was one of the Duke's household before arriving here and his being hired was never in question."

"People are so odd sometimes," Lydia said. "So often they are embarrassed at being wrong, and they say all manner of things to save face. It would be amusing if it were not so sad."

"It is not as if they can deceive you, miss." Ellery retrieved the box of cosmetics. "I will fix this for you."

Lydia sat still as Ellery powdered her cheek. No one could deceive her—almost no one, she chastised herself, remembering Mrs. Ruskin. She hoped devoutly that Lord Craythorne would bring the Ruskins to justice. That might restore her confidence in her talent. Perhaps her embarrassment at being tricked put her solidly in company with those who dissembled or lied to protect their self-esteem.

The house seemed unexpectedly empty, though Lydia did not Discern any obvious reduction in staff. Perhaps it was that normally at this hour, Lady Craythorne would be entertaining guests, or Lord Craythorne would be closeted with his informants, and neither of them were present—though they might just be asleep still.

She called for cold meats and cheeses, not wishing to burden the kitchen staff with a demand for a more elaborate meal, and ate distractedly, Discerning the servants as they moved about the mansion. None of them showed any sign they were still disturbed by the previous night's evacuation, though she guessed if she were to speak to them on the subject, their emotions would become more volatile.

She had almost finished her meal when she heard the front door open and Discerned Lord Craythorne's approach. Eagerly, she shot to her feet, then decided she wished to appear calm and not as if she had been waiting all day for his return. Lord Craythorne's emotions were once more focused on some challenge, yellow-green with mingled excitement and intellectual passion. Lydia resumed her seat and pretended to be eating. But Lord Craythorne swept past the closed dining room door in the direction of his study. Embarrassed at having set up a tableau that no one would see, Lydia hurried after him.

Lord Craythorne heard her footsteps and turned, smiling when he realized who had followed him. "I believed you would still be abed."

"I slept long enough—oh, your Grace, tell me you have news?"

"Let us sit. There is currently no hurry. In fact, let us go to the library instead." His smile widened. "It has become our unofficial council of war chamber, do you not agree?"

"I only know it is congenial, and that your emotions are more expansive there." Lydia arched her eyebrow. The gesture was harder than it looked. "If the library makes you more likely to share confidences, then I will agree to it being anything you like, officially or unofficially."

That drew a laugh from the Duke. "I had not considered that. How fortunate that you keep your own counsel so readily, as I am sure you will not spread my secrets abroad."

They crossed the foyer to the stairs, which rose to a small landing before doubling back on themselves to end at the first floor. Lydia eyed Lord Craythorne and decided to broach a subject she hoped he was willing to discuss with her. "You have not spread your secret yourself," she said. "I imagine one does not begin a typical conversation with 'by the by, I have discovered an Extraordinary Scorcher talent, how has your day been?'"

She had hoped to make him laugh again, but guilt and shame and a little mulish anger rose up within him, and Lydia was taken aback at her inadvertent presumption. "Your Grace—" she began.

"Let me pretend I have privacy from you, Miss Wescott, and do not comment on what you Discern," Lord Craythorne said.

His anger did not grow, and she Discerned nothing that meant his words were chastisement, but his cold rebuff hurt nonetheless. "Then I will not," she said, hoping her light tone did not convey her emotions.

They walked to the second staircase in silence as Lord Craythorne struggled to master himself. Finally, he said, "Do you believe this is something I ought to tell others?"

"I do not believe you should keep it a secret," Lydia replied. "And—"

"And, what?" Lord Craythorne asked when she did not immediately continue.

"I cannot reply without disregarding your wishes." Lydia did not look his way, but his guilt surged high enough she guessed it showed in his expression.

Lord Craythorne sighed. "Forgive me. That was foolishness, telling you not to speak what you Discern. It is not as if I can stop you—no, do not look so!" He put a hand on Lydia's wrist, gripping her gently but firmly. "That was no criticism, merely a statement of fact. I meant that I am a fool to try to ignore what I feel, or to pretend you do not know my innermost heart simply because you say nothing."

Lydia examined his face and his emotions, his mud-brown remorse, and an unfamiliar pang shot through her, an emotion she had no name for. "I would rather not give you pain," she said, hoping to offer him relief.

"I would be a fool twice over if I rejected your counsel on the grounds that it holds a terrible mirror up to my secret hopes and fears." Lord Craythorne shook his head. "Advise me, please, and if I ever again ask you to keep my secrets from me, ignore that request."

"You are daring, your Grace," Lydia said with a smile.

"Merely unwilling to risk being a fool again. Now, what did you intend to say?"

Lydia cast back in memory. "I believe you are ashamed that your fear of your talent, of being thought wild and uncontrolled simply because you are a Scorcher, prevented you from discovering the truth for many years. Now the idea of admitting to it embarrasses you. You also dislike notoriety, and this will make you notorious indeed. Though 'notorious' sounds so underhanded and villainous, so perhaps that is the wrong word. But I believe you take my meaning."

"I do, and you are correct on all counts, as usual." Lord Craythorne held the library door for her. "It is foolishness, I know."

"Not entirely foolishness, because there is nothing wrong with a desire for privacy." Lydia seated herself at the table and folded her hands in her lap. "And I apologize for raising the subject."

"You need not apologize. Friends should not be afraid to broach certain subjects with one another."

"I meant because the discussion of your Extraordinary talent distracted us from what I truly care about learning. What of the Raven's Rest? Did you find Mr. Suggitt? Or the Ruskins?"

Lord Craythorne dragged the chair opposite Lydia away from the table, but did not sit, instead leaning heavily on it as if he were too weary to support his own weight. "We were not in time to capture anyone at the Raven's Rest. However, the innkeeper provided us with valuable information, and my men tracked Suggitt to his bolt hole and apprehended him."

Lydia sat up straight in excitement. "And the Ruskins?"

"Disappeared, for now. I hope an interrogation of Suggitt will produce their location." Lord Craythorne finally sat, slumping in his chair as if his weariness had grown stronger. "How strange," he said, regarding Lydia closely. "I believed it was impossible to have more than one talent, and yet I am certain I have developed an Extraordinary Discerner's ability."

Lydia, confused, said, "Your Grace?"

"I mean," Lord Craythorne said, "your eagerness to participate in that interrogation is palpable."

Lydia blushed. "I suppose I should not reveal myself. But there is nothing wrong with wishing to be of use!"

"Of course not. And, as it happens, I intend you to be there. Suggitt almost certainly knows of your talent, and I daresay he fears what you will Discern. Had you not requested it, I believe I would have insisted on your presence." Lord Craythorne's smile was wicked. "These Libertymen have led me a merry dance, and I find myself wishing to turn the tables in as dramatic a manner as possible."

Lydia smiled back. "Your Grace," she said, "I wish for that as well."

CHAPTER 27

IN WHICH ANOTHER INTERROGATION LEADS LYDIA TO LAMENT HER LOT

A t nightfall, Lord Craythorne called for the carriage. Lydia, waiting with him in the foyer near the hearth with its blazing fire, said, "At the risk of encouraging you in conventional thinking, should I perhaps have Ellery join us? Except I cannot see a reason for her to participate, and now I fear you will say I must stay behind to protect my reputation."

Lord Craythorne eyed her in some amusement. "Why, Miss Wescott, surely as a fallen woman you should have no care for your reputation?"

Lydia scowled. "I do not see why a woman's honor is tainted by being alone with a man to whom she is neither related nor married. It is as if society believes we are all so wanton as to—"

"Pray, do not complete that sentence, as I wish to retain some illusions about your delicacy." His smile broadened, and he added, "As it happens, I intend that no one who matters will see us, and we *are* engaged to be wed, so if anyone does choose to pour out opprobrium on either of us, it is not as if that censure will stick."

"Just so you do not change your mind. Oh, how I hope Mr. Suggitt's information leads to capturing the Ruskins!"

"We will find them, never fear." Lord Craythorne fixed his attention on the fire, and the flames dipped and bowed as if stirred by a nonexistent wind.

Lydia observed this curiously. "What a, well, extraordinary talent to have. Fire is so volatile, and being able to control it must feel wonderful. To have such power, I mean."

"I fear to me it is still an unknown, for the most part. Fire still burns me if I touch it, which makes me wonder whether my inattention to my talent for all those years has hampered it, or made me defective in some way." The fire stretched high up the chimney like soft wax drawn out in a long string, then collapsed on itself and separated to burn in a ring that danced upon the logs.

"If you are capable of doing something so elaborate as that, your Grace," Lydia said, "I doubt you need fear you are defective. Perhaps the talent grows with use. Mine certainly did."

"I should speak to Lady Enderleigh. She must have answers." Lord Craythorne sighed deeply. "I am ashamed of how reluctant I am to share this news. It feels like cowardice."

"It is simply that you are a private person and accustomed to keeping your own counsel." Lydia tugged her pelisse closer around her shoulders as the footman opened the front door, letting in a gust of icy air. "Besides, Mr. Suggitt is currently more important than you are. Or —no, perhaps that is wrong, because he is a criminal and a traitor and you are a duke who is neither. And yet—oh, I am saying this all wrong."

Lord Craythorne gestured to her to precede him. "I understand your meaning. Perhaps that should worry me."

"You are not very funny, your Grace."

Darkness had fallen early due to heavy clouds obscuring the sky, scudding along propelled by the brisk wind. Lydia huddled deeper into her wrap and wished her shoes were stouter. No one had thought to put a hot brick on the floor, and her toes felt cold enough she was sure the chill radiated up her legs and through her body. Across from her, Lord Craythorne sat silently, apparently impervious to the cold. She eyed his Hessian boots with envy.

They rode through the streets, not speaking. Lord Craythorne's emotions were nothing but confidence and mild anticipation, as if they were going nowhere more exciting than a play or an evening with nodding acquaintances. Lydia's own emotions were more tumultuous. She reminded herself that she should appear calm and confident and not give away any of her excitement.

She watched Lord Craythorne again. He was looking out the window and seemed unaware of her scrutiny. The passing lamps threw his visage into light, then darkness, then light again, making him seem to flicker as they rode. She liked his profile, how with his curly hair and aquiline nose he looked like the better class of Roman emperors. The idle image made her giggle.

Lord Craythorne stirred. "Will you share your amusement?"

Lydia shook her head. Impulsively, she said, "Why do you give me so much respect, your Grace? I am little more than a girl, and I am not always fully tethered to reality, and no one ever believes someone like me might have opinions or ideas worth listening to. And yet you have always treated me as an equal, not as someone in need of protection, even when I was a stranger to you."

Lord Craythorne rubbed a hand over his chin in a thoughtful gesture. "Do you suggest I should not?"

"Of course not! But—very well, I should not pry."

He chuckled. "I told you once I speak to you as if you are male and my peer, and you have never been offended. I find your candor and eagerness refreshing, and I value the way you see the world."

"But you are not like Colin—my brother respects my talent, but he remembers my past and he wishes to protect my future. You must be unusual yourself, your Grace. Thank you."

Lord Craythorne's smile faded. "I know not how unusual I am, but I have always been surrounded by sycophants whose true opinions I cannot trust, and to find someone who is not only honest with me, but forces me to be honest with myself...perhaps few men wish for such a friendship, but to me, it is invaluable."

His words warmed Lydia's heart. "I assure you," she said, "you are one of a rarefied few. Most people who know of my talent fear what I will Discern. Though most people live bland and harmless lives, and their fears are outsized by comparison to reality." She sighed. "I dislike being feared."

"That is something we have in common," Lord Craythorne said. "I believe—but we are here. I would like you to remain silent at first while I ask questions. Let Suggitt become increasingly apprehensive about what you might discover. If he proves recalcitrant, we will change our strategy. Do you understand?"

"Of course, your Grace. And I suggest you ask him questions that can be answered with a 'yes' or a 'no,' as those answers are easy to Discern."

Lord Craythorne nodded. He assisted Lydia out of the carriage and guided her with one hand on her elbow toward the building they had stopped in front of. "I will do my best."

The modestly-sized red brick house they now approached was made grander by a row of white pillars along its front façade, smooth and appearing to bulge in the middle. An elaborate wrought iron lantern hung above the double doors, casting a wan yellow light over the doorstep and the walls immediately to either side. In that light, the red brick appeared orange, a not very attractive color, but one so warm Lydia shivered with the contrast between it and the still-frigid wind that made the lantern creak as it swung from its chain.

Lord Craythorne opened the door without knocking and ushered Lydia in. The foyer beyond had a tall ceiling, but was not nearly so comfortable as Lord Craythorne's home; there was no grand fireplace, no welcoming chairs, only a pair of lamps on the far wall and a chandelier with half its candles extinguished. The three lights cast ominous shadows across the walls and floor and gave Lord Craythorne a villainous look.

Lydia swiftly assessed the house, which was small enough to be entirely within her range. There were only ten people in or around it in addition to herself and Lord Craythorne. Three of them paced in circles around the house outside, their emotions damped by the cold but still keenly alert and anticipatory. Two were below stairs, their idle beige interest focused on chores or cooking, probably. Four made a knot of emotion upstairs, some of them alert, some of them bored. And one individual was afraid, a dull pulsing brown surrounded by those four. It was not a sharp, immediate fear, but one that suggested the person had been afraid for a while and was becoming too weary to care.

"We must hurry, your Grace," Lydia said, and headed for the stairs.

"Hurry? Is something wrong?" Lord Craythorne caught up to her easily.

"No—well, yes—it is not precisely wrong, it is just that I can tell Mr. Suggitt is losing his fear of what you might do to him, and we must act before he becomes indifferent, as I do not wish for you to torture him."

"*Torture?*" Lord Craythorne put a hand on Lydia's arm, bringing her to a halt. "No one has spoken of torture."

"Then perhaps it is your men who will do it. I do not mean to accuse you."

Lord Craythorne let out a choked laugh. "He will not be tortured, Miss Wescott. When he can give us no more information, he will be taken to the city jail and held pending trial. What do you take me for?"

Lydia blushed. "I suppose life is not like a dramatic novel."

"I should hope not," Lord Craythorne said. "Imagine how much more trouble the world would be in if villains roamed free to harass innocent maidens such as yourself."

The upstairs hall was as dimly and unnervingly lit as below, but Lord Craythorne walked confidently to the second door on the left and opened it, bowing Lydia in. It was mostly bare, furnished with only one elegantly carved and gilded table pushed into a corner. The four men whose emotions she had Discerned stood or paced throughout the room, armed with pistols and short blades. They stopped mid-step and came to attention at Lord Craythorne's entrance, surprise at Lydia's presence taking the place of alert anticipation.

Lydia looked past the Duke at the fifth man. He was bound securely to a kitchen chair whose back was to the door. At the sound of the door opening, he tilted his blindfolded head as if straining to hear more clearly, or possibly trying to see down the sides of his nose. His fear increased, but not by as much as Lydia liked, as far as getting information out of him went. She recognized his red hair and broad shoulders from the investiture ball, when Mr. Ruskin had chastised him for his brash speaking.

Now that Lydia knew the truth about the Ruskins, that interaction seemed very different. She had believed Mr. Ruskin did not appreciate Suggitt's disruption of the ball, but more likely Mr. Ruskin had not wished him to speak of their true allegiances so loudly. She told herself she could have had no reason to suspect Mr. Ruskin then, but she could not help imagining how things would have played out differently had she known to accuse him immediately. She would not have been locked in a madhouse to rot, for one.

Lord Craythorne walked with slow, deliberate steps to stand in front of Suggitt, gesturing for Lydia to stay back. He regarded his captive for a moment, to Lydia's Discernment calming his excitement. Then he snatched the blindfold away.

Suggitt shook his head as if emerging from deep water. Though Lydia could not see his face, his emotions lay bare to her, easily Discerned. Apprehension suffused him, as did fear he endeavored to suppress, and disdain, which worried her. Disdain indicated someone who intended to brazen out his situation.

"Abel Suggitt," Lord Craythorne said. "You and your fellow Libertymen attempted to burn down the Viceroy's palace so you might seize power. You incited simultaneous riots in several other cities as part of this coup attempt. You are responsible for the deaths of seventeen men attached to the palace, and I hold to your account the many other deaths, injuries, and destruction caused by your mob."

"You've no proof," Suggitt sneered. "I wasn't anywhere near the Viceroy's palace. You're holding me captive against the law."

That was a lie that blazed so bright Lydia might almost have read by it. She shook her head when Lord Craythorne glanced her way.

"Bold words," Lord Craythorne said. "The punishment for treason is death. I am willing to commute that punishment to transportation if you are forthcoming with information about your co-conspirators."

"I'm no tattle-mouth," Suggitt said. "Go ahead and make me. I will say nothing, no matter how you torture me."

"If you are no Libertyman, then you have nothing to tell," Lord Craythorne said, "so your words have already betrayed you."

Chagrin momentarily flooded through Suggitt, but he regained his composure quickly enough Lydia might have admired him had he not been a foul traitor. "I'll say no more," he said.

Lord Craythorne regarded him thoughtfully. "Unfortunately for you," he said, "you need not speak to give me information." He nodded at Lydia, who startled out of her contemplation of Suggitt's emotions. She controlled her sudden attack of nervousness and walked to where Suggitt could see her.

Suggitt's eyes widened, and his expression became almost comically frightened. "I see you have guessed the identity of my associate," Lord Craythorne said, his voice remaining calm and implacable. "Perhaps you had something to do with how Mr. and Mrs. Ruskin attempted to make her disappear."

Suggitt's eyes moved rapidly as he looked from Lydia to Lord Craythorne and back to Lydia. He remained silent.

"He did not," Lydia said. "They told him of my talent and what they intended, though. I believe he had other responsibilities."

Suggitt's mouth fell open. "That—" he began, swallowed, and said, "Stay out of my head, woman!"

"It is your emotions that betray you," Lydia said, "and I am no mind reader as Extraordinary Speakers are said to be. Which is not as fortunate for you as you imagine. Do not bother speaking. Your Grace?"

She could tell Lord Craythorne was having trouble controlling his amusement, but his demeanor was as unruffled as ever. "Have the Libertymen plans for another attack?" he asked.

"No," Lydia said, watching Suggitt's face carefully. It was gradually reddening as if he was holding his breath, though in fact he breathed loudly and heavily through his nose. His lips, by contrast, were a white pinched line that looked near to breaking as he held back words. His efforts to suppress his emotions were comical, as he clearly believed willing himself not to feel was as easy as whistling for it. Lydia, who had years of experience in suppressing emotion, almost sympathized with him.

"Did Mr. Ruskin give any further orders to you or your compatriots?" Lord Craythorne watched Lydia instead of Suggitt. His regard gave her an odd, uncomfortable sensation, as if despite the circumstances she and he were the only ones in the room, and Suggitt was merely a figment of the air.

"He is confused by that question," she said. "Is not Mr. Ruskin your leader?"

Suggitt laughed. "Don't know everything, do you, girl?"

"Really, it is better you not speak if you wish to confound us," Lydia said. "Your Grace, he believes *he* is the ringleader, but I am certain that is untrue."

Lord Craythorne's gaze turned on Suggitt. "You, the leader of the Libertymen? Unlikely. Mr. and Mrs. Ruskin have played you for a fool. They abandoned you to capture, gave you the impression that you are more important than you are—what a perfect tool."

Suggitt abruptly wrenched at his bonds, jerking forward and making Lydia take an involuntary step back, though she was well out of his reach. The men surrounding them brought their pistols to the ready. Suggitt ignored them. "I am no man's tool," he snarled.

"No, I believe your conjecture is correct, your Grace," Lydia said. "He is not incompetent, I daresay, because if he was the one who arranged for all those riots, he succeeded very well. It was not his fault the Ruskins kidnapped me and accelerated those plans—well, it is perhaps somewhat his fault, in the sense that he was complicit—though he did not participate in the kidnapping, so possibly I am still wrong—"

"I understand, Miss Wescott," Lord Craythorne said, again suppressing mirth. Lydia scowled at him, but he was already staring at Suggitt again as if he truly could penetrate the man's skull to lay bare the thoughts beneath. "How much of what you just said is true?"

"Oh, all of it, he is very proud of what he accomplished and annoyed that his careful plans were disrupted." Lydia regarded Suggitt closely. "Mr. Suggitt, does your father know of your affiliations?"

Suggitt's red face paled.

"So he does not, I see. Would he approve if he did know?"

"Miss Wescott—" Lord Craythorne was confused, though he did not show it.

"Lord Craythorne, the elder Mr. Suggitt has no connections to the Libertymen, but he harbors an admiration for their work," Lydia said.

"I cannot say if that makes him a danger, but I believe the government should know to watch him carefully."

"Thank you, Miss Wescott, but let us stick to the matter at hand. Mr. Suggitt, have I convinced you that attempting to conceal information is pointless? I repeat my offer: give us the names of your fellows, and you will receive transportation to Australia rather than the hangman's noose." Lord Craythorne gestured, and one of the men holstered his pistol and set out paper and ink at the lonely table.

"Do your worst," Suggitt said. "You'll have to take the names from me by force, for I won't betray those whose only crime is wishing for freedom from damned aristos like you." His fear surged through him, forcing Lydia to take a deep breath and suppress her own emotions.

"Miss Wescott, a word?" Lord Craythorne drew her to the door and then through it, shutting it quietly on the tableau within. "I doubt it is feasible to list off the names of every man in Washington who might be complicit, and that is what it would take for your Discernment to identify the Libertymen, am I correct?"

"You are, your Grace." Lydia sighed. "I should not wish for mind reading to be possible, for it could not fail but to be used for evil, but I do wish it in this circumstance."

"I understand, and I agree." Lord Craythorne sighed as well. "The best I believe we can hope for is to learn where the Ruskins went, as those are names we *do* have."

"Do you have an idea, your Grace?"

Lord Craythorne gazed at the door as if he could see through it. "I do."

He opened the door and ushered Lydia back inside. "Mr. Suggitt," he said, taking slow, deliberate steps until he stood before the bound man. "I cannot applaud your methods, but it might surprise you to know I sympathize with your desire to see your country self-governing."

Suggitt's eyes narrowed. "That won't work, either. Pretending to be on my side. I suppose next you will say you are opposed to Britain's hold on its colonies?"

"No, I will not." Lord Craythorne paced in a slow circle around Suggitt, his hands clasped behind his back. "America is not ready for freedom. Your own George Washington saw it. He was a patriot like none other, and he knew the insistence of some Americans on maintaining the foul institution of slavery would tear this nation apart were it to achieve independence. He swore he would not see his beloved country destroyed."

"Washington was a fool and a traitor," Suggitt spat, craning his neck trying to follow Lord Craythorne's movements. "And you know nothing of American interests. Slavery is essential to the South's economic prosperity."

"We will have to disagree on that point," Lord Craythorne replied calmly. "The issue at hand is the Libertymen's lust for power disguised as altruism. You claim—"

"That is a lie!" Suggitt shouted. "It is England who craves power. Excessive taxation, quartering of soldiers in our houses without our permission, a puppet government—"

"You claim you wish to better the lives of Americans," Lord Craythorne continued, raising his voice to override Suggitt's, "and yet your rioters destroyed American businesses and houses, not British ones. Did those who suffered thank the Libertymen for that?"

"Necessary losses," Suggitt said. His uncertainty did not sound in his voice.

"No, because before that, your men disguised themselves as Iroquois to conceal their true intentions as well as to bring the Six Nations into conflict with England. Though it is not England who would suffer from war with the Haudenosaunee, but Americans. Ordinary Americans who wish only to live in peace." Lord Craythorne stepped closer, looming over Suggitt. "I question whether your organization, such as it is, has anyone's best interests in mind but its own."

"We do what we must." Suggitt still sounded defiant, but despair welled up in him, and Lydia had to make herself a void to keep from being overwhelmed at this crucial moment.

"Do you?" Lord Craythorne sounded more arrogant and dismissive than Lydia had ever heard him, though it was all a front; his true emotions were confident and assured of victory. "Then I suppose Mr. Ruskin's actions reflect what *he* must do in the name of American freedom."

"You think to trick me. I will give nothing away."

"Do you know how we found you?" Lord Craythorne clasped his hands behind his back and turned away, taking a few slow steps before turning on his heel and pacing the other way. "The barman at the Raven's Rest saw the benefits of helping those pursuing a criminal. He was very forthcoming."

"Traitor," Suggitt breathed.

"One always underestimates the perceptive powers of a barman. He was forthcoming about other things as well." Lord Craythorne's voice grew quieter, but the room was silent except for Suggitt's heavy breathing, and his words sounded like the lash of whips in the still air. "How Mr. Ruskin met privately with others, not in your presence. How he gave orders that were counter to the ones he gave you. How Mr. Ruskin's behavior to you did not match his behavior at other times. Mr. Ruskin played you for a fool, Abel Suggitt. You were never anything but a pawn."

Lydia held her breath. Lord Craythorne was not telling the truth, or at least not the whole truth. His complex emotions revealed he was guessing rather than lying, though it was a near thing. She could not look at Suggitt in fear of giving the Duke's game away.

Suggitt's fury and fear were so strong Lydia could not imagine how they were not palpable to everyone in the room. "More lies," he shouted. "You think to turn me from my purpose—"

"Irrelevant," Lord Craythorne said. "You were a useful tool, and as Miss Wescott has pointed out, you were skilled at provoking riots. But you were meant to be caught. Mr. Ruskin believed our capturing you would distract us from him, permitting him a clean escape." He was guessing more fiercely now, and Lydia admired his coolness and the rapidity with which he spun his suppositions. She could have done the same, though she would not have been guessing.

Suggitt's uncertainty grew again, fighting with his fear and anger. "I gave Ruskin his orders," he said, and this time he did not sound certain.

"He let you believe that," Lord Craythorne said. "And when the plan went sour, he and his wife escaped. Leaving you, well, in this position." He swept a hand downward, indicating all of Suggitt.

"No. We were to—" Suggitt's gaze flicked to Lydia, and he shut his mouth.

"You have a rendezvous," Lydia said. "Mr. Suggitt, you should tell Lord Craythorne where that is. Mr. and Mrs. Ruskin are dangerous. You may be a patriot, but I do not believe they are."

Suggitt's heavy breathing subsided, and his ruddy complexion faded to its usual tan. "I will not give anyone away," he said.

Impulsively, Lydia stepped forward. "Consider what the Libertymen have *not* accomplished due to last night's action, Mr. Suggitt. The people are resentful of their property and homes being destroyed, and they do not lay the blame on British soldiers, but on their fellow Americans. Whose idea was the riots? Yours, or another's? And what might that other person have wished to accomplish?"

Suggitt's fear and uncertainty became wariness. "Ruskin is a patriot," he said.

"A patriot who has done untold damage to your organization," Lord Craythorne said. "The Libertymen are not my concern at the moment. I wish to apprehend Mr. Ruskin. Why should you remain loyal to someone who betrayed you?"

Suggitt lowered his head. "We were to rendezvous at a certain location here in Washington. But Ruskin will not be there, not if it is known I was captured. I do not know where else he might go."

"That is a lie," Lydia said. "Please, Mr. Suggitt, do not imagine you can deceive me. Tell us what you know."

"Very well, it is more true to say I do not know *precisely* where he is," Suggitt said. He sagged in his bonds, desolate and abandoned and ashamed, all of which Lydia hated to Discern in anyone, even a hardened traitor. "He has two other residences, in New York City and in Philadelphia, but he may have returned to England. Now, release me."

"That was not the agreement," Lord Craythorne said, "and you know if I let you go, I will merely have you followed to your compatriots. You will stand trial for your crimes. But if your information proves valuable, I will speak on your behalf."

"I told the truth," Suggitt said, this time staring at Lydia. "Tell him."

"He speaks truth," Lydia told Lord Craythorne. "And I believe he knows specifics of the locations he mentioned."

Lord Craythorne crossed to the table and took up the pen. "Then let us hear more."

Lydia stayed close, fearing Suggitt would lie now that she had vouched for him, but he gave directions and descriptions without once veering into deception. When he finished, Lord Craythorne gathered up his pages of notes and said, "Thank you for your cooperation, Mr. Suggitt. See that he is made comfortable in a cell, gentlemen."

In the carriage, Lydia said, "What is to be done now?"

"I will set my men to investigating each of these places." Lord Craythorne folded the papers and tucked them away inside his coat. "*You* will have dinner, and then sleep. And before you protest, let me remind you that this is not a task you can assist me in. Take pride in how you have served your country tonight."

"Very well," Lydia sighed, making the Duke laugh. "Oh, yes, laugh if you must, but *you* have the more exciting part to play."

"It is not as if I will accompany my men on their raids," Lord Craythorne said. "In fact, I must wait on their information. One can hardly call that exciting. But I believe the Libertymen's threat is nearly over, so perhaps there is no more excitement to be had."

"I should not wish for things to be otherwise," Lydia said, "as excitement can mean danger. But I daresay I shall have trouble sleeping tonight!"

CHAPTER 28

IN WHICH AN UNEXPECTED ENCOUNTER CUTS SHORT A SHOPPING EXPEDITION

Despite her words, Lydia slept soundly, waking at nearly noon from a dream that shredded to filmy nothing as she tried to remember it. All that remained were emotions that in her dream could not overwhelm her: sorrow, the deep aching sorrow of a terrible loss, and longing for something she could not have. She lay blinking up at the canopy, filled with sorrow of a different kind. If only she knew the way of remaining herself in the face of others' emotions! Her time in that unnamed asylum proved the solution she had depended on for years was imperfect, and yet she knew of no other way to protect herself.

Eventually, feeling as weary as if she had not slept at all, she made herself ignore her sorrow in favor of something real. Lord Craythorne must surely have news of the Ruskins.

She dressed quickly and hurried downstairs, but a voice from Lady Craythorne's drawing room stopped her from descending to the ground floor. She entered the drawing room and made her curtsey. "Your Grace, good morning."

"It is a fine morning, what is left of it," Lady Craythorne said, but without any hidden criticism of Lydia for having slept late. "I intend to pay calls this afternoon, and I wish for you to join me."

"Of course, Lady Craythorne."

Lydia's stomach chose that moment to rumble its demand for food. Lady Craythorne smiled, but made no comment. Instead, she said, "I suppose you will wish to purchase wedding clothes? Oliver has not said when you are to be married, but under the circumstances he will not wish to delay."

That made Lydia forget her hunger. "Wedding clothes?" she said, feeling rather stupid. "But I—it is not as if—I had not considered the matter, your Grace."

"It is unfortunate your mother cannot be here, as such activities are a peculiar pleasure, planning a daughter's future." Lady Craythorne's voice sounded indifferent, but Lydia perceived in her a keen curiosity. She could not now remember what she had told Lady Craythorne about her mother, whether she had revealed any of that part of her past, and for a moment, memory struck her so hard it felt like a physical blow to the chest.

She calmed her breathing and made a decision. "My mother has no interest in my life, nor in seeing me ever again," she said, "and for my part, I do not wish any contact with her."

Lady Craythorne raised her eyebrows. "Indeed," she said. "Then that is why you have not seen her in four years."

"She feared my talent, and tried to drive it out of me," Lydia said. "I prefer not to speak of it."

"Then we will not." The curiosity that impelled Lady Craythorne's questions sharpened, but to Lydia's surprise she did not pursue the matter. "If you wish, I will accompany you."

"Accompany me?"

"In your tour of the warehouses for your wedding clothes. You cannot continue to dress as a young maiden when you are Duchess of Craythorne." Lady Craythorne was now suffused with pleased satisfaction at her proposal. "I would be pleased to guide you."

"Well, I—that is most generous of you, your Grace. I would appreciate that." Apprehension crept over Lydia, the sense of an impending doom drawing nearer. She could not deny the accuracy of Lady Craythorne's words, but she did not know how she was to purchase anything on the small sum she had for her needs in the colonies. Now she wished she had not been so cavalier in her dismissal of Colin's offer to escort her to America. She might have sent word via Speaker, and he could have brought enough—oh, what a coil!

"We will Bound to New York City tomorrow morning," Lady Craythorne was saying. "Washington is all very well, but all the most fashionable modistes are in that city, and I have credit with all of them. And it will be enjoyable seeing the sights."

"We will not return to London?"

Lady Craythorne shook her head. "There are ladies I wish to visit in New York, and the city is not so provincial that you will suffer for having bought your clothes there."

Lady Craythorne's affability made Lydia suspicious, but she could imagine no way to press her for details. Then she decided she did not care about politeness. "You are remarkably cheerful, your Grace, and I cannot fathom why you should be so kind to me."

She expected Lady Craythorne to burst into outraged denial, but the Dowager Duchess's emotions were calm, if tinged with remorse. Lady Craythorne tapped her fingers lightly on the arm of the divan. "I would tell you I am fond of you, but you would know it was not entirely true. That is, I am not sure I am able to feel fondness for anyone, not after so many years of bitterness and resentment. But you are to be my daughter, and I admire you, and perhaps that is better than fondness. I wish to support you—there will be those who criticize you for your hasty marriage, and others who will snub you, and you do not deserve any of that."

She stopped tapping and curled her hand into a loose fist, still resting it on the divan's arm. "You do not love my son," she said after a moment's pause. "Tell me, what do you feel for him?"

Startled, Lydia said, "Well, I—he is kind to me, and treats me with respect, and that gives me such happiness. I like talking to him, even when he teases me, and—I suppose I honor him for what he has achieved. We are friends."

To her surprise, amusement welled up in the Dowager Duchess that Lydia could not explain. She had not said anything humorous. Lady Craythorne did not so much as smile, however, merely said,

"That is as much as any mother can hope for when her son chooses a bride."

Lydia considered asking her about her amusement, but before she could say anything, Lady Craythorne rose and said, "You should eat something, for I intend to pay many calls today, and I would prefer you to be adequately fortified, given that everyone we visit will wish to congratulate you on your very fine catch." Her amusement surged. "I am just prideful enough to take pleasure in Lady Fanshawe's humbling. She did so wish for her daughter to attach Oliver. I almost wish for an Extraordinary Discerner's talent, to sense her chagrin more directly."

"I should not encourage your pride, but I admit to anticipating that visit with a great deal of pleasure, now that I know Dorothea will not be hurt by my engagement." Lydia smiled. "She is happier now that she has admitted—but I should not say more, only that she does not love Lord Craythorne and had given up on appealing to him regardless of her mother's wishes."

"I am glad you have become friends. Lady Dorothea is in a terrible position." Lady Craythorne's genuine pity for Dorothea relieved Lydia's mind. She had not meant to comment on her friend's emotions.

"At any rate—excuse me, I am being addressed," Lady Craythorne said, and tilted her head back in the attitude of a Speaker receiving mental communication. Lydia took the opportunity to hurry downstairs. For the first time in her life, she looked forward to paying social calls.

⚜

THE FOLLOWING DAY, SHE PERMITTED ELLERY TO CHOOSE AN elegant morning gown, one that made her look respectable and mature, someone deserving of fine wedding clothes. Ellery's eye for fashion was excellent, and Lydia observed herself in the mirror as Ellery pinned up her hair and felt, if not confident, at least not as if she were pretending to a rank she did not deserve.

She had believed, before paying calls with the Dowager Duchess the previous afternoon, that discussing her engagement with others would make it seem more real. But Dorothea and Miranda's poorly concealed astonishment had made her instead feel awkward, as if she had invented Lord Craythorne's proposal to make herself more important.

Lydia had done a little discreet digging to learn what was known of her abduction, whether the truth of her talent had been revealed. Dorothea knew only what she had learned third hand from Lady Fanshawe, wildly exaggerated, with no mention of Discerners. Miranda's mother Mrs. Adams, one of Lady Craythorne's reticulum, had been present for Lord Craythorne's demand to be left alone with Lydia, making Miranda's information more accurate but no less dramatic.

"Of course I do not believe anything but the best of you," she had said in a low, confiding voice while her mother and the Dowager Duchess were talking nearby, "but it does seem so odd, Lord Craythorne insisting the house be cleared. Surely, if he—" She had blushed. "I should say no more."

"It was all a misunderstanding," Lydia had said. "I was quite ill, and he wished to protect me from prying eyes while a doctor was fetched. We were not intimate."

Miranda had blushed harder, and her curiosity increased to new heights. "And now you are to be wed." she had said. "That is so peculiar. I wonder that—but I suppose those of low minds will assume the worst, and this is for your protection."

Lydia had seen how badly her friend wished to gossip, but she could say no more without revealing her talent. So she had merely said, "It is not terrible, as Lord Craythorne and I are friends," and then changed the subject to music.

Now she reflected on those conversations and sighed, prompting Ellery to inquire, "Is something wrong, miss? Perhaps you would like your hair arranged differently?"

"No, it is lovely. I simply feel a stranger to myself. I had forgotten how it is to be stared at and whispered about. When I left the Magdalen Asylum, so many of those I met knew I had been mad and made assumptions about my character. It is unpleasant to know exactly what those around you assume about you, particularly when those emotions are cruel or mean-spirited."

"And now they whisper their assumptions about what passed between you and his Grace that require you to be married." Ellery laid a few spare pins on the dressing table and stepped back.

"Yes. I wonder now if we might have simply weathered the criticisms—but no, Lord Craythorne has suffered as much as I, in how his peers believe the worst of him, and I could not permit that to stand." Lydia rose and settled her skirts. "Now, of course, he cannot withdraw his promise to me, and I cannot break our engagement without making things worse."

"It is not so terrible," Ellery protested. "Marrying must be better than living as a spinster in your brother and sister-in-law's house."

"Perhaps." Lydia again regarded her reflection and pinched her cheeks to put color in them, avoiding the cosmetics concealing the still-dark bruise. "For today, I intend to enjoy myself in choosing gowns. Lady Craythorne has been so obliging, I wish not to disrupt this new understanding we have between us."

But when she joined Lady Craythorne in the drawing room, she was dismayed to Discern the lady's irritation. Just as she determined the irritation was not directed at her, Lady Craythorne said, "Our trip must be delayed by an hour or more, as there are no Bounders available to convey us to the city. It seems they are all engaged on government work. I shall have no time for my proposed social visits."

"It must be something important, for all of them to be busy," Lydia said.

Her voice must have sounded unnaturally calm, for Lady Craythorne's irritation immediately ebbed, joined by embarrassment. "I should not be resentful," she said, "as our personal desires are not important by comparison to the Viceroy's trip to oversee the repairs to New York's Government House after the riots. My annoyance is for the necessity of it—that those horrid Libertymen believed themselves entitled to kill and destroy in the name of freedom."

Lydia Discerned Lord Craythorne's approach, but said nothing. An unexpected memory of Abel Suggitt proclaiming his ideals struck her, and to her surprise she sympathized with the man, now languishing in a cell awaiting trial. "I do not think it is so awful for Americans to wish to have their own country," she said, "but they tried war to gain their freedom and failed. I cannot help believing they must try peace, instead."

"I have no sympathy for them, as they benefit tremendously from England's influence and resources," Lady Craythorne said. "Perhaps in another fifty years they will have thrown off the pernicious influence of slavery and will deserve their freedom."

"If we can stop these Libertymen permanently, perhaps it will be sooner than that," Lord Craythorne said as he entered the room. "I am here to inform you ladies that the Bounder will be at your disposal in twenty minutes, if you will wait outside the Bounding chamber?"

"Has he been told where and when to meet us for our return?" Lady Craythorne asked.

"That, you will have to settle with him. I did not like to make assumptions as to how long it takes to assemble a wardrobe." Lord Craythorne smiled at Lydia. "I fear I have not had time to return to England for a special license, but I imagine political matters here will be settled enough for me to do so by the end of next week. I hope that is satisfactory."

"I am not impatient, your Grace," Lydia said. At his expression of disbelief, she controlled a blush and added, "Very well, in *this* matter I am not impatient, and you should not make fun—oh, now you are even more amused! How dare you!"

Lord Craythorne laughed. "I understand you better every day, Miss Wescott. I assure you my amusement is not mocking, but then I believe you know that."

Lydia Discerned that Lady Craythorne was suppressing a smile. It seemed everyone around her found her funny that day. "I do, your Grace, and I suppose it is now your right to laugh at my inconsistencies, so I do not mind."

"I promise I will never mock you." Lord Craythorne smiled and made a shallow bow that encompassed both Lydia and his mother. "You are both invited to dine at Government House, if you prefer, but if you choose to return here, simply instruct the Bounder as to time and place."

"That is kind of the Viceroy, and if Miss Wescott is not too tired, we will attend." Lady Craythorne's genuine concern for Lydia's health stopped Lydia from protesting. She had given enough indications of her assumed frailty that Lady Craythorne could not be criticized for believing them.

Instead, she said, "Yes, I would like that very much."

"Very well. I must leave for New York City now, but I hope to see you this evening. Lieutenant Danniell is waiting for you in New York. I have instructed him to accompany you."

"Surely that is unnecessary," Lady Craythorne protested.

"The city still suffers unrest as a result of the riots. It is true, you will likely not venture into the areas worst affected, but I do not take chances." Lord Craythorne bowed again and left the room. Lydia followed his progress down the stairs until he abruptly blinked out of her Discernment range.

She expected Lady Craythorne to suggest reading, or that Lydia play the pianoforte, but instead the Dowager Duchess led the way downstairs to the short hall leading to the Bounding chamber. The hall was unexpectedly busy with servants passing between the offices and the main house, most of them housemaids who nodded in shy acknowledgement of Lady Craythorne and Lydia but did not stop to curtsey. Lydia amused herself Discerning the household, noting the varying degrees of calm or intense interest or occasional boredom that characterized the servants' emotions and Lady Craythorne's barely controlled impatience to be off. As Lady Craythorne was no longer annoyed, her impatience was an emotion Lydia did not believe she needed to challenge.

It seemed much longer than twenty minutes before the Bounding chamber door opened and a young man with tousled blond hair poked his head out. "Your Grace," he said, "if you will join me?"

Lady Craythorne was already moving. She entered the Bounding chamber, the door closed, and a second later she and the Bounder vanished from Lydia's Discernment. Lydia waited. Again, the door opened, and the Bounder extended a hand to Lydia. She had just enough time to wonder why he wished to leave from within the chamber—a Bounder could Bound from anywhere he liked, but had to arrive within a Bounding chamber—when the blond man unceremoniously put an arm around her waist, lifted her with ease, and—

floating weightless through nothing, empty as air—
they were elsewhere.

The air smelled damp, much more so than Washington, and that combined with the chill in the air made Lydia shiver. The Bounder released her and said, "It is a cold day indeed, miss. I hope you do not intend to walk far."

"So do I," Lydia said. The ground where they stood was concrete, not wood planking, and was unexpectedly grimy, as were the canvas walls of the Bounding chamber in which they had arrived. She caught a glimpse of the Bounding symbol painted on the left-hand wall—a stylized eagle with wings upswept as if stooping to prey—just before the Bounder opened the tent flap and bowed. Lydia exited swiftly.

She found herself out of doors on a narrow street lined with identical houses no taller than two stories. Each had a door of glossy polished oak that looked finer than the houses themselves. Their windows were clear glass that ought to have reflected the sunlight at this hour, but the street was narrow enough that the sun's rays did not penetrate farther than the roofs. The smell of damp was stronger now, and past the houses Lydia glimpsed a wide river whose ripples caught the sun as the windows did not, turning the water glassy greenish-grey.

Lady Craythorne waited a short distance away, her attention fixed on a point farther along the street, next to a tall soldier in scarlet with white facings and a lieutenant's epaulette. He was scanning the street and barely gave Lydia any heed.

"Come, it is not much of a walk," Lady Craythorne said, and put her words into action without waiting for Lydia's response. Lydia recollected herself and hurried after her.

She had never imagined Lady Craythorne walking anywhere, but it turned out the Dowager Duchess's words were correct, for after no more than half a minute's walk the lady turned right into a side street. Lydia slowed, gawking at the arched and pillared façade past which the street extended a short distance to a building taller than the nearby houses. It had no conventional door, but looked as if its front had been sheared off to expose the rooms within. Its high roof let in light through a dozen glass-paned skylights, illuminating the interior clearly.

Lydia drifted forward, fascinated. It looked exactly like any London street, with storefront windows and signs bearing shop names, and now that she was closer, she saw paving stones rather than floorboards. But the entire thing was roofed. She had never seen anything like it.

"Miss Wescott, do not dawdle," Lady Craythorne said, returning to take Lydia's arm and urge her along.

"What is this place?" Lydia said. "It is truly astonishing. I believed we were going to choose fabrics at the warehouses."

"It is New Berkeley Exchange," Lady Craythorne said, "and I am surprised at your astonishment, as there are at least two similar establishments in London, both larger than this one. It is true there are only a few linen-drapers in the Exchange, but Mrs. Adams assures me the lack is made up for by the presence of many milliners and jewelers and the like, so we need make only the one trip."

"Why, Lady Craythorne, almost you convince me that you do not enjoy shopping!"

Lady Craythorne's lips curved on one side in a wry smile. "I consider it a necessary evil. I prefer visiting and conversation to spending hours debating with oneself over a muslin gown or a cotton one. Though if I must do so, I prefer to do it in company."

"I am not fond of shopping either, though—" Lydia gasped. "Look, a music seller! I would so enjoy purchasing a new piece of sheet music."

"Then we shall make that your reward. Come, the drapers are at this end." Lady Craythorne nodded at a sign halfway down the arcade.

Lydia soon understood that not enjoying shopping was for Lady Craythorne an understatement. The Dowager Duchess passed through the linen-drapers' shops like a whirlwind, selecting fabrics only to set them aside as not suitable to Lydia's pale coloring, draping others over Lydia's shoulder with calculated approval. Lydia found she enjoyed Lady Craythorne's intervention, for the lady chose well, and Lydia needed only confirm her choices.

Having selected the makings of ten gowns to be sent to Lady Craythorne's modiste— "That will be a visit for another day," Lady Craythorne assured Lydia, who had begun to wonder if the Dowager Duchess's energetic rapidity of pace meant she intended them to accomplish every errand required of a bride in a single afternoon— they visited a number of glovers, milliners, lacemen, and a linen shop, where Lydia was supplied with more shifts and assorted undergarments than she had ever believed necessary. She declined stays in favor of convenables, which made Lady Craythorne first appalled, then curious, and after the shop owner had explained the undergarments a third time, she unbent enough to say she would consider them for herself in future.

Each purchase was wrapped and marked for delivery to Government House, where it could be transported to Washington at leisure. Lydia had imagined Lieutenant Danniell would carry their parcels, but Lady Craythorne did not ask him to, and when Lydia considered the matter further, she realized he could not protect them if he was burdened with parcels.

She was increasingly sure Lord Craythorne had been overly cautious in sending Danniell with them. Lady Craythorne did not appear to intend to leave the Exchange, and it was so placid despite the many shoppers thronging the arcade she could not imagine they were in any danger.

When they left the shoemaker's shop, with Lydia the proud owner of three new pairs of boots and half a dozen pairs of dancing shoes, Lady Craythorne sighed and said, "I believe we are finished. If you would like to visit the music-seller's shop, I am in need of a jeweler."

Danniell stirred from his silence. He had not spoken the whole time, and now his voice startled Lydia with how high-pitched it was given his size. "You should remain together, your Grace," he said. "I cannot protect you if you separate."

"That is admirable thinking, lieutenant, but surely you can see we are in no danger?" Lady Craythorne gestured with a sweeping wave that encompassed all of the Exchange. "And it will be for but half an hour. Miss Wescott, you have a pocket watch?"

Lydia indicated that she did possess such a thing.

"Then we will meet at the entrance in half an hour, and after that I believe we deserve some refreshments. The American ladies of my reticulum are very fond of Black's tea shop." Lady Craythorne turned and walked away. Danniell, looking horribly conflicted, cast his gaze on her retreating form, then on Lydia.

"Go with her, lieutenant," Lydia urged. "The music-seller's is only a few shops away, and I will be quite safe."

Scowling, Danniell hesitated a moment longer, then hurried after Lady Craythorne.

Lydia watched him go. She felt momentarily bereft, surrounded by strangers who had no interest in her, men and women walking past in the beige-yellow of mild excitement or the green of avarice or in some cases ruddy irritation with a companion or a shopkeeper. To counter the feeling, she walked swiftly to the music-seller's shop. It was one of the smaller shops, and racks and cabinets filled its confines, making it feel even smaller than it was.

Lydia turned down the shop owner's assistance with a smile, so pleased to be done with the necessary shopping she did not even care about his mild lust centered on her. She had no particular song in mind, and in fact hoped to make a serendipitous find rather than pick something she already knew. She browsed the cabinets, idly flicking through popular songs. Many were duets, which she could not use until she returned home to play them with Prudence. Still, it was enjoyable to play through the melodies in her head and imagine how they would sound when played for true.

The light in the arcade dimmed, and she glanced out the store front at the skylights. Clouds had passed overhead, but she was not in a position to see whether they were rainclouds or high, thin cirrus sheets blocking the sun temporarily. Then she gasped and dropped the music she was holding. Outside, strolling past as if she had not a care in the world, was Mrs. Ruskin.

Without a second's hesitation, Lydia left the shop to follow her.

CHAPTER 29

IN WHICH LYDIA'S INTERVENTION MAKES MATTERS WORSE

Lydia was not so startled that she failed to take precautions against Mrs. Ruskin's seeing her. She stayed well back, always keeping at least two other shoppers between herself and her quarry. Mrs. Ruskin never looked behind her. She wore an attractive bonnet of cream and scarlet stripes, matching the dark red of her redingote, and between that and her height—for Mrs. Ruskin was tall for a woman—Lydia had no difficulty keeping the woman in sight.

Mrs. Ruskin threaded her way through the crowd, which had grown in the time Lydia had been within the shops, and exited the arcade, turning right past the pillared façade. When Lydia emerged, she was several yards ahead, walking briskly if not rapidly down the street. Lydia hesitated only a moment. She ought to tell someone, Lieutenant Danniell if no one else, but if she turned back, Mrs. Ruskin would escape into the city. Following her, at a safe distance, was the only reasonable course of action.

The streets were thin of pedestrian traffic, the few passersby indifferent to anything but their own concerns, and at first Lydia's heart raced in fear that Mrs. Ruskin would turn for some reason and see her. She reminded herself that if that happened, it was not as if Lydia was in any danger; Mrs. Ruskin would likely just flee.

The houses surrounding the Exchange gave way to taller buildings, all of them apparently businesses of some sort, though not shops. Only a few were labeled, and those bore simple brass plaques next to their doors rather than large signs enticing customers. Lydia did not pay more than the barest attention to them, as following Mrs. Ruskin without revealing herself was difficult.

It did not occur to her until they had been walking for nearly five minutes that she was now hopelessly lost. She refused to let herself fear. Again, nothing terrible would happen were she to lose sight of Mrs. Ruskin. She would retrace her steps—except she had not been paying attention to anything but Mrs. Ruskin, and did not perfectly remember the route she had taken. Very well, she would ask directions to the Exchange, or to Government House, and however disappointed she would be at letting Mrs. Ruskin elude her, at least she would be safe.

Gradually, the edifices lining the street grew larger, their façades dressed stone rather than plaster, and more people thronged the streets. Lydia ignored their mingled emotions, a striking tangle of indifference, calm, excitement or keen intent, with a few notes of brown despondence. Mrs. Ruskin still did not turn around. Plate glass windows revealed shop merchandise, all of it displayed in such fashion as to indicate the objects were quite costly. A carriage rattled past, startling Lydia with its noise. She glanced at it, then back at Mrs. Ruskin, who at that moment rounded a corner. Lydia hurried after her.

When she reached the corner, Mrs. Ruskin had disappeared.

Lydia took a few more steps along the new street and surveyed her surroundings. Ahead, two elegantly-dressed women entered a shop, their emotions excited and slightly avaricious. The plate glass window next to the door revealed that the shop sold perfumes, combs, and other items with which ladies might adorn themselves. Mrs. Ruskin was nowhere in sight.

Lydia kept walking, looking in all directions for a glimpse of the cream and scarlet bonnet. The street was wide, big enough for two carriages to pass one another with plenty of room to spare. On the far side, more shops towered over the pavements. Mrs. Ruskin had not crossed the street; she could not have done so in the moment before Lydia rounded the corner after her, not without being still visible.

Frustrated, Lydia stopped near the door of the next shop, a watch-maker's, and consulted her own watch. With a jolt of horror, she realized it had been nearly half an hour since Lady Craythorne had left her. It would appear Lydia had disappeared completely. She would have to hurry back the way she had come, and hope Lady Craythorne stayed at the Exchange rather than setting off in search of her.

She turned—and met the implacable gaze of Mrs. Ruskin.

Shock rooted her to the ground. Mrs. Ruskin's emotions were as calm as if they were chance-met acquaintances. Her smile was so pleasant Lydia did not at first observe the small pistol she held, nearly concealed by the folds of her redingote, pointed directly at Lydia's chest. "Miss Wescott," she said. "What a surprise to find you here."

Lydia swallowed. No words came to mind that were not inane. "I did not believe you saw me," she finally said.

Mrs. Ruskin pursed her lips. "These plate glass windows are a marvel. They work as mirrors in the right light. I have been watching you follow me for some time, waiting for my moment—then I merely stepped inside that shop and let you pass. Simple, really. I wonder that the possibility did not occur to you."

Lydia chose not to be drawn by this. "What now?" she said, hoping she appeared as calm as Mrs. Ruskin felt. "Will you shoot me here in the street?"

"Of course not." Mrs. Ruskin looked Lydia up and down. "But I also cannot have you run to where you might warn someone of my presence. No, I think on the whole it is best you come with me." She took a step forward and pressed the pistol into Lydia's side. "Go on," she added, indicating with a nod the direction that Lydia should walk.

Lydia did not move. "I will flee. You will have to shoot me to get me to go with you."

"I will not shoot you," Mrs. Ruskin said. "I will shoot...one of them." She nodded at the passersby, the ignorant, oblivious passersby who saw nothing amiss with their little tableau. "That woman in the fur-trimmed pelisse, perhaps? Or the child walking with her? Which would you like your recalcitrance to condemn to injury or death?" She smiled, still so sweetly. "More likely death. I am a fair shot."

"No," Lydia said, then cursed herself for sounding so afraid. Mrs. Ruskin would use her fear against her. "No, I will go, but do not—"

"That direction," Mrs. Ruskin said, sounding so satisfied Lydia wished she dared slap her. "Walk until I tell you to stop."

Lydia walked. Her heart raced once more, this time with fear and apprehension she suppressed. She should not let fear rule her, not when she needed to remain clearheaded.

Ahead, the buildings loomed over the street, blocking the afternoon light so only their tops caught the sunshine diffused by the lowering clouds that promised rain. One building in particular caught Lydia's eye; it was shorter than its neighbors, which still made it a good three stories tall, and very wide, with windows taller than Lydia and a great arched entrance flanked by rows of white pillars. The flat roof was ringed with odd crenellations better suited to a medieval castle. Carriages stopped in front of the building occasionally, and men in formal dress emerged from those carriages to enter through the arch.

When Lydia was nearly opposite the arch, a woman in the dark grey of the War Office's Extraordinary Movers plummeted from the sky to land on the flat roof, disappearing behind the crenellations, and moments later a man dressed in a similar costume Flew away from the roof. Lydia held her breath. It had to be Government House. If she could distract Mrs. Ruskin, she might make her escape—and Mrs. Ruskin would shoot an innocent. Lydia knew enough of the woman to guess she would do this regardless of whether it brought Lydia back.

"Go inside here," Mrs. Ruskin said. Lydia stopped. "Here" was a building opposite Government House, a mansion with ornately carved pilasters giving the appearance of columns holding up the triangular frieze above the double doors. Lydia opened the door, considered shutting it in Mrs. Ruskin's face, was again aware of the pistol thrust into her side, and proceeded to enter the mansion.

The foyer beyond was brightly lit, brighter than the shadowed street outside. Lydia's footsteps rang out on the white and black tile, echoed shortly by Mrs. Ruskin's. Mrs. Ruskin shut the door with a slow, deliberate motion Lydia tried not to feel had sealed her doom. To distract herself, she examined her surroundings. The walls were paneled in dark wood against which the many lamps reflected like tiny suns. Doors to left and right, elaborately carved with fanciful scenes of tilled fields and cavorting lambs, stood slightly ajar, while a hall straight ahead led deeper into the house. Stairs carpeted in plush navy blue led up to a balcony surrounding the foyer on three sides. Lydia Discerned no one else present.

"Upstairs, all the way to the second floor," Mrs. Ruskin said. She prodded Lydia in the back with the pistol. The small muzzle pressed into her like a knife point. Fear returned, this time fear for herself. She could run nowhere. She had no choice but to do as Mrs. Ruskin said or bleed to death on the white and black tile.

As slowly as she dared, she ascended the stairs, going rapidly over possibilities. She could not run past Mrs. Ruskin to the front door. She could not take the pistol from Mrs. Ruskin, who was larger and likely stronger than she. She might run ahead, but with no idea what or who waited above, that might only make her situation worse. She made herself breathe slowly and kept walking. She would see what Mrs. Ruskin had in mind, and formulate a plan then.

She expected the stairs to terminate on the first floor, at the balcony, and for Mrs. Ruskin to direct her to a second staircase, but at the first floor landing, more stairs immediately continued up. Still carpeted in dark blue, they smelled of fresh lacquer, Lydia guessed from the handrail, which felt slightly tacky. She saw only a glimpse of the first floor hallway, extending to the left of the stairs; unlike the foyer, no lights illuminated it past the landing, and Lydia saw only vague outlines of closed doors and darker patches that might be portraits on the walls. Then the stairwell closed in around her again.

The second floor was as dimly lit as the first, and Lydia left the stairs and stopped, unwilling to walk into darkness. The presence of two other people somewhere nearby increased her reluctance. Mrs. Ruskin's gun pressed more firmly against her back, sending another thrill of fear through her. Then her captor took her arm and guided her forward, with the gun never wavering, to a door near the stairwell. "Open it," she said. Lydia, hating herself for her complicity in her own abduction, did so.

The room beyond was bright by comparison, though after Lydia's eyes adjusted to the difference, she realized it was because three large windows not obscured by drapes let in a pale grey pre-storm light. Cold air gusted against her body, and a second glance showed that the center window was open, letting in the smell of oncoming rain. Out the window, she saw the crenellated flat roof of Government House, and as she watched, another Extraordinary Mover plummeted to land somewhere among the chimneys that had not been visible from the street.

Two dark shapes were silhouetted against the window, and in the next moment, Lydia recognized Mr. Ruskin as the man on the right. The man on the left, short and burly with a heavy brow and thick waist, looked vaguely familiar. Lydia's memory of the investiture ball suggested he had been one of Abel Suggitt's companions, but she was not certain.

Mr. Ruskin stood upright from where he had been crouching. "What are you doing with *her?*" he exclaimed. "Are you mad?"

"She followed me home. May I keep her?" Mrs. Ruskin laughed, a merry sound that chilled Lydia in how it perfectly matched her cheerful emotions.

"Hannah," Mr. Ruskin said, approaching Lydia the way he might an angry dog, "we are so close to success. Why did you not dispose of her?"

"I could not exactly shoot her on the street, my dear." Mrs. Ruskin sounded shocked. "And I could not permit her to warn anyone in Government House of our presence. Nor can I shoot her now, unless you wish the noise to draw attention to this room?" She shook her head, apparently sorrowful, though her true emotions were nothing but pleasure. "Time enough to kill her once we have achieved our goal."

Mr. Ruskin scowled. "Which may not be today. We have seen nothing of that traitor Monroe, nor any activity that might herald his arrival."

Lydia looked past Mr. Ruskin at the second man, who had not moved. His attention was fixed on something outside the window. Lydia noted that the window had been shattered rather than opened and saw the rifle in the stranger's hand, held where he might aim it in seconds. "You wish to kill the Viceroy," she said. "That man intends to shoot him."

"And now I cannot release you, not now you know our plan," Mrs. Ruskin said merrily. "Oh, how silly of me. I never intended to release you. I should not have given you false hope."

"I know what you intend," Lydia said, her mouth dry. Strangely, Mrs. Ruskin's cruel taunts helped her control her fears. There might be nothing she could do to prevent that little pistol from ending her life, and while she did not intend to lie down and make it easy for her captors, having accepted what might be her fate strengthened her.

She made herself attend to the emotions nearest her. Mrs. Ruskin's cheerfulness did not matter, as the woman's emotional state did not reflect her intentions. Mr. Ruskin's anger was the sort that indicates one's expectations are thwarted, anger and frustration and a little fear. Tense anticipation mingled with excitement characterized the stranger's emotions. He, at least, had no worries connected to killing a man.

"Where are my manners? Miss Wescott, you should sit." Mrs. Ruskin removed the gun from Lydia's back and gestured with her other hand. Lydia was not stupid enough to believe that made her safe.

The room was scantly furnished with only a sofa, a matching armchair, and a sideboard whose lower doors did not close properly. Lydia took a seat on the sofa, and Mrs. Ruskin sat beside her, the terrible little pistol still pointed at her. Lydia clasped her hands in her lap and made herself breathe calmly.

"We know of this place," she said in a conversational tone, and was pleased her voice did not shake. "Abel Suggitt told Lord Craythorne of your New York residence. It is only a matter of time before you are apprehended."

"As if I am fool enough not to realize my residence in this city is compromised," Mr. Ruskin said. "This house is merely convenient for what we intend."

"You say you are no fool, and yet your plan is foolish," Lydia retorted. "Killing the Viceroy will not give you American independence. It will simply mean the British government will never stop chasing you."

"You know nothing," Mr. Ruskin said, turning back to the window and flattening himself against the wall beside it so he could not be seen from the outside.

"We have plans," Mrs. Ruskin added. "The Viceroy's death will spark a revolution, here and throughout the colonies."

"Say nothing more," Mr. Ruskin said.

"I will be dead soon—can I not know the truth?" Lydia asked. "It is not as if you will permit me to run free where I might tell someone."

"I believe that qualifies as a dying woman's last request," Mrs. Ruskin said with a laugh.

Mr. Ruskin shrugged. "Do as you wish, Hannah. It will be over soon in any case."

Mrs. Ruskin lowered the pistol, but did not shift her finger from the trigger. "Once we kill the Viceroy," she said in a low, confiding voice, "our allies among the Six Nations will join our people in attacking key places throughout the colonies. The British Army is not at full strength here thanks to so much of their effort being spent in Europe, chasing the remains of the Grande Armée. They will fall to us easily. By the time they regroup, we will control the American government. And this time, the war will not go their way."

"But the Haudenosaunee swore they did not attack before," Lydia said, "and I know those so-called Iroquois warriors were Libertymen disguised as a feint."

A flash of annoyance shot through both the Ruskins. "That fool Suggitt," Mr. Ruskin said. "He should not have taken the initiative. That ruse nearly destroyed everything."

"It is not as if he was in our counsel to know the actual plan," Mrs. Ruskin said. "Though it is true he is a fool. I don't suppose your Lord Craythorne had him killed?"

Lydia shook her head. "He will be tried and sentenced to transportation."

Mrs. Ruskin shrugged. "I suppose that satisfies me. I always prefer that my enemies live to suffer, if that is possible —after all, death is over in an instant, is it not?" She waved the gun's muzzle in a little circle, still aimed at Lydia. "How unfortunate you will not be in a position to tell me whether or not that is true."

Lydia noticed that the stranger's intensity of emotion had diminished slightly, suggesting he was listening to this conversation. That might mean he was inattentive to anyone arriving at or leaving Government House. "But I do not understand," she said, making herself sound as young and naïve as she could, "why the Iroquois leaders denied their connection to the attack if they are on your side."

"A miscommunication," Mrs. Ruskin said airily. "Much like the one that led to your interment in that madhouse. James Parker believed you knew more than you did, and that you were about to reveal our identities to that hound of King George's. Speaking of fools." She did not say whether she meant her informant, or Lord Craythorne, was the fool, but Lydia guessed she meant both.

"How did James discover my talent?" she asked.

Mrs. Ruskin smiled, a reflective, thoughtful expression, and her control of her emotions slipped for the briefest moment. It was enough that Lydia had to suppress a gasp that would have given her new knowledge away. "James was a skilled sneak. He seduced your maid to gain her trust and thus her information about you, and he eavesdropped on your conversations. I wonder that you did not notice. You must not be as skilled with your talent as we were led to believe."

Lydia moistened dry lips. She recalled, now, the time when she had accused Lord Craythorne of murdering his wife, how in her distraction she had not given heed to other emotions. Anyone might have lurked nearby and she would not have known. "James 'was' a skilled sneak?" she asked.

The smile broadened, and again Mrs. Ruskin's memories made a crack in her emotions. "I have no use for those who fail me," she said. "James was useful for a while. And then he was not. You cannot fault me for disposing of a broken tool, can you?"

Lydia drew in a deep breath. "No," she said. "But I can despise you for so callously ridding yourself of your lover."

Surprise shot through Mrs. Ruskin. Mr. Ruskin straightened, his confusion evident on his face as well as in his emotions. "What was that?" he said.

"A silly ruse," Mrs. Ruskin said, sounding bored and indifferent though her heart raced. "She wishes to confuse us. Pay her no mind."

The stranger's emotions were a far more complex tangle, surprise and anger and, unexpectedly, jealousy. Lydia suppressed a smile and put on her most innocent expression. "An Extraordinary Discerner cannot be lied to, Mr. Ruskin, and Mrs. Ruskin's emotions are very clear. She was intimate with James Parker."

Mr. Ruskin took a few steps toward the sofa. "You lie."

"She was the one who gave him his orders," Lydia guessed, and saw by Mr. Ruskin's face she had landed on the truth. "They were frequently in each other's company. Mrs. Ruskin was the one who recruited him, wasn't she? I am certain those meetings look very different to you now, sir."

With his brow creased in agonized indecision, Mr. Ruskin turned his attention on his wife. "Hannah?"

"She lies, Adam." Mrs. Ruskin still sounded unconcerned. "You know me better than anyone. Do you not believe you would have noticed if I were unfaithful?"

"I don't—I cannot say," Mr. Ruskin said.

Lydia assessed his tumultuous emotions and decided to press harder. "Mr. Ruskin, I regret that you had to learn of your wife's infidelity this way. And you, Mr.—I beg your pardon, we have not been introduced."

"Babbage," the man said. He was breathing heavily, and his hand clenched the rifle so hard the tendons on his arms stood out like taut ropes.

"Mr. Babbage, I pity you, too. I imagine Mrs. Ruskin promised that she was yours alone, did she not? And that once Mr. Ruskin was gone, you could be together openly. How unfortunate that Mrs. Ruskin was so free with her favors."

Babbage and Mr. Ruskin stared at one another. Mrs. Ruskin laughed. "Come, now, you see that she was almost successful," she exclaimed, and raised her pistol. "I believe I will risk this shot alerting someone."

"Hannah, look at me," Mr. Ruskin said in a hoarse voice. "Look at me and swear it is a lie."

Mrs. Ruskin lowered the pistol. "Of course it's a lie," she said. "I have always been faithful."

"You treacherous whore," Babbage snarled. He dropped the rifle and lunged for Mrs. Ruskin. Mr. Ruskin shoved him aside. Lydia leaned back, pressed herself against the arm of the sofa, and brought both legs around to kick Mrs. Ruskin in the chest.

The attack shoved Mrs. Ruskin out of Babbage's reach. Lydia was already moving, wrestling with Mrs. Ruskin for the pistol. She was terrifyingly aware that while Mrs. Ruskin's finger no longer rested on the trigger, it was far too close to it for Lydia's comfort. Then Mr. Ruskin was dragging her away, and Babbage had both hands on Mrs. Ruskin's arm, pushing her into the sofa cushions.

The sound of the pistol discharging shattered the air, echoing in the sparsely furnished room like a thunderclap. Babbage jerked and stumbled back. Then he let go of Mrs. Ruskin and collapsed, clutching his stomach. Terror and pain coursed through Lydia as if she had been the one shot. She was too overwhelmed to fight Mr. Ruskin when he gripped her more firmly and shook her the way a terrier does a rat.

Mrs. Ruskin swore viciously. "Damn him for a jealous fool," she said. "Now one of us must do the deed."

"You killed him," Mr. Ruskin said, somewhat breathlessly, but his grip did not slacken, and Lydia, recovering herself, did not attempt to break free. "We needed him, and—how dare you play me false? How many men have there—"

Mrs. Ruskin was looking out the window and held up a hand to silence him. "This is not the time. The Viceroy is here. We can discuss that vixen's lies later." She swept up the rifle and examined it, then knelt at the window and brought its barrel to rest on the casement.

Lydia did not stop to ponder her options. At the moment, there seemed to be only one.

She stomped her heel hard on the toe of Mr. Ruskin's stout boot. Her own boot was not as sturdy, but the attack startled him into loosening his hold. Twisting free in that instant, she swung her joined fists at his nose. Mr. Ruskin cried out and stepped back, clapping a hand to his face. Lydia raced toward Mrs. Ruskin, not slowing as she neared, and slammed into her, knocking her back.

The rifle went off nearly in Lydia's face, deafening her. Mrs. Ruskin's lips moved in silent invective, based on the fury raging through her. Lydia dropped, bearing Mrs. Ruskin down beneath her slight weight and slamming her head into the floorboards. She swiftly rolled to one side and got to her knees. Mrs. Ruskin lay unmoving before her.

Lydia crawled to the window and hauled herself up. Below, the street looked like a pot overflowing with boiling water, dozens of men and women rushing about in apparent panic. She was too far away to Discern their emotions, for which she would have been grateful had she not been so weary, empty of anything but dull relief.

A knot of people on the steps of Government House were the only still figures in the street. Lydia saw two men she recognized from the Viceroy's palace, and then noted the Viceroy, standing tall and apparently calling for help. Everyone else surrounded a very still figure on the ground. Lydia's heart constricted. Mrs. Ruskin's shot had not killed the Viceroy, but someone else had not been so lucky—

The crowd shifted, revealing the fallen man. Lydia took in the familiar frock coat and boots, the curly hair, and the blood spreading across his chest. Mrs. Ruskin had shot Lord Craythorne.

CHAPTER 30

IN WHICH LYDIA IS
OVERCOME ONCE MORE

A hard hand squeezed her upper arm, dragging her away from the window. "What have you done?" Mr. Ruskin demanded. Fear and anger warred within him. He pressed the back of his other hand to his nose, which streamed blood, and leaned against the wall where he could not be seen from the street to look out the window. "You have ruined everything."

Lydia could not speak. The sight of that still figure lying in the street would not leave her imagination. Lord Craythorne shot. Impossible. Any minute now he would fling the door open and demand the Ruskins surrender.

Mr. Ruskin swore viciously under his breath and dragged Lydia away, shoving her at the sofa. He knelt beside his wife and shook her. "Hannah, we must flee. They are coming," he said. "Hannah, collect yourself."

Mrs. Ruskin groaned and rose to support herself on one elbow. "That chit of a girl spoiled my aim, but I am sure I got the shot off in time."

"The Viceroy lives. We must *go*, do you not understand?" Mr. Ruskin hauled Mrs. Ruskin to her feet and put his shoulder beneath her arm for support.

"No," Mrs. Ruskin said. Her emotions, which had ebbed while she lay semi-conscious, surged into anger and then a terrible vicious glee. Lydia was on her feet in an instant and racing for the door. She barely managed to avoid Babbage's body, sprawled in a pool of blood; she could not tell if he was dead or merely dying and found she did not care.

She had her hand on the knob when Mrs. Ruskin grabbed her by the hair and hauled her backward. Lydia screamed at the unexpected sharp pain and clawed Mrs. Ruskin's hand, trying to get free. The grip tightened. Desperate, Lydia stopped trying to pull away and instead slammed into Mrs. Ruskin, knocking her back a few steps.

The pain in her head subsided. Mrs. Ruskin grabbed her by the shoulders and shook her until she cried out. Both the Ruskins' anger suffused her, and she tried to make herself a void and could not. Emotions, her own and the Ruskins', rose up with her, overwhelming her, and she cried out again, this time in fear for herself.

"Yes, scream if you must, it makes your pain sweeter," Mrs. Ruskin snarled. Lydia, barely aware of her surroundings, could not resist as the woman dragged her to the window. Cold air blew briskly through the open hole, bringing with it spatterings of rain. Lydia struggled again to get free, but Mrs. Ruskin's grip was tighter than a clamp and as implacable.

"Hannah, leave her. We must make our escape," Mr. Ruskin said.

"I will not be satisfied unless I have my revenge," Mrs. Ruskin said.

From some distant, sane corner of Lydia's mind came the understanding of what Mrs. Ruskin intended to do. She could no longer see anything for the colors that tumbled about her vision, red and yellow and deep, passionate green that had nothing to do with love. Blindly, she swung her elbow into Mrs. Ruskin's stomach, and the woman released her with a great *ooph* of breath.

Lydia could not remember what she had meant to do. Run, fight, run, fight—and then once more the figure of Lord Craythorne lying in the street presented itself in stunning clarity, and rage built up within her, a natural rage that entwined with that of Mrs. Ruskin until it filled every part of her. She screamed and launched herself at Mrs. Ruskin, bowling the woman over with her attack.

Mrs. Ruskin was taller than she, outweighed her, but Lydia in her fury fought like a maddened cat, clawing and kicking and tearing at Mrs. Ruskin's hair until Mrs. Ruskin screamed as well. Harsh breaths tore from her lungs, abrading her throat, or possibly she was still screaming. Then other hands were pulling her away, and Mr. Ruskin's voice came from a point near her right ear: "Hannah, for God's sake—"

Mrs. Ruskin got heavily to her feet. Her face was bloody from long, deep scratches, her bonnet was gone, and her hair was tangled beyond redemption, but in her heart there was nothing but a fury that matched Lydia's own. Lydia strained against Mr. Ruskin's hands, desperate to bash her enemy's head against the floor. She was breathing so hard her chest hurt, but it was a distant pain, far removed from the anger thrilling through her.

Swaying slightly, Mrs. Ruskin walked forward until she was face to face with Lydia. "You dare," she whispered. Then she slapped Lydia so hard it knocked her head back and left her temporarily stunned, unable to resist when Mrs. Ruskin once more took hold of her. She wrestled Lydia free of her husband's hold and dragged Lydia to the window. Lydia recovered and struggled for freedom, but the rush of power her anger had given her was fading, and she felt weaker than she ever had before.

"We haven't failed," Mrs. Ruskin said in a hoarse, raspy voice. "But it will not matter to you, ever again."

The open window gaped at Lydia's back. Her legs pressed against the wall beneath it. Mrs. Ruskin shoved, and Lydia lost her balance. For a moment, her legs clung to the windowsill and she imagined herself hanging from it upside down, watching the street spin over her head. Then she was falling.

She had enough time to wonder if dying would hurt less if she maneuvered herself to land on her head rather than her back, and then she struck the ground. But it did not hurt at all. The street was not hard, but soft, with give like a good mattress.

She opened her eyes and looked up. There was the window she had fallen from, far closer than it should be, and a short distance above that, a man hovered in midair. He was dressed in the dark grey of an

Extraordinary Mover in the War Office and looked very concerned. "Miss, you look as if you were attacked," he said. "Who are you?"

"Mr. and Mrs. Ruskin are escaping," Lydia said, as hoarsely as Mrs. Ruskin had sounded. "Do not mind about me. You must capture them."

"Who are Mr. and Mrs. Ruskin?" the Extraordinary Mover asked, puzzlement joining his concern.

Lydia felt like screaming again, but her throat did not wish to cooperate. "Lord Craythorne will—" she began, and a terrible aching misery filled her chest, one she tried desperately to ignore. He would not thank her for being overwhelmed when it was imperative the Ruskins be caught. She refused to remember that he was no longer in a position to thank anyone for anything.

"Lord Craythorne was shot," the man said. "I must set you down, miss, so I can investigate where the shot came from."

"They are already gone," Lydia said with as much force as she could muster. "You must Fly *now* to capture the Ruskins, they tried to kill the Viceroy and shot—" She swallowed tears. "Why do you not understand?"

The man glanced at the open window, and Lydia fell an inch or so before he caught her again. "The shots came from inside," he said.

Lydia ground her teeth. "You are a marvel of perspicacity, sir. Set me down and go after them!"

"You need not be rude," the man said, embarrassment and anger taking the place of concern. Lydia did not care if he felt insulted.

The Extraordinary Mover rotated her into an upright position and brought her gently to stand on the ground, then released the invisible grip he had held her with. Lydia staggered, catching her balance, then ran for the mansion's front door. Inwardly, she screamed at herself for her foolishness. She had no weapon and was not strong enough to apprehend the Ruskins. But she could not bear to do nothing, not when Lord Craythorne—

She slammed the door open and then held still, listening, watching. She heard no footsteps, saw no change in the ground floor such as open doors that had previously been shut or lanterns guttering in the wind of someone's passage. Then, down the dark hall that led past the staircase, she saw a distant light. Without considering what it might be, she ran toward it.

The light took shape as the outline of a door the farther she ran. Lydia pushed herself harder, and then had to stop as the light vanished, leaving her in near-total darkness. She turned to look back at the foyer, where the lanterns burned, then groped her way along the hall until she bumped into a wall head first. Rubbing her forehead with one hand, she patted the wall in search of a door frame or a knob.

Her hand finally fell on the curve of a latch. She tugged at it, managed to depress the mechanism, and pulled the door open. Grey, stormy light blinded her for a moment, and she blinked her eyes until they cleared.

She stood in an alley that ran behind the houses, narrow and stinking of animal waste and urine. At the far end of the alley, two figures were just disappearing around a corner. Lydia raced after them.

She pelted around the corner at full speed, slapping one hand against the wall to steady herself as she pivoted, and jerked away instinctively as a shot cracked the still air and a pistol ball struck the wall near her head, sending chips of stone flying. Mrs. Ruskin stood several feet away, lowering the pistol. A terrible animalistic snarl emerged from Lydia's throat, and she sprang after her prey, fury once more filling her. That woman had killed Lord Craythorne, and she would pay for that and all her other crimes.

Mr. Ruskin was urging his wife to move, move now, and then all of them were off running again. The alley let out on a wide street, not as wide as the one fronting Government House, but one filled with pedestrians and carriages who were not inclined to move aside for running strangers. Lydia dodged through gaps between passersby with ease, feeling fleeter of foot than a deer and more agile than a mink. She realized she was gaining on her prey just as Mrs. Ruskin shoved an elderly woman, hooking her ankle so she fell to the ground with a cry of pain right in Lydia's path.

Lydia did not pause; she gathered herself and leaped over the woman, dodging two men who came to the old lady's aid. For a moment, her eyes met Mrs. Ruskin's, and a clear note of fear edged out the cunning anger that characterized the woman. Lydia smiled. Mrs. Ruskin turned and ran, faster than before. Not fast enough.

But now Mr. Ruskin had seen Mrs. Ruskin's ploy, and he too began shoving pedestrians so they would stumble into Lydia's way. Lydia had to slow to avoid the obstacles. Inwardly, she cursed, as she had no breath to spare for words. Thunder rumbled, and seconds later lightning speared across the sky, heralding the rain that began to fall in hard, stinging drops.

Lydia ran wide of the crowd, into the street, where all she had to dodge were carriages and horses. Now she ran faster, once more gaining on the Ruskins. Her feet ached, her chest hurt from the pounding of her heart and the rapidity of her breath, and she was beginning to feel the pain from her fight with Mrs. Ruskin, but she refused to give up even though she had no idea what she would do when she caught them.

Then she saw Mr. Ruskin wave his hand at a passing hackney, and her heart pounded with fear as well as exertion. If they rode instead of running, she would lose them entirely, for she could not outrun a carriage. She pushed herself harder, but they were climbing inside, the driver had snapped the reins, and the carriage accelerated away from the curb. Lydia slowed to a halt and stood watching the carriage disappear, conscious of the Ruskins' triumphant glee. The rain beat upon her head, not yet a downpour but harder than a sprinkle, dreary and discouraging.

Then, to her astonishment, the hackney stopped abruptly some fifty feet away. Lydia waited for the Ruskins to emerge. Instead, the horse and carriage rose slowly into the air, coming to a halt about twenty feet off the ground. The horse jerked its head, tossing its mane and making distressed noises, but its legs were as still as if they were bound together.

Stunned, Lydia drifted forward along with dozens of other people, all of them watching the miraculous carriage. The driver sat as if frozen, though the shifting of his legs and the way he covered his head with his coat said he was not held the way the horse was. Muffled cries came from within the hackney, and its doors rattled but did not open.

"I hope you are right about this, miss," said a voice from behind

Lydia. She whirled around to see the Extraordinary Mover, hovering at the same height as the floating carriage, his gaze fixed on it. He did not look as if he noticed the rain. "I can be severely punished for interfering with civilian transport."

"You stopped them," Lydia said, still stunned.

"You *were* pursuing those two, and you did suggest it was Lord Craythorne's desire to see them apprehended," the man said. He descended to alight next to Lydia. The carriage remained where it was, though now hands were gesticulating through the carriage windows.

"These are the leaders of the Libertymen," Lydia said. "Capturing them was Lord Craythorne's purpose." She belatedly recalled that Lord Craythorne's involvement in rooting out the conspiracy was at the very least not spoken of, and was possibly a great secret, but it no longer mattered.

"Then I should report their capture," the man said. "If you will permit me, I will carry you as well, miss."

Lydia shook her head, then realized how very tired she was, and that moreover she had once more not paid attention to her route and was lost. "Yes, thank you—I beg your pardon, we have not been introduced. I am Miss Wescott."

The man's eyes widened. "Miss Wescott? I recall your name. You are engaged to marry Lord Craythorne."

Are engaged. Not *were* engaged. "Lord Craythorne was shot," Lydia said, feeling stupid. "I saw. He looked—I believed him dead."

"He may be—I beg your pardon, Miss Wescott, that was insensitive." The man's contrition was visible as well as palpable. "I do not know what happened, but the bustle surrounding him was not the sort of attention one gives a corpse. I do not believe the shot killed him outright."

Relief tried to overtake Lydia, and she suppressed it, not wishing to hope and have that hope dashed by cold reality. "Please, let us hurry, Mr...."

"Hammond," the Extraordinary Mover said. "Hold still, and do not resist, as that makes Moving more difficult."

Lydia obeyed. Hammond Flew back into the sky, and moments later the same pressure that had caught her when she fell out the window gripped her, hugging her legs and hips but leaving her upper body free. The force wrapped her gown tightly around her legs, preserving her modesty, though she found she did not care much who saw her. Lord Craythorne might yet be alive. Once more she suppressed the giddy happiness that tried to overwhelm her.

Hammond Moved her to where he could keep everything in sight, carriage and Lydia and all, and they flew very high, higher than the tops of the buildings. It astonished Lydia that all her running had brought her only a few streets away from Government House. She shielded her face against the rain that battered her more strongly and watched Hammond Fly close beside the hackney, apparently speaking to the driver, who nodded now and again as if in agreement. The horse's eyes were wild, and it quivered, inspiring pity in Lydia. She knew little of horses, and animals did not feel emotion the same way humans did, so she could not Discern its fear, but it was visible none-theless.

They reached Government House, where the street in front of the building was empty save for a dark red stain in front of the doors grad-ually turning pink with rainwater. Lydia looked at it once and then refused to see it again.

The carriage descended, causing the passersby to scatter, and Lydia sank lower until she and the horse and the carriage all touched ground together. No, that was not accurate; the horse continued to float a few inches above the pavement. Hammond alit and called to a man standing nearby. The man looked startled, but in moments he and Hammond were gathering other men to stand around the horse, calming it as Hammond gently released his grip on its legs. The horse continued to quiver, but did not fall, and shortly its master stood beside it, soothing it.

Lydia walked to where she could see the Ruskins within the carriage. They had stopped waving their arms and trying to break down the doors and now sat staring straight ahead, apparently emotionless. Anger and humiliation surged through Mr. Ruskin as well as jealousy, presumably because he now had time to contemplate his wife's infidelity. Mrs. Ruskin's fury raged within her, but Lydia now had control of herself and did not fear being overwhelmed.

She considered speaking to them, taunting them at being captured, demanding they reveal the details of their plan or the names of other Libertymen, declaiming noble sentiments about real freedom that would be memorialized for history. But her knowledge that Lord Craythorne might not be dead made all those other desires tawdry. So she merely turned away and entered Government House.

The entrance hall was unexpectedly cold, nearly as cold as outdoors. Lydia shivered and rubbed her arms, which reminded her that she was nearly wet through. Now that the crisis was over, she felt sore and bruised and weary beyond belief.

She looked about her, hoping for direction. The place looked more like a mausoleum than a mansion, its pillared hall greyly lit by windows above the front door and the walls a blank, unadorned white that also looked grey. Rain beat a tattoo against the windows, loud enough to echo through the room. She was alone in the foyer, though two of its four doors were open and she saw movement within each of those rooms and Discerned the presence of others.

Uncertainly, she pushed open the left-hand door and then stood in the doorway, waiting to be noticed. The three men within did not at first look up. One sat at a table, pen in hand; another sat nearby, reading from a sheaf of papers he held; the third rummaged in a desk drawer, muttering to himself. He was the first to see Lydia, and his reaction made her feel even more conspicuous and out of place; he dropped the seal he held so its wooden handle bounced as it hit the floor, and his eyes widened as if Lydia were a specter and not a human woman.

"Miss, you look—" He collected himself and came toward her with his hand outstretched. "Who did this to you? Sit, pray, and permit me to call Dr. Wootton." He removed his frock coat and placed it around her shoulders.

"I—" Lydia caught herself before she could protest she was uninjured. "It was Mrs. Ruskin. She and Mr. Ruskin are the leaders of the Libertymen Lord Craythorne was pursuing. She pushed me out of a window."

The other two men had risen and were staring at Lydia in horror. The man with the pen set it aside and hurried to offer Lydia his chair.

"Walker, see to it," he said, and the man who had mentioned a doctor left the room. "Miss—I beg your pardon, but may I ask your name?"

"It is Wescott," Lydia said. "Please, tell me—"

"Miss Wescott," the man said, sounding even more horrified. "You are—that is, Lord Craythorne announced his engagement to a Miss Wescott this morning—are you she?"

Lydia nodded. The chair was hard and angular, but she had never felt anything so comfortable. "Please, I must know. Lord Craythorne was shot, but is he...?" She could not bring herself to finish that sentence.

The two men exchanged glances. "Lord Craythorne is still under the care of the Extraordinary Shaper Dr. Mansfield," the first man said. "I fear we cannot reassure you. Dr. Mansfield is quite competent, however." That he did not say everything would be all right filled Lydia with cold dread.

Footsteps heralded the appearance of the third man, Walker, who was accompanied by an elderly man dressed in an ugly frock coat and pantaloons that had seen better days. "This is Dr. Wootton, miss," Walker said. "He will see to your care."

Dr. Wootton, for all his slovenliness, had a kind smile, and his hand was gentle as it took hers to help her rise. Lydia did not like to lean heavily on someone so old, but his step was firmer than she expected, and she found that, like it or not, she needed assistance.

They walked slowly up the stairs and down a long hall that smelled of astringent cleanser and tallow candles to a door that, when Dr. Wootton opened it, turned out to lead to a bedroom. It smelled of disuse rather than tallow, and when the doctor opened the drapes, the grey light revealed a four-poster bed with no drapes covered in a patchwork quilt and an armchair pulled up before a small round table, both covered in a light layer of dust.

Dr. Wootton guided Lydia to the chair and helped her sit. "You were quite badly beaten, my dear," he said, frowning. "But it appears you gave your assailant a fight." He raised Lydia's hand and examined the nails, which Lydia now realized were bloody.

"I am not so bad off," she said.

"Nevertheless," the doctor said, and proceed to examine her. He tutted over her arm when it proved she could not raise it higher than her chest, but eventually said, "That shoulder should be looked at by Dr. Mansfield, to be safe, but otherwise I see nothing wrong with you that Time will not repair." He smiled, an expression twenty years younger than he was, and added, "Ah, the resilience of youth!"

Lydia did not return his smile. "I believed Dr. Mansfield was attending to Lord Craythorne. Do you know anything of his condition?"

Dr. Wootton's smile vanished. "I have complete faith in Dr. Mansfield," he said, "but you must know, a shot to the chest is quite complicated to Heal. Are you acquainted with Lord Craythorne?"

Superstition gripped her, the feeling that if she said she was engaged to marry Lord Craythorne, that admission would cost him his life. "Yes," she said. "I am Lady Craythorne's companion."

Dr. Wootton patted her hand. "You should rest," he said. "Lady Craythorne has been summoned, and she will arrive shortly."

Lydia nodded. She stood, feeling as old as Dr. Wootton, and removed Walker's frock coat and draped it over the armchair. When Dr. Wootton was gone, she pulled the patchwork quilt off the bed and wrapped it around herself, then lay on the bed and curled into a ball. The quilt warmed her, though she was not completely comfortable thanks to her wet gown and draggling hair. It was still enough to stop her shivering.

Her aching body kept her from drifting off to sleep, and memory made her even more wakeful. Lord Craythorne shot, and possibly dying. She could not stop herself remembering how she had spoiled Mrs. Ruskin's shot, and how that meant she was responsible for Lord Craythorne's death. She indulged in that misery for a moment or two before controlling herself. She had stopped Mrs. Ruskin from killing the Viceroy, and it was pure bad luck that the wild shot had struck anyone. Lord Craythorne's death was Mrs. Ruskin's fault, not Lydia's.

Here in the still room, with rain against glass the only sound, Lydia could not avoid facing what she had managed not to consider: Lord Craythorne might be dead. Her dear friend, gone forever. How he had become so dear in such a short time, she did not know, but she had so many memories she could not believe they had not known one another forever. The way he looked when he teased her about her abominable lack of poetic sensibilities. The library table set on fire when she had accused him of killing his wife. How he never treated her like a child or an inferior, even when he might justifiably have done so.

Grief welled up in her chest, and her throat ached with unshed tears. The unmistakable sensation of emotion threatening to overwhelm her surged, and she suppressed it desperately, embracing the void so completely she had no sense of herself. There was no Lydia, just the terrible, aching misery of loss.

She did not know how long she was lost to herself, but eventually she jerked awake to a hand on her shoulder. Lady Craythorne stood over her, her face very still. The room was darker than it had been, and it was difficult to see more of Lady Craythorne than her face. "Miss Wescott, wake up," she said.

Lydia blinked away blurriness from her eyes. Lady Craythorne's emotions were muted with tiredness, but she was not cheerful or relieved, and Lydia's heart constricted once more. "Is Lord Craythorne —" she said.

Relief suffused the Dowager Duchess. "He lives," she said. "He will require more Healing, and he has not yet woken, but—Miss Wescott!"

Lydia gripped Lady Craythorne's hand in stunned surprise. Blackness flooded her vision, and she heard no more.

CHAPTER 31

IN WHICH LADY CRAYTHORNE IS A BETTER DISCERNER THAN LYDIA

Lydia came to herself after what seemed like only a moment to find Lady Craythorne chafing her wrist and calling out for Dr. Wootton. "No, I am well," Lydia said, "I was just so relieved. No one would say anything, and I was sure he would die."

Lady Craythorne settled herself on the edge of the bed, still holding Lydia's hand. "It was a near thing. It is fortunate Mr. Monroe travels with an Extraordinary Shaper as a matter of course. Dr. Mansfield is a miracle worker."

"I must thank him," Lydia said. "I could not bear it if Lord Craythorne were gone."

Lady Craythorne's eyes narrowed. "You are good friends."

"We are. At least—I do not know what he considers me." Lady Craythorne's regard made Lydia uncomfortable. The Dowager Duchess's emotions were placid, but sharply focused in the way emotions were when a person was intent on learning a thing.

"And you enjoy his company," Lady Craythorne continued.

"Of course," Lydia said, more confused than before.

"You speak freely with him, and are unafraid to challenge his assumptions."

"Your Grace, I do not understand." Lydia pushed herself to a sitting position. "Is there some meaning to this recitation?"

The Dowager Duchess smiled. "How unfortunate," she said, "that you cannot Discern your own emotions." She rose. "I will return when the Bounder arrives. We will take rooms in a hotel near here until Oliver is well enough to return to Washington. And I believe the Viceroy wishes to speak with you regarding your spectacular capture of the Libertymen's leaders."

Lydia suddenly recalled what else had happened that day, and guilt swept through her. "I hope I did not give you too much worry, running off like that. I saw Mrs. Ruskin, and I could only think of stopping her —but I should have considered more how my disappearance would look. Please, forgive me."

Lady Craythorne scowled. "You should certainly beg my forgiveness. After I assured Lieutenant Danniell that we were safe! Anything might have happened to you!"

"Oh, then you are not angry," Lydia said, relieved.

"You are impertinent to Discern my emotions," Lady Craythorne said, but she was still only moderately annoyed. "No, but I was terribly worried. It was nearly an hour before I discovered where you were, thanks to my having added young Mr. Walker at Government House to my reticulum. It was a precaution I hoped we would not need." She sniffed imperiously. "Nevertheless, you are not to do such a thing again."

"It will not be necessary, I hope." Lydia touched her hair, which must be hopelessly tangled. Her scalp hurt, and her various bruises seemed to have doubled in size, but Lord Craythorne was alive, and she did not care about her physical pains now.

⁂

FOUR DAYS PASSED IN WHICH LYDIA DID NOT SEE LORD Craythorne, though he was awake after the second day and, according to Lady Craythorne, aware of his surroundings by the third. "He is still abed, and betrothed or not, it would be inappropriate for you to visit his bedchamber," Lady Craythorne had said.

Lydia had agreed. Awkwardness flooded through her when she considered seeing Lord Craythorne in such a state. He was possessed of such a powerful presence, was so vibrantly alive, she did not wish to diminish him by witnessing him in a weakened condition. It was foolishness, but she was nevertheless relieved at Lady Craythorne's forbiddance.

Lady Craythorne spent most of her time at her son's side, so Lydia was left to her own devices. She spent those days sitting at the window of her hotel room and watching the street below. Most of the passersby were beyond her range, which comforted her. She could not forget how she had lost control in her fight with Mrs. Ruskin. Giving in to her emotions—how undisciplined she had been, how lost to all reason. The memory frightened her, tied as it was to memories of Magdalen and that unnamed madhouse. If she had no control, so much better to feel nothing, no natural emotion that might be amplified by those emotions she Discerned into madness.

On the fourth day, she was startled by a knock on her door and Lady Craythorne's entrance without an invitation. "The Viceroy would like to meet with you," she said. "I have just Spoken with Mr. Walker. Mr. Monroe invites you to join him at Government House this afternoon."

"I will be happy to speak to him," Lydia said. "But I am not sure what I might say. It was Mr. Hammond who apprehended the Ruskins, and I did nothing but fight a losing battle and be thrown out a window."

"Mr. Walker did not provide details." Annoyance filled Lady Craythorne at this. Presumably she believed the Government House Speaker should be more respectful of the Dowager Duchess of Craythorne. "Lieutenant Danniell will call for you at two o'clock. That is the extent of my information."

"Perhaps that is all there is to tell."

"Perhaps." Lady Craythorne sniffed. "I am off to sit with Oliver again. He has done very little but eat and sleep the past two days, but Dr. Mansfield says he has turned a corner and will be on his feet by tomorrow."

The idea cheered Lydia out of the dread uncertainty the Viceroy's summons had filled her with. "I am so glad."

Lady Craythorne's emotions sharpened into amusement, but she said no more, instead leaving the room as abruptly as she had entered. Lydia stared at the closed door as if she might see the retreating figure through it. She could not understand why her relationship with Lord Craythorne was so amusing to the Dowager Duchess. With a shrug, she turned back to the window.

At two o'clock, she was dressed as formally as she could manage with her limited travel wardrobe and waiting for Lieutenant Danniell. The lieutenant behaved as properly as ever, and looked indifferent about his escort duties, but he was intensely curious about Lydia. She did not know if it was curiosity about her role in apprehending the leaders of the Libertymen, or her betrothal to Lord Craythorne, or even why the Viceroy wished to speak to her, but she chose not to interrogate him. She still felt rather disconnected from reality. She, Lydia Wescott, of no notable family, to meet face to face with the Viceroy of the American colonies! It was nearly as intimidating as meeting the King himself.

She followed Danniell through the imposing foyer of Government House, which still looked bleak though the day was sunny, and up stairs and down halls until Danniell opened a door at the end of a hall and said, "Miss Wescott, you will wait here."

Lydia had expected the door to lead to Mr. Monroe's office, but instead the room was an antechamber, furnished with cushioned chairs and a thick rug patterned in gold and blue. A second door opposite the one by which she had entered hung ajar, and even had she not Discerned the presence of three people beyond it, she would have known she was not alone by the sound of quiet conversation and the occasional movement as of papers shuffling.

Paintings in ornate gilded frames hung on the walls, mostly portraits of severe-looking men who might be previous viceroys. Lydia knew too little of American history to recognize any of them. One painting, though, caught her eye; it was a landscape of green and gold fields and handsome trees, beyond which a distant city could be seen. Lydia recognized Oxford from her time at Magdalen, as that asylum was within an easy distance of the great university city. The sight calmed her nerves, which grew more disordered as she waited.

She walked around the room, too nervous to sit, and imagined histories for the men in the paintings. Several of them wore powdered wigs as had been popular a few decades ago, and Lydia pretended they were dressed up to attend on the King before his madness took him. The one with the rosy cheeks might have been a landowner of repute, determined to convince the King to award him greater favors in the form of more land. Lydia did not know any landowners, but it was her impression that they liked adding to their property.

It felt like an hour, but was more likely only a few minutes, before the other door opened fully and a man emerged. Lydia recognized him from the investiture ball; he had not been introduced to her, but he had frequently been at the Viceroy's side. "Miss Wescott, I am Frederick Wainwright," he said, bowing. "Pray, enter." He was only moderately interested in her; most of his attention was on his desire for food.

Lydia curtseyed and passed through the doorway.

Her first impression of the Viceroy's office was that his desk was the biggest she had ever seen. It was closer in size to a table than a true desk, with thick curved legs ending in carved lion's feet and a top easily three inches thick. She could not imagine how they had got it through the door. It had to have been constructed within the office.

She was engrossed enough in her appraisal of the desk that she did not notice the Viceroy had risen from his chair behind it. His words caught her by surprise. "Miss Wescott. Thank you for joining me. Won't you have a seat?"

Lydia remembered the people she had Discerned and brought her attention back to the office. The Viceroy was as tall and attractive as she remembered. His companion was shorter and had a face that looked as if it had been caught in a wine press, but his emotions were placid in a way Lydia liked. The second man bowed and exited the room, leaving the door open.

The Viceroy waved a hand, and Lydia realized there were two chairs as large as the desk positioned facing it. "Thank you, your Excellency," she said. "Is that how you are addressed? I have heard that reference, but now I am not certain."

The Viceroy smiled, and his attention on her became that of a fond elder amused by a child's antics. Lydia managed not to scowl at him. If he was the type to misjudge her because of her age and apparent frailty, she would soon disabuse him of that notion.

"That is the correct term of address," the Viceroy said, "but you may call me simply Mr. Monroe. We do not stand quite so much on ceremony in America as they do in England."

Lydia sat, and immediately discovered the depth of the chair meant if she sat fully back, her feet would dangle like the child Mr. Monroe clearly saw her as. She scooted forward to sit on the chair's edge.

"Before I begin, I should inform you that I know your secret talent," Mr. Monroe said. He sat behind the desk, towering over its surface like a mountain overlooking a plain. "Lord Craythorne believed I needed to understand your capabilities, in the event I might make use of you myself."

Lydia controlled her irritation at his manner of speech, though she deeply disliked being considered a tool. She was certain that had not been Lord Craythorne's suggestion. "I am sure Lord Craythorne knows best what will suit, sir. And I assume you have not been so careless as to spread the news about."

Mr. Monroe's smile broadened. "He also said I should expect you to speak candidly, and that I should not take offense. Is it true you can Discern lies?"

"It is, Mr. Monroe. But I hope you do not intend to test me here and now. I am not a performing animal."

"I did not intend to imply as such."

Lydia raised one eyebrow in the way her brother often did. "In fact, you did, your Excellency. You are not convinced I can do what Lord Craythorne has told you, and you further do not believe Discerning emotions is as useful as all that."

Mr. Monroe's eyes widened. "Yes, you should be astonished," Lydia said, pressing the attack, "and I believe embarrassment is also warranted. But you should not fear me. I do not spread what I Discern abroad."

The Viceroy leaned back in his chair. "I apologize," he said, and now his amusement was gone. "I misjudged you, despite what the Duke said."

"Most people do," Lydia said, "and I confess I trade on that sometimes. But I prefer not to be underestimated by those with whom I work."

"Including me?" Mr. Monroe's intent expression did not give away the turmoil that still filled him.

"If you wish. Though I do not know how I might be of service."

"You were instrumental in capturing Mr. and Mrs. Ruskin," Mr. Monroe said. "That is service aplenty."

Lydia shrugged. "I was captured by them first, so I do not know how much praise I deserve. It was Mr. Hammond who stopped them."

"Hammond followed you through the streets, as he did not know the Ruskins to recognize them from above. Had you not been so dogged in pursuing them, they would have vanished." Mr. Monroe grew thoughtful. "But you say you were captured?"

"Mrs. Ruskin saw me following her—following her the first time—and she had a pistol. But I did very nearly escape." Lydia smiled, remembering how she had turned her Discernment to her advantage in manipulating the Ruskins and their compatriot Babbage. "Do you know their plan, sir?"

"I know they intended to kill me, and that you prevented it. For that, I am personally in your debt." Mr. Monroe leaned forward now. "What more can you tell me?"

"Mrs. Ruskin told me your death was to be the signal for the Libertymen to attack key cities, aided by their Iroquois allies. She implied it was the Haudenosaunee government they had joined with." Lydia gasped. "I should have told you before! Perhaps the Iroquois have already attacked!"

"Be at ease, Miss Wescott. The Ruskins have revealed much under questioning, and you are not the only source of my information. And I have had a delegation from the Haudenosaunee. They are interested in making a more permanent peace." Mr. Monroe's emotions became tinged with satisfaction. "Though your information puts a new light on the manner of their approach. I daresay they only wished to act against America if they were supported by the Libertymen."

"Does not that make them opportunists, and untrustworthy?"

"Opportunists, yes, but untrustworthy—on the contrary. We now know what their intent was, and that permits my government to treat with them advantageously." Mr. Monroe smiled. "I believe we will have many years of good relations with our northern neighbors."

"I am so glad. I fear I have been preoccupied these past days, or I would have come to you immediately." She had been so caught up in Lord Craythorne's recovery and her own fears she had not given much thought to the Ruskins.

"Yes. I understand from Mrs. Ruskin's interrogation that the shot that nearly killed Lord Craythorne was meant for me. I hope you do not blame yourself for how that shot went awry."

"No, sir. Not any longer." Guilt still struck her occasionally, but with every report from Lady Craythorne of her son's recovery, that guilt lessened.

"Then there is nothing left but for me to thank you again, and express my regret that your marriage will take you back to England. I can now sincerely say that your talent is remarkable, and that I wish it might be employed here in America." Mr. Monroe rose, prompting Lydia to do the same. "But I imagine you believe you have the better end of the bargain."

Lydia offered Mr. Monroe her hand. It was swallowed up in his much larger one. "Yes, sir, I do," she said, and was surprised to realize that the idea of marriage was not only no longer strange, but something she anticipated with great pleasure.

"I have considered long how I might show my gratitude to you for saving my life," Mr. Monroe continued. "I cannot offer you a position in my administration, and money would be so tawdry. And it is not as if any reward is the equivalent of a human life. But Mrs. Monroe has spoken to Lady Craythorne, and the Dowager Duchess suggested something you would appreciate."

He opened a drawer and removed a flat box covered in black velvet. "I hope it will suit. I fear I know nothing of ladies' jewelry, to Elizabeth's despair."

Curious, Lydia took the box. It was hinged on one side to open like a clamshell. She lifted the lid and gasped. The necklace within was of silver and three linked ovals of green jade, carved so delicately they looked like spun sugar. Lydia brushed the silver chain with her fingertip. "This is from the museum," she said. "Lady Susan Cotterell's Chinese jewelry. I cannot accept. It belongs to the colonies."

"When I explained to the curator what I had in mind, he was very obliging. It seems he is of the opinion that the Cotterell collection would be of more value if it was worn instead of preserved in a museum, gathering dust," Mr. Monroe said.

"That cannot be the fussy little man I met," Lydia said without thinking.

Mr. Monroe laughed. "You mean Mr. Schotton. He is perhaps a little too proud of his connection to the museum. No, Mr. Alcott is more openminded. He will use the money with which I purchased this to expand their collection of textiles, which is a worthy use in my opinion."

"Then I will not reject your gift, if you are sure—" Lydia touched the jade ovals. They felt smooth and a little soapy and warm like something alive. "But it helps that I do not wish to reject it. This is beautiful."

"Then we are both satisfied." Mr. Monroe came around the desk to stand next to the door. "Thank you for your service to the government, and I wish you well."

"Thank you, sir." Lydia shut the box and tucked it under her arm, decided that made her look like a message runner, and ended by holding it carefully in one hand.

Lieutenant Danniell waited for her in the antechamber. In his usual silent manner, he escorted her out of Government House and back to the hotel. Lydia, still awestruck by the Viceroy's gift, observed Danniell's placid alertness with amusement. He did not know that he was escorting a very valuable piece of jewelry. She imagined herself wearing it, possibly on her wedding day—

That image nearly brought her to a halt. Only Danniell's imperturbable gait kept her walking with him. She had finally become accustomed to the idea that she would marry, if she could so casually make plans as that. But it was marriage to Lord Craythorne that suited her, not marriage in general. She was certain of that.

The doorman at the hotel opened the door for Lydia and her escort, tipping his hat as was his custom. Lydia smiled at him in return. She felt at peace with the world, though the hotel was never terribly warm, and despite its newness the carpet in the foyer gave off unpleasant whiffs of mildew wherever one stepped. It was otherwise quite lovely, though not as nice as Lord Craythorne's Washington mansion. The prospect of returning there cheered her unexpectedly—but the Libertymen threat was ended, so they would all return to England soon. That filled her with rather more trepidation, as it was an unknown. Perhaps Colin was correct that she liked to make her nest and stay comfortably in it.

Very few people remained in the hotel during the day, and she Discerned mainly those outside on the street, as well as the doorman and the hotel employees and a handful of guests on the floors above. She was preoccupied with thoughts of her beautiful necklace and paid her surroundings very little heed. The two men conversing near the stairs did not draw her attention at first, as she was bidding farewell to Lieutenant Danniell. They ignored her as well.

As she turned to make her ascent, her eye fell on the one of the pair facing her. To her shock, it was Mr. Rutledge. She only barely took in his partner's appearance—tall, but not so tall as Mr. Rutledge, broad shoulders, curly hair—and then another jolt ran through her. Lord Craythorne. But surely Lady Craythorne had said he would not be on his feet for another day?

She gazed at him, grateful beyond measure that he was well. In a moment, he would notice her, but for now, she would enjoy watching him unawares. Sweet, unadulterated happiness swept over her. How she had missed him!

His head tilted slightly as he listened to something Mr. Rutledge said, and her heart gave a funny little thump at the memory of how often he had looked at her that way, listening or speaking or teasing her. A moment's fear struck her that perhaps those moments of accord could not last, and then she recalled they were to marry, and her heart beat faster with excitement.

Out of nowhere Lady Craythorne's knowing smile, her secret amusement, came to Lydia's memory. Why Lydia's fondness for Lord

Craythorne should amuse the Dowager Duchess so, she still did not understand. Lord Craythorne was kind, and generous of heart, and quick of understanding, and he cared about what made Lydia happy. There was no reason she should not appreciate those qualities and so many more that made him who he was, and no reason her heart—

Lydia drew in a sharp breath. Finally, she understood what the Dowager Duchess had hinted at, and felt like a fool. She had not known her own emotions, indeed. "Oh," she said, faintly, and then in a louder voice, "*Oh.*"

The noise drew both men's attention. Mr. Rutledge was surprised, Lord Craythorne puzzled. He turned, and his eyes widened. Then he smiled. His puzzlement disappeared in a rush of emotion, warm and tender and so joyful Lydia took a step back in astonishment. She had Discerned this emotion before, had seen Colin's love for Clemency and hers for him, but it had never been directed at her before. And now it swept over her in a rich green wave, enticing her, twining with her own newfound realization until she believed she might die of happiness.

Lord Craythorne took a step toward her. "Lydia," he said, extending his hand.

Lydia's gaze moved from his face to his outstretched hand. Then she turned and fled.

CHAPTER 32

IN WHICH TAKING GOOD ADVICE REWARDS LYDIA BEYOND ANYTHING SHE DREAMED POSSIBLE

She heard Lord Craythorne call her name again, Discerned his feelings of love being supplanted by surprise and then a terrible aching sorrow and humiliation that made her own heart ache. To her relief, he did not follow her. The last thing she Discerned from him before she fled out of range was the inward-turned tension that accompanied physical pain. The fleeting thought that she had caused him to relapse vanished unheeded, though she could imagine no other reason for him not to pursue her. It did not matter. She had to get away.

She ran until her chest ached with a more physical pain and her legs and feet were sore, and then she stopped with one hand on the nearest wall for balance, sucking in air as if she were drowning. The wall was of granite, rough against her palm, but she welcomed the little pain. It was a distraction from memory.

Lord Craythorne loved her. And she, to her everlasting surprise, loved him.

She realized she still clutched the velvet box and wrapped her arm around it, holding it close to her chest. The soft velvet contrasted with the hard stone wall so completely she felt torn in half, one side rough and cold, the other warm and soft. Men and women passed her, some of them looking at her curiously, most of them indifferent to her presence. She had believed her turmoil was visible, but it seemed only a Discerner could tell that her heart was broken.

If she were anyone else, discovering that she loved the man she would marry, and that he loved her, would be cause for rejoicing. They would share that love and make a beautiful life for themselves. But she was an Extraordinary Discerner. She could not permit herself to experience strong emotions, anger, hatred, fear...love. She had already been carried away by it in Discerning his love for her, that sense of being tangled up and swept away by her love for him so that she could not tell where she began or ended. She could not bear being mad again, not even such a sweet madness as that.

As her breathing slowed, she looked around herself. She had believed she was hopelessly lost, as she had paid no attention to her path as she ran, but to her relief she was still on the same street as the hotel, a few blocks away. Her relief vanished as she realized she did not know where to go. Returning to the hotel, to face Lord Craythorne, made her ill. He loved her, he surely knew she had Discerned his love, and she had run from him. She could never explain what had motivated her in a way that would lessen that betrayal.

She shivered as a chilly wind brushed her face. Fortunately, she still wore her warm coat and had not gone running into the street dressed only in her muslin gown. Even so, the air was cold despite the sun, and she should go indoors as soon as possible. She might find a tea shop, or a bookseller—except she had no money, had left her reticule in her room on the grounds that she did not need money to visit the Viceroy. Perhaps a stationer's shop would not mind if she browsed, or she might pretend interest in a hat.

Lydia sighed. There was no point in putting off the inevitable, and waiting might even make the upcoming meeting worse—for she could not ignore or avoid Lord Craythorne indefinitely. She turned and trudged back to the hotel.

As she neared the front door, her heart sped up until it was beating nearly as rapidly as it had when she ran. She imagined Mr. Rutledge and Lord Craythorne still in the foyer, waiting for her, planning her chastisement. But the foyer was empty save for a few hotel employees and one elegantly-dressed woman speaking sharply to a man in a suit. Lydia recognized him as the hotel manager. He was listening politely, but in his heart he wished the woman to the devil. Lydia could hardly blame him. She did not know why so many people believed they were entitled to take out their wrath on their inferiors—or perhaps it was that they could not Discern the hurt and humiliation they inflicted. It was difficult to chastise someone when you felt the injustice of the chastisement as if you were the one receiving it.

She avoided the rude lady and mounted the stairs slowly, like a criminal approaching the gallows. Which was ridiculous. Lord Craythorne would not shout at her; no, he felt betrayed and wounded, justly so, and Lydia would have to experience those emotions in the knowledge that she was the one who had caused them.

No one waited to apprehend her in the hall, though she Discerned the presence of four people in the Dowager Duchess's room next to hers. She entered her own room and closed the door with relief, ignoring the tiny voice that berated her for being a coward. She set the necklace box on her bedside table and dropped into the chair near the window where she had sat all those days watching the crowds pass. Next door, two of the four people were intent in the way people become when they are conversing on a subject both care about. That would be Lady Craythorne and possibly Mr. Rutledge, if he was in New York City on business, though Lydia did not know what he might have to say to Lady Craythorne. Another was placid and a little bored; that was likely Lady Craythorne's maid Bisset.

The fourth was Lord Craythorne, distinguishable as always by his muted emotions. Lydia made herself attend to his emotional state, which was exactly as she had predicted, hurt and miserable. Her heart ached with the desire to go to him, to tell him of her love and explain —but he would not understand. She barely understood it herself. If only he had gone on indifferent to her, or she to him! They might have remained happily married as friends...but that was impossible now.

The door opened, and Ellery entered. "Miss, are you feeling well?

You look very ill. Should I fetch you water, or perhaps you should lie down?"

Lydia shook her head and returned to watching the street. "There is no cure for what ails me, Maud."

Ellery, to her surprise, giggled. "I apologize, miss. It is just that you sounded like someone in a melodrama."

"That is not far wrong." Lydia sighed. "My life has become the stuff of farce, and I cannot imagine how it might be made right."

Ellery came to stand beside Lydia. "Will it help if you tell me, miss?"

"It cannot hurt. Maud, I have fallen in love with Lord Craythorne, and he loves me."

Ellery covered her mouth to hold back a gasp. "Oh, miss, that is wonderful!"

"It would be for anyone else. I cannot love someone who loves me." Saying the words aloud made her feel empty inside. "I Discern his love, and it—there is no way to explain to someone who is not a Discerner what it is like to be tangled up in emotion. That is how I become mad, losing myself. It does not matter if it is a happy or sad emotion, only that it is a strong one, because that is what overwhelms me. And I know of no way to stop it."

To Lydia's surprise, Ellery sat on the edge of the bed facing her. "But you must feel those strong emotions all the time," she said. "The ones you Discern, I mean, belonging to others. How is it you are not overwhelmed all the time?"

"I refuse to permit myself to feel," Lydia said. "If I do not feel anger myself, for example, I cannot become confused by someone else's anger."

Ellery's brow furrowed. "I beg your pardon, miss, for speaking bluntly, but that seems a terrible way to live, never feeling anything."

"I don't—" Lydia paused, contemplating. "It is not *every* emotion. Just the powerful ones."

"It is still terrible." Ellery's calmness was threaded through with sorrow and a trace of pity. "You are human, and humans feel things. I believe it is what makes us who we are."

"But I am different."

"Not that different." Ellery leaned forward. "Miss, Charles and James both broke my heart, but as much as I wish they had been the men I believed they were, I do not wish never to have felt the pain of their betrayal. My father always liked to quote that psalm—the one about weeping lasting for a night, but joy coming in the morning? And he said joy is sweeter when it comes after sorrow, because we have the memory of not having it. I believe he was right."

"It is not as if I wish to feel no pain, Maud!" Lydia exclaimed. "I *cannot* lose myself again, I cannot, do you not understand? What is the point of experiencing anger or sorrow or even love if I am no longer sane enough to appreciate what comes after?"

"I don't know, miss." Ellery wiped her eyes, making Lydia wish she dared weep as well. "But you have gone all these years suppressing your emotions. Perhaps you need to embrace them, instead."

"I told you—"

"You said we were friends, and if that's true, I will be bold." Ellery stood and stared down at Lydia. "If what frightens you is being lost, confused between your emotions and other people's, then perhaps all you really need is a way to identify your feelings separate from those. And I believe, if you can do that well enough to know which emotions to suppress, you should be able to find those emotions and hold to them instead." She turned and left the room before Lydia could say anything in reply.

Lydia watched the door close and then sat staring at it, numb to her core. Ellery knew nothing of the matter. She was not an Extraordinary Discerner nor even an ordinary one; she could not know what it was like to experience the emotions of others, how overwhelming it could be. It was easy for her to talk of embracing emotions rather than suppressing them, because for her, suppressing emotions was not how she survived.

But Lydia could not dismiss one thing Ellery had said: *if you can do that well enough to know which emotions to suppress, you should be able to find those emotions and hold to them instead.* It had not occurred to Lydia that to suppress her emotions, she had to know the difference between her natural emotions and Discerned emotions. She could not suppress them otherwise. And the problem was, had always been, the moments when that distinction was lost. So Ellery might be correct. It might actually be a matter of doing *something* to keep that distinction. Suppressing emotion—or embracing it.

Lydia got up and lay on her bed fully clothed. This was ridiculous. She would likely only drive herself to madness, and even a temporary madness frightened her. But she recalled the sensation of Lord Craythorne's love for her, how in the moment before it began to overwhelm her it had enfolded her in pure joy. She wished for nothing less than to feel that again, now and every day for the rest of her life. She dismissed the possibility that her rejection of him had destroyed his love. Even if that were true, she could not bear to go on as a void.

She curled into a ball and focused on the emotions surrounding her. Those in Lady Craythorne's room remained as they had been, placid or intent or sorrowing. Lydia focused on the last of those. Lord Craythorne's misery broke her heart the more because she Discerned him trying to suppress it. Her own sorrow filled her and began to twine with his.

Instinctively, she began to make herself a void, emotionless and separate. No. Not again. She closed her eyes. What did she feel? That terrible ache at having hurt the man she loved when he clearly expected nothing but reciprocal love from her. She had rejected him in the worst way possible—no. His pain was not what mattered now. *What did she feel?*

She let herself sink into her misery. It was not the same as his. She could tell the difference—she was not sure that was true, but she willed it to be so. She was an Extraordinary Discerner, she had mastery of her talent as no other Discerner did, and if she could Discern lies and the secrets of others' hearts, she could certainly Discern her own!

She embraced her sorrow so it flooded every part of herself, building and building like a wave poised on the horizon until it surged, carrying her away. It was not like being overwhelmed, that terrible tangle of others' emotions and her own; it was pure and untrammeled, and she knew in that instant this was truly her own emotion and no one else's. A cry burst out of her, surprising her, and then she was sobbing in earnest, grief and misery pouring out of her in tears.

The last time she had wept, she was in the throes of madness. She could not remember ever weeping when she was in her right mind, and certainly not weeping as she did now. It hurt, tearing at her chest and throat and swelling her eyes, and she welcomed it as it swept away her confusion and filled her with the knowledge that *this* was real, *this* was her true emotion.

As her weeping wound down, she hugged her knees to her chest and tried to calm her breathing. And as she breathed slowly, in through the nose, out through the mouth, she became aware again of those in her vicinity. She still Discerned Lord Craythorne's pain, but this time it was clearly distinct from her own, as if emotions were visible and a line had been drawn around his. There was no color to it, which seemed strange, but she chose not to dwell on that small mystery.

She drifted for a while, testing the boundaries of this new perception against all the emotions within her range. The experience she had in suppressing her emotions felt as if it had been inverted, as if instead of a void, she was...well, whatever the inverse of a void was. It was not something that could be described with words. And yet she was confident that this new approach would not desert her, for all it was barely tested.

She sat up and wiped her eyes, then rang for Ellery. When Ellery entered, Lydia was at the dressing table tidying her hair. "Maud, will you ask Lord Craythorne to join me?"

Ellery eyed her skeptically. "Miss, you look disheveled. Are you sure you wish him to see you like this?"

"I cannot wait longer or I will lose my nerve. Please, Maud, do as I ask."

Ellery nodded and closed the door.

Lydia Discerned Lord Craythorne's changing emotions and was aware when his misery increased. That his sorrow deepened at the prospect of seeing her made her stomach tighten into a burning knot. But she would not be a coward, and regardless of the outcome of this conversation, she would have done the right thing.

The door opened, and Lord Craythorne entered. His face was smooth, expressionless, but his unhappiness battered at Lydia until she focused instead on her own emotional state so his faded into the background. She nodded to Ellery, who quietly closed the door on them both.

Lydia stood. "Will you sit, your Grace?"

"I do not believe," Lord Craythorne said, still dispassionately, "that this will be an ordinary, civil conversation."

Lydia's knees shook, and she held herself still and did not resume her seat. "It may not be much of a conversation at all. I simply have two things I wish to say to you, and I do not expect a response. But I could not bear it if I did not say them."

Lord Craythorne inclined his head as if suggesting she get on with it.

"Your Grace," Lydia said, "I behaved abominably to you. I Discerned your love for me, and I turned my back on you, rejecting your implicit offer. I was afraid, but I should never have done that. Not to a friend."

Her words roused Lord Craythorne's sorrow and hurt, and her heart ached more to Discern his state. Despite her newfound control, her sorrow tangled with his, and she paused, breathing in deeply and willing her confusion to flow out of her with her exhalation. Once more, she embraced her own pain and let it swell over her so his receded slightly from her Discernment.

When she had regained control, she said, "That is the first thing. I apologize for running away and hurting you. This is the second thing." She drew in a deep breath and lowered her head so she was looking at his boots and not his expressionless face. "The reason I ran is that I love you, and my love for you tangled with your love for me until I feared becoming mad. I could not bear that, not again. I know it is not something you will understand, and I thank God that you do not, for I would not wish that madness on anyone."

Lord Craythorne shifted as if he meant to speak, and his sorrow became tinged with surprise. Lydia held up a hand for silence. "You see," she went on, "I have never loved before, and I have never been loved before, not the way you love me, or did love me before I rejected you—oh, I do not know what I am saying! I do not ask your forgiveness, because that might mean I believe you should not have been injured. I simply wish you to know that I did not flee because I despise you. I feel—it is so much the opposite of despising I do not know a word for it."

She waited for him to say whatever she had forestalled, but he remained silent. His emotions now swirled together, sorrow mixed with confusion and surprise in a way Lydia did not understand. Nervously, trying to fill the space between them, she added, "I release you from our engagement—I do not wish for you to consider yourself obligated, not after what I have done. And I will ensure everyone knows I am the one who broke it off, so you will not be censured— though perhaps that will make you seem a figure of pity, and that would be wrong—or possibly you would like me to blacken my own character, so you—"

"That will be unnecessary," Lord Craythorne said.

His emotions shifted toward amusement, and Lydia risked a glance at him. He was smiling, the faintest curve of his lips, but unmistakably a smile. The tiniest thread of hope twined about her heart, and she crushed it. She Discerned no love in his heart, only the sort of humor that rises from a sense of the ridiculous.

"You are laughing at me," she said, concealing her despair.

"I am not," Lord Craythorne said. "Despite extreme provocation."

"It is all on the inside," Lydia said. "Do you believe my apology is nothing more than a source of amusement, your Grace?"

"No." Lord Craythorne shook his head slightly. "No, it is, in fact, the most heartfelt and convincing apology I have ever heard."

"Then why are you laughing? You know you cannot conceal your emotions from me."

Lord Craythorne let out a deep breath. "Because," he said, taking a step closer, "I know of no other woman who would be so overcome by her feelings for me her only choice was flight or madness. I cannot decide if that is a tremendous compliment or deeply disturbing."

"Perhaps it is both," Lydia said, breathlessly. He could not hate her if he could find her amusing—or perhaps that was untrue, and she truly had no hope at all.

"And yet I am here, and you do not appear to be mad," Lord Craythorne said, his mirth dissolving. "What does that mean?"

His emotions were becoming clearer, less muddled, but what Lydia

Discerned gave her no relief. "You are afraid I no longer love you," she said.

"What have we discussed about you commenting on my private emotions?"

"*You* said that I was not to protect you from yourself, your Grace."

Lord Craythorne again shook his head, this time slowly, as if helpless against fate. "Very well. Yes. I fear you do not love me, and I fear that you do. If you were so distressed that you ran from me, how do I know that will not happen again?"

Lydia's hands shook, and she clasped them together to still them. "I do not know if I can explain—Discernment makes no sense to those who are not Discerners—you cannot say how it is you control a fire, can you? And this is much the same. But I am certain, your Grace —" She drew in a deep breath and let it out slowly. "I am certain I have true mastery of my talent now where before I had only the barest of control. And I would not have gained that mastery had I not the best of incentives."

Both Lord Craythorne's eyebrows raised. "And what is that?"

Lydia lowered her head again. "The prospect of loving you, and being loved in return, now and for all the days of my life."

As she spoke, surprise overtook Lord Craythorne, and then his emotions were a glorious tangle of relief, and happiness, and that beautiful love centered on her. "You *do* love me!" she exclaimed, cutting off his words as he opened his mouth. "Oh, I am so glad!"

"*I* am not," Lord Craythorne said, rather grouchily. "A man likes to be able to speak his love, not have it spoken for him."

Lydia smiled. "Forgive me," she said. "Go ahead. I promise to be suitably overjoyed at your declaration."

Lord Craythorne laughed and closed the remaining distance between them. "Do you know," he said, taking both her hands in his, "you were my first thought upon waking from being Healed. In the moment before I opened my eyes, I wished I might find you there at my bedside, and the depth of my unhappiness when I did not made me realize you meant much more to me than a friend and companion. I have never been so annoyed with my mother than when I asked to see you and she refused on the grounds that such a visit was inappropriate."

Lydia blushed. "The idea of visiting your bedchamber discomfited me, and I believe now that was the beginning of my awareness that I love you. It was such an intimacy, you see."

"I understand. I doubt anyone else would." His smile vanished, leaving him looking so somber Lydia would have assumed the worst had she not been basking in the depth of his love for her. "Perhaps I should have known all along how I cared for you. I imagine I could not readily see beyond my terrible past to a glorious future. But I assure you, Lydia Wescott—" He took her in his arms and held her close— "I love you for everything you are, your rambling asides and lack of poetic sensibilities and all."

His closeness took her breath away. "Then I suppose I should not break off our engagement."

"You are forbidden to do so. Imagine what a figure of ridicule that would make me. Poor Lord Craythorne, rejected by the girl whose reputation he ruined." Lord Craythorne smiled, a rather impish expression that with his curly hair gave him a satirical appearance. "I should never find another woman to marry, and my mother would have to intervene, and we all know how well that worked out before."

"I would rather marry you than remain unwed in my brother and sister-in-law's house. They are wonderful, but they will not kiss me as I am certain you intend to." Despite her bold words, saying this filled her with uncertainty. Suppose she was wrong, and she could not, in fact, distinguish her emotions from his during such an intimate gesture?

Lord Craythorne raised his eyebrows again. "You seem very certain of yourself. Suppose I do not believe in kissing before marriage?"

That dispelled Lydia's fears. "Need I remind you, your Grace—"

"Oliver. Please."

"Very well—need I remind you, Oliver, that I know your innermost heart?"

He pursed his lips in pretended introspection. "It occurs to me that you cannot possibly be as innocent as you look, not if you are privy to the basest desires."

"I hope you do not think less of me for that. In truth, everything I know of love comes from observation and not experience." Shyness overcame Lydia again. She recalled all the times she had observed men and women in passion, how amused she had been to be a secret witness to desire. Those memories felt tawdry now.

"Lydia," Oliver said, resting his fingers beneath her chin and tilting her head so she had to look at him, "what you have seen and felt does not matter, only who you are. And I promise that will always be true."

His hand shifted to caress her cheek, and then his lips touched hers gently, so gently that she did not expect the surge of passion and joy that swept over her with his kiss, stunning her with its intensity. For a moment, she was lost, unable to distinguish between his love and her own, and then she seized hold of her emotions and let them sweep her away. He kissed her again, and she responded eagerly, feeling as if she swam in an ocean whose warm waves carried her up and down with every kiss.

She became aware of a growing urgency within her, her body warming unexpectedly and demanding that she touch him, feel his skin against hers. Just as she realized the strength of that urge came from his emotions as well as hers, Oliver kissed her forehead and then held her close, cradling her head against his shoulder. He was breathing as raggedly as she, and she giggled and said, "I did not realize it would feel like *that*. It is so different when one is a participant rather than an observer."

"It seems Discernment has its limitations," Oliver said. "And I have yet to procure a special license for us. Would you prefer to be married here or in England, darling?"

"Those kisses say America, and tomorrow, but Colin and Clemency will not forgive me if I marry anywhere but from our parish church." Lydia lifted her head to gaze into her beloved's eyes. "And then we can begin our life together. Extraordinary Scorcher and Extraordinary Discerner."

Oliver frowned. "Do you intend to declare your talent openly, then?"

"I find I have had enough of secrecy," Lydia said. "There are so many things I might do if I am publicly an Extraordinary Discerner.

My desire for the excitement of clandestine missions has faded. I had enough excitement when Mrs. Ruskin threw me out the window."

Oliver's arms around her waist stiffened. "Mrs. Ruskin did *what*?"

"Oh. I assumed you were told." Lydia hugged him close. "It seems we have much to talk about. Do you know it is my fault you were shot? That is, I did not shoot you, and I did not mean for Mrs. Ruskin's shot to go awry—well, I did, but I only meant for her not to shoot the Viceroy—"

Oliver silenced her with a kiss.

CHAPTER 33

IN WHICH LYDIA'S HAPPY ENDING IS UNLIKE ANYTHING SHE IMAGINED

"**A**n Extraordinary Discerner," Dorothea said. She set her teacup down without looking at the saucer, and the cup clipped the edge of the saucer, causing tea to slosh over the side. All her attention was fixed on Lydia.

"You concealed your talent," Miranda said. She held a half-eaten cake in her hand as if she had forgotten it was there.

Lydia had never been so grateful for a talent that permitted her to Discern her friends' emotions and guide her in a response. She had considered not telling them, reasoning that they were rarely in England and it was unlikely they would meet again after Lydia returned home. But that was not the act of a friend.

So she paid close attention to their emotional reactions rather than the smooth, polite faces they wore. Miranda was startled and curious. Dorothea's emotions were resentful and a little fearful. That those feelings no longer appeared in color, Lydia believed was a result of her new, true mastery of her talent; now she simply Discerned others' emotions, and there was never any question which ones were her own.

In the face of those emotional reactions, Lydia chose to speak circumspectly rather than responding to what they did not say. "I apologize for the necessity. It was not you I concealed—well, yes, I did, I mean that I could not reveal my talent to those I, well, spied on, and that meant concealing it from everyone."

"And you spied on us?" Dorothea said. Her emotions were building toward an outburst.

"Of course not. It was the Libertymen I spied on. And I did not expect that you and I should become friends." Lydia hoped she was saying the right thing. "I believe if my ruse had had to go on for very long, I might have brought you and Miranda into my confidences."

"Oh, but suppose *we* were Libertymen!" Miranda exclaimed.

Dorothea snorted in an unladylike way. "We could not be Libertymen, Miranda. That is perfectly ridiculous."

"Very well, suppose our parents or close friends were Libertymen, and we accidentally revealed our knowledge to them," Miranda said, undeterred. "Obviously Lydia could not tell us the truth. It does not mean we are not friends."

"People fear my talent," Lydia told Dorothea. "They fear I will Discern their secrets and tell the world—or they fear my knowing what they keep hidden, simply because it is an intimate thing they do not wish to share. And it is true I cannot help what I Discern. But I am very good at keeping secrets, and I promise I do not act on them. Please, do not be angry."

Dorothea scowled. "Then you knew my feelings for Lord Craythorne."

"I know how they changed when you were finally permitted to have your own opinion, and not your mother's," Lydia said. It might be too blunt an assertion, but Lydia knew Dorothea prized plain speaking, and the way Dorothea's emotions became calmer proved it was the right thing to say.

"*I* say it is more exciting that you were a spy," Miranda said. She took a small bite from her cake and chewed thoughtfully. "I wish I could be a spy. So many adventures!"

Lydia recalled her thirty-six hours in the madhouse and the sight of Oliver bleeding to death on the steps of Government House. That the doctors responsible for her interment had been imprisoned, charged with kidnapping, and Oliver was not dead, did not lessen those horrors. "Not all adventures are the sort one wishes to experience," she said. "But your desire is not impossible. Some of what I did depended on my youthful and innocent appearance rather than my talent."

To her surprise, Dorothea smiled in a rather knowing way. "I am sure Mr. Sabot appreciated that. Of course, he has been arrested as a Libertyman sympathizer, but I understand he has begun a new poem inspired by a Miss W."

Lydia blushed. "I suppose there is no way to stop him."

"Well, I intend to use my father's connections to speak to someone in Government House—though we leave for London in a few months, so perhaps that should wait." Miranda ate the last of her cake. "I will not sit idle waiting for someone to marry me."

"Not even Mr. Cavanaugh?" Dorothea teased.

It was Miranda's turn to blush. "Mr. Cavanaugh has his career to consider first, though he has been most flattering. It will be a year or more before he can seriously contemplate marriage. And if I can serve my country during that time, so much the better."

Lydia observed Dorothea's emotions taking a turn toward down-heartedness and guessed what troubled her friend. "I would like very much for you both to visit me in England," she said, "perhaps for an extended visit? Lady Craythorne is kind, but she is my mother-in-law. It would be much more enjoyable to attend social gatherings with those of my own age, especially since there are many who would like to entertain the new Duchess of Craythorne." She paused, caught up once more in the beauty of her new situation. "It is still such a peculiar notion."

"Not so peculiar, given that you were much in the Duke's company, however you might protest otherwise," Dorothea said. Her mood had already altered into introspection, and Lydia hoped she was contemplating meeting eligible young men far from her mother's oppressive presence.

"Yes, Lord Craythorne says we ought to have known this would happen," Lydia said with a fond smile. "In my defense, I am not very good at knowing my own emotions, as I am so buffeted by the emotions of others."

"Then it is settled," Miranda said. "We will come to you in a month's time—you will be returned from your wedding trip by then, yes?"

"We are to be married in a week, after returning to England." The warmth of her love again suffused Lydia, and she realized in the next moment that it was not solely her own feeling. "There is Lord Craythorne now," she added, turning to face the door.

"That will take some getting used to," Miranda murmured to Dorothea.

The door opened, and Oliver said, "I beg your pardon, I did not realize you were entertaining guests."

"We were just leaving," Dorothea said, setting her half-drunk cup of tea aside and rising. "Congratulations, your Grace, and I wish you both very happy."

"Thank you, Lady Dorothea, Miss Adams," Oliver said.

He stood back to permit them to exit, then came fully into the drawing room to meet Lydia, who had risen to meet him. "I am glad your friends are so perceptive as to see I wish to be alone with you," he said, taking her hands and drawing her close for a kiss. "They did not seem angry over your revelation."

"No, they took it well." Lydia leaned against his shoulder and sighed deeply. "I have invited them to stay with us for a long visit. I hope you do not mind."

"Craythorne House is large enough to accommodate more than two extra guests, though I hope you will refrain from filling it with friends." Oliver ran a hand gently down her back to rest at her waist. "Privacy will become impossible."

"At the risk of making myself a figure of pity, I must point out that Dorothea and Miranda are my only friends to whom I am not related. So you need not fear." She tilted her head back to regard him. "You are in good spirits. Does that mean our time here is over?"

"It does. There are likely still pockets of Libertymen resistance, but with Mr. and Mrs. Ruskin captured, their leadership is gone, and the Viceroy's agents make careful note of any hint of rebel sympathizing. There is still work to be done in England, as Lord Deverell was not the only Englishman interested in promoting American independence, but

I believe the threat to the King and the Prince Regent, at least, are also ended."

Oliver's satisfaction at having achieved his goal warmed Lydia's heart. "Is it wrong of me to say I understand their desires?" she asked. "The American colonies are thriving, and they are so far from England, I can quite see why their people might wish to rule themselves."

"There is nothing wrong with that, and you are not alone," Oliver said. "It is a contentious subject in Parliament. There are many who wish not to lose the bounty of resources America provides the mother country, but there are many more who see the justice of giving the colonies freedom."

"Then why do they not? It is the question of slavery, yes?"

"It is." Oliver looked and felt grim for a moment. "The buying and selling of slaves is already illegal in England and her colonies, and it is only a matter of time until Parliament declares slavery itself illegal."

"I do not understand how slavery is not illegal if buying and selling slaves is."

"There are enough men in Parliament with holdings in America and the West Indies that depend on slave labor for their profitability that I fear greed is more powerful a motivator than doing the right thing." Oliver's bleak mood deepened. "And Americans in the South are in the same position. They must learn how to survive in an economy not based on the enslavement of human beings. And England will not release them until they do."

"I understand. I do not believe everyone does. Mr. Suggitt, for one."

"Abel Suggitt is no longer in a position to drive policy. And I believe I have made his father sufficiently afraid for his son's life that he will rethink his own politics, or at least his expression of them."

Lydia smiled. "You are so satisfied with yourself right now I should conjure an absurd request, to take advantage of your expansive mood."

"You forget, my love, I am inclined to do anything you ask, regardless of my mood," Oliver said, and bent to kiss her once more.

THE FOLLOWING MONDAY, LYDIA STOOD IN FRONT OF THE MIRROR in her own bedroom at Emeraude House and held one of her new gowns against herself, examining the result with a critical eye. "This will not suit," she told Ellery. "It is quite the wrong color to match my necklace, and is a trifle too informal for church."

"You should wear the green one, miss," Ellery said, offering it draped across her arms. "Though the weather has been so cold, perhaps the grey silk would be better."

Lydia took both proffered gowns and awkwardly held them over each shoulder so the jade and silver necklace was clearly visible. "I believe you are right about the grey silk. And the green is not quite the same shade as the jade."

"That is not entirely true, they are the same color except that the gown is much paler," Ellery declared.

Lydia moved closer to the mirror and peered at her reflection. "You have a very good eye for color, Maud."

"I consider it a useful skill." Ellery accepted both gowns from Lydia and hurried to fold the green one away, draping the grey one over the foot of the bed. "And I will use that skill to trim your wedding bonnet, now that you have chosen a gown for that day."

Lydia straightened the gown she wore, which had become rumpled after she had tested so many possibilities. "I am so impatient. It seems Thursday is forever away, and there is so much I wish to do beginning Thursday. Be married, embark on our wedding trip, return to Craythorne House to welcome Dorothea and Miranda...if only Thursday were today!"

"If that were so, miss, you would be a woefully unprepared bride," Ellery scolded, but with a smile.

Someone knocked on the door, and before Ellery could reach it to open it, Clemency walked in. "I apologize for bursting in on you," she said, "but you have a caller I believe you will wish to meet."

"A caller for me?" Lydia's social status had improved substantially upon the announcement of her talent, her intended marriage, and her subsequent elevation to the nobility, and she was accustomed to being thronged with callers. Clemency's interest and approval, though, was unusual, as was anyone calling before noon. "Who is it?"

"It is Lady Enderleigh." Clemency's emotions were subdued excitement, the anticipation of a pleasant encounter in the immediate future. "She is a lovely woman, and I believe you will like her."

England's first Extraordinary Scorcher in a century, though no longer England's only Extraordinary Scorcher. "You are acquainted with her, yes?"

"I am. We are not close, but I consider her a friend." Clemency smiled, and her emotions became reflective of memory. "We met in a rather dramatic fashion, and she is among the few who know of my nocturnal habits pursuing criminals."

"Then—is she here because of my talent, or Oliver's?"

Clemency shrugged. "You are the one more likely to know the answer to that. I suggest you ask her."

Lydia contemplated this as she walked downstairs to the drawing room, the pleasant one. Oliver had not said if he had been introduced to Lady Enderleigh, and she suspected that meant he had not. She could not imagine why Lady Enderleigh would call on her before calling on Oliver, or inviting him to meet with her, or—it was simply unusual, however one looked at it.

Lady Enderleigh rose from the sofa nearest the fireplace when Lydia entered. She was a striking woman, with chestnut brown hair and grey eyes made fierce by her heavy eyebrows. But her smile was pleasant enough, and she extended a hand to Lydia, saying, "Miss Wescott, thank you for seeing me."

"You were curious," Lydia said, Discerning Lady Enderleigh's emotions, which were placid enough, but bore a tinge of anticipation that sharpened into curiosity.

"I was—but you are polite not to comment further," Lady Enderleigh said. "I understand an Extraordinary Discerner cannot help what she Discerns. It is not so easy as ignoring a sound or a sight."

"That is true. Please, won't you sit?" Lydia sat in the chair opposite where Lady Enderleigh had been sitting, and Lady Enderleigh resumed her seat.

"I am sure you are wondering why I called on you," Lady Enderleigh said. "Curiosity, yes, but I hoped also to enlist your help. I am reluctant to approach Lord Craythorne directly. We are both

MELISSA MCSHANE

Extraordinary Scorchers, true, but he is yet unmarried, and I know him only by reputation, and even were neither of those things true, it is still awkward for a lady to make overtures to a gentleman."

"Oliver—Lord Craythorne will not mind," Lydia said, "but I understand you. And you would also like to know why he has not reached out to you, whether it is social unease or a fear of his talent or something else."

Lady Enderleigh smiled. "Your talent is remarkable. You understood all that from my emotions?"

"Most of it. I am skilled at extrapolating from what people feel to what they have in mind that might prompt those feelings." Lydia glanced at the fire, which seemed to reach out long, thin fingers to Lady Enderleigh.

"Well, it is true. I imagine Lord Craythorne was very surprised to discover his Extraordinary talent." Lady Enderleigh pursed her lips reflectively. "It is not a comfortable talent. Fire burns—at least, it took time for my talent to advance to the point that fire does not burn me. Is Lord Craythorne the same?"

"It has been only two weeks since he discovered he is an Extraordinary. So far, fire still burns him. Perhaps you know what he should expect."

Lady Enderleigh shook her head. "I do not recall how long it was between my manifestation and that development. I can say that he will know when it happens, and he should be wary of becoming angry or frightened until then." She smiled again. "Something you can assist with, I am sure."

Lydia laughed. "Lord Craythorne is in command of his emotions to a remarkable degree, but I take your meaning."

"Then—" Lady Enderleigh leaned forward slightly. "I would enjoy making Lord Craythorne's acquaintance, if you would make introductions?"

"I would be pleased to, Lady Enderleigh," Lydia said.

"Please, call me Elinor." Lady Enderleigh turned her head to observe the fire, which shrank from her gaze. "I would like us to be friends. My husband has always said there is a bond between Extraordinaries that does not exist between us and ordinary talents, something that encourages us to connect intimately upon very short acquaintance, and I have found this to be true."

Lydia had already noticed herself how comfortable she was talking to Elinor. "I would like that as well," she said. "And...do not tell Lord Craythorne I said this—I would never betray his confidences, of course, but this is one I believe needs sharing only with you—I hope you will help him embrace his talent. He has gone so long despising it, and even fearing it—but you are so confident, I know you can teach him the same."

"I will," Elinor said without hesitation. "I selfishly wish him to find joy as an Extraordinary Scorcher, as I benefit from no longer being the only one of my kind. Perhaps you understand what it is like to be stared at as an oddity."

Lydia nodded vehemently. "Oh, yes."

She had as usual been aware of the others in the house, but now she recognized Oliver's approach, and her heart leaped in anticipation. "Have you time now?" she asked. "For an extended visit, I mean. Because Lord Craythorne has just arrived, and I know he will wish to speak with you."

Elinor's heavy eyebrows rose. "Your Discernment is that powerful? How useful, to be aware of anyone's approach."

Lydia smiled. "This is the one whose approach I will always be happy about," she said.

⁂

Time was more peculiar than Discernment, Lydia reflected. Monday, Tuesday, and Wednesday had passed slower than candle wax melting; Thursday, by contrast, had flashed by so quickly it was over almost before Lydia could appreciate its beauty. Her family's happiness and lingering surprise at her marriage. Standing with Oliver in the drafty chapel. Floating along on their combined joy at being made one. The feel of the jade and silver necklace against her throat, warm like a living thing caressing her skin.

Now she rode with Oliver in his own carriage to Craythorne House, her hand in his warmer than the rest of her. Ellery had been correct; the weather had not changed, and the evening would have been dreary had Lydia not been so deeply content. Oliver's satisfaction matched her own.

"How peculiar," she said. "I would have imagined we would be joyful, or excited, or even anticipatory. Instead, we are both as peacefully happy as if this were a marriage of ten years' standing rather than ten hours."

Oliver's hand clasped hers more tightly. "I cannot explain it. Perhaps anticipation has wearied us to the point of being unable to feel anything more exciting than contentment."

Lydia raised one eyebrow. "Oh? And what have you anticipated, your Grace?"

"You are the Extraordinary Discerner. You tell me," Oliver said with an arch smile, and Lydia blushed despite herself.

The carriage came to a halt, and Oliver handed her down and then hooked her arm through his. "Are you certain you wish to travel, my dear?" he asked. "You are the one who said you prefer to make your nest and stay in it."

"That is true, but I will have many years to make this my nest," Lydia said, "and I believe two weeks' journey to see the sights of Europe will not disturb me."

"Well, in either case, I have something to show you, if you will come with me to the drawing room." Oliver's placid happiness deepened and became tinged with anticipation, though not the anticipation of intimacy he had suggested. Lydia, curious, walked up the stairs with him.

The drawing room was dark, but candles flared into life when they entered. "That is remarkable control, Oliver," Lydia exclaimed.

"I have been practicing," Oliver said with no small measure of pride.

He led Lydia to the far wall, where a framed picture hung between two vases holding fresh lilac branches. Lydia glanced at it, then took a longer look. "It is from the watercolor book," she exclaimed. She had paged through it so many times she felt it belonged to her—well, now it did—and the image she saw was as familiar to her as her own fingers.

One of the pages had been removed and framed as Lydia had often imagined doing. It was of a small brown wren, delicately drawn in perfect detail, sitting in a nest equally intricate in rendition. But that was not all; within the frame, beneath the wren, were inscribed several verses of poetry. The handwriting was bold, but suited the wren's delicacy perfectly.

Lydia stepped closer to read the words in the low light. "I know this one," she said, delighted. "'A Valediction Forbidding Mourning.' Did you pen this?"

"I like to believe my penmanship is of the highest quality," Oliver said, "and it would not be much of a gift if I passed off half of its construction to another."

Lydia trailed her fingers down the lines and paused before the end. She read aloud:

If they be two, they are two so
As stiff twin compasses are two,
Thy soul the fixed foot, makes no show
To move, but doth, if th' other do.

"That is us," she said. "Moving together as one."

Oliver nodded. "I hoped you would see it, though I do not intend to be often away."

"No, not that." Lydia put her arms around him. "But such is life that we will not always be in perfect harmony, and I intend *that*—" She nodded at the poem— "to remind me that we are one even when we believe otherwise."

Oliver drew her closer. "Then shall we repair upstairs, and see how close we may become now that we are wed?"

"You are nearly a Discerner yourself, my love," Lydia replied.

THE TALENTS

The Corporeal Talents: Mover, Shaper, Scorcher, Bounder

MOVER (Greek τελεκινεσις): Capable of moving things without physically touching them. While originally this talent was believed to be connected to one's bodily strength, female Movers able to lift far more than their male counterparts have disproven this theory in recent years. Depending on skill, training, and practice, Movers may be able to lift and manipulate multiple objects at once, pick locks, and manipulate anything the human hand can manage. Movers can Move other people so long as they don't resist, and some are capable of Moving an unwilling target if the Mover is strong enough.

An EXTRAORDINARY MOVER, in addition to all these things, is capable of flight. Aside from this, an Extraordinary Mover is not guaranteed to be better skilled or stronger than an ordinary Mover; Helen Garrity, England's highest-rated Mover (at upwards of 12,000 pounds lifting capacity), was an ordinary Mover.

SHAPER (Greek μπιοκινεσις): Capable of manipulating their own bodies. Shapers can alter their own flesh, including healing wounds. Most Shapers use their ability only to make themselves more attractive, though that sort of beauty is always obvious as Shaped. More subtle uses include disguising oneself, and many Shapers have also been spies. It usually takes time for a Shaper to alter herself because Shaping is painful, and the faster one does it, the more painful it is. Under extreme duress, Shapers can alter their bodies rapidly, but this results in great pain and longer-term muscle and joint pain.

Shapers can mend bone, heal cuts or abrasions, repair physical damage to organs as from a knife wound, etc., make hair and nails grow, improve their physical condition (for example, enhance lung efficiency), and change their skin color. They cannot restore lost limbs or organs, cure diseases (though they can repair the physical damage done by disease), change hair or eye color, or regenerate nerves.

An EXTRAORDINARY SHAPER is capable of turning a Shaper's talent on another person with skin-to-skin contact. Extraordinary Shapers are sometimes called Healers as a result. While most Extraordinary Shapers use their talent to help others, there is nothing to stop them from causing injury or even death.

SCORCHER (Greek πιροκινεσις): Capable of igniting fire by the power of thought. The fire is natural and will cause ordinary flammable objects to catch on fire. If there aren't any such objects handy, the fire will burn briefly and then go out. A Scorcher must be able to see the place he or she is starting the fire.

Scorcher talent has four dimensions: power, range, distance, and stamina. Power refers to how large and hot a fire the Scorcher can create; range is how far the Scorcher can fling a fire before it goes out; distance is how far away from him- or herself a Scorcher can ignite a fire; and stamina refers to how often the Scorcher can use his or her power before becoming exhausted.

The hottest ordinary fire any Scorcher has ever created could melt brass (approximately 1700 degrees F). When she gave herself over to the fire, Elinor Pembroke was able to melt iron (over 2200 degrees F).

Scorchers are rare because they manifest by igniting fire unconsciously, in their sleep. About 10-20% of Scorchers survive manifestation.

EXTRAORDINARY SCORCHERS are capable of controlling and mentally extinguishing fires. As their talent develops,

Extraordinary Scorchers become immune to fire, and their control over it increases.

BOUNDER (Greek τελεταχύς): Capable of moving from one point to another without passing through the intervening space. Bounders can move themselves anywhere they can see clearly within a certain range that varies according to the Bounder; this is called Skipping. They can also Bound to any location marked with a Bounder symbol, known as a signature. The room must be closed to the outdoors and empty of people and objects. Bounders refer to the "simplicity" of a space, meaning how free of "clutter" (objects, people, etc.) it is. Spaces that are too cluttered are impossible to Bound to, as are outdoor locations, which are full of constant movement. It is possible to keep a Bounder out of somewhere if you alter the place by defacing the Bounding chamber or putting some object or person into it.

An EXTRAORDINARY BOUNDER lacks most of the limitations an ordinary Bounder operates under. An Extraordinary Bounder's range is line of sight, which can allow them to Skip many miles' distance. Extraordinary Bounders do not require Bounding signatures, instead using what they refer to as "essence" to identify a space they Bound to. Essence comprises the essential nature of a space and is impossible to explain to non-Bounders; human beings have an essence which differs from that of a place and allows an Extraordinary Bounder to identify people without seeing them. While Extraordinary Bounders are still incapable of Bounding to an outdoor location, they can Bound to places too cluttered for an ordinary Bounder, as well as ones that contain people.

The Ethereal Talents: Seer, Speaker, Discerner, Coercer
SEER (Greek προφητεία): Capable of seeing a short distance into the future through Dreams. Seers experience lucid Dreams in which they see future events as if they were present as an invisible observer. They may or may not be able to recognize the people or places involved, so Seers tend to be very well informed about people and events and are socially active. Their Dreams are not inevitable and there is no problem with altering the timeline; they see things that are

the natural consequence of the current situation/circumstances, and altering those things alters the foreseen event. Just their knowledge of the event is not sufficient to alter it.

No one knows how a Seer's brain produces Dream, only that Dreams come in response to what the Seer meditates on. Seers therefore study current events in depth and read up on things they might be asked to Dream about. Seers have high social status and are very popular, with many of them making a living from Dream commissions.

An EXTRAORDINARY SEER, in addition to Dreaming, is capable of touching an object and perceiving events and people associated with it. These Visions allow them not only to see the past of the person most closely connected to the object, but occasionally to have glimpses of the future. They can also find a Vision linked to what the object's owner is seeing at the moment and "see" through their eyes. Most recently, the Extraordinary Seer Sophia Westlake discovered how to use Visions attached to one object to perceive related objects, leading to the defeat of the Caribbean pirates led by Rhys Evans.

SPEAKER (Greek τελεπάθεια): Capable of communicating by thought with any other Speaker. Speakers can mentally communicate with any Speaker within range of sight. They can also communicate with any Speaker they know well. The definition of "know well" has meaning only to a Speaker, but in general it means someone they have spoken verbally or mentally with on several occasions. A Speaker's circle of Speaker friends is called a reticulum, and a reticulum might contain several hundred members depending on the Speaker. Speakers easily distinguish between the different "voices" of their Speaker friends, though Speaking is not auditory. A Speaker can send images as well as words if she is proficient enough. Speakers cannot Speak to non-Speakers, and they are incapable of reading minds.

An EXTRAORDINARY SPEAKER has all the abilities of an ordinary Speaker, but is also capable of sending thoughts and images into the minds of anyone, Speaker or not. Additionally, an Extraordinary Speaker can Speak to multiple people at a time, though all will receive the same message. Extraordinary Speakers can send a "burst" of noise that startles or wakes the recipient. Rumors that

Extraordinary Speakers can read minds are universally denied by Speakers, but the rumors persist.

DISCERNER (Greek ενσυναίσθηση): Able to experience other people's feelings as if they were their own. Discerners require touch to be able to do this (though not skin-to-skin contact), and much of learning to control the skill involves learning to distinguish one's own emotions from those of the other person. Discerners can detect lies, sense motives, read other people's emotional states, and identify Coercers. Discerners are immune to the talent of a Coercer, though they can be overwhelmed by anyone capable of projecting strong emotions.

An EXTRAORDINARY DISCERNER can do all these things without the need for touch. Extraordinary Discerners are always aware of the emotions of those near them, though the range at which they are aware varies according to the Extraordinary Discerner. Nearly three-quarters of all Extraordinary Discerners go mad because of their talent.

COERCER (Greek τελενσυναίσθηση): Capable of influencing the emotions of others with a touch. Coercers are viewed with great suspicion, since their ability is a kind of mind control. Those altered are not aware that their mood has been artificially changed and are extremely suggestible while the Coercer is in direct contact with them. By altering someone's emotions, a Coercer can influence their behavior or change his or her attitude toward the Coercer.

Coercers do not feel others' emotions the way Discerners do, but can tell what they are and how they're changing. Many Coercers have sociopathic tendencies as a result. Unlike Discerners, Coercers have to work hard at being able to use their talent, which in its untrained state is erratic. However, Coercers always know when they've altered someone's mood. Coercers do not "broadcast" their emotions, appearing as a blank to Discerners. Because Coercion is viewed with suspicion (for good reason), Coercers keep their ability secret even if they don't use it maliciously.

An EXTRAORDINARY COERCER does not need a physical

connection to influence someone's emotions. Extraordinary Coercers are capable of turning their talent on several people at a time, and the most powerful Extraordinary Coercers can control mobs. The most powerful Extraordinary Coercer known to date is Napoleon Bonaparte.

HISTORICAL NOTE

I never actually thought I would set one of the Extraordinaries books in America. Almost all the development I did of my alternative history centered on England and Europe, and as I wrote at the end of *Beguiling Birthright*, the series was meant to end with the defeat of Napoleon. When that event happened two books early, I had to do some rethinking. I realized I was interested in revealing some of what had changed in my version of events that went beyond the mention in *Burning Bright* of the "Great Colonial Conflict" that ended with the American colonists losing the Revolutionary War.

However, as Lydia's story developed, it became clear that much of that development didn't have a place in her story. I had wanted to write about the Haudenosaunee (Iroquois), whose nation in my history holds sovereign territory north of New York State, but Lydia never has a reason to travel that far north. Details of their fictional culture and relationship with England will have to remain a mystery.

The subject of slavery and how it related to the events of the American Revolution is far too complex for me to address in this story, and as with earlier books, I didn't want to write as if I understood personally how it affected the millions of men and women enslaved and brought to the US. At the same time, I couldn't ignore the abhorrent practice entirely, as it's my feeling that even the existence of magical talent would not stop some people from continuing to see others as things because of their skin color. So, in the end, I decided I should not make the book hinge on slavery's abolition, and stuck only to the references that occur throughout the story. Mr. Ruskin's mention in Chapter Eleven of slaves developing talent and turning it on their former masters is still the thing I most regret being unable to make a more present scene in the book.

With *Discerning Insight*, the main Extraordinaries series comes to an end: eight talents, eight women, eight books. I see potential for further adventures set in this world, but that will have to wait for a future time. Until then, thank you, reader, for joining me on this journey.

—Melissa McShane

ACKNOWLEDGMENTS

As always, this book was made better by careful reading by Jacob Proffitt and Sherwood Smith, the latter of whom, in addition to general comments, made some key suggestions about describing Lydia's talent I found extremely valuable. Any mistakes remain my own.

ABOUT THE AUTHOR

In addition to the Extraordinaries series, Melissa McShane is the author of nearly fifty fantasy novels, including *The Book of Secrets*, first in The Last Oracle series; *Pretender to the Crown,* first in the novels of Tremontane; and *Company of Strangers*, first in the series of the same name. She lives with her family in the shelter of the mountains out West, along with two aging and demanding cats and a library she barely keeps under control.

You can visit her at her website www.melissamcshanewrites.com for information about her other books and new releases.

For more detailed information sent to your inbox, including news on Melissa's upcoming new series The Books of the Dark Goddess, you can sign up for her newsletter here.

facebook.com/melissamcshanewrites
x.com/mmcshanewrites

ALSO BY MELISSA MCSHANE

THE EXTRAORDINARIES

Burning Bright

Wondering Sight

Abounding Might

Whispering Twilight

Liberating Fight

Beguiling Birthright

Soaring Flight

Discerning Insight

THE BOOKS OF THE DARK GODDESS

Silver and Shadow (forthcoming)

THE LAST ORACLE

The Book of Secrets

The Book of Peril

The Book of Mayhem

The Book of Lies

The Book of Betrayal

The Book of Havoc

The Book of Harmony

The Book of War

The Book of Destiny

THE NOVELS OF TREMONTANE

Pretender to the Crown

Guardian of the Crown

Champion of the Crown

Ally of the Crown

Stranger to the Crown

Scholar of the Crown

Servant of the Crown

Exile of the Crown

Rider of the Crown

Agent of the Crown

Voyager of the Crown

Tales of the Crown

COMPANY OF STRANGERS

Company of Strangers

Stone of Inheritance

Mortal Rites

Shifting Loyalties

Sands of Memory

Call of Wizardry

THE DRAGONS OF MOTHER STONE

Spark the Fire

Faith in Flames

Ember in Shadow

Skies Will Burn

THE CONVERGENCE TRILOGY

The Summoned Mage

The Wandering Mage

The Unconquered Mage

THE BOOKS OF DALANINE

The Smoke-Scented Girl

The God-Touched Man

Emissary

Warts and All: A Fairy Tale Collection

The View from Castle Always